FORBIDDEN TO THE DESERT PRINCE

MAISEY YATES

THE CHRISTMAS HE CLAIMED THE SECRETARY

CAITLIN CREWS

MILLS & BOON

First published in Great Britain 2022
by Mills & Boon, an imprint of HarperCollins*Publishers* Ltd,
1 London Bridge Street, London, SE1 9GF

www.harpercollins.co.uk

HarperCollins*Publishers*
1st Floor, Watermarque Building,
Ringsend Road, Dublin 4, Ireland

Forbidden to the Desert Prince © 2022 Maisey Yates

The Christmas He Claimed the Secretary © 2022 Caitlin Crews

ISBN: 978-0-263-30107-6

11/22

This book is produced from independently certified FSC™ paper
to ensure responsible forest management.
For more information visit: www.harpercollins.co.uk/green.

Printed and Bound in Spain using 100% Renewable Electricity
at CPI Black Print, Barcelona

FORBIDDEN TO THE DESERT PRINCE

MAISEY YATES

MILLS & BOON

For the readers.

You're why these books exist, and I'm so thankful.

CHAPTER ONE

Run.

ARIEL HART STARED at the text message on her phone. For just one breath.

Then she sprang into action. She had known this moment could come. She'd known to be prepared for it.

"Darling," her mother had tried to reassure her, *"he's been imprisoned for years. He may have died in captivity. You don't know if he'll come for you."*

But she *had* known.

Her father had meddled in affairs he never should have and he'd used her as a chess piece and…

No time for self-pity, Ari, get it together.

She changed her clothing, quickly, taking off the cashmere sweatpants and equally soft cable-knit sweater she was wearing, trading them out for a pair of black leggings and a black hoodie that felt stiff as cardboard. She put the hood up over her white-blond hair and tucked each strand beneath it. She slipped on a pair of black trainers, picked up her black duffel bag and looked around her beautiful Parisian apartment one last time.

She'd felt safe here.

It was tranquil. Beautiful. All pale pinks and soothing tans. That she now looked like a cat burglar seemed an affront to the subtlety of the space.

She'd made a life here. Started her career.

For years she'd lived looking over her shoulder. Moving all the time, using assumed names. But about seven years after she'd…stopped. It was in the back of her mind that it could happen, she still had a go bag. But it had seemed unlikely. She didn't know if Riyaz was alive. She didn't know if Cairo was alive.

That was one reason she and her mother had taken it on themselves to simply…be wary. How could you call the police or an embassy about a potential threat from another country by persons who had not threatened you, in all actuality, and might in fact be dead?

But in her heart she'd known.

That he could come for her in search of revenge, or marriage.

And she didn't want either.

She'd leave it all behind now.

She'd be a fugitive, not a fashion designer.

But there was no space for pity. Not now.

It was possibly a matter of life and death, and there was no time to feel sorry for herself in the face of that.

She'd felt sorry for herself twenty years ago when she'd discovered—at age eight—that her father had promised her to a stranger. She'd felt sorry for herself, wandering the glittering halls at the palace in Nazul, looking at all the glorious mosaics and sitting by the fountains, the scent of orange blossom in the arid desert air.

And when her father had used the access he'd gained to the palace to assist in a coup that overthrew the royal family of Nazul and left the sheikh and sheikha dead, one son thrown into a dungeon and the other...

Missing.

Cairo.

She didn't think of him often, or at least, she tried not to.

The younger brother, the one with a ready smile and engaging dark eyes, so unlike the one she was promised to marry. The boy who had become her friend. Her confidant. Her first heartbreak.

When she was thirteen, she'd been sitting in the courtyard one day, baking in the sun and sulking, and there he'd been.

"Not enjoying yourself, ya amar?"

"It's very hot."

"It is the desert."

"I want to go back to Europe. I hate it here."

"Europe? You're American, Ari, are you not?"

"We spend half the year in Paris."

"Ah, how very nice."

"Nicer than this."

"Tell me, are you angry at this place? Or at its intent for you?"

"It's all the same."

"I don't think that's true. If you look around you might see that the place and the purpose are not one in the same. And perhaps...you might enjoy aspects of your time here."

And then he'd reached up and picked an orange from the tree above and handed it to her.

"Whether you wish to like it or not, the trees yet grow fruit. It cannot be all bad. Think on that, ya amar."

My moon. He had called her that for some reason she had never been able to figure out.

He said it as if to mock her and yet she'd always felt such an odd tangle inside her when he said things like that.

Cairo had been the closest thing to joy on those trips to Nazul. Though it had gotten thorny and complicated when she was twelve, and he thirteen, and he had suddenly grown very tall, and she'd found it hard to speak to him.

It had been such a funny thing. One year she'd gone to visit and they'd run around the palace like wild, feral things like they had since she was eight. And the next... she'd been shy around him. They'd had one whole year of barely speaking.

But that day she hadn't hidden from him. That day, he'd given her an orange.

And from there something else had blossomed between them. Something tender and precious and aching. She thought she might be in love, and she knew it was impossible. After five days she'd gone back to Paris. And the day after that...

The world had ended. At least in Nazul.

The heir, her fiancé, Riyaz was taken prisoner. Held as collateral.

And Cairo?

He had either been killed along with palace resisters, his body discarded as if he were nothing, not even important enough to be identified.

Or he had disappeared.

It didn't matter now. Riyaz was out. And that meant...

He would either seek to claim his bride or his revenge, and she wanted no part of either.

The sins of her father were his to pay, not hers.

But she would still have to face consequences.

She put on her backpack and headed to the door, and opened it.

And stopped.

He was there.

Standing there. Taller, broader and just plain more than when last she'd seen him. It wasn't Riyaz, or a cavalcade of soldiers, like she'd seen in her nightmares. It wasn't the monster she had trained herself to fear, to run from.

It was *him.*

Cairo al Hadid.

Very much alive.

And in her hallway.

"Ya amar," he said. "I have come for you."

Sheikh Cairo Ahmad Syed al Hadid had been a man without a country for far too long.

Perhaps that was not an accurate portrayal of the situation. He had a country. And he had not forgotten. He had made it his mission to take down the invading forces. All these years, he had not forgotten. The screams of his mother. The dying bellow of his father as he took his sword and did battle, though it was futile. Because he was King of Nazul, and he would have never let it fall without a fight. And it would never have fallen if not for the betrayal.

A betrayal at the hands of the Hart patriarch. Dominic Hart had gotten greedy. He had taken his connection to the royal family of Nazul, and he had decided instead to take the money of a vicious warlord in order to betray the al Hadid family.

The man had been an Eastern European mercenary who'd decided he was done running missions and gaining power for others, and had decided to take power where he could for himself. He'd chosen Nazul because it was rich in natural resources, and small enough, with few enough allies on a global scale that he would face few consequences for his actions.

But Cairo had seen that there were consequences. That man had been on the throne these past years, and Cairo had taken great joy in ending his reign. In watching his face when Cairo and his army for hire had stormed the palace and he'd known.

He'd known.

Cairo was not there to take prisoners.

Bloody battles had a cost. Revenge had a cost.

But Cairo owed that debt. He still owed a debt.

His life, his desires, his body, his soul. They were not his own. He'd lost his right to a life that belonged to himself all those years ago on a desert night when he'd made a mistake that had cost everything.

And so he'd lived these past years knowing this moment would come, and that when it did, he would give all to see his country restored.

To his brother sitting on the throne, as the rightful leader of Nazul.

He'd escaped the palace that day.

But he'd known he would return.

He had moved to England and begun using the name Syed al Shahar, his mother's family name. He had used his wit and his understanding of systems to get himself into the finest schools on scholarship. From there, he had begun to build an empire.

And people might know Cairo as a playboy, businessman and mogul, but they did not know that he had been a boy who had watched his family die in a palace in a far-off desert kingdom that made few headlines.

What was yet more global unrest, after all? It had been a blip on the radar of the news media in Europe and the United States, for what did they care? People killing each other in a country that none of them wanted to visit anyway.

That was how they ranked their concern. Did they wish to vacation there? Or was the country in question potentially going to invade them? If not... A cruel footnote in the history of a world filled with cruel histories. Unremarkable. And yet, it had changed his entire life.

He had known, though.

He had *known* that Riyaz had survived. He had felt that in his bones. Either way, Cairo's loyalty was to Nazul. And he had built his empire on the foundation of wanting nothing more than to destroy the men that had killed his family. That had taken his legacy.

And he had known that if his brother truly were being held captive, then he must be rescued. Cairo would always come for him.

He might be Syed to the world, but he had always been Cairo.

Always.

He knew what he had to do. All the parties, all the excess...it was never for him. And if it successfully helped to burn away the memories of what had happened in Nazul?

He did not mind having those memories blurred.

He didn't need them sharp to fulfill his mission.

He knew who he was. He might have indulged himself in the pleasures to be found in the world. It had started as a way to gain access to parties and by extension, to people.

But he found that he had an endless capacity to work hard, and to pursue divine degradation even harder.

And so he had built himself an empire. One that allowed him to move freely between nations. Collect allies and data, and many other things that aided him in this overthrow of the overthrowers.

He'd also found himself in many rooms with men who were dangerous and lacked scruples. He'd saved a girl from one of those rooms.

Brianna Whitman.

He'd helped her escape the fate set out for her by her father, sent her to school, and she'd become an accomplished life coach for people who had come from difficult circumstances, and while he found all of that to be modern, soft nonsense...

It had seemed less nonsensical when he saw his brother for the first time in fifteen years. He'd hired Brianna then, to go and try to help him. Coax him back to the world, to the position of his birth. She was there now, trying her best to help him become the man he was meant to be, rather than the beast he'd been fashioned into through years of isolation.

Riyaz was free. But Riyaz was not... He was certainly not fit to rule. He was blunt and he lacked even basic manners. He had spent the years in the dungeon reading and honing his body into a war machine. He was a strange mix of things, his brother. Well-read, for he'd had nothing to do in the dungeon but read, and he'd done so to keep his language alive. He had also worked out exhaustively to avoid letting any part of him atrophy.

But he had no practice of applying these things in the real world. He could hardly hold a conversation, let alone engage in matters of global diplomacy.

Cairo's taking of the palace in Nazul was a secret. To the nation, to the world. They'd power, but they continued to operate in stealth mode, particularly as he figured out when he could present Riyaz to the people.

They would have only one chance to do so.

Riyaz could not be seen as weak mentally. He could not be seen as affected by what he'd endured. The people would want a strong, triumphant return.

When Riyaz had been freed from the dungeon, Cairo had been there.

His brother had been dressed in near rags, his hair and beard long. Cairo had expected to find him weak and pale, but Riyaz had been built of pure muscle and rage. He refused to go outside. He refused to sleep in a bed. He spent much of his time in the dungeon still.

He had asked for two things upon his freedom.

A cheeseburger, and Ariel Hart.

Ariel...

The name had been a jagged, whispered memory to Cairo.

But he had known just where she was.

He had always known.

He had thought of going to her, many times. And yet he'd known there was only ever one circumstance under which he could see her again. If Riyaz wanted her.

And Riyaz wanted her.

So Cairo would do what Riyaz had asked. He owed him that.

"You had to know that I would come for you," he said.

"I…"

She was beautiful. She was orange blossoms in a mosaic garden that he had not seen in more than a decade. She was rich, perfumed air. She was a moment in time he could never have back.

It was the impact of her that shocked him. For Cairo was dead to most things in the world. He felt rage, and he felt desire, he had felt something larger than himself when Riyaz had been freed from the dungeon.

But this… Her… She was incredibly beautiful. She surpassed that which she had promised to become. For she had always been lovely.

Her robin's egg blue eyes were wide as she looked up at him. She was dressed as if she was ready to run. She had been warned.

"Are you here to kill me?" she whispered.

"No," he said. "That would be far too basic, and I am a civilized man."

"And not dead," she pointed out.

"No. At least not last I checked." He looked at her yet more intently. "Did you think that I was?"

"I did not discount it." She looked away, and he was certain he saw regret in her eyes, sadness. But he was not swayed by it. "I know the fate of the rest of your family."

"Riyaz lives."

She nodded slowly. "Is that why you're here? Because of Riyaz?"

"Yes," said Cairo. "I am here on behalf of my brother. You don't seem shocked that Riyaz is alive."

"There were rumors. That he had been kept alive and imprisoned in the palace. Collateral of some kind. I do not fully understand."

"Neither do I. But can one understand the will of a madman? Your father is included in that."

"My father's betrayal of your family was not something I had any idea of."

"And I have no designs to blame you for it. You were a mere child."

"So were you."

He regarded her for a long moment. He had not felt like a child. Not since he had escaped the palace that day. He had known then that all he could do was survive. He'd had to. For he was the only remaining, living member of his family that was not being held in captivity. Survival was not an option. It was a directive.

"Then, you aren't here for revenge?"

Revenge would be a much simpler task. Revenge he'd taken already and it had been easy, cathartic.

Ariel had never been easy for him.

But atonement required sacrifice.

And she was that.

"No. I'm here to ensure that the contract is honored. My brother has been freed, and he needs a wife."

"I don't suppose there's any chance of you trying to find another one."

"No. There is not. You were promised to my family, and my family has lost too much of what it is owed. I will not see this ended as well."

She tossed her hair, looking every bit the haughty American socialite he had always thought lurked beneath the rather sweet, large eyed demeanor that she had always portrayed when she came to visit Nazul. But it was not genuine. He could see that just as easily. She was trying to be brave.

"It seems a bit like crying over spilled milk," she said.

He was not a cruel man. But he was not a man who knew how to bend either. And there were certain things he refused to suffer. Fools, attempts at manipulation, and attitude from the woman whose father had engineered the murder of his parents.

"It is not milk that has been spilled, *ya amar*, but blood. The blood of my parents. And it is not spilled milk that causes anguish even now, but lost years. Fifteen years Riyaz has been in the dungeon. Fifteen years. Without human contact. With nothing. While I made the weapons that would claim his freedom. And you wish to speak to me in cliché. Let me return one for you. An eye for an eye. A tooth for a tooth. A life in captivity… For a life in captivity."

What she wanted didn't matter here. It could not matter. Softness here, with her, was unforgivable. A mistake made once before and never again.

Never again.

And then he reached out and took her by the arm, propelling her from her apartment. But she did not move quickly enough, so he lifted her off the ground with ease, cradling her in his arms as if she were a bride he were to carry over his own threshold. Laughable. She was not for him. She never had been. Always, from the beginning, she had been meant for Riyaz. And Riyaz had been robbed of… Absolutely everything.

It was that which fueled him now. The rage that he

felt on behalf of his brother. And the need to atone for his part in it.

He was dimly aware that she was punching him. But her fists were like pebbles against an oak. Of no consequence. His family had suffered. His only punishment had been to see it, when he'd deserved the same death.

All these years, he had lived a life. A life that was fueled by his need for revenge. A life that was purgatory, but a life all the same.

And she… She had been here in Paris. She had been everywhere. Living unfettered by the horror that had taken place at the palace. He did not pause to wait for the elevator, rather he carried her straight down the stairs of the old building, down and out to the street where his limousine was idling against the curb.

He opened the door on his own, and all but threw her onto the plush seat. He closed the door firmly and locked them in. "Drive," he said to his driver.

The man was paid well enough not to question anything. Which was good, because Ariel began to protest. And did not stop.

"He's kidnapping me," she said to the driver.

The driver's ice-cold glance connected with Cairo's in the rearview mirror. And then Cairo slowly put the divider up between the front and the back of the car.

"He does not care," said Cairo.

"Cairo, what good does it do to have me marry your brother?" She looked around wildly, as if something suddenly dawned on her. "You don't really want me to marry him, do you? Am I going to be publicly executed or something? Since my father is already dead?"

"I told you already, it is not revenge I'm after," he said. "Public execution is barbaric. Your father was barbaric, Ariel. And if he were alive, perhaps I would treat him as he treated my family. It is a travesty that he was able to die so neatly. A heart attack. Bland, nondescript and far too quick. My mother screamed in agony. My father fought until his very last breath." She had the decency to look cowed by that. "It is not so simple as having you pay for his sins. It is about the restoration of Nazul. You were part of an original promise that was made to my country, to my brother. Your father was part of fracturing the peace of our country, the rightness of the world. What better image to present to the people than to see Riyaz back on the throne, with you as his bride, as if none of the bad things had ever happened?" He nearly laughed. For there was no erasing the past, no matter how beautifully you tried to gild the present. "Most importantly of all, it is what Riyaz has asked for." Though he wasn't sure his brother saw it how he did. But he had a plan in place to protect Ariel and please Riyaz. "The responsibility of restoring Nazul is mine."

"How is it yours?"

"Riyaz has been in a dungeon for fifteen years, how do you suppose he is?"

For the first time she looked subdued. "How is he?"

"Not well," he said. "When it becomes public knowledge that he lives…"

"It is," she said.

"I do not believe that it is."

"My mother knew. She texted me and she told me to run. Because Riyaz was out."

He paused for a long moment. "There must be somebody inside the palace with a connection to your family."

"Unlikely."

"We brought back many of the old staff who once worked there. Perhaps it was a mistake."

He was hell-bent on making things as they were. It was the only way. But in this… He had clearly miscalculated. Thankfully, however, it had not been leaked to the media at large. But who knew what Ariel's mother might do with it. She had never seemed like a craven or greedy woman, but then, neither had her husband. And he had been secretly plotting to aid in the overthrow of their family.

Yes, Cairo had learned at a very early age that you could not trust anyone.

"Regardless," he said. "We are attempting to ensure that Riyaz is ready. To face the public. There is a team with him now, and they are working with him."

"Are we going to the palace now?"

He was silent for a moment. "No. We must be certain that he is… For all that you might think that I am barbaric, that I would oversee your public execution, it is actually not my goal. So until I have made certain it is not my brother's, I will be keeping you safe. With me."

"With *you*?" She spoke the word as if it were laughable.

"Yes. I take my position in the monarchy very seriously. Riyaz is the heir, and I am the spare. But I was also the one who was spared captivity. It is my job now to use what I have to support him."

"And what is that?"

"Social graces," Cairo returned.

"I don't know that they've been on the best display."

"My apologies for your struggle," he said.

"Cairo…"

"You knew. You knew I would come for you. You

were prepared to run. Your mother was prepared to text you to run. Do not act surprised by it now."

"I had rather thought that murder would be the aim."

"No. So you should be relieved."

"I'm not."

He looked at her, hard. "This was always how it would be. You knew that. You knew it when you were a child. You know it now. The al Hadid family is an inevitability. We are the sun in the desert. You cannot outrun us. And you cannot extinguish us. Your fate is sealed."

CHAPTER TWO

THE SUN WAS so hot today. She felt like she might die of it, but she waited in the garden anyway. She waited and waited because she knew eventually...he would come.

"There you are, ya amar."

She looked up, the throb of her heart painful. "Cairo."

He'd told her she could call him by his name, and it had felt like a gift.

"Ari..."

The nickname on his lips made her feel a new kind of warm.

"Why doesn't Riyaz ever come out?"

"He's the heir. He's going to be the sheikh. Do you prefer his company to mine?"

She bit her lip. "I should."

His boyish grin became wicked. "But you don't."

If you could expire from panic, or perhaps have all the energy zapped out of you because you were in a state of heightened terror, then Ariel felt as if she had achieved that state. She had given up trying to talk to him. That snatch of memory was a lie. A joke.

That Cairo was long gone.

In many ways, he was dead, like she'd always imagined he was.

Because this wasn't her friend. This wasn't the boy she'd loved.

Her heart clenched tight.

Her father was responsible for this.

When she'd been a child, she'd been protected from the world. She'd had tutors at home, and she'd been well educated. She'd traveled all over. She'd been wealthy and comfortable. But she hadn't realized that the choices her father had made for her weren't…normal. Not in modern society.

She had been upset that she'd been promised to marry a sheikh, but her father had explained that people like them often had to make choices, alliances and marriages that others didn't. It was how you protected wealth, it was how you stayed safe, that was what he'd told her.

She'd accepted it then.

She couldn't say she was accepting of this now.

But there was some part of her that felt compelled to face this.

To see it through.

Even to the point of just…understanding what had become of Cairo over the course of all these years.

Or she could jump out of a moving vehicle and try to run for it.

They clearly weren't going to a major airport. They had passed Charles de Gaulle an hour ago, and she had no idea where they were headed. She also knew she didn't really have a hope in hell of getting away from him. She didn't have a phone. She could not be tracked.

She had her backpack, which did have money in it, and if she could escape…

But then she would have to run, and he would only catch her. She should've been training to physically run, but she had been so certain that she would have time if this ever happened…

You were hoping it would never happen.

Yes. And it was a complicated hope. Of course it was. Because she had never wished lifelong captivity on Cairo. But of course, she had not wished to be caught up in their world again.

The whole of that world? Or just the version of it where you were promised to the wrong brother?

She shoved that thought aside and closed her eyes.

Cairo was alive.

He wasn't dead.

And so there she was, slumped in the corner of the limousine, and when they finally pulled in to the empty airfield, she was still trying to find…something to hold on to. She'd thought the longer she sat with him, with this, the more real it would seem.

But no.

It all felt less and less possible as the minutes ticked by.

And then she saw it. Shiny and sleek, cutting quickly through the air before descending smoothly, the sound it made following behind it.

"My private jet," he said.

"Right," she responded. "Naturally. Of course you have a private jet."

And she looked at him and realized. She had seen him. She had seen him in the media before. In society pages. But not under the name Cairo.

He was not the sort of playboy who posed for photos. There were often distant shots of him on yachts with half-naked beauties, sunglasses obscuring his face. She had not recognized him in those photos, though she'd be lying if she said she'd never stopped and given them a second look.

How could she not have realized it was Cairo? She'd looked twice at stories about Syed, because Cairo was the only man who'd ever made her look twice.

"Where did the name Syed come from?" she asked.

"One of my many names," he said, a grin curving his lips. "For a royal is gifted with many. And easy enough to adopt so that I could fly under the radar."

"You're a billionaire." She said it like an accusation.

"Yes," he said. "Staging a reverse coup isn't cheap."

"*How?* People don't just…become billionaires."

"I had advantages. I had already taken on board the finest education the world had to offer, from the palace, of course. And then… I knew the right things to say. Knew some people to go to who could help me. Help me become somebody new. Help me navigate the system in England.

"I had nothing. Nothing but who and what I knew when I escaped. And now I have much. Much that I will pass on to my brother and to my people."

"So the plane doesn't belong to the royal family. It's yours."

"Yes, it is."

She felt overwhelmed then. Swamped by just how unmatched she was.

He was international businessman Syed al Shahar, and he was one of the most famous and highly sought-after men in the world. He had allies in every corner, and more than that, resources. And they would be going back to a country where he was a prince. A sheikh. And there… Well, there she would have no allies at all.

She was an ant compared to him.

Her father had been nothing but a trifling fool who'd had no idea what he was messing with.

And he had condemned her and her mother to a life of worry.

He had condemned Cairo's family to death.

No. She would never forgive him. And hadn't.

He had made so much money betraying them. Her mother had taken much of it in court. And they had never spoken to him again. He had died alone. So for all that Cairo knew of her father's demise, she was not certain that he was aware of that.

She didn't feel like telling him now. Because it felt a small part of her power. If he did not know everything about her. Unless…

"You've always known where I was, haven't you?"

"Yes."

"Why did you only come and get me now?"

It sounded small, and a bit like a plea, and she hated herself for it.

"I felt it reasonable to allow you to have a life while there was a life for you to have. One of your choosing. But there are things bigger than you at play here. Bigger than me. Choice is not for us. You have done quite well for yourself in the fashion industry."

"Thank you for noticing," she said.

The fashion industry was cutthroat, especially in Paris. And she knew that her position in it was enhanced by her father's position in society, made extra grim by the fact that she was no longer speaking to him when he died. And yet it was still his name that she often traded on.

But she had ambition, and it was the way the world worked.

"I particularly like your jewelry."

"Thank you," she said. "Although I can't tell if you're being serious or not."

"I am. I have an appreciation of art," he said. "Why would I lie?"

"Only because I did not think that you would be concerned with such things."

"Many of my mistresses have enjoyed your pieces."

She looked at him. His dark eyes were filled with fire she could not divine.

And she didn't know why, but the statement about *mistresses* made her stomach feel hollow. It was something of a reminder of the gulf between them. But then, there had always been a gulf between them. She could remember when they were young, there had always been something shining in his eyes, a knowledge and mischief that she could not quite get a grasp on.

But then, Cairo had never been hers to grasp. They had a strange friendship back at the palace, but it had never been easy. It had always felt as if there was a wall between them, by some necessity.

"It is nice that you are such a conscientious paramour," she said. Rather than any of the other things that had crowded her throat.

"Let's go," he said, opening the door of the limousine, but she remained resolutely stuck to the spot.

"Are you really going to make it this difficult?"

"Should I make it easy?"

Tension stretched between them, and he reached across the space and pulled her to him.

His body was hard, hot. And suddenly, she wanted to lean into it. Into his strength. Into the way that he held her closely.

It was the strangest thing.

This urge to surrender.

So she struggled. Against herself more than anything, but he did not seem bothered by it. Not at all. He extracted her from the limousine and carried her to the doors of the private plane.

And he hauled her right up the steps.

She kicked and struggled, and there was a smiling flight attendant on board. She looked at the other woman in disbelief. The other woman simply smiled. "Can I get you some champagne?"

"Are you…" she asked. "This man is *kidnapping* me."

She only grinned wider. Like a terrifying fem-bot. "Sheikh Cairo is of course the ruler of that which he surveys, and the reigning power in this facility. I assure you that it is functionally impossible for him to kidnap anyone in this sphere."

"I assure you it's not," she said, still wiggling as he set her down on one of the seats inside the cabin.

"Champagne?" the woman asked again.

"You're all shocking," she said. *"Complicit,"* she added for good measure.

"No champagne then?"

"Of course I want champagne," Ariel snapped.

And she let the grinning woman pour her a glass of champagne, and she felt slightly like she'd lost some sort of battle, but she was on the plane with or without a drink, so she might as well indulge.

She took the glass from the woman, who smiled and turned to Cairo. "None for me. You may go."

He didn't use her name or accept her services and Ariel felt slightly irritated that she'd accepted.

And the woman vanished. Just as he'd commanded.

"Do you have her under a spell?"

"Yes, Ariel. That spell is called power." He reclined in his chair, his hands behind his head, tightening his shirt over his broad, muscular chest.

She was trying to wrap her head around the fact that this was both Syed and Cairo. When she'd seen him at her house he'd been recognizable only as Cairo. It was the impact of him, his eyes, and the fact he'd appeared right after her mother's text.

But now, with him on the private jet, sprawled out like a man waiting to be served, she saw the infamous playboy and businessman. She was shocked they'd never moved in the same circles; in fashion she interacted with many men like him, and as he'd said, he bought her jewelry for his mistresses.

But it was by design. She knew that. She didn't even have to ask.

"You've changed," she said.

"I would hope so," he responded, his tone dark. "My parents were murdered and I was separated from my brother and my homeland. I ought to have changed."

For the first time, regret and pity swamped the rest of what she felt. Overtook her concerns for herself.

"I'm sorry. For what you went through, I really am. I felt like I lost something that day too."

His eyes went hard, and she knew she'd miscalculated. "You were never happy there."

"I wasn't happy I was being forced into marriage. Show me a girl who would be?"

"My brother is the ruler of Nazul. Many women would line up for the chance."

"I never wanted to be a wife. By which I mean I never wanted to be defined by that. My mother's whole identity was my father. She just…went along with everything he said. She loved me, she loves me. But she… she doesn't know how to make up her own mind. She doesn't take a stand, ever. She's never known how to be alone or single. It's why we don't see each other very much now. She's had two husbands since my dad." She shook her head. "Why would I want that? Maybe I wouldn't have wanted to get married at all. Maybe I don't like men. No one ever asked me."

His lips curved upward, his head tilting to the side. "Do you not?"

"Do I not what?"

"Like men."

She'd wondered about it, in her years since leaving Nazul. There hadn't been a single man who'd turned her head in all the years since Cairo had offered her an orange. She'd been a girl then, and it was distant enough memory that she sometimes wondered if she'd imagined it.

"I like my work," she said. "I like choosing. I like being free. I like cashmere sweatpants and evenings at home alone. I like ice cream and costume dramas and I really do not think I will make a good wife or a good sheikha."

"You didn't answer my question."

"I gave you all the information you need."

She could tell he wasn't used to people talking to him like that. His jaw went stiff, his hands tightening on the arms of the chair he sat in. Fine. He had already kidnapped her. He had already taken her memories, her best and sweetest memories, of Nazul and turned them into something else.

She'd wept for him.

She'd loved him.

The boy.

Not the man he was now.

"Why do you need to know? You don't care what I like. You don't care what I want."

"A good point."

"Would my lack of interest in men keep you from marrying me off to your brother?"

"No. This is not about you. It's about what Riyaz has asked for. What he feels is best for Nazul. You do not matter at all, apart from that which you symbolize."

And like that, all the pity for him evaporated. "How dare you? How dare you speak to me like that, as if you can simply…"

"Oh, forgive me, Ariel, do you find it confronting that you have to live a life you didn't choose? I'm not your audience."

"Such a caustic tone is a bit basic, don't you think?"

He arched a dark brow. "I am anything but basic, *ya amar*. And I think you know that."

Ariel knew how to pretend to be fine. She knew how to pretend to be bored even when she was nervous. She had learned how to navigate the often harsh fashion industry, and that had been easy compared to recovering from what her father had done. To living with the knowledge that her freedom might have an expiration date on it. And well, Cairo was right about one thing. That information was not new. Not in the least. She had known that she would be married off to somebody from the time that she was a child. Then her father had committed that horrible act and she'd been worried the retribution would fall on her head. It was only in the small window of her life that she had allowed herself to imagine that her fate might not be fixed.

So yes. She knew how to pretend to be bored. She knew how to banter with people who actively wished her ill. She did not allow herself to be affected overly much by the opinions of others. Because she alone knew her own strength. She had to.

She would love to say that she had been close with her mother in the years since her father's death. She'd wondered at the time if she might change when the structure of the family changed. But it was like the whole thing hadn't been a release, more that it had dissolved everything.

His betrayal. His death.

They had never been able to be whole again after all of that.

And it was as if it was easier for her mother to go off and have her own life. They spoke on the phone. They texted. But Helene seemed much happier with distance between them, and Ariel didn't see the point in fighting that. There were too many things to fight. And she had chosen in these years to focus on herself and her goals. Because…

Well. Because of things like this.

He was watching her. Far too closely.

"Do you think that you might be able to read my mind? And even if you could, would it matter?"

"One should always attempt to know as much is possible about the person they find themselves thirty thousand feet in the air with, don't you think?"

"I don't know what I think. In fact, I think I won't know what I think for the duration. I would rather give you nothing." And that was true. She wanted to hide all of her feelings. Her fears. Her desires. The strange, tangled up grief that she had felt for him for all these years.

She wanted to hide it all.

If he wanted a vessel, a symbol, then she could be that. And give him nothing of what she was.

And what will the point of your life be then?

She wished that she had an answer to that. She suddenly felt sad. Bleak. Because what had the point of any of it been? She had built her life up to a certain place, and now would have to abandon it. So what had been the point of building it up at all? Giving herself a taste of a life that she could not hold on to. A taste of the life that she could not claim or keep.

And apparently Riyaz wasn't in his right mind.

"You're afraid," he said.

"You say that as if it's a flaw?"

"Not at all. Simply an observation. I told you. I'm not going to hurt you."

"You seem to think that the only way a person can be hurt is with a sword. I had a life."

"So did I. And I abandoned it."

"Have you sold all of your holdings? Are you releasing hold on everything that you've built?"

"Of course not. It is advantageous to my country to keep it. But it will not be my primary focus. My days of traveling around the world and doing as I please are at an end. I was always working to accomplish the goal of taking back Nazul, but I knew I would have to get back to my other life. The life from before. Which was also disrupted. We are not guaranteed the life that we plan, are we? You will forgive me for not feeling sympathy where perhaps you think I should. It is this… This generation. This modern world. You think that you can simply pursue your own selfish version of happiness, and that you are guaranteed such a thing, entitled to it. But we are entitled to nothing. I am royalty and I learned that. I learned that as I watched my parents died. As my brother was taken away from me. As I had to run, knowing that it was the right thing to do even though it felt like cowardice. I wanted to stay and fight to the death as my father did. That was what I wanted. Hero's death. But I had to find a way to make a hero's life, did I not? Because of Riyaz. And so… That is what I'm doing."

"A hero's life," she said softly. And she knew that she would be revealing herself with her next words, so she chose them carefully. "And yet, for all that I have heard of you in the guise of Syed, you have chosen a playboy's life. And as you admitted to me, you've had many mistresses. How does that match up with what you're telling me? How does that equate to heroism? How do you look at yourself and see what you claim?"

"I did not say that I looked at myself and saw a hero. I am in pursuit of it. There is an inequality that I must balance. I had fifteen years of freedom while my brother was in chains. I had fifteen more years of life as my parents have laid in the graves. I can never wholly right this." His eyes went blank. "But as of now, I live in service, in an attempt to make amends of some kind."

"Where are we going?"

"I have a home in the mountains near my country. It was a way that I could sneak in with the enemy unaware. A compound that my brother does not know exists."

"I'm confused. Are you doing things in *service* of your brother, or are you *afraid* of your brother?"

"I do not fear him. But I also do not know his frame of mind. I do not know how deeply his time in the dungeon damaged him. That, I await, before I go crashing in to his world."

She looked at him, and then she saw the boy that he had been. The boy who had come and sat with her at the fountain. The boy who'd cared. He was worried about his brother. And she should not feel any sympathy for him. None at all. She should not feel… He had kidnapped her. What was the matter with her? Why was she finding ways to justify his behavior? To excuse him?

Was it because he was handsome?

No, it was because he was handsome that she wanted to fling herself out of the plane. Because for all these years no man had turned her head. For all these years she had told herself that the tied up, twisted up feelings that Cairo had once made her feel were locked away in the past. And yet, he was here. And she was tied up. Twisted up.

There was a syndrome for feeling sympathy for one's captor. She was a modern enough woman to be aware of it.

Except he has been something more to you. And you can't un-know that.

And your father did destroy his family.

Her father had claimed that he had not known that the men who were there to take over the country would kill the royal family. He had claimed that. But even at fourteen, she had not found herself to be that naive. She knew better. Her father could not possibly have believed that his betrayal would not have resulted in the deaths of the family. He had to know. And yet...

She wondered if he told himself that. She wondered if he told himself that there was nothing he could've done. That he had believed in good faith and done what he needed to do to keep his family safe. It was the narrative that he had told them. That he had been put in an impossible position where they were threatened.

It was only that... She had not believed it. Neither had her mother. What they had believed was that he had wanted that money, and it superseded the influence of the royal family, after all, the royal family would cease to have influence if they were deposed... And that was the issue. It seemed very much like he had known what would happen. And perhaps he had felt that it would happen no matter what, and there would be no gain for him at all if he didn't help.

But there was no honor in it. And she could never respect it.

And that created a strange sort of responsibility inside of her for Cairo's feelings. No matter that she had shouted at him that it wasn't her sin, it was her father's. Perhaps in the same way that he felt responsible for his bloodline, for Riyaz, she felt responsible for her father.

Not responsible enough to marry Riyaz. But...

"How much longer?"

"So impatient. You must remember my country is beautiful."

"I barely remember it at all," she lied.

"You were to be the queen. Did you not find that an intoxicating idea of the future?"

She shook her head. "No. I never wanted power. And when you are being moved about by powerful men, I do not think that the promise of the throne feels powerful at all." She looked at a spot, just behind his head because looking at him was always a mistake. "I was always being maneuvered. And I was very aware of it. I never thought that there was power to be had for me."

"And if there was?"

She met his gaze again. "What do you mean?"

"It remains to be seen, how Riyaz will do."

"So what, you think that I might need to…"

"I don't know. But you are successful. You are more than a socialite now. And that… I think that that is a boon. There is an appearance of modernity to you as a choice, and the country is in bad need of some. It's been cut off from the outside world for fifteen years after being nearly crushed beneath the bootheel of a dictator."

"Oh. Well. I didn't know that you are aiming to bring the country into the modern era. The whole forced bride thing seems to belie that."

"*Appearances*, I said."

"Yes. You are all about those, aren't you?"

"Life is all about appearances, Ariel. I appeared to be a simple orphan boy, and managed to construct a new identity for myself as a result. I appeared to be an international playboy without an original thought in my head, and therefore was able to get close to the enemies of my family. I appeared harmless. Therefore I was able to inflict great harm when necessary. Appearance is all life is."

"I don't believe that."

There was a core of steel running through his words. It made her tremble. It frightened her.

He was not the man that he once had been. But then, she had known him as a boy. He also wasn't the playboy that he appeared to be, she did believe that. She believed him capable of great ruthlessness. And she did not ever want to fall on the wrong side of that. But at the same time... There was something about him, about the way that he was. The way that he was put together. It made her tremble.

It called to something long forgotten inside of her.

Whispered across her skin like an orange scented breeze.

She shut her mind down. She was panicking, that's what she was doing. She was seeking desperately for something... Something other than panic. And that was twisting it all into this... Whatever it was. She refused to name it.

Refused.

"There is a bedroom at the back. Why don't you sleep? For when we land, we will be assessing the situation. And you will begin training."

"I'm not a dog," she said. "'Go lie down.' 'Begin your training.'"

He said nothing. And so she sat, sipping her champagne slowly and staring straight ahead. And even when she became utterly exhausted, she refused to sleep.

Because she would not give him the satisfaction of having successfully given her a command.

CHAPTER THREE

WHEN THE PLANE descended over the mountains, in a strip of land that fell between countries, onto the hidden airway concealed by a pass, he felt like the blood of his ancestors had risen up within him. The battle cry of a warrior echoing through his body.

It had nothing to do with Ariel being at his side.

He was home. And he had returned home a victor. As he had known he must. Ariel was still sitting across from him, staring, though he wondered if she had lapsed off into some fugue state. She certainly didn't want to give him the satisfaction of being reasonable. Pity for her, he was neither satisfied nor dissatisfied by her display of temper. He had bigger things on his mind. And indeed, there were bigger problems set out before himself and his nation.

Ariel was meant to be a solution.

Atonement.

She did not possess the power to become a problem.

Riyaz had demanded her. Cairo would fulfill the promise.

After the plane landed, the door opened, and she remained. Sitting. Looking straight ahead.

"If you have the idea that I will not take you in hand

and bodily remove you, I believe I have already disproven such a notion."

"Why must you make everything about you?"

She stood and disembarked on the plane on her own two feet, and he could only stare.

He remembered her well from his time at the palace, though he had spent many years attempting to not remember at all.

He tried not to remember that life. For it created an ache in his chest that had no home. It could not.

He could not allow such a thing to take up residence within him. No. Not when he himself was far too essential to this cause.

There could not be a moment of self-pity. And so, he did not cast his mind back. But she... She forced him to think of those days.

He thought of his brother, as he had once been. His older brother, his idol in every way. Much more serious than he had ever been.

And the only sticking point ever in their relationship was one that Riyaz had not known about.

His eyes drifted to Ariel.

What a foolish boy he'd been.

He had loved it when the sulky American girl had come to stay with them. She was beautiful.

She had been quite the most singular thing he'd ever seen with her aqua blue eyes and pale blond hair. Her lips were the most delicate shade of pink, and his thoughts of Ariel had been his very first thoughts that were quite so... Specific. He had thought of kissing those lips.

Devouring them.

As a teenage boy, it had made him ache. She had

made him ache. And she had been for his brother. And so, all he had been able to do was… He remembered stolen moments in the garden, and he was certain they had not been quite the same for him.

And now?

She was no less beautiful. She was singular.

Of course he had kept tabs on her. But the photographs of her in the media did not do her justice.

And he marveled at his own behavior. Buying her jewelry for his cast-off lovers. In many ways, he wondered if it was an intentional nod to that first experience of desire.

Of course, she was twenty-eight years old now. Likely the innocence of youth had long been banished for her, as it certainly had for him.

She is no concern of yours. Not beyond bringing her here.

As a green boy, he'd let himself get far too close to temptation.

He'd been playing with fire. But he knew better now.

She was here for Riyaz. Nothing more. She had always been for Riyaz.

It was only a twenty-minute ride by helicopter from this home down to the palace in the capital city. They were close. And yet, Riyaz did not know of their presence.

Necessary.

He needed to speak to Brianna. And he would. Soon.

"Come," he said.

"Where?" She looked around them. And he knew what she saw. Forbidding, harsh wilderness, which seemed to have nothing hospitable to it at all.

"It is an oasis. In the desert."

"You are delusional," she said. "I have a feeling you would call a thimbleful of water an oasis in the desert if you thought you could use such assertions to manipulate those around you."

"Perhaps I might," he said. "But in this case, it is not a thimbleful. Follow me."

There was a thin trail that wound its way through the mountain passage. They were arid mountains, with twisted olive trees covering the rocky surfaces. Scrub brush down beneath. The sky was an insipid sort of blue, washed pale by the heat of the Arabian sunshine.

"Are there snakes?" she asked.

"I would have thought you'd know. There are snakes everywhere. One must always look out."

She looked at him, those turquoise eyes regarding him closely. And he could see that she was not certain whether he'd spoken in metaphor or not. "Literal and figurative," he clarified.

"Of course."

He led the way, but paused for a moment. "The plane is already gone. If you attempt to run… There is but one place you can go. And it contains me. Think on that."

"I'm not stupid enough to run away from you in the desert."

"That is a relief."

"If I was going to attempt a reckless runaway situation, I would have leapt out of the car."

"That begs the question… Why didn't you?"

"If I had managed to survive the fall without injuring myself, I would not have been able to outrun you. What is the point of suffering the humiliation of such a thing if I can't even really escape?"

"A valid question."

"I wish that I could ask you what happened. How we ended up here. But the sad thing is I know the answer. And so… I'm just following you."

"The best decision, you will find."

They came around the corner of one of the black craggy outcroppings, and there you could see, glinting in the sun, a sheet of glass. The front of the house.

"What is this?"

"My fortress."

It was a stark, black box. All tinted windows in the front that kept out the harshness of the desert sun, but provided a brilliant view of their surroundings. It was part of the wild landscape. And it was also a shelter.

"You can only get in if your palm print is programmed to allow you to do so." They walked up to a mighty gate that cordoned off the property from the surrounding land. He pressed his palm against a flat black box at the gate, and it gave them entry.

"Are there any vehicles here?"

"Yes," he said. "But like the gate, you will not be using them unless you have custom access."

"One might be tempted to call you paranoid," she said.

"One would be tempted to respond that my paranoia is earned. Do you not think?"

She said nothing. And he was gratified by the fact he had won this round. Or perhaps she really was getting tired now.

As they approached the home, its massive structure shaded them, and he walked up to the door and placed his palm against the sensor he knew was there. It unlocked.

It was all black inside, flooded with light. "This is…"

"It's extraordinary," he said. "I am aware. I have been working on it for many years. A place for me to set up operations as I worked to amass a team to take out the corrupt leadership of my nation, and free my brother."

"How did you… How did you do that? You're one man. You're not an army."

"That is correct. I am only one man. But I am Sheikh Cairo, and the protection of my country is my sworn duty. My loyalty to my brother is unparalleled. Do you know what the function of the second son is in a traditional royal family?"

"You were to join the military. To become the commander."

"Yes. Did we have that conversation once?"

She shook her head slowly. "We didn't. I asked Riyaz once, when he went walking with me out at the fountain."

"Did my brother walk with you?"

She looked at him. "Yes."

He had not known that. The sensation that assaulted his chest was a shock to him. Why should he feel… Anything over the fact that his brother had taken walks with the woman that had been promised to be his wife? It was good and right that Riyaz should do so.

It was only that he had assumed the two of them did not have a connection then. He had thought… He had thought the connection was his. And his alone.

It mattered not. She was not his. Not then. Not now.

Part of him wanted to take her back to Paris then. She would not be within his reach, but she would not be within reach of Riyaz either.

The deep desire to do just that shook him down to his core.

He would not. He would not falter, not now. He couldn't trust himself. Could not trust himself especially when it came to her.

He could see she did not want this, but…to give in to her needs would be to deny Riyaz.

And it would be to indulge himself.

That weighted the scale. It meant he had to persevere in this. To give Riyaz what he wanted.

To deny Ariel in this was also to deny himself. And if he'd learned one thing from his failure fifteen years ago…

It was that he had to deny himself at all costs.

"Aisha," he called out.

A small woman wearing traditional robes appeared. "Please show Ariel to her room. Have a bath drawn for her. She and I are to dine together tonight. Where we will speak of future plans."

"I did not agree to have dinner with you," she said.

Something like a flame ignited in his gut.

"I think you still do not understand the situation in which you find yourself, Ariel Hart.

"You do not have a choice here. You are in this territory between countries. Traditionally, it is no man's land. But now? It is my land. And in it you will do as I say. In it, I am lord and master. You will go, you will bathe. You will perfume your skin, you will put on jewels and that gown that is befitting of a royal woman in this country, and we will speak of the future."

A challenge glittered in her eyes, and he knew that whether he wanted to or not, he was going to have to see where the challenge led. For he could not ensure that she would do as he asked unless he put her in the bathtub himself and scrubbed his hands over her skin.

The idea sent a jolt of unexpected lust through him.

Lust was something he felt on his own timetable. He had spent a great many years exorcising demons in bed. He had found that anonymous sex did a lot to banish unpleasant memories. But there were times when he indulged and times when he did not. He had spent years availing himself to every perversion known to man. The sheer variety of it all had turned him rather jaded. And it was best to be jaded, he found. For that allowed him dominion over his sexual desire. So having it rise up now with little warning or control was… It was unacceptable.

He gritted his teeth and tamped it down. His boyhood desire for Ariel had been that of an untried lad. He had not known what it was like to sink into a woman's body, and so she had consumed his thoughts. He knew now. From every angle and every position. There was no mystery left. And yet, Ariel felt like a mystery.

She belongs to Riyaz.

Yes. She belongs to Riyaz.

He snapped his fingers, and Aisha put her hand on Ariel's arm.

"Come along," she said.

"I will," said Ariel. And then she turned aqua eyes on to him. "But only to get away from him."

As if that would affect him. He felt nothing. The sooner she understood that, the better.

CHAPTER FOUR

SHE WAS TRYING not to be impressed by the grandeur of this place. At first she had thought it terribly ugly. A large, shiny box out in the middle of these unforgiving mountains.

But she could see the beauty once she was inside. The way the windows captured the sunlight, while protecting them from the harshest aspects of it. The way it showed them the mountains, the trees, the wild landscape below, while concealing the house from view.

It was an architectural wonder.

A huge part of fashion was appreciating the elements of design, and this house was… It was truly remarkable.

The woman was at least a head taller than Ariel, but she moved with a ruthless efficiency that belied her size. She opened up a door in the hallway, black like everything else, and Ariel's mouth opened when she saw the room. It too was black. The floors, the walls. But the ceiling had a graphic, brilliant wallpaper on it with large magenta flowers. A chandelier hung from the ceiling. The bed that stood at the center of the room was gold, with plush, velvet coverings in different shades of pink.

"What is this room for?"

"It has always been for you," she said. "Sheikh Cairo

has been preparing this place for this inevitability for many years."

The words echoed within her.

Riyaz had demanded her. But Cairo had prepared a room for her.

As if it had been fate.

No.

He had never been her fate. That was all magical thinking, the kind she'd let herself fall into as a girl.

She wasn't a girl anymore.

"Has he?" The words came out scratchy.

"Yes. I will just go run your bath. The bathroom is just through there. You will find a selection of clothing in the armoire. You may choose that which you wish for dinner." The woman disappeared, and a moment later she heard water running.

She opened up the gilded, mirrored armoire, and inside found a myriad of jeweled, ornate dresses.

They were halfway between contemporary and traditional dress, each one of vibrant color, with gems stitched into fashionable designs.

The designer's heart within her quickened. This was inspiration. Down to the depths of her soul.

And she felt... Privileged to get to put on such clothing. But she didn't want to give him the satisfaction of knowing that.

She might be enjoying elements of this, but he didn't need the satisfaction of knowing that.

She touched a brilliant blue gown. It had a matching top that would bare her midriff, and a skirt with a high waist that looked as if it would hug her hips and flare out around her knees.

She selected it and carried it into the bathroom. And

what she saw in there stopped her cold. It was not a simple bathtub. Rather more of a pool, with gold taps, the farthest most edge simply a window that looked out at the desert below.

"I will leave you," the woman said. "The water is scented with oil, and you will find different scrubs at the edge just there."

"Thank you," Ariel said.

It was funny how, even now, her manners seemed important. What a strange thing that was. Though none of the staff here had been rude to her. Other than the whole…not caring that she'd been kidnapped thing.

It made her feel compelled to be polite.

The woman left, and she began to undress slowly, shivering as she realized she stood naked there in front of the windows, gazing out at the wilderness. There was no one and nothing there, of course.

The sun spilled into the room and illuminated her naked body, gold poured out on her curves. It warmed her.

And it felt to her a rather wanton thing. And she had never played the part of a wanton in her entire life.

It was thrilling. Standing there looking out with her body exposed, and she could not say why. But it was like she was on the precipice of flying. On the edge of freedom.

You are not free. You're a captive.

That sobering thought cut off the strange fantasy she'd found herself caught in, and she began to walk into the water.

She moaned as the warmth enveloped her body. She really was exhausted. The bath was deep, and huge, and she swam to the window. She was still entirely exposed. Even covered in water.

She thought of Cairo, his intense, hot gaze, and she felt her nipples go tight, her breasts get heavy.

Something began to throb between her legs.

And she was so tired she couldn't even shut the feelings away.

In her mind's eye, she saw him hand her the orange again. But this time, it was Cairo the man. And she was naked. In a pool of water.

His eyes were hot. Dark with hunger…

She had to wonder if she was here because he'd forced her, or if because part of her had waited fifteen years to be with Cairo again…

She gasped, snapped herself back to reality and went over to the scrubbing salts.

She put some on her hand and began to work them vigorously over her body, abrading herself, punishing herself for such thoughts.

She shivered. Then she rinsed herself and got out of the water. She dried herself on the plushiest towel that had ever made contact with her skin, and put on the heavy, jeweled garment she had chosen for herself.

A moment later, there was a knock at the door. "I am here for hair and makeup," said a woman that she had not yet seen before.

"I'm sure that isn't necessary."

"You are having dinner with *him*." She said the pronoun as if it were capitalized. Singular. "Of course it is necessary."

What was it about this man? All of these employees talked about him as if he was the sun and the moon.

And she decided she would ask the woman just that.

She wasn't too polite to not be nosy. She sat down in a chair in front of the mirror.

"How many of you work here?"

"At least fifty are employed here. To keep house, to cook, to take care of the grounds. As security."

"And why are you so loyal to Cairo?"

"He saved us," the woman said, admiration over-taking her voice. "After the royal family was deposed, many politically connected families were in danger. And there were some of us who were impoverished be-fore, and in danger of going hungry. He ran missions where he smuggled many of us over the border. And he ensured that we were well cared for afterward. Sheikh Cairo never forgot his people. And now, he is on the verge of bringing us home. On the verge of restoring that which the locusts have eaten. He is our savior."

"No wonder he has a god complex," she said. But a knot had begun to form in her chest, because she could not deny that what he had done was good.

And why was he treating her as he did?

"You are going to marry Riyaz," the woman said. "We pray for our sheikh."

"Yes," she said. "I will too."

She had to hope for…something to come from Riyaz. Compassion that Cairo certainly wasn't showing her. Something.

She hadn't had a choice about whether or not she came here. She didn't have a choice about whether or not she'd be sent to Riyaz. Cairo hadn't saved *her*. And if Riyaz wasn't sane…if he was bent on vengeance, well, she didn't know what that meant for her fate.

CHAPTER FIVE

"HE ISN'T WELL."

He looked at Brianna's worried golden eyes. "No improvement?"

"He does not sleep in a bed, Cairo. He outright refuses the meals that we serve. He works out, punishing his body day and night…"

"I have freed him," Cairo said. "I do not understand why he persists in acting this way."

"Because in his mind he is still in a cage, Cairo. And I do not know how to reach him."

"I have faith in you," he said.

Brianna's expression softened. He had often thought that perhaps if he were to marry a woman it might've been her. But he worried that she had been treated too harshly, and he wanted to protect her. Not expose her to more harm.

Brianna deserved a different sort of man. A man who could love.

His own had been killed one night out in the desert.

She deserved to be well rid of him and Riyaz as soon as she finished her work.

He knew that she admired him. He knew that he would've been able to seduce her easily. But he actually knew her. Cared for her. So he had never done so. She was more a sister to him. Though he knew the description would likely cause her distress.

"It's difficult," Brianna said. "I can't force him to talk about what he doesn't want to remember."

"Keep trying."

He heard footsteps and looked up over his phone screen. And there she was, standing in the doorway. Her presence was a punch of pure adrenaline that took his breath away. The blue that she was wearing made her eyes look like jewels lit on fire. And it was the strip of her revealed midriff that caused his body to stir. How long had it been since such a simple show of skin on a woman had created such a response in him? Perhaps never.

"Let me show you something."

Her eyes went round. "What?"

"A secret." She looked at him as if he were magic, and he felt like he'd won a prize, even though he knew that he was risking much by taking her hand this way and leading her down the cool palace corridor.

He pushed open the door to the room that held the wedding gems.

He didn't know why he wanted to show her these.

Perhaps because he found himself imagining giving them to her.

But they would never be his to give. Not to her or anyone.

"What are they?" she asked, approaching the glass case, her eyes alight with wonder as she looked at the jewels. Bracelets, a necklace, glittering ruby red. And the red silk scarf...

"Wedding jewels. For the sheikha and the sheikh."
Her eyes met his then, and he saw pain there.

"I have to go," he said, ending the call abruptly.

"Was that one of your lovers?" Ariel asked.

She said it casually. But she sounded jealous.

"Did you not hear what we were speaking of?"

Ariel shrugged. "I heard a woman's voice."

"I do not ever speak to my lovers on the phone. There is never a reason to. That was one of my oldest friends. She is overseeing Riyaz."

"And?"

"Progress is yet to be made. But I trust her."

"So you do trust some people," she said.

"I rescued her," he said. "She is bound to me. Who better to trust?"

"You have a habit of that," she said. "Rescuing people, I mean."

"What makes you say that?"

"The woman who did my hair and makeup. She told me. About how everyone in your employ was smuggled out of the country. That you saved them."

"Brianna is not from Nazul," he said. "But yes."

"Brianna," she said. "Is that the woman with Riyaz?"

"It is. She is a very dear friend."

"Forgive me," she said. "But you do not seem like the sort of person who has friends. Though I will concede that perhaps I only feel this way because of the way that we reconnected with one another."

"Glad I could surprise you," he said.

What he did not like, was the way his body was responding to her. It was very deep and elemental. And it was unacceptable. The way that he had once felt about

Ariel was immaterial. And it should not be bleeding into this present moment. But she was… Stunning. No photograph or media had prepared him. He had any number of beautiful women. Of course he had. He was a man with money and influence. A man with power. It was an aphrodisiac, even without what he knew to be physical attributes that women enjoyed.

But there was something different about her. There always had been. He despised that. That there should be something singular about this woman.

It made no sense as to why. "Come," he said. He stood and held out his hand. Determined to touch her now, because he would defy this attraction between them. He would make it his own. Force it into submission. He was not controlled by his body.

It was one of the assets of years of hedonism.

For him, there was nothing yet to discover.

Except for her.

Women were all the same. He placed that thought firmly in his mind. She did not reach out to take his hand, so he took it on his own.

A sharp gasp exited her lips, and she looked up at him, her eyes wide.

"Come," he repeated. "We will go to dinner."

"All right," she said, tilting her chin upward. Her hand was soft. It was the bland list of observations. Women's hands were often soft, and Ariel did not do manual labor. Why would her hand be anything but soft?

And yet he had not expected her palm to feel as the silken petal of a desert lily. He had not anticipated that it would be something beyond mere softness, but a home that seemed to slip beneath the barrier of his soul and create in him a dry well of longing that was like a man who needed drink in the desert. The sensation that one might die if they could not satiate that need.

Oh, yes. He had expected that she would be soft. But he had not expected this.

Ruthlessly, he shut that down. And he led her from the seating area where he had been speaking to Brianna, into the dining room. The table was laid with a grand feast. Traditional meals of his country.

It was one of the many benefits he enjoyed for having rescued so many people from his homeland. There was a great deal of incredible traditional cooking in his life, and he did not take it for granted. For his people had been overrun. His people had been oppressed these many years.

Seeing where the spirit endured was part of what had given him motivation. Strength. Hope. For as much as he was dark, gritty and forged in the iron of pain, hope resided. It must.

One did not seek to seize back the throne without hope. Even now, the endeavor that they were undertaking with Riyaz required hope.

For Riyaz had suffered unimaginably. And Cairo had to cling to hope that they could bring his brother back from the brink. There was no other option.

Not for his country, and not for him.

Cairo was the only family Riyaz had left. Cairo and Ariel were the only remaining links to the past beyond the food on this table. Beyond traditions and remembered songs and stories. The whisper from the window that reminded him of his mother's voice.

Riyaz was all he had.

He looked up at Ariel. "I hope this is to your liking."

"I… I don't know why I feel the need to reassure you," she said.

"I don't know. Do I seem a man in need of great reassurance?"

"I just find it interesting that I am compelled to ensure that I'm not rude to my kidnapper."

"Perhaps because you know I am not your kidnapper. Rather, your trustee. Your guardian."

"Please." She sat down in the chair just to the right of the head of the table, and he took his place at the head.

"Is it to your liking?"

"Is my answer important? Yet again, I did not think that my preferences signified."

"Oh, they change nothing of note. But they may actually change the menu. So it would not be the worst thing in the world for you to voice your opinions on the cuisine."

"It looks lovely," she said. "Truly. And there, now I have successfully done something to ease the monster of rising Stockholm syndrome inside of me."

"Stockholm syndrome? Have you begun to sympathize with me?"

"Don't go that far."

"But would you like some jeweled couscous? Perhaps some lamb?"

"Yes."

He did the honors of dishing out the feast. And he presented her a plate laden with delicacies, and he was gratified when he saw the rising hunger in her eyes. And he felt an answering hunger rising inside of him that had nothing to do with food. This woman had always fascinated him. She was something quite a bit beyond anything he'd ever experienced before. And always had been. Yet again he wondered if that had something to do with the fact that when he'd met her he had been nothing more than a virgin boy. A boy who knew nothing about desire. Whose first taste of it had been when sitting near her. Was it possible that it was simply such an experience that was so formative that one never truly moved beyond it?

Perhaps it was his punishment, for his sins.

Or perhaps it was just a reminder of his weakness.

"I do not wish to fight with you," he said. Because there was no point to that. She could fight him all she wanted, but his mission would not change. If she thought she might wear him down, she was incorrect. If she thought she might eventually appeal to some sort of sympathy inside of him, she was incorrect there as well. He did not possess any. He could not feel sorry for a woman who was bound to a life of finery and protection. He would see no harm done to her, and she would enjoy an elevated position. There were true hardships in the world. Having choice taken away from you was hardly one of them. Especially not when the cage you would be put in was so finely gilded.

Everyone had cages.

"Why do you wish to know anything about me?" she asked.

"Because. We are to be family. Should we not know one another?"

"Then you tell me first. How did you decide to start a chain of hotels that would make you a billionaire? How did you get into property management, and innovation? How did you know that it would make you the kind of successful that you needed to be in order to claim your country again?"

"I looked at the success of other men who had done similar things. Men who had come up from nothing. And I used the information that I had about what made men envious. Exclusivity. I lived the life of a royal, so I understood luxury. And I understood the way wishing to feel connected to luxury could drive some men insane. And so I cultivated that angle. I manipulated human nature. Because if there is one thing that I have learned it's that humans do not change. And that they can always be exploited for your purposes."

"So, no part of you feels passionate about the luxury travel industry?"

"Every time I walked into one of my own hotels I was very aware that my brother—if he was still alive— was being kept in appalling conditions. Every time I made a place for the wealthy to enjoy the heights of luxury, I was aware that my brother might be in chains. In many ways I was simply creating reminders. All around me, all the time. No. I do not feel passion for anything other than what I have done now. So now you know me. My story." He leveled his eyes on hers. "Now you can tell me yours."

"I love beautiful things. I always have." She looked down. "And I suppose I am a very shallow girl. For I have always liked the way beautifully cut clothing made me feel."

"Very nice. What a sound bite. Is that what you would say to the media?"

She looked up at him, her expression hard. "What does it matter?"

"You can continue to fight me, but the result will be the same. Will it make you feel better?"

"Perhaps nothing will make me feel better."

"That seems a reasonable response."

"Do you expect me to be reasonable?"

"No. I simply felt we might talk."

"I'm not a thirteen-year-old girl, Cairo. Not anymore. You can't bait me with an orange and a charming smile. We have gone beyond that."

"Can we pretend? For a moment. The last time I ever wanted to know what another person thought or felt was in that garden. And it was you. So perhaps you could indulge me for a moment."

He did not know where that moment of raw honesty had come from. He was not certain that such a thing had even existed in him before this moment.

And yet he found that it was true. Whether he could identify what it had come from or not.

She did not speak for a moment. And then she lifted her head. "Because I watched my mother have to come to terms with the fact that she married a monster. I watched her go from believing that she had a beautiful, perfect life, to being appalled by the realization of what my father had done. And she had to somehow keep her head held high. She would wake up in the morning, and she would feel... Destroyed. By what he had done to you, to me. By what he had done to us. And then she would put on the right shade of lipstick. A proper dress. A just so pair of earrings, and she would conquer the day regardless of what was going on inside of her. It was like watching a warrior suit up for battle. And I could appreciate then, the way that women wielded power when they did not have a sword. I watched my mother survive a very difficult betrayal, and whether or not you recognize that what happened hurt us too... It did. I was always interested in art and design, but the way that design could change the way my mother carried herself, the way that fashion allowed her to find some strengths, that is what propelled me in that direction. Perhaps I wanted to find some of it for myself. But at any rate I found that I was quite good at it."

"And you feel passion for it," he said.

"Yes," she said. "I do. I feel immensely passionate about seeing my work, my heart, come together like this. I worked so hard. So hard to get where I am. It's painful to leave it behind."

"And lovers?" He had not meant to ask that question, and it bit the edge of his tongue. The idea of a man putting his hands on her body... It did something to him. Twisted something in his soul. And yet, was his task not to bring her to his brother so that his brother might have her? Of course it was.

He bit down until he tasted blood.

It did not matter what he wanted.

"Why do you insist on asking me about things that do not matter? You don't care that I love fashion. And you don't care why. You don't care if I have a lover. You want only what you want. You do not care for me one bit."

"I have not been able to afford to care for a thing beyond the liberation of my country, and my brother."

"Well, what, then? What then—now that you have accomplished it?" she asked.

"I continue to fight."

And he would do so from his own cage.

Everyone had a cage.

His was to keep him away from her.

CHAPTER SIX

"Show me the desert."

"You hate the desert," he said.

"But you don't. I want to understand."

"All right, but we could get in trouble."

She knew they could. She had sensed that as their friendship deepened. As her feelings for him became more and more difficult. As it became clear to her she...

She thought he was the most beautiful boy she'd ever known, and she wanted to hate Nazul with all that she was, but she could never hate Cairo.

"I don't care," she said. "Show me."

She didn't know why she found this conversation so... Infuriating. Perhaps it was the way he pretended that he cared. The way he acted as if her feelings mattered even a little bit. When she knew they did not. He was going to do exactly what he wanted to, no matter what she said to him. There was no appealing to his better nature. That nature did not exist. *The boy that you want him to be doesn't exist.*

She had to confess, even if to herself, sitting there feeling guiltily sated from the meal that he had just put before her, that she had felt a sense of... Jealousy twisted up inside of her when she had overheard him speaking to that woman.

When she talked about Stockholm syndrome, in part, she wasn't kidding. And she didn't like it one bit.

But his raw, masculine beauty called to her. As did something about being here in the desert. She thought of the way that she had stood before the window, naked. The way that she'd felt… Thrilled by it.

And just then, she felt a surge of something wild within her.

"Would you show me the desert?"

She hadn't meant to ask that, in quite those terms. She hadn't meant to echo the conversation from that last day. Oh, that last night.

How she'd wished she'd kissed him that last night.

But she'd been fourteen. Engaged to his brother. Even if it was against her will.

Even if it had been him she'd desired.

She *didn't* want to kiss him now. She ignored the throb in her body that called her a liar.

"Excuse me?"

"I wish to tour the grounds," she said, rephrasing. "We did once sit outside in the gardens at the palace, did we not? When I felt hopeless about the future. About my position in your country. About everything. We sat there in the blossoms, and we talked like human beings. I just… I want to go outside for a moment."

"As you wish," he said, standing and looking at her with distrust. She didn't know what she wanted, but she knew that her heart was pounding like a bird trapped in a cage. Or rather, like what she was. A woman caught in a trap.

One thing she knew… She would fight.

Because if she did not she wouldn't be able to re-spect herself.

It was a slow dawning realization that while her mother had always been kind to her, she had been pas-sive. She had been passive in her own life, and in Ar-iel's. And Ariel feared that in many ways she'd fallen into that same passivity. Acceptance.

Her mother had accepted a husband who had decided their daughter would have a political marriage, and who knew what other red flags she'd ignored? She'd ex-pressed sympathy for Ariel's desire to not marry Riyaz, but in the end had done nothing to stop it.

She had told Ariel to be on guard for Riyaz's return, and yet had treated it like an inevitability, and Ariel could see the echoes of this in her own life.

Yes, as a young girl she'd accepted what her father had told her but eventually she'd begun to want her own, separate things.

When she'd been bundled up to go to Nazul every year she had complained, she hadn't fought.

When she'd been fourteen, she hadn't fought. She'd wanted to kiss Cairo, and she hadn't done it. She'd wanted him and not Riyaz and she hadn't done a thing about it. It wasn't a kiss she needed now, but the spirit remained.

She did not want to marry Riyaz. She didn't want the life that had been prescribed to her, and she would fight, even knowing she couldn't win.

She would fight because it would make her some-thing more than a captive.

She had to be brave now, where she hadn't been be-fore.

He went behind her chair and positioned himself so

that he could pull it out for her while she stood. It was such an odd thing. The way that he played the part of a gentleman even while holding her against her will.

He took her arm, as if he was a man taking her out for a night on the town, and not a walk out in the desert.

He led her back to the spacious entry, and out the front door, which only opened because of the touch of his palm.

Yes. She even needed him to get outside. She was right to try this. Right to do it.

She made a somewhat decisive move away from him as the evening air enveloped her. "It's beautiful," she said, spinning in a circle. What she had said about clothing had not been wrong. She felt powerful in this dress. She felt like the sort of woman who could do whatever she wanted. Who could bend the universe to her will.

And she would try. She would try, no matter the cost.

She looked around and took stock of her surroundings. Took another step to keep herself just distant enough.

And then thunder rolled, out there in the desert, echoing off the mountains all around them.

"What is that?"

"A storm. We shouldn't stay out here. They rage hard and fast."

One fat drop of water landed on her face. Then another. "Just a moment," she whispered.

"Ariel…"

And that was when she ran. She ran like the desert contained her salvation and she had no choice but to fling herself into it, arms wide open. Water hit against her body, cold and harsh, and she ran.

She ran, in jeweled slippers and a gown made of silk

that clung to her skin. She ran even though she could not win. She ran because it was the only way she would ever be able to continue to look at herself in the mirror day in and day out for the remainder of her life, which she would no doubt spend as a prisoner.

A prisoner.

She ran. Tears streaming down her face. And when she felt a strong arm grab her around the waist, and when she found herself being spun, her back hitting firmly against the rock wall of the mountain behind her, with a wall of male muscle in front, she let out a sob of distress.

Everything in her rebelled against this moment. Against this man. Against the inevitability of it. She pounded her fists against his chest. And let out the most vile string of curses she'd ever said in all her life.

"I hate you," she shouted. "I don't want to be a prisoner for the rest of my life." She hit him again, and he simply stood fast, holding her still with ease. The storm that she unleashed upon him was a tiny, wrecked gull raging against the tempest.

"I will not be a prisoner for the rest of my life."

She shrieked it. Shouted it. Until she felt the tide beginning to turn inside of herself. Until she felt the power begin to turn and shift within her.

Until she felt herself begin to change. Until the words took on new meaning. Until she recognized the power within them. The power within herself. She had known that she wouldn't escape, out here in the desert. She had known. But she had to do it to prove her mettle. To prove her might. To prove that she was not a wilting flower who would go into the heat to die, but rather a gem who would only become stronger through fire and flame.

"I am not a prisoner," she said. "I'm Ariel Hart. I'm a world-renowned fashion designer. And I did not betray you. I don't deserve to be held against my will, to have everything that I have worked for stripped away from me. I don't deserve it, and I refuse to be punished for the sins of my father. I demand that you give me a life, or I will never stop trying to run. Because as long as I'm in a cage I will kick against the bars, I promise you that, Cairo."

"You are a fool," he hissed, moving closer to her, the rain sliding down over his handsome face. So close. So close. "You would die out here. Me capturing you is the kindest thing that could happen."

"I'm not afraid. I'm not afraid to challenge death. To challenge the desert. I have never been afraid. Always, the men around me have sought to manipulate my life. To decide who I am and what I can do and how much I can be. And only with my father gone, only with your brother in prison, was I able to pursue a life of my own. I went and made myself a success, and I had to spend those years hoping that…"

"Hoping I was dead?"

Never that.

Oh, never that.

Even standing here now, awash in her rage and indignity, she'd never want him dead.

It was the worst part of all of this. Her connection to him. The fact that she could never be fully certain if the reason she hadn't jumped out of that car back in Paris wasn't to save herself the road rash, but to give herself some time with him.

If the reason she'd run now, knowing she would be

caught, was because part of her didn't want to be free of him.

"I deserve it," she said, to herself as much as him. But she didn't know now what she thought she deserved. It was tangled up in all this heat. In him. "And I will fight for it. I will not simply become your docile princess."

He gripped her hard by the shoulders, his hands biting into her. "What is it you want? Do you want the moon? Is that it?"

Ya amar.

His moon. He had called her that before. It was a memory that haunted her, for there was no other word for it. The kind of memory that kept her trapped. The kind that made it so no other man ever piqued her interest.

The kind that let him into her dreams.

"Shall I climb up there and pull it down for you?" he continued, a rough rage in his voice she didn't understand. "I cannot do that any more than I can grant you your freedom. This is a set path."

"I wish to be allowed to retain my work. I wish to have freedom. I will not be kept in a palace as a symbol. I'm more than a symbol. If this is to be my life, then this life must contain all that I desire."

"And that is?"

"My career, as I said. But I will need the freedom to travel."

"And if you escape?"

"That is simply it. I cannot be treated like a prisoner. If I'm not treated like a prisoner, perhaps I will not behave as one. But if I am, then I promise that is all you will get from me."

"What do you need here, now?"

"I need a computer. I need access to email and the internet. I need a phone. I cannot be kept away from the outside world."

"Once we get to my country. Then you may have those things. But not before then."

"If you do not trust me…"

"You just tried to run away out to the middle of the desert at night. You could've been bitten by a viper. Worse. There are jackals out here. You would make a nice meal for them."

"I told you. I'm not afraid."

"Perhaps you were not afraid because you have never seen someone die. But I have, Ariel. I fear it. I saw no peace in it."

She was silenced by that. "But you will give me those things when we're back at the palace?"

"Yes."

"And if Riyaz does not wish for me to have these things?"

"Riyaz is having to learn how to… Be a real boy. For lack of a better way of describing it. He will acquiesce to what I tell him is appropriate."

"You are certain?"

"I will see that it is so. I told you, this is not a punishment. It is the fulfillment of what is right. I am not holding you captive."

"Am I free to go?"

"No. But you are not…in danger. No harm will come to you. My aim is not to crush you. We will continue to discuss the terms of this as we await further clarity on the situation."

And she knew that she had won a victory. She knew

that the wildness of the desert, the wildness in her, the way that they echoed around and within each other, but it was the truth of who she was. That it was what she was meant to be. She had to listen to the wildness at her core.

That wildness would guide her. And it would make sure she had a life. Even if…

Her thoughts trailed off. He was still touching her. His hands on her shoulders. His face close. He was beautiful. This man who was her enemy. This man who held her captive.

And she did not mean held her captive by holding her prisoner. But rather, kept her captivated by the intensity in his dark gaze.

And it was funny that when she thought about her future, what she thought was in terms of what she might have to give up. Her career. Her freedom. Her travel. But what she could not think of was being married to Riyaz. Not only because she could not imagine the man—she hadn't seen him since he was sixteen years old. But also because… Cairo would be her brother-in-law. And Cairo might elicit inside of her a mix of reactions, but many of them were not appropriate for a man who would hold that position and title.

Had she ever been running from Cairo?

Had it only ever been Riyaz? Was that why she was here now, feeling all of these things?

"Let us go back to the house," he said.

She was soaked through to the bone now. Tired. Exhausted.

"Let go of me," she said.

"Only if you promise not to run."

And she wanted…she wanted to kiss him. Or maybe

more accurately, she wanted to live a life where she *could* kiss him.

Hadn't that always been what she'd wanted?

Hadn't it always been what she was denied?

No matter whether she was fourteen and promised to his brother, a free woman in Paris promised to no one, or an escaped prisoner in the desert…

In none of those lives had kissing him ever been possible.

"I can't promise that," she whispered.

"I promise you your freedom when we get to the palace," he said, his voice rough. He moved his face even closer to hers, his lips so close, so very close. "Now promise me you will not run."

There was a heartbeat, a space, a breath, where she thought to defy him.

Or herself.

She didn't not know which.

"I won't run," she said instead.

And when he let go of her, she could swear that she saw relief in his dark gaze, and she wondered why. She would not try to run again. Not tonight. Because he was right. Because there was death out there waiting in the desert, and she did not wish to court that level of danger. Her running had not been about that. It had been about being willing. Willing to risk everything for freedom. And perhaps she would not be able to gain all of her freedom, but she would not live as a prisoner. That would be her rallying cry. That would be her declaration.

It was clear to her, however, that whatever it was she felt burning in her now… He felt the same.

The realization made her stomach hollow itself out.

And she decided there was a limit to the wildness that she would chase in the desert. She might be willing to tempt death by running out into nothingness, but she would not tempt him.

The idea made her shiver.

"Cold? Imagine how cold you would've been if you were out sleeping on the desert floor. You would not have fared well in a flash flood."

"I wouldn't have slept for long according to you. There are jackals out there. Though I suspect that there might be jackals where I'm headed too."

He grinned then, his white teeth gleaming. "If I intended to eat you, Ariel, you would know."

The hardness in his voice called to something feminine in her. The dangerous edge to his tone like a blade slicing against her tender skin. And she shivered. This time, definitely not from the cold.

"When you say that Riyaz is not well…"

"We will not discuss him tonight." They arrived back at the house, and he allowed her entry. There was a mirror just at the entry, and she looked at it and saw herself. Her hair askew, her makeup having run down her face. She looked a misery. And she had imagined that there had been something like heat between them back there. The idea was laughable. If the clothing had felt like her armor only an hour ago, it felt like a costume now. Not fitting of the bedraggled, ruined creature that stood there looking in the mirror now.

"I need to sleep," she said.

"I'm glad that you finally think so. You had a long day."

"Yes."

And as the years stretched on in front of her, she wondered if every day would feel this long.

And when she looked at Cairo, the feeling that was created inside of her was more confusing than she would like to admit.

"Change into dry clothes," he said. "And sleep. For in the morning, we must begin to see to your education."

And as she watched him walk away, his clothes clinging to him because of the rain—yet he looked no less imposing for it—she realized she would comply.

Because Cairo needed this.

And one thing she had never been able to turn away from was him.

She wasn't choosing Riyaz.

But part of her was choosing Cairo.

Or perhaps had chosen him all those years ago in Nazul.

Perhaps what really held her here was not the vastness of the desert or the power of the al Hadid family.

But feelings for Cairo that had grown like orange blossoms in the unforgiving sun when she had been far too young to fear their power.

CHAPTER SEVEN

SHOW ME THE DESERT...

He cursed himself as a fool for the entire rest of the night. The memory of her skin beneath his hands...

He never should've let her go outside. He never should've let her get in a position to run. Less still, should he have negotiated with her.

Weakness.

Ariel Hart had always been an unforgivable weakness.

It was time for breakfast now, and the spread of pastries and very strong coffee that was laid out on the table was mocked by the fact that she had not arrived on time as he had bid her to. If she had run again in the night...

But the house was locked up, and you could only get out if your palm print matched those programmed into the security system. So she could not have done so.

You are soft for her. You always have been.

He gritted his teeth. He was not a stupid boy anymore.

He would not be. It was unacceptable. He would not be soft for the woman, because there was no room for softness in him. In his life. In this world.

Finally, she appeared. She was wearing a pair of

high waisted olive green pants with safari pockets and a white shirt. Her hair was tied low on her neck, a white silk scarf holding it back. She looked simple, with no makeup on her face. And yet she made everything in him go tight. And he remembered what she had said last night. About her mother. About armor. About the way clothing made her feel as if she had the strength to face down what she must. He could see how it was true now for her. Could see the way that she had dressed herself today, quite different from last night. Last night her clothing had been a distraction. Glittery, sensual.

Today, they were a riff on the masculine. Much more no nonsense. She had come to negotiate today. Not distract him with her body, and yet, distracted he remained.

"Good of you to join me."

"Apologies. I found that I rather took longer in the bath than intended. It is a beautiful bath."

And her words force the image into his mind of her naked body gliding through the water.

Lust kicked him, square and hard. He could not believe that she had chosen her words by accident.

But why? Why would she choose to goad him like this? Was he the only one remembering the past, or did their shared memories haunt her too?

He had to accept the idea that he might be reading something into their interaction. Something he had never done in his life. Not even once. When a woman wanted him, he knew.

"I'm not sure what you intend to teach me," she said, sitting down at the table and reaching out, piling pastries onto her plate before grabbing the coffee pot and pouring herself a measure of strong, dark liquid.

She took a sip, took a bite of croissant, then sighed.

"You seem an entirely different woman than the one I left last night."

"A mental breakdown can do wonders for the spirit. Sometimes giving into despair is the beginning of fighting your way back up."

"Funny, I'm not sure I trust you."

She shrugged, then licked some sugar off her finger. He felt the action echo along his length and nearly cursed out loud.

This was unconscionable.

He could not want her. She was for Riyaz. Riyaz, who would have to be tamed into something much more civilized before he could ever go near her. Riyaz who… It was entirely possible that Riyaz had not touched a woman in sixteen years. And then… Given his age when he was taken into the dungeon… It was entirely possible he never had. He looked at Ariel, and he wondered what that might mean for her. If that would mean a brutal, unpracticed experience for her.

She was a beautiful woman. Undoubtedly she'd had her share of lovers. He could only hope that her skill would compensate for the lack of it potentially found in Riyaz. He did his best not to think of it. "I'm asking you again," she said, "what is it you intend to teach me? Because you know that I was schooled in the customs of your country from the time I was a child. I spent summers there. I learned the language. I have been in training to be the sheikha for years. So what is it that…"

"There were things you were never taught. You had not been walked through the customs that would be present at the wedding. The dance. It is important that you know. It is important that you walk in armed. Is it not?"

And he wondered who this was for.

This was education Riyaz would be doing if he was not being put back together. And so… He would do this. She was afraid. She did not want to lose everything. She did not want to leave it all behind. That was understandable. He would see her well prepared to go toe to toe with his brother. To be the bride at the spectacle of a wedding that they would be throwing. The wedding that would signal their true return to power. The sheikh is dead. Long live the sheikh.

"I didn't realize…"

"There is a maze of customs to navigate. And strengthening the customs of the nation is part of my sworn duty. Showing them that all is well. The wedding must go off without a hitch."

"You are truly not used to anything opposing you."

"Very rarely has anything tried. Except you."

"So I'm to get princess lessons?"

"It is more than that. You are correct. You cannot live as a prisoner. It will not do. You must be strong, you must be traditional, a symbol of all that was good, and a symbol of all that is now better."

"How nice for me. And what do you get to be a symbol of, Cairo?"

"Endurance. Of never giving up. Hope. While Riyaz is a symbol of our strength. He is not broken. Not truly. I will not allow that to be so."

He couldn't let it be the end of his brother. The truth of him. If Riyaz was broken beyond repair then Cairo's life didn't matter at all.

"You love him."

"I always have. He is my older brother. My idol. My

future king. When we were younger… He had both everything and nothing that I wanted."

He realized the words could not make sense to her. But it was true. He had never envied Riyaz's duty. Not ever. He had envied him Ariel. But that was all. Yes. He had envied him Ariel. But mostly… He had simply admired his older brother. Seen him as a great and glorious leader. And the best older brother. Strong. Intelligent. Quick with it. He had seen Riyaz but briefly in the time since he had been extracted from the dungeon. He spoke with no concept of what was appropriate and what was not. It seemed at times he lived to be deliberately provocative, and yet he could see there was nothing so calculated in his brother. He acted on animal instinct. And there were rages…

Yes. The rages.

"I will lay down my life to protect him," Cairo said. "Already, I have sacrificed many years to protect him. I will continue to do so."

"It's quite sad," she said suddenly, her eyes going vacant.

"What is?"

"I don't have anyone in my life I feel that way about. I'm defending my… My business. I love my business. I love what I do. I'm so very passionate about it. But it was not piecing a country back together. I'm angry at you, Cairo. But I cannot deny that you have done more with your life than I have with mine. In sheer terms of what you have given to others. Every employee that I have met is slavishly devoted to you, and it is because of what you've done for them. And then you really mean it. You're giving everything for Riyaz. And I was weeping in the desert over my fashion label."

"It is a gift," he said slowly, "to have such dreams, Ariel. A gift to be allowed to want things. You should not feel ashamed."

His own desires were not allowed.

"I think I understand you better now. My mother… She might be my style icon. But… We are not close. Not really. What happened with my father was too difficult. She was heartbroken by his actions. They separated. And then he died. And it was all just awful. Layers upon layers of heartbreak. For what? So that he could have money and power. He did not love us more than that." She took a shuddering breath. "And then he died. He didn't even get to spend the money. Not much of it. He died without family. I think my mother felt broken by that. Truly. To where even spending time with me became painful. Because I reminded her of the time that was spent in your country. Of my father's pursuits. Of that which became more important than us. And the lives of your family. Riyaz has been in a dungeon for the last fifteen years, and I think that you still may have a stronger bond with him than I do with my mother."

"It is a tragedy. All around. On every front. But I will see it restored."

"When do these lessons begin?" She finished her cup of coffee and poured herself another.

"Now."

"Please do let me finish my coffee."

"You can bring it with you."

Her eyes flickered, but the corners of her mouth turned upward. "I don't see a to-go cup."

"Bring the fine china. Much more eco-friendly than a disposable cup anyway.

Her heart was racing. There was something about

the conversation they'd just had that set her alight. And now she was being ushered into a massive room with windows floor to ceiling, with the promise that Cairo would be with her shortly.

It was early yet, so the sun wasn't half as punishing is it would become later. She could see the bright and arid desert below, and something began to throb between her thighs. Shame ignited within her, and she looked back and saw Cairo, and the feeling intensified. She'd had a host of erotic dreams last night. The kinds of images that had never plagued her before. Not once.

It was unendurable. Maybe it was because the specter of the fact that she would…

That she would presumably be sleeping with Riyaz loomed over her head.

She knew about sex. She was a woman in the world, after all. She worked in an industry that was practically saturated in sexuality. Naked models were always strewn about backstage off the catwalks, and she did fittings on beautiful people in every position along the gender spectrum all the time. She simply didn't react to it. It was part of work. Meanwhile, they were all sleeping with each other in various combinations, and seemed to take it quite casually. Ditto the commentary on it. She was often treated to graphic details about somebody's sexual exploits.

And yet, it had remained theoretical for her. She had attributed it to early trauma and all of that. The fact that she had been bound to a man that she didn't choose from the time she was a child. Oh, yes, she had given herself a great many reasons for why her sexuality was just a little bit dampened.

Except she was beginning to wonder if that was the

case. Or if it had simply gone into hiding until she could see Cairo again.

Because she still remembered that day. That sun-drenched day in the desert…

Was that why even the desert aroused her?

Was it because of him? That was the most disturbing thought she'd ever had.

She heard decisive footsteps behind her and she turned to see Cairo step into the room. "It is a good view," he said.

"Yes. A great view of the landscape that wants to kill me."

"It doesn't want to kill you. It doesn't think of you at all. But if you were to walk into its jaws, it would not hesitate to swallow you whole."

There was something about those words. Something about the way they landed. Like a pomegranate seed at the center of her chest. And then it began to expand. As if it was growing into an entire tree. Blossoming inside of her, twisting and divining throughout her entire body. She felt invaded. By his words. By his scent. By his presence. "The wedding ceremony in Nazul lasts for three days. The bride and groom meet one another at the altar, and they extend their hands."

Without thinking, she moved her right hand forward.

"Not your right," he said. "The left. That is the hand for making vows. Unbreakable promises." He reached out with his left hand and took hers. He turned his palm slightly, then wrapped his fingers around hers, and reflexively she did the same. Then with his right hand he took a silken scarf from his pocket. "When the bride and groom take hands like this, their hands are then tethered together."

She remembered this. The silk scarf. Red and brilliant, behind the display of wedding jewelry he had shown her at the palace.

She'd been hurt that he'd shown it to her. She'd felt like he was reminding her that she was marrying Riyaz.

And not him.

But now he was standing before her, holding the scarf. And she couldn't breathe. "It is symbolic of the fact that the words that you speak will bind you," he continued. "That even if you release your hold, it is those words that hold you there. The bride and groom do not kiss. They speak vows, the scarf is tied. And then…" He reached out and pressed his thumb against her forehead. "With your thoughts." Then his thumb slid down to her lips, and her breath caught. "With your words." And then down yet again to the center of her breasts. Her breath froze. "With your heart. Serve me only."

"I…"

"And then you."

She took her hand and lifted it to his forehead, but she realized that her fingers were trembling. "With your thoughts. With your words." She could not bring herself to make full contact with his mouth. But then he grabbed her hand and pressed her palm flat over his chest. "With your heart. Serve only me."

And she felt changed. It was an awful feeling. Terrifying. And there was nothing that she could do about it. She felt as if she had made vows to him. In this very room. And when she looked up and looked into his eyes… Her breath seemed to freeze in her chest altogether. It was more intimate than a kiss.

At least she imagined it was. She had never been kissed.

She wondered now for the first time if it was because of the kiss she'd never given him. If her body was still waiting for it.

She swallowed hard and pulled away, the silk scarf around their hands unraveling as she did. "Those are very interesting vows."

"I have always thought they were romantic. My parents were in love. Very much."

"Then why did they arrange a marriage for Riyaz?"

"Their marriage was arranged," said Cairo. "Love followed. They believed that was the path to love."

"Oh."

"For them it resulted in the greatest love imaginable, so why would they consider another way for their children? They saw it as a sort of fate."

"I see." Except she didn't, and her whole body still burned.

"After that there is the feast. It will be outside in a big tent that includes the entirety of the palace. All families. Regardless of wealth and status. Food will be brought out to the villages as well. The celebration will be spread everywhere. For everyone. It is a wedding. And weddings are about abundance. Abundance of joy. Abundance of food."

"And after the food?"

"Let us worry about it tomorrow. Tonight…we will have a feast."

CHAPTER EIGHT

"THE DESERT AT night is beautiful."

She looked at him instead of the moon and the stars. She looked at him like he was the moon and the stars.

"I told you that it was. Not as hot. But dangerous. You have to be careful. You cannot come out here alone."

She clung to his arm, and he felt a rising tide of desire. It frightened him. He was not a stranger to sexual arousal. But he had never felt that for another person. Not like this. Not while he was with them. "I wouldn't. I promise. I won't do anything dangerous, Cairo. I wouldn't want to be out here without you anyway."

She smiled up at him. And the moon made her face glow. She had never asked why he called her his moon. Because in the desert, in the dark, on a clear night, a full moon was a gift. It could light your way. Guide you. That was what she felt like to him. She felt like far too much. Far too special. Far too important. She could be his friend. They could always be friends. Of course they could. But she would marry Riyaz someday. And he would not be able to walk alone with her. He would not be able to touch her.

And he found himself reaching out then to touch

her face. "Ariel," he said, her name a whisper when he didn't mean it to be.

Her eyes went round and glassy, and they reflected the stars. As if she was made of them.

"Cairo," she whispered.

He wanted to kiss her. But he knew that he couldn't. Not ever. He should not have ever showed her those gems. He should never have let himself think about putting them on her body. He should never have allowed himself to dream, even for a moment, about binding her to him.

It was forbidden.

She had been told to dress for a feast. A wedding feast. Apparently, she was being prepared for what would happen on day two of the wedding.

The idea made her uneasy. She dressed in a pink gown tonight. With long billowing sleeves and glimmering turquoise jewels sewn into the fabric. It swished when she walked, a mermaid shaped gown with a high waist.

It covered almost every inch of skin. And yet, it revealed the shape of her figure in a way that made her feel… Well. She felt quite sexy, and she'd never given much thought to how she felt about her own appearance. Not really.

When she walked into the dining room, he was not there. But Aisha was.

"He is waiting for you outside in the garden."

"Oh," she said.

"I will show you."

Of course, Aisha would have to show her, because

she knew she couldn't exit any part of the palace without an approved palm print. She had tried.

But then, she didn't feel all that inspired to try to run again. Not after…

She thought of what happened last night. Running in the rainstorm. Fighting against him like that. He was a strong, solid wall of muscle. A strong, solid wall of man. There was no running from him. No opposing him. Not really.

Aisha pressed her palm to a doorway she hadn't gone through before, and it opened. There was a garden back here. Landscaped and beautiful, surrounded entirely by the mountain. Private. It was lit up now, even in the darkness. Glowing mosaic lights casting colorful sunspots everywhere. The ground was tiled in white and blue, and there was a fountain at the center. And fruit trees. Like the palace in Nazul. Like the palace where she and Cairo had sat together. And there he was. Wearing a white shirt tucked into black pants. The shirt was unbuttoned midway down his chest, and she could not help but admire his stark, tanned skin, and the contrast with the pale fabric. He looked strong and beautiful. Vital.

She swallowed hard. Everything had felt upside down from the moment he had come back into her life. He had kidnapped her after all. Turned everything a different way.

It had also been like he'd returned from the dead. She had always hoped that he lived. But she hadn't known. And for the first time, she allowed herself to feel a rush of gratitude that the boy she had cared so much for was still alive. Even if he had grown into a man whose purposes opposed her own.

He said he wouldn't make you a prisoner.

And maybe she had to accept that as a compromise. Except, of course some women got to live their entire lives in freedom.

You've had over fifteen years of freedom. And you built a wonderful business with it. But what have you done with your personal life?

She had never been in love with anyone. Not anyone but him.

She ignored that treacherous thought. It wasn't that she was in love with him… Maybe she had thought that she was. And maybe it had kept her from moving on. Even now, his masculine beauty left her speechless. Even now it appealed to her in a way that no one else ever had.

He was so strong and solid, and she was torn between wanting to fling herself at him and hit him again like she had done last night. And… Throw herself at him and cling to him. To move her hand over that flash of bare skin of his chest. To feel his muscles, the heat of his skin, his chest hair.

She blinked, and then turned to look at Aisha, but the other woman had melted away, leaving her there alone with Cairo.

"This is the feast that we will have for the wedding," he said, gesturing to a table behind him. She hadn't even looked at the table. She had been so focused on him.

So focused on the reality that what she had done with her freedom had been… Very, very limited. All this time she could have done whatever she wanted. Taken whichever lover she chose. She hadn't. Because a part of her had never left Nazul. Whatever she told herself, a part of her had never been truly free, and it wasn't simply a matter of waiting for Riyaz to escape the dungeon. It was something deeper than that. Much, much deeper.

Something she couldn't bear to examine. Not now.

"Come, my moon. Have a seat." He held the chair out for her. It was a glorious chair. Golden mosaic like everything else in the garden. And she found herself obeying his command, taking her seat at the table. "Spiced lamb," he said. "Couscous with mint. Lemon rice. These will be the traditional things you will find at your wedding feast."

"I see."

There was a cake as well, at his end of the table.

"What is the cake?"

"Saffron. Honey and orange."

Orange. The tang of it settled on her tongue even without having tasted it. The promise of it.

And it reminded her of that day in the garden. And this reminded her of that night long ago.

When he had touched her cheek. They had very nearly kissed that night. She had always been sure of it. The idea had often terrified her. Because she had wondered… Though they were young… She had wondered if Cairo would have ever actually touched his mouth to hers if they would have ever been able to stop at a kiss. Or if passion would have carried them to a place where the consequences might have been far-reaching for her. Especially since… Days after that night she had left. And then his family was gone.

She began to serve herself food, trying her best to banish thoughts from long ago.

"How did you find out when it happened?"

She looked up at him, his dark gaze measured there from across the table.

"My father told us. He told my mother and I as if we should be proud. He knew that I had never wanted to marry Riyaz, so he thought that I would… Celebrate. That he had gotten money for betraying your parents. For helping their enemies figure out how to get into the palace. For helping them find their weakness. We were both… Horrified."

She remembered throwing herself to the ground and weeping until she could not breathe. She hadn't wanted to marry Riyaz. She hadn't been happy there in Nazul. But the sheikh and sheikha had never been anything but kind to her, and Riyaz, though serious and distant, had never been an object of hatred for her.

But it was Cairo. The thought of Cairo, bleeding on the mosaic tile that had broken her.

"I asked about you. My father said that no one had ever found your body. But that you were presumed dead. Cairo, I…"

"Your father was shocked that you and your mother did not praise his perfidy?"

"Yes. And I think even more shocked when my mother left him over it. He had thought that money was what she wanted. It wasn't. I know that my father understood loyalty. I don't think he understood love. My mother could not stay with a man who had caused so much pain. And I… I could never look at him again." *I felt like I died that day with you.*

But she did not say that last part out loud.

Instead, she looked down at her plate, and then back up at him. "How did you escape?"

"It wasn't easy. There was a battle. Intense and bloody. My mother was killed. My father raised his sword to fight. And he took down many of the men who invaded the palace. Before he died, he whispered to me that I had to survive. That I had to run. He said they had not killed Riyaz but that he had been taken prisoner. Sometimes I… Over the years, I wondered if he had lied to me. If he had told me that to keep me from staying and dying. If he had given me a mission as a gift. It was a despairing thought. I needed to believe that my brother lived. But there were persistent rumors that he was a prisoner. And I hoped in those rumors."

"But how did you escape?"

"It was a melee. I knew a secret entrance out to the gardens. I slipped away in the fighting and got free of the palace. There were soldiers—enemy soldiers—stationed in the garden, but… You remember the orange tree."

"Yes." Of course she did.

"I climbed the tree to escape over the wall."

"But what was out there beyond the wall?"

"The desert. When I speak to you of the harsh sun, the jackals, of flash floods and freezing nights, it is because I have survived in the desert. I walked until I escaped over the border into Turkey. And from there I was able to gain safe passage to England as a refugee. There were many people who left Nazul around that time. By the time I arrived there, I was unrecognizable as Cairo. I had lost so much weight and was chapped and weathered from the sun. There was a man who gave me fake papers. Syed. The name that you had seen in the media. That was when I adopted that name. That is how I escaped."

"It sounds… Awful."

"It was. It was only the thought of Riyaz that kept me going. For a great number of years. And then… I went

to school, and I made friends. I started my own business and began to earn money. I of course discovered
pleasures of the flesh. And the pleasures of alcohol. I
was… Rudderless for a time. And I will not say that I
am proud of everything that I did. I felt that there was
no reason to leave any stone unturned when it came
to substances or sex. It was like a delayed response to
surviving the massacre. A celebration of being alive.
Or perhaps a punishment to my body for doing so. And
then gradually I became adept at figuring out how to
work my way toward staging the next coup for Nazul
and pleasing myself. I became quite good at the balance."

It was funny, for even though she felt as if she had
left desire and attraction behind in Nazul along with
him, and even though she had not done the same thing
he had, it felt much like the same. For the way he talked
about sex was as if it were a self-medication of some
kind. Not so much about desire as it was about the need
to blot out unfortunate memories. It didn't sound like
pleasure.

Not really.

He spoke of it as if it were any sort of drug.

And she wondered what other damage had been
done to him. Wondered what else had scarred his soul.
Changed the course of who he was. Because the fact
was…

She might have escaped her betrothal to Riyaz, but
she had never really escaped Nazul.

They finished eating, and then were brought a fresh
pot of coffee to go alongside the cake.

The staff melted away again, leaving them alone.
And suddenly, it did not feel like a rehearsal for any-

thing. It simply felt like she was out in the desert at night with Cairo. Much like that night when they had been teenagers.

Her body ached with it.

She looked up at him, and pain bloomed in her chest.

Pain for what he had been through. Pain for what he had lost. Pain for what the two of them had lost. For they both had lost something that day.

He picked up the cake, and moved around the table, coming to sit in the chair beside her, and she found her breath freezing at the base of her throat. He pushed his fork into the end of the cake and brought it up to her lips. "Try it."

His eyes never left hers as she parted her lips slowly and took the cake inside. As the sharp, citrusy flavor burst on her tongue. It felt intimate. Sitting this close to him while tasting the decadence of the dessert. The moon was bright. And the stars shone with vibrance. And then he reached out and touched her cheek.

"Cairo," she whispered.

He had made a mistake. This was a dangerous game. He should not have brought the meal outside…he should not have set this up at all. Princess lessons? She did not need to practice eating dinner. And yet… He had felt that he wanted to do this. For her. With her. He could not quite credit it. Could not quite figure out what he had been thinking, except he had felt compelled to give her something.

Her breakdown in the desert, and then the tension the following day when he had bound the scarf around her hands…

It was like when they were young. And he had felt

compelled to give her something nice. To make up for the fact that she was somewhere she did not wish to be. Except now was he not the captor? Except now was he not the one who had brought her here? Not her father, but him. He was her jailer in many respects, and he had no right to think that he could bribe her with cake to make it all better when what she wanted was to return to Paris. But there was no question of that, any more than there was a question of…

His chest went tight.

She looked up at him, and he saw the stars in her eyes. And he remembered. Remembered what it was like all those years ago when he had looked down at her and seen…

Hope. A future. One that he could not have, but one that he was desperate for all the same. The need to kiss her now was almost unendurable.

But she belongs to Riyaz.

Riyaz had demanded her. Payment for his suffering. The bride price. The daughter of his enemy.

Satisfaction for that which he had endured.

For that which Cairo bore blame.

How could he touch her?

She was here because he was bound to do what Riyaz had asked. Because he had to deny himself.

But in this moment he could not look at her and see that. She was simply Ariel. As he had seen her then. The gown she wore showed none of her pale, enticing skin, and yet he was bewitched by it. By the way the fabric clung to her curves. By the way it revealed the shape of her body. He ached. When he had been a boy, he had no practice restraining himself, but he had no knowledge of what touching a woman entailed either.

He knew now. He also should have better restraint.

And yet he found the knowledge far outweighed any self-control he might have acquired in the last few years.

So he touched her face, moved his fingertips over her lips. Her eyes fluttered closed.

"Cairo," she whispered. He leaned in, slowly. Slowly, for he wanted to prolong the moment. Prolong the breath before the sin. And just as he stopped, a breath before her lips her eyes opened. And his world was filled with aqua stars, and it was as if a shard of glass had been pressed into his heart and turned hard. It was painful, being this close to her. "I wonder," he whispered, "if you might taste of orange."

And then he curved his hand around the back of her head and closed the distance between their mouths.

She was citrus and softness and years of longing. She was the innocence of a kiss between two teenagers, and the carnal knowledge of a kiss between two adults who knew full well that what they were doing was wrong.

And he could not stop. He angled his head, deepened it, parted her lips beneath his own and slid his tongue against hers.

She gasped, and it gave him the opportunity to gain yet more ground. To take it deeper.

"Cairo," she moaned.

"Ariel. *Ya amar.*" He kissed her deeper. Harder. His body straining against the confines of his pants. His need like a dark, driving force.

He wanted her.

He wanted to strip her naked there beneath the moon. A pagan sacrifice to his selfish desires.

He wanted her.

Bring back Ariel Hart. She is what I want. She is what I'm owed.

It was Riyaz's voice, echoing in his head that brought him back from the brink. He pulled away from her, his breath ragged. Painful. "No," he said. "No. This is not possible. You are my brother's."

"I am not your brother's," she said. "I never have been. I'm my own, Cairo."

"No. You are the payment for your father's betrayal. You are the satisfaction of what was done to my family. Riyaz has demanded it, and he will have it. And if you think that you can turn my head with a kiss, you are sadly mistaken. I have had more lovers than you can count. Do you think you can tempt me? Do you think you can distract me?"

"Clearly I can," she said, her face blank.

"I'm sure you've manipulated men with your body in the past. It is a lovely body. A lovely mouth. But I am not one of those men. My honor demands that I fulfill what my brother has asked. And I will see it done. Pleas from your mouth, and cries of pleasure from your lips, will not deter me from my goal."

"Cairo," she shouted as he stood up.

He turned to face her.

"Is that what you think? That I'm trying to manipulate you?"

"Why would I? Perhaps you always were. Perhaps you always sought to use me to escape from your engagement to my brother."

"I thought we were friends. Then. Back then I thought we were friends."

"Perhaps we were. I cannot remember back that long. I cannot remember being quite so innocent."

"Maybe the years have not jaded me in the same way they have you. Maybe I didn't go out and take every lover available to me. Maybe…" Her words became rough, and he could see tears in her eyes. "Maybe I never forgot you. Did you ever think of that?" He turned away from her, turned away from the guilt that was twisting his chest. And he went back into the house, leaving her outside.

If she ran…

She wouldn't run. Somehow, he knew she wouldn't run.

He went into his study, took out his phone and called Brianna. "How is he?"

"Cairo…"

"How is he?"

"He is… Demanding. Uncivilized. Rough."

He thought of all those things being directed at Ariel.

As if you've treated her any better.

"He hasn't hurt you," he said to Brianna.

"No," she said quickly. "No, he hasn't hurt me. I don't think he would…"

"And what about Ariel? Do you think he would hurt her?"

"He thinks that she is his… Compensation. I don't think that he would hurt her."

"You're telling me you think it's safe for me to bring her back?" he asked through gritted teeth.

"You might give it a couple of days. But soon." There was a strange note to Brianna's voice, but he could not read it.

"I need to ask you something else about my brother. Do you know if they…? Has he spoken to you about his time in the dungeon?"

"Yes. Quite distinctly."

"And did he tell you whether or not they brought him women?"

"I…"

"Did they bring him women while he was in the dungeon?"

"No. They didn't."

"Thank you."

"Why did you…"

"I simply want to know what I'm bringing her into."

There was a long pause. "What is your relationship to her, Cairo?"

"That is absolutely none of your business," he said.

He hung up abruptly, her words echoing in his ears, the softness of her kiss impressed upon his mouth.

They had not brought women to his brother while he was in the dungeon. That meant… Unless he'd supplied himself with lovers since he had been released…

It was possible, but unlikely that he would have heard. If his brother had begun bringing a parade of sex workers into the house, it was quite likely that Brianna would have mentioned it. Likely that it would have signified.

And he worried about what it might mean for Ariel. If Riyaz would have any idea how to please a woman.

Do you worry how you just hate the idea of any other man's hands on her?

It did not matter what he liked or didn't like. She belonged to Riyaz. He had made a promise. And he had to keep it.

No matter how enticing she was.

No matter that he had given in to temptation in a way that he had not done even when he'd been a boy.

But his chest still felt like it was full of glass. And he did not know what could be done about it.

CHAPTER NINE

HER LIPS STILL felt swollen the next morning. She touched them before she moved. She was lying cocooned in the large bed in her room, covered by velvet blankets. The desert sun had risen, the open windows allowing the light to pour in. But it might as well have been night, out in the garden, for all that her body still burned with Cairo's touch. She didn't understand how he affected her so. And she could not…

She was all bound up in this. In this confusion. In the desire to touch him again, kiss him again. In the knowledge that he was sending her off to marry his brother in spite of this connection between them.

And somewhere in all of that was her freedom, a distant, hazy memory.

Her life in Paris before Cairo had taken her. Before he had stormed back into her life. Why did she feel more free in his arms than she ever had at any other time in her life? She wasn't free. She was a prisoner. She was being forced to live this life. Being forced to…

Her heart was pounding hard. She got out of bed and opened up her closet, looked inside of it. She took out another white shirt, and a pair of khaki high waist pants. She'd gone for that specific Katherine Hepburn look yesterday, and she was happy to repeat it today. The sensuality of the dress from the night before… Yeah. She didn't want that feeling. Not again.

She carried the clothes into the bathroom with her and filled the tub. She looked out on the desert, naked. And the same sensual promise that she felt the first time whispered over her skin.

The thing that scared her the most was that even if she were to escape now… What was there to go back to? A career, yes. Though, Cairo had made it sound as if it was all right for her to carry on her career even as the sheikha. But she wasn't sure that she was the same person. When Cairo had so abruptly disappeared out of her life it was like a thread had been cut. And she had been set on a new path, the severing of that past connection painful and abrupt. And now it was as if she had gotten a chance to pick that thread up again, golden and beautiful, and see who she might have been if she had kept moving along it. Except… It wouldn't have been Cairo that she kissed. She would have married Riyaz. A man she couldn't even picture now. She wondered what the face of that taciturn boy looked like now that he was a man. A man that had spent the last sixteen years in a cage.

But Cairo was all she could see. Cairo was all she could want. Her heart throbbed.

Was he her enemy anymore? She wasn't sure. He wanted something for her that she didn't want for herself. But within that, he wanted her.

And that was something she simply didn't know what to do with.

She bathed herself, her skin perfumed by oils in the water. And then she got dressed, putting her hair in a low bun before heading down to breakfast. He wasn't there. She sat at the table by herself and wondered if they actually would have a lesson today, or if he would avoid her after the kiss.

The kiss. It had scalded her from the inside out.

She ate quickly, and caffeinated, and then went into the room where they had said those vows yesterday. And there he was. Standing with his back to her, looking out of the window. An echo of what she had just done upstairs. An echo that made her body tremble.

"And what is the lesson today?"

He turned, and the impact of his glory left her breathless. His features were sharp, his brows straight and dark. His nose like a blade. His lips... They had done inestimable damage already.

"Dancing," he said.

She looked at him, and she nearly laughed. Because the idea of him dancing seemed absurd. He seemed twice as likely—even dressed in his custom cut suit— as he was to pull out a sword and start a battle. But he reached out his hand yet again. And she thought that if she had to touch him one more time she would be burned.

She did not know how she could go on. Then, he was taking her hand again.

"It is similar to dances you may have seen or done. It is on a three count. Something like Latin dance."

"All the dances will be like this?"

"No. But the important dance is that which takes place between you and Riyaz. Your groom."

"Right. My groom."

He wrapped his arm around her, with one hand firmly clasped. And they were suddenly pressed tightly together. Her breasts to his chest. His eyes didn't leave hers. And he began to slowly count. "One. Two. Three."

And with that count came movements. Slow but decisive. A pause, then a turn. "One. Two. Three." The slow decisive turn carried them swiftly over the tiled floor. She could not remember the last time she had danced with anyone. Maybe she never had. Maybe it just felt like she should have. She hadn't had a normal childhood. She hadn't gone to school dances. Not even after her parents divorced. Not even after the engagement to Riyaz had presumably ended with his captivity.

This was the first time she had ever been danced with. And while she had touched men during garment fittings. It wasn't the same as this.

This was Cairo.

The only man to ever hold her in his arms.

The only man to ever kiss her.

And it took her a moment to fully realize, but she suddenly had the sense for what this dance mimicked. The movement, the rhythm.

It was like lovers.

A husband and wife. Consummating. Coming together. How could that be? Such an intimate promise to make before all those people.

And yet, she supposed it was as old as time. Hadn't they hung sheets out the window to prove the woman's virginity back in medieval times?

The thought of a sheet bearing her blood being suspended from a window made her wish she were dead. But then, she imagined that her inexperience with the rhythm just now betrayed her as a blood spot would. Just the same.

Abruptly, he ended the dance. Abruptly, they stopped

moving. "Yes. Just like that." He stepped away from her, and he seemed to take her breath with him.

"And then what?"

"Then the bride and groom depart the festivities."

"You said that the wedding lasts three days."

"Yes. It does. But of course…the marriage must be consummated. Otherwise, it is not legal. That night, after the vows ceremony and the dance, the bride and groom depart to consummate."

"I'm sorry… You… Are you going to hang a sheet out the window with my virgin's blood on it as well?"

"What?"

"You heard me."

"I do not think that in this day and age anyone would suspect that a modern, beautiful woman such as yourself to be a virgin. Also, no. As it is not the Middle Ages."

He really didn't know? Even after the dance… He didn't know. She had sort of imagined that he might… Watch her. Have observed something of her life while he was keeping tabs on her. But apparently not. If so, he might know that she never entertained any men. That she didn't have lovers.

"So I'm simply to go off with a stranger… I have not seen Riyaz in sixteen years. And I'm supposed to show up at the palace, ready for a wedding, ready to consummate…"

Panic was beginning to swell in her breast, and she could feel herself going beyond sanity. "I hardly need princess lessons, Cairo. What I could use are lessons on how exactly I'm supposed to cope with that. How exactly I'm supposed to cope with the idea that I'm going to go from having only been kissed just once to…"

Everything around them went still. His expression was flat, his eyes dark. There was a fire in them that nearly terrified her. It wasn't like anything else she had ever seen.

This stillness. She realized what it reminded her of then. A predator. Lying in wait in the grass. Waiting for its prey to make the wrong move. Or perhaps the right move.

"You what?"

"Don't make me repeat it. I'm not ashamed of it. Nor am I embarrassed. But the reality is you are teaching me… Pomp and circumstance. All of these things are for show, the ceremony. And I am expected to… To have another person inside of me. Someone that I don't even know. I don't… I have never…"

He reached out, his hand grabbing hold of her chin, his touch was scalding. "Are you telling me that you are a virgin?"

"It's not like I go around thinking of myself that way," she said. "But it is becoming more and more difficult to avoid the word. Given that I am suddenly, very suddenly faced with the reality of what is before me."

"You have only kissed a man once?"

"Last night," she said, her whole body hot.

"Do you not like men?"

"No, that isn't it. It's just that it hasn't… I have not had the desire. Or…found the person who…"

"Forgive me. But I do not understand. You see, opportunity for me has always been quite present, and desire never short."

"Well, that's you. That isn't how it works for me. I don't know what to tell you. I've never…"

She couldn't tell him. She could not tell him that

there was a bright and warm day that lived in her mind where he had handed her a piece of fruit, and it had felt like the world had gone still. Where he had stared at her, and she had understood for the first time what it meant to be attracted to another person.

And that nothing that had ever occurred since then had matched it. How could she tell him that? Especially when it wasn't true for him. He'd slept with everything. Everything that moved. That was what the tabloids said, that was the impression that he had given.

The moment had not meant to him what it did to her, so why indulge herself by thinking of it? And why admit to him that it mattered at all?

"This could be a problem," he said.

"Why? I would've thought that you would crow about it. I mean, doesn't it complete the whole barbarian trophy, being brought back to your king? A virgin at that."

"You know how to please yourself?"

"I…" Her mouth dropped open, and then snapped back shut. Suddenly, a pulse began to beat hard between her legs.

"Do you know how to please yourself?" His voice became dark, slick. Coated in honey. It made her tremble. Made her entire body feel weak. They should not be talking about this. Except… Who was here to make such rules? He was in charge.

He was in charge.

"I have not… I have not given enough thought to it to explore that particular…"

"You have not brought yourself to orgasm?"

"No."

And for the first time she was forced to confront how deeply she had shut down that part of herself. Perhaps it was because of the arranged marriage. Perhaps it was because of her father's betrayal of the person she was supposed to marry. Perhaps it was thinking Cairo was dead.

She didn't know, because she had not pondered it overly much, because it was… Distressing. Tangled around this trauma in her past that she had wanted to pretend wasn't trauma at all. She had wanted to pretend that she had gone on to be successful and that was all that mattered. That she was fine. That all was well.

And yet she could see that it wasn't. That it never had been.

"This could very well be a problem."

"Why?"

"My brother has been locked in a dungeon for sixteen years," he said. "He's not… If he has…"

"What are you saying? You think that your brother is a virgin as well?"

"It is entirely possible. And if not, then what manner of sexual contact has he had? Prostitutes? If they sent someone down to service him…"

"You don't really think that happened."

"I don't know. But I was counting on you having enough sexual experience that you would be able to… Ease the way between the two of you."

"Well, I don't. So if you're going to give lessons, Cairo, perhaps those are the lessons you should be giving."

The volley that was set out between them was… It was explosive. Dangerous. And she knew then and there that she had not been imagining the banked fire in his eyes. She knew that last night when she had wept with him holding on to her shoulders, she had not imagined the magnetic force between the two of them.

He wanted her. He wanted her. And that was the way of it.

He wanted her, and it was not imaginary. And she wanted him.

And she was supposed to marry his brother. She didn't want to.

And he wouldn't waver.

And then there was the fact that he was… He didn't seem to possess human feeling. Neither of them did, she was certain of that. For if Cairo spoke of Riyaz as being broken, then she could rest assured that he would be even more difficult.

And she'd wanted Cairo from the beginning.

His was the kiss she'd wanted all those years ago.

The one she hadn't been brave enough to claim.

"Do not say things like that."

"Why not?"

And yet again, she felt the wildness. The wildness pushing at her spirit. It was an accident but today she had dressed like Katherine Hepburn. Like she had a safari to go on. A lion to tame. She had known that she would need strength today.

And she had dressed accordingly. But she remembered the power she had felt, standing naked before the windows. With the wilderness in front of her. And she was suddenly seized by another urge.

You are insane. You've been kissed once. You don't have any experience.

That was true. But she had been right to run. It had gotten him to listen. Perhaps it had even gotten her some sympathy. So she would not question her instinct.

She began to unbutton her shirt. Slowly, purposefully, and she let it fall from her shoulders.

Then she unclasped her bra and let it fall as well.

She didn't dwell on the fact that he could see her. Rather she dwelled on how good it felt to have the air on her skin. The desert before her.

Cairo was the desert. She realized.

Cairo was the sand and the sky and the sun.

Cairo was Nazul. He always had been for her. And always would be. She unbuttoned her pants, unzipped them, kicked her shoes off as she pushed the pants and underwear down her legs.

And she was naked before him, as she had been before the desert.

But she understood now. That they were one in the same. Understood now, that this was why it felt right. That this was why it mattered.

And then she stood, completely naked and unashamed. "If you wish to teach me something of value. Teach me about pleasure."

CHAPTER TEN

IT WAS LIKE the whole world caved in on itself. Like the sound and the ever-loving fury had come to collect. In many ways, he was a man of discipline. And in many ways, a man of none. In many ways he was a man without equal, a man who would not be tested.

But the problem with Ariel was she had been trying him and testing him since he was a boy. The problem with Ariel was that she was symbolic of all that he hoped to achieve.

And the problem with Ariel was that she had just professed her innocence. And what would that mean? He was to give her beautiful virgin body over to his brother? A man who was little more than a beast?

To atone for his sins, he would compound them by giving her to Riyaz as if she was his to give, and maybe...

Maybe it would be better to let her choose him now. For this.

To be the first.

You know that isn't why you're bending here. It isn't for her. It's for you.

It didn't matter why. She didn't even know how to pleasure herself. And he... He was brought back to that moment when he had entered the jewel room. When he had shown her the crown. The necklace. The bracelets. He remembered the way that he had wanted to put them on her. The way he had wanted to take the silken scarf and wrap it around their hands.

As a boy, that had been the highest expression of his desire. As a boy, it had been his version of wishing to take her to bed, he supposed. He wanted to kiss her. That much she'd known.

And now here she was, naked before him. In her body was a glorious splendor that he had never seen before. The smooth cast of her skin. Pale pink nipples and high, firm breasts. The indent of her waist, the flare of her hips. But the shape was unimportant. It was that it was her. That was what mattered. That was what signified. It was what made her irresistible. It was what made her...

His.

He gritted his teeth together and curled his fingers into fists.

And he wondered... What she hoped to gain from this.

Riyaz never has to know.

No. He didn't. And he didn't know when he was going to be able to deliver her to Riyaz. But the beast within him hated those options. The beast within him roared against it. And yet he realized it would not be better. Not ever. The idea of any other man putting his hands on Ariel destroyed him.

But he had promised her to Riyaz. He had promised that he would fix this.

Fix this nation... He could not be what Ariel wanted

or needed. And so the plan would have to remain in place.

But he could have her.

In the meantime, why could he not have her?

To teach her. To show her what her body could feel.

He refused to finish the thought. Refused to go down that road. For it was a fury within him.

She took a step toward him, and the crack of desire that went through him was like a bolt of lightning.

And if Riyaz had not requested her specifically, he would've abandoned the plan then. Would have given her a chance to run. Either away from him or to him.

But Riyaz wanted her. Had asked for her by name, when he had spoken of nothing else from the past.

His brother seemed set on carrying out the plan as it had been laid out before them, so how could he deny him that?

But now…

He had taken this pause to ensure Ariel's safety.

He wished to ensure her safety in all things. He reached out his hand, brushed his fingertips along her cheek, and down, cupping her breasts and moving his thumb over her nipple. Her head fell back, her lips parting, a raw sound escaping her lips. "This is what you want?"

"Cairo…"

"You want to finish this thing that began to burn between us when we were children, is that it? Even knowing where it will end?"

"Cairo…"

"Why? Tell me your game. If this is simply a way that you think you can manipulate me… I cannot be manipulated, Ariel, and I will not be. I will not be taken in the way that my father was by yours. I will not yield. I owe my brother the life that he has missed, and he has demanded you. Thus, you will be given to him."

"But you're tempted," she said.

"Yes, I'm tempted. I'm tempted to show you all of the things that your body can do. Everything that it can feel. I am tempted to touch you until you're crying out my name. Until you are beneath me, with me buried inside of you. Yes, I am tempted. But to give in to the temptation will mean nothing. And you must understand that."

"I want a choice," she said. "It was always decided for me that Riyaz would be my husband. And it didn't matter that you were the one that I preferred."

Somewhere in all of that, he wanted to ask her. If she wanted the choice so badly why had she not made it when she was living life on her own? She could've been with anyone that she wanted to. She had not been. And he had to wonder why.

But the questions were lost in the feel of her soft skin beneath his palm. They were lost as lust clouded his vision. Overtook every reasonable thought. Made him more beast than man.

And here he was concerned that his brother would be too rough with her. Not have a care for her needs.

He found that he was on edge. Beside himself. Beyond himself.

He moved forward, one hand still on her breast, and with the other, cupped her chin. He stared at her for a long moment. Deep into those aqua eyes. And then he dipped his head and claimed her mouth.

He had wanted her, wanted this, since they were children, but he would not have known what to do with the electrical storm that it created.

It was almost too much for him now. A man of jaded tastes. A man who had taken more lovers than he could count.

Yes. He would have to see her in the palace, knowing that she could no longer be his. Knowing that she now gave her body to his brother. But the alternative was to see her, never having been inside of her.

She tasted of oranges. Strong coffee and a brightness that he had long since given up believing in. If he were honest, she tasted of his failure. But in the moment, it felt only like triumph. She felt like salvation. And much like when his plane had descended in these mountains, he wanted to roar. He was not in his brother's kingdom. Not now. He was in his own. In his element. And he was holding her in his arms. And she was his. He claimed her. Her soft naked body pressed up against his.

And the years were erased. Except he was a man now, and she was a woman. And he knew what he wanted of her.

"Let me show you," he said. "Let me show you what you can feel. Let me show you what your body can do." He put his hand between her legs and found her slick with wanting, and he continued to lick into her mouth, mirroring the exploration happening between her thighs. She was slick and eager, and he slid his thumb over the source of her pleasure, relishing her gasp of desire.

And he realized, as her pleasure coated his fingers, that everything had changed. That there was no question of her being given to his brother, or anyone. She was his. It did not matter what agreement his father had drawn up with hers. It did not matter what he owed Riyaz, what Riyaz wanted or what he'd asked for. She was his. She had been from the moment he had first seen her. No other man had ever touched her body, and no other man ever would.

She belonged to him. And if he had to wage a war…

To have her, that he would. To stake his claim on her body.

He pushed a finger inside of her and she made a small, sweet sound of desire.

He worked his finger in and out of her tight channel, need pulsing within him.

How he wanted her. How she belonged to him. He marveled at it.

Had it always been this? And had this always been fate? Had he ever really intended to get her for Riyaz, or had he always been intent on claiming her for himself?

Perhaps this was what he had been waiting for all along. His. His woman. It was his turn to take his place in the palace as well. He should also take a wife.

Intense possessiveness poured through him. "Mine," he said, the word hard. He added a second finger to the first, and her knees buckled. He tested her, teased her. And he could feel her entire body begin to tremble.

"Come for me," he growled.

He pressed his palm against the sensitized bundle of nerves at the apex of her thighs and she gasped, her knees buckling. And only he held her up.

"Cairo," she whispered.

"You are not a prisoner," he said, withdrawing his fingers from her body, rubbing his thumb over her lips. "You are my lover. You belong to me."

He picked her up off the ground and carried her out of the ballroom. She was stark naked. And she clung to him.

If any of the staff saw them, they quickly melted into the background, making themselves invisible. They would betray nothing. He knew that. He almost expected her to gasp with maidenly modesty at being paraded through the public space bare as she was. But she didn't. She only clung to him. And he was intent on making her his own.

Nothing else mattered. Nothing. He carried her up the stairs, and into his bedroom. One entire wall was a window that looked over the valley below.

The room felt exposed, though nobody could see up this far to see inside. And anyway, no one would ever be out in that unforgiving part of the desert. He set her down, on the highly polished floor, just in front of the window. He held her chin, guided her to look straight ahead. "Do you see? Down there, and ahead. That is Nazul. That is Riyaz's domain. But this here… This is mine. And while you are in it, you are mine as well. Do you remember when I showed you the jewels?"

"Yes. The jewels meant for Riyaz's bride."

"Yes. I showed them to you because I had a fantasy. Of putting them on your wrists. Your head. Your neck. Of binding your hand to mine. I was but a fourteen-year-old boy. I knew nothing of life or the things which might happen in the future. I only knew that you belonged to Riyaz, and could not belong to me. But I wanted you to."

"I thought that you showed them to me to remind me. I didn't think…"

"Perhaps I was attempting to remind myself, but I do not think I was half so present. What I wanted, what I truly wanted, was to betray my brother."

And now… He had lived his life in service of freeing Riyaz. He would demand her payment. Yes. She would be his bride. His. He would bind her wrists with a red scarf before all the nation. And then he would bind her wrists with it in their room, his willing supplicant. Not a prisoner.

"From up here you are the queen of the desert," he said. "Look at the way the light shines on you. You have nothing to hide. You are beautiful. Glorious. Did you not take a lover because you did not know?"

She looked at him. "I didn't take a lover because I didn't care to. It is that simple."

"But I can feel your desire. The evidence of it still is coating my fingers."

She shivered. "Perhaps it is because I left my desire with you. It is a scary thought. That you hold the key to my desire. I did not wish that it were true. When we knew one another we were innocent. At least, it felt innocent to me."

"It was," he said. "I was drawn to you. I thought you were beautiful. But I did not think of stripping you naked. I thought of kissing your lips. I thought of marrying you, but not of taking you to bed. And now… I am consumed by the idea of thrusting inside of you. Deep and hard. Feeling your tight wet body closed around mine. Would you like that? My possession?"

"Yes," she whispered.

"You understand that there will be no question of you going to Riyaz after this?"

She looked wide-eyed and confused. "There won't be?"

"No. You will be giving up the throne in exchange for the knowledge of my body. Does that seem a fair trade to you?"

His body ached. Pulsed with desire. He needed her

to say yes. He needed it more than he needed his next breath.

"Yes," she said.

"There is no turning back from this. There will be no remaking the moment into something else. We are not children trading oranges in a garden."

"I understand."

He wondered if she did. But he was past the point of talking. He took her hand and pinned it to her lower back, walked her up toward the window, sweeping her hair to the side and exposing her neck. Then he pinned her other hand with the first, holding her fast with one hand wrapped around both of her wrists. He kissed her neck, and she arched forward, her breasts pressing against the window. He grunted in approval. This game of both possessing her and making a show of displaying her appealed to something darkly possessive within him.

He himself was not a modest man. He had never thought much of engaging in intimacy and semi-public places if the opportunity presented itself. But he could not say that he had ever taken particular pleasure in it either. But there was something about this moment. The declaration of it. The pleasure deferred that made it feel like a rush. A flood of excitement that overtook everything.

"Imagine, if the sands below were filled with adoring subjects. Watching how I worship you. Gazing upon your beauty."

He heard the sound of her swallowing hard in the silence of the room.

"It excites you."

"I don't know why."

"Because you like that I make you like this. Only me. Is that true? Do you wish the world to know that only I make you so wet? That only I could ever entice you to such sin?"

"You arouse me, it's true. But I like to think that I'm wild enough to stand naked before the desert all on my own. Aren't I the one who asked for this?"

"It's true you did. You are a wild woman in your soul. And I find that it is a beautiful thing."

She would not have made a sheikha. She was too… Untamed. She was not what Riyaz needed. But for him… For Cairo she would be perfect.

He pulled her away from the window, turned her so that she was facing him, and still keeping her wrists captive, brought her against his body, claimed her mouth in a deep, hard kiss. "You're beautiful," he said. "And mine."

"You said that," she whispered.

"And I will keep saying it. Until it is a tattoo on your soul. Until you know it as well as you know it is time to draw a breath lest you perish. You were always mine, Ariel."

And it was good that he was doing this. Because the alternative would be to betray his brother once he had already taken her as his wife. Cairo knew his limitations, and Ariel Hart was the hardest of those limitations. She was the one thing he could not resist. The one thing he could not endure.

And he would've had her. "Was that your first orgasm?" he asked, his mouth close to hers.

Her cheeks turned pink, and she nodded slowly.

"Did you like it?"

"It makes me want things. Wild things. Things I never would've thought I could want."

"Yes. That is the problem with pleasure. It can turn us into strangers to ourselves. Can make something that would not sound appealing at all the most enticing thing on earth. I wish to feast upon you. Lay you open on that bed for me and lick you until you scream my name."

Interest sparked in the depths of her eyes, and she shivered. "What are you waiting for, then?"

He growled and lifted her up, setting her down on the center of the bed and forcing her knees apart. He looked down at her, the flushed, swollen heart of her, slick with her desire for him. "Tell me who is about to pleasure you, Ariel."

"Cairo," she said.

"I gave you an orange in the garden to show you the pleasures of my country. And now I will feast upon you like you're ripened fruit, to show you the pleasures of your own body. I will give you everything good. I take care of what is mine." He pressed his thumb against the pearl between her swollen lips and rubbed it slowly across that sensitized flesh. She moaned and shook, and he slid his thumb down and penetrated her slowly. Then he leaned forward, kissing her inner thigh before sucking the source of her pleasure into his mouth until she cried out. He licked her, savoring the flavor of her as he moved his fingers in and out of her body.

"Cairo," she said, her voice trembling.

"Yes," he growled. He did not feel like a civilized man. He was the barbarian warrior of his people's past. And he had claimed a woman. She was his war prize. Not Riyaz's. She was his. He had claimed her. He was the one that had righted the wrongs that had been done against their family. It was not Riyaz's fault that he had been a prisoner. That his hands had been bound and he had not been able to claim revenge. But Cairo had done so. He had deposed the imposters. The woman should be his.

And he would claim that honor before his brother. He vowed it.

He licked and sucked, rubbing two fingers within her slick channel until she found her release again. And then again.

Until she was begging him to stop. Even as she clung to his shoulders to keep him from moving away.

She was becoming ready for his possession. And the idea of it caused his masculinity to harden painfully.

He moved up her body, kissing her stomach, sucking her nipple deep within his mouth. She had the most perfect body. Because it was hers.

"Are you ready for me?"

He was still fully clothed. And he moved away from her, taking his shirt off slowly. He watched as her eyes widened, as hunger darkened them.

When he removed the rest of his clothing, he saw a bit of fear there. He was not a small man. It was true. But her fear turned to hunger after only a moment. She sat up, moving to the edge of the bed. She kissed his stomach, down to his Adonis belt and to the sensitized crown of his arousal, where she ran her tongue around the head of him before taking him inside of her mouth. He growled, gripping her hair with his hand. And pushed himself deeper into the welcoming heat of her mouth. He should have a care because of her innocence, he thought at first. But then... She should know. She should know what sort of man she was allowing into her bed. There was something to be said for starting as you meant to go on. And now that she was his...

Theirs was not a gentle desire. Why pretend that it was?

He rocked his hips forward and back, and she took him as deep as she could, swirling her tongue around his length as she did.

When he was close, too close, he moved away from her. He put his hand between her legs and found her slippery for him still, and he kissed her mouth, moving her back onto the bed as he positioned himself between her thighs. He pressed himself to the entrance of her body and entered her slowly. She closed her eyes, arching her back up off the bed as he moved into her, inch by agonizing inch.

He growled as he thrust fully home, and she gripped his shoulders hard, digging her fingernails into his flesh. He took the pain as his due, as he was certain the breaching of her maidenhead had caused her pain as well.

This should hurt. It was right that it be painful. They had waited so long. It should be everything.

He might have taken his share of lovers, but he had never had Ariel. And that made it new. Singular. Set apart from every other experience. And every other person.

He had given himself over to a life of hedonistic pleasure, something, anything to drown out the pain of what he had lost. The only way that he had been able to function for a great number of years was to blot everything out. Drink. Sex. Oblivion was the name of the game.

But this was not oblivion. Here, he was present. Here,

it was sharp. Real. The feeling of being inside of her was not like anything else.

And he began to move. And he watched as the slight discomfort on her face transformed. Bloomed into wonder. And he felt that same bloom echo inside of himself. They were both of them brilliant. Made new in this storm of desire.

She wrapped her legs around his waist, a raw cry shattering the silence of the room. And she hadn't even come yet. Each thrust made her whimper. And he found himself growling in response. And then he felt it. The ripples of her next release. The promise of her completion. Then he let himself go. He held her hips as he drove into her, hard, ruthless. And when she screamed with pleasure, he allowed himself that same rush.

But it was not a blur. Not a blessed moment of nothing as it often was. Instead, it was her. Ariel. Everything.

A heightened sense of his partner, rather than an isolated moment of release.

Even his own pleasure was somehow about her. And that was a revelation.

She looked up at him, soft with a small smile on her lips. "Well, if I would've known that it was like that I might not have waited so long."

"Believe me," he said, his voice rough. "That was singular."

"Good."

"There is no question about you marrying Riyaz now…you know that."

"You said. And I... I decided. But I don't know what it means."

"We are still going back to Nazul. But instead of marrying him... You will marry me."

CHAPTER ELEVEN

SHE FELT LIKE she was in a state of shock. She had just lost her virginity and quite spectacularly to the man that had haunted her dreams and fantasies for the better part of her life.

And now he was... Now he was telling her that she was going to marry him. And not his brother.

But nowhere in any of this had she ever been given a choice. Not about anything.

He gave you a choice. He told you. You were choosing to not be with Riyaz.

Still. It was a limited set of options.

And yet...

She couldn't imagine leaving Cairo. Not after that.

But when it came right down to it she didn't know him.

And the fact that she had feelings for him made all of this feel much more fraught. She didn't care for Riyaz. Had never kissed him or made love to him. Marrying him had felt like something hollow she could not wrap her mind around. But it hadn't felt... Like it might shatter her.

That was the thing. She had no feelings for Riyaz. She had far too many for Cairo.

She didn't know what she wanted. She couldn't imagine going back to Paris and acting as if this had never happened. It wasn't even her goal. Not anymore. But she also couldn't… She couldn't fathom… She couldn't imagine how they had gone from him being so set on handing her over to Riyaz to this.

"Surely you must have known the moment I put my hands on you that you were mine? It was foolish of us to deny it. This has been… I see it now," he said. "I see it now with clarity. This has been inevitable. You and I have always been on this path. Perhaps I survived to find you."

The words were almost romantic, except they sounded tortured. Torn from him as if by force.

"Cairo… I don't understand. You've never made any indication that you wish to marry anyone in…"

"I will marry you. For it must be decisive. And I must claim you. You must be mine. There is no opening for Riyaz to have you then."

"And what will you do?"

"I will marry you before taking you to the palace. We had our wedding feast after all. And our wedding night."

"How will you do that?"

"I will get a preacher to come and marry us, obviously. Clergy are not so hard to come by. I will have one flown in."

"Why?"

"There's nothing he can do."

"I thought that him being the sheikh meant that he could do anything he wanted."

"Perhaps. But I believe that he will respect it. He will

respect that I have claimed you in this way. It is something he can understand."

"You speak of him like he's an animal."

"Not an animal. But a warrior. He has spent these long years turning himself into a weapon. But so have I."

"Cairo... What of love? Of children?"

"I did not use protection when I took you. Children may be an inevitability of the passion that we find between ourselves. Love has nothing to do with marriage." He looked at her, his black eyes dark. "Passion has nothing to do with love. Fate is not love, is it?"

"I don't know," she said. "But I..."

"And what love have you seen in your life? Did your father love you? Did he love your mother?"

"I don't know. I don't know. I haven't seen it."

"Do not worry about love. Think of what I can make you feel."

"And my career?"

It didn't actually seem that important in the moment.

"You may have whatever you wish. My moon, I will not keep you prisoner."

"But you won't let me go either."

He shook his head. "No. I will not."

"That is being a prisoner, Cairo. Just one with privileges."

"Then I will be your jailer as well as your husband. I had hoped that you might decide for yourself that you wished to stay."

She wasn't sure she wanted to leave. That was for certain. But just for a moment... Just for a moment she imagined what it might have been like if the two of them would have met on a busy city street. If he would have asked her to dinner, and she would've said yes. If they would've gone to the movies and eaten popcorn. And he would've kissed her goodnight on the doorstep, and she would have done something wild like have sex with him that first date, and felt just slightly guilty but not regretful. And made a promise to see him again. And again and again. She wasn't sure that she wanted to leave him. But she wasn't sure how she felt about him issuing life sentences. And she just wished...

She just wished that she might have been a different woman. And him a different man. She just wished that it might've been... Fate that had brought them together in a different way. And not this hard and sharp reality. Not Stockholm syndrome.

Maybe it had always been Stockholm syndrome.

"I will have someone here to wed us by nightfall."

"Cairo..."

"I will not leave any room for this to fall apart. I will not leave any room for him to take you from me. That is all."

And this was her life, she realized. Being caught between two impossible alpha males. This man, who sought to bend the world to his sheer will in spite of the fact that he was not—by birth order—the heir to the throne of his country.

And his older brother who was.

And she didn't know why in the world both of them were so hell-bent on having her.

She wondered if any of it was actually about her. Even for Cairo. And he always just wanted what his brother had? Had it always simply been about... Being denied something that he wanted because of birth order? She knew that he wanted her. Physically. It was apparent. The passion between them had been intense, and even if she did not have experience, she knew that it was real. And extremely hot. She knew that.

But that didn't mean that it wasn't spurred on by something else. A more complicated emotion than even he realized.

He would tell her that he didn't have emotions. And she knew that he had been through more than she could understand. She knew that while she had been hurt by what had happened to his family, it wasn't the same.

She did know that.

At least, she hoped she did. She hoped that he was choosing this, as she had chosen him.

"I must go see to some business."

"I see." He kissed her. Rough and hard, it tethered her to the moment. Tethered her to the earth. He wanted her. Whatever else existed beneath the surface, he wanted her. That was… It was something. It was something good to know anyway.

"You see. All will be well."

The hours passed slowly. The first thing that arrived was not a clergyman, but a gown. White and lace. And definitely not something traditional. It was long-sleeved, with a high neck, but the lace was see-through. The petals of the flowers would just cover her nipples, but only just, and her skin would show through the fabric. The woman who had done her hair and makeup the first day she had been in residence appeared. "Cairo has requested that I see to your preparations for the wedding."

"Do you not find that strange?"

The woman ducked her head. "No. I've seen the way

he looks at you. Since he first brought you here. I know that he intended for you to marry the sheikh. But I could see that he had passion for you. You are very lucky. He is a wonderful man."

The way the woman said it was tinged with jealousy, and even though it wasn't a pointed or mean jealousy, it made Ariel feel just a little bit guilty. They had up-ended a whole lot of things.

She styled Ariel's hair expertly, and did her makeup so that she looked fresh-faced and glowing. As for the dress... The only thing she was given to wear under-neath it was a white thong, which made the entire thing seem rather like extremely fancy lingerie.

Everything was covered. But only just.

She had a feeling that her groom would not be in anything quite so scandalous.

But just the thought of him in a dark suit cut around the lines of his body made her mouth go dry.

In fairness, what women found sexy was slightly different than what men found sexy. She didn't wish to see him in see-through mesh.

Her lips twitched, and so did her body, in such a way that she thought maybe she wouldn't mind it. But then, she didn't mind the look of Cairo altogether.

The moment of levity was welcome. Because oth-erwise she just felt... Blindsided. By everything that had happened.

And yet at the same time it felt... Like that thread had been tied back together. There was a great knot at the middle, and you couldn't untangle it without undo-ing the bond. It wasn't seamless. And it spoke to the fact that there had been a number of years between this moment and the last when they had been together.

But still… It did feel like a continuation of something. Like a piece of herself had been restored, that had before been lost.

Maybe she did have to accept the fact that Cairo was her fate.

"He is outside," said Aisha after Ariel went downstairs.

"Will you… Will you let me outside?"

"You can do that yourself," the other woman said, smiling.

Ariel walked slowly to the door and extended her hand. And it gave way to her.

Her heart expanded in her chest. That was a sign of something. Of trust. A prisoner with privileges.

She tried to tamp down her reaction to it.

She walked outside into the heat, the sun painting the sky pink as it began to set on the horizon. And there was Cairo. Standing there with a man in robes. And there was a horse beside him, with a garland around his neck. As if he too had been dressed for the wedding. He looked at her, his gaze filled with heat, and she couldn't help but be swept away in the moment.

"My moon," he said. "Give me your hands."

She did so. And the officiant handed him two cuffs. He put them on her wrists. Then the officiant handed him the necklace, and he fastened it around her neck.

And what he took out next was not a crown, but a simple circle of gems, with a teardrop ruby at the center. And slowly, very carefully, he pinned it to her hair, the gem resting at the center of her forehead. Where he had touched her with his thumb that day in the ballroom.

"And now we can begin," he said.

The officiant then took the red silk scarf and bound their hands together. But this was not a rehearsal. This was real. They were real.

"With your mind. With your mouth. With your heart. Obey me." She found herself nodding as he made the commandments, as he touched her with his thumb. And then she returned the proclamation. "With your thoughts. With your words. With your heart."

"And though we now remove the scarf," the officiant said. "The words have bonded you. Hold hands through life, but remember, even when you let go, these promises are meant to keep you, bound to one another. Bound to your union, to your commitment. There is nothing that can undo a spiritual bond such as this one. You are husband and wife. And there is none but death that can separate you. And even then, your souls will find one another amongst the stars."

And he released the scarf from around their hands. But she could still feel it there. And they held on to each other still.

"Thank you," Cairo said. "I trust you will file all necessary paperwork upon your return?"

"Yes. Though I will have it sent to no school until your brother's fire cools. And I will remain in Turkey until that point."

"I do not blame you. Thank you again."

And then suddenly she found herself being swept up onto the back of a horse. She gasped as Cairo lifted her from the ground and set her in front of him. And with a decisive, masculine command, he spurred the horse into a gallop. And on they went. He held on to her, his arm around her waist as they tore through the desert sand, a cloud of earth billowing behind them. She couldn't have asked him what they were doing if she wanted to. He wouldn't have been able to hear her over the sound of the hoofbeats, and she wouldn't have been able to shout it into the rushing wind.

They rode across the sands, away from the house, away from everything. And the farther and farther they got from everyone else, the more it felt… Right. The less she felt a prisoner. And then she saw it, in the distance, just as the sun dipped entirely behind the mountain and blanketed the earth in darkness.

There was a stake and a feeding trough set out there for the horse, and a bonfire lit there as well. There was a spread of food next to it. And she had a feeling that whoever had set it up must have just vacated, as it might otherwise have been a target for animals.

"And here is where we will spend our wedding night," he said, bringing the horse to a stop.

But it was the tent that caught her focus. Large and elaborate, with brightly colored tapestries all along the outside.

She could feel his heart raging behind her, and her own beats in a fiery response.

"Why?" It was the only thing she could think to say. And she wasn't sure why it mattered. But she was curious. Why not go to the sumptuously appointed rooms back there?

"Because the desert has always called to us, has it not?"

Her heart surged in rebuttal of that statement. "I used to hate it here."

"No. You didn't. You hated feeling bound in the face of such wildness. But you are not. Not with me. Here we are free."

He helped her off the horse, and then took their steed and tied him to the wooden post outside. Then he took her hand and led her inside the tent. The tent was one large room with a star shape on the roof, and a hanging lantern made of fractured glass at the center. There was a large, sumptuously appointed bed at the center of it. Scarves hanging around the frame. It was entirely there for sex. And she had a feeling so was Cairo. The dress that he had chosen for her certainly suggested that. "There is an oasis just past the tent. There may be animals at it, but they will not bother us."

"Why do you think that? Because you're with me?"

"Yes. And they would not dare." He began to take his clothing off, slowly, and she watched him, rapt. He took his white shirt off first, exposing acres of bronzed muscle. His abdominal muscles shifted as he began to undo his belt, as he took his shoes off and everything else, leaving him completely naked to her gaze. And aroused. He was glorious. A warrior made into sensual reality right before her. His arousal was strong and thick, his thighs well-muscled. And everything feminine within her reacted to the sight of him.

"Take off your dress. And then we will walk to the oasis."

"What?"

"You have wanted to walk naked in the desert this entire time. You want to be like this in the open. It excites you."

And she felt ashamed just then. Only slightly. But why? Why should she? She had never known what to do with her sexuality, because it had never felt like it was entirely her own. She had been put in a situation where she was meant to give herself to a man she hadn't cho-

sen. And when she did meet a man she actually cared
for… He was forbidden to her. And then she had thought
he was gone and…

It just wasn't easy. Any of this. It was terrifying and
exciting all at once.

And the truth was, even if Cairo had given her limited options, when it came to wanting him, there was
no doubt about the fact that she did.

She wanted him. That was simply the truth of it.
There was no coercion when it came to her desire for
him.

And maybe… Maybe he was right. Maybe this was
what she wanted. Maybe she wanted it so badly because she had never felt like her sexuality, her body was
her own. But that was the strange and amazing gift of
wanting Cairo. It was a rebellion. And… By wanting
her in return, he had also rebelled. It was a heady realization indeed. He had wanted nothing more than to
serve Riyaz, than to give him what he wanted, but he
had rebelled entirely by doing this. And with that truth,
she could see her own power.

Clearly. Absolutely.

So she began to slowly take her gown off, revealing
her bare curves beneath, the brief pair of underwear,
which she took off quickly. She had never been ashamed
to be naked in front of him.

"Come," he said, taking her hand and leading her
out of the tent.

The night air kissed her skin, and her heart began
to beat faster, as she thought of that trip into the desert
when they had been young.

He looked at her, the smile on his face almost boyish, and it made her wonder if he was thinking of the

same thing. They walked slowly, even though the ground was soft.

"If when we were teenagers... If I had kissed you..."

"It frightens me to think of what might've happened," he said. "We would've been too young for such an explosion of passion, don't you think?"

"I do," she said. "And yet I'm not sure that would have stopped either of us."

"I'm not sure we would have known how to stop."

"We're both nearly thirty, Cairo. And we did not stop when we touched. We definitely wouldn't have had the maturity to do it then."

"True." He tightened his hold on her hand. "But you are my wife now. And we can do whatever we please. You are no longer forbidden to me."

The words were dark and delicious. They made her shiver.

They came over a small hill, and that was when she could see the pool of water. Two jackals out on the edge looked up when they approached. But the little dogs scampered off into the distance as they approached.

"I told you they would not make nuisances of themselves. They have no real desire to interact with a person, at least not unless we are in much worse shape. They prefer an easier fight." He held his hand out to her. "Come. Into the water."

The water was warm from the sun, just perfect, and she took his hand and allowed him to lead her into it.

He wrapped his arm around her waist, and dragged her deeper, held her as they floated, chest to chest, the sound of the waves lapping against their skin calming and arousing at once. "And I would have you beneath the light of the moon," he said.

"And I would let you."

Right now they felt like younger versions of themselves. Less complicated versions of themselves. Without murder and kidnappings and betrayal between them. But perhaps this was the truth of them. As they might have been without such complications.

And for tonight, she would revel in it.

"When a warrior took a bride, he would bring her out into the desert to consummate. So that the entire tribe would not hear the sounds of their pleasure. Of course, a hazard of living in tents is that you often did hear the lovemaking of others. But that first night… Warriors and kings were able to keep the cries of their women to themselves. That is why I brought you out here."

"I don't care if anyone hears."

"I know you don't. And neither do I. But still… It seemed right."

It did. She didn't need any further explanation. It just did. He stood them both up, and he began to move his hands smoothly over her water slick skin. She sighed, as he moved his hands up to cup her breasts, to tease her nipples. "You are a goddess. A temptress. And I ought to love you for it. But I cannot. I ought to love myself, and I cannot. For I have one. I have one you." She knew that she should object to that. To such masculine, possessive language. And yet she found she couldn't. And she gave up trying by the time one hand moved around to cup her rear, then moved deeper, delving between her thighs, teasing her. Penetrating her.

She gave up all resistance after that. And she simply surrendered.

He lowered his head and suckled her nipple between his lips, drawing her in deep as he continued to tease her with his finger.

She rocked her hips against him, found the blunt head of his arousal, used it to soothe that sensitized bundle of nerves between her legs.

She rocked her hips as he pushed two fingers within her, and her orgasm unraveled within her. She gasped, calling out his name.

And then he swallowed her cries with a deep kiss.

She collapsed against him, and he lifted her up out of the water, carrying her back to shore. All the way back to the tent.

The bonfire yet raged, and there was food there for them still. But there was also a blanket spread out in the sand, and he laid her down upon it. Water dripped from her breasts, sliding down slowly, the cool sensations making her long for the touch of his hands. Then again, anything would make her long for the touch of his hands.

She was bare, open to the sky, and just the thought of it made her internal muscles pulse. And then there he was, above her, every inch the hardened warrior. He knelt down beside her, kissed her mouth, her neck, down to her breast again, down her stomach, until he found himself between her legs. He seemed to enjoy doing that. Seemed to enjoy the taste of her, and she loved the way that he licked her deep.

She rocked her hips restlessly in time with the wicked pass of his tongue, his teeth, the deep, rough penetration of his fingers. Two, and then three, which made her gasped. She rolled her hips along with him, begging, pleading his name toward the sky as if it were a prayer.

When her orgasm hit, it hit hard. Her internal muscles clenching around his finger as she cried out.

He removed them, and then slid them into his own mouth, licking them clean, a little ripple of need making her whimper as he did so, his dark eyes never breaking contact with hers. He lay down on the blanket beside her, then gripped her hips, and settled her over him, guiding her slowly onto the blunt head of his erection. And she took him in, inch by inch. "You are free. Ride me."

She let her head fall back as she began to let her hips rock, as she moved up and down, setting a torturous rhythm that both pleased and tormented them both.

Out there in the open air, she cupped her own breast, toying with her nipple as she moved over him, allowing him to watch her as she tightened her own pleasure.

"Put your other hand between your legs," he said roughly. She did so, rubbing at the source of her desire there before stroking her fingers along either side of where he penetrated her. Making them both cry out.

She didn't have experience. But she wanted him. And she had no shame in that desire. And it was the lack of shame that made everything feel brilliant. That made it all feel wonderful. That made everything she did seem right and make sense.

Suddenly, he growled, reversing their positions so that he was over her. And she gloried in that. And the dominance of it. She had enjoyed where she sat, so she could take him in and give him a show as well. But she loved his weight over her, the strong heat of that steel within her. The way his eyes blazed down into hers. And then he began to move, each thrust within her hard and fast taking her breath away.

Oh, how she needed this. Needed him.

And suddenly, pleasure began to ripple within her. And she climaxed before she even knew that it was building, her shocked scream of pleasure echoing around them. And he followed closely behind, lowering his head and growling like the most ferocious beast of the desert. She felt him pulse within her, felt him spill his seed deep.

And she rocked her hips in time with the pulsing of his release, wringing out every last bit of pleasure between the two of them.

And then they lay there. Naked and unashamed beneath the night sky.

"I told you you would like the desert at night," he said, his voice rough. "It only took me sixteen years to show you why."

"And I have wondered about that old unfulfilled promise so many nights since," she whispered.

She dragged her fingers over his chest, luxuriating in the muscle, the heat, the crisp hair.

All the textures of who he was.

"Come, my bride," he said. "You must be hungry."

They sat naked in front of the fire and ate their wedding meal. Different than the one they had had the other night. This one was much more rustic, but no less delicious. And she was ravenous.

Then he doused the fire and took her inside, made love to her over and over again in the big bed, until the sounds of morning began to be heard through the canvas walls.

And then she clung to him and slept. And she knew, as she drifted off to sleep, that she had made her choice.

She was no longer a prisoner. She chose him.

CHAPTER TWELVE

HE THOUGHT HE was dreaming. But there was a sound. Persistent and rhythmic, and it did not stop. In fact, it only seemed to be getting closer. And closer. And then the walls of the tent began to move. A mighty wind flexing them inward. He sat up. Ariel was pressed to his side, naked, her bare bottom scooted as hard up against his morning erection as possible.

And even in spite of the fact that there was something happening, what he found he wanted to do was roll her over onto her back and claim her. But he could not. Because…

Suddenly, the last vestiges of sleep and sexual drugging faded.

It was a helicopter.

It was his brother.

"Dress," he said quickly. He put on a pair of pants, and Ariel began to silently scramble behind him, putting the white wedding dress back on that she discarded the night before. It revealed too much of her body, but nothing could be done about that.

He heard the moment the helicopter landed.

He could hear a woman's voice. Sharp and persistent. Brianna.

And then the tent flap opened, and a dark figure blotted out the sun.

Riyaz.

His dark hair was shoulder-length, he'd refused to cut it. His frame massive and uncompromising. He had scars on his face that twisted his formerly easy good looks into something much more challenging to behold.

And just behind him was Brianna. Her red hair scooped up into a ponytail, her eyes wide.

"And here I find you. With mine," said Riyaz.

"My apologies," said Cairo. "She is no longer yours. I have married her. And we have consummated it. Quite thoroughly, you will find."

"So I see." He looked around the tent, his gaze assessing. And it was impossible to tell what Riyaz thought about anything. It always had been. But he was yet more inscrutable after all his years of being locked away. Brianna touched his arm, and he saw his brother's entire body react. It went stiff, and then…calm. "What is it?" he asked, looking at her.

"You don't want to kill your brother," she said.

He took her chin in his hand. "I know that, *habibti*. I don't intend to." Then he turned back to Cairo, and there was no softness remaining. "The dungeon might be suitable."

"The dungeon. Is that what you think? And will you throw Ariel there as well?"

"I am the sheikh. I could marry her if I choose, regardless of whether or not she is bound to you." It was the most words he had ever heard Riyaz use in a sentence since coming out of the dungeon. It seemed as if Brianna's work with him had been quite accomplished.

"Or I could throw her in there with you. Or… Take two wives."

"Two wives."

"Yes," he said. "For I have already decided who I will marry."

"You said that you wanted to marry her," Cairo said, gesturing to Ariel.

"I said for you to bring her to me. I said it was what I required. I did not say why. I had thought that I might marry her. But I have decided on another course of action."

"What is that?"

"I'm marrying Brianna."

Brianna's eyes went round.

"Riyaz…"

"It will be no argument," he said. "You are mine. Or have I not made you so these last days?" Brianna's face turned red. And it did not take a great detective to figure out exactly what had been going on between his good friend and his brother.

"The situation is complicated, I see," Cairo said. "How dare you burst into my wedding tent given that you already decided what you plan to do?"

"I have not said yes," said Brianna. "I'm not yours. I don't live here. I'm not a citizen of this country. I don't…"

"You're mine now," he said. "Our bodies do not lie. You have lain with me, and you will be my wife."

Brianna was getting redder and redder. "Can you please not announce…?"

"You have stormed into the aftermath of my wedding night," Cairo said to Brianna. "Why should you be embarrassed to have your own activities commented upon?"

"Cairo," she said. "I'm sorry I…"

"You know, both of you could ask the women around you what they want," Ariel said. "Just because a woman sleeps with you it does not mean she wishes to marry you. Just because she is born doesn't mean she wishes to marry you. Just because her father says."

"Yes," said Brianna. "Exactly that."

"It is done," said Cairo. "You are my wife."

"I'm not his wife," said Brianna.

Riyaz looked her up and down. "You will be. Soon. Perhaps we might find someone out here to do the deed."

"You cannot get married in a desert," said Cairo. "You must have a wedding that is symbolic for the people."

"You do not get to order me around. I have spent enough time in captivity."

"But are not concerned at all about putting others in captivity," said Ariel. "I'm pleased that you're alive, Riyaz," she said. "But it doesn't give you license to act like a monster."

"Monster or not. You're both coming with me. Back to Nazul. These games have gone on long enough. It is time I begin my rule."

And that was how Ariel found herself bundled up in her see-through wedding dress and put into a helicopter. She could scarcely fathom what was happening to her. And she didn't think that the other woman had any idea of what was happening either.

The helicopter ride was short, as Cairo had said it

would be. She thought of all the clothing she had left behind at the house in no man's land. Another life that she had to leave behind because of the dictates of these men.

She looked at Brianna—she thought that was the other girl's name—and the other woman looked back with a strange sort of wide-eyed misery.

She wondered what sort of life Brianna had left behind to be here. What sort of life she had not intended to leave.

The helicopter touched down in front of the palace. Golden and bright as she remembered it. It was strange how much the same it looked. It didn't seem like it should be possible. It had been polluted. Perverted by the violence and death of the royal family. By the fact that Riyaz had spent years living in the dungeon. And yet it had the audacity to look the same. They got out of the helicopter. And suddenly, there were servants ushering them into the palace.

"I must speak to my brother," said Cairo. "Brianna, please stay with Ariel."

Brianna looked mutinous, but then the two men left, and Ariel and Brianna were ushered into a plush sitting room. There were drinks sitting there. Something that looked like lemon with mint in it. She thought of resisting it, but then also thought that it might be a bit spiteful for no real reason. So she poured herself a measure of liquid.

"I take it you didn't expect to get a proposal."

Brianna's eyebrows shot up. "Was it a proposal? I thought it was a command."

"I think in their world that passes as a proposal. At least in my experience."

"They seem to think that getting naked with them means a proposal."

Ariel laughed. "Well. Yes."

"I loved him, you know."

She looked at her. "Riyaz?"

Brianna shook her head. "Never mind. Never mind. It's all very complicated now. And…"

Cairo. Brianna meant Cairo. Because of course they knew each other. That was the woman that he had spoken of that he had saved. The one he had talked to on the phone.

Ariel felt both guilty, and possessive in the moment.

But Cairo was her husband, so there was no reason to go being territorial about it. Especially not when Riyaz had already made proclamations about the fact that they were to get married. Unless…

"Cairo said that he was very… He's dangerous. He didn't hurt you? He didn't force you…"

The redhead's face went a scalding shade of strawberry. "He didn't force me to do anything. I was… A willing participant. He is… Complicated. And I somehow managed to get swept up in the complication."

That undersold the situation.

"And what are we to do?"

"I don't know."

CHAPTER THIRTEEN

CAIRO FACED HIS BROTHER, who sat on the throne, looking ill-suited to the position. Their father had been sophisticated. Always well-dressed. Always well-groomed. Riyaz looked like a relic from another time. And a rather dangerous one at that.

"Are you going to kill me?"

"No. Enough blood has been shed in these halls. I am deeply uninterested in killing you over a woman that I do not want. I want Brianna."

"Does Brianna want you?"

"She seems to want me well enough when she is naked with me."

Cairo did not especially wish to think of his friend that way. Or his brother.

"She did not seem particularly like she wishes to marry you, though."

He waved his hand. "Neither did Ariel. Did she wish to marry you?"

"That's different."

"Why? Because Brianna is your friend, and you feel possessive of her?"

"Did you only decide to have her to get at me? Was she collateral?"

"Do you love her?"

"No," said Cairo. "Not like you mean."

"She loves you."

Riyaz looked… Mystified by that. Haunted by it.

Guilt stabbed his chest. "She doesn't really. She idolizes me because I rescued her. It is not the same."

"It is. She would've chosen you. Though… She cannot resist me. These are inconvenient things. Bodies. I have had no prior experience with it. It is… Intoxicating."

Yet again more information than Cairo had wanted about his brother and his friend. "Marry her then," he said. "But you must have a ceremony that gives the country hope. And you cannot have a bride that looks as though she is being forced."

"I will handle it. And there will be no consequence for you and Ariel. It is also a good thing, I think," he said slowly. "Yes. It is a good thing. Her marrying you or me… The end result is the same. It puts to right something that was wrong. It does not allow her father to have the final say, and it… It may heal something. For our people."

"You are not quite so far gone as you allowed me to believe."

"I was," he said. "Brianna is remarkable."

Brianna might not love Riyaz, but he had the feeling that Riyaz loved Brianna. Whether or not his brother would openly apply that word to it or not. "We will announce your marriage, and my upcoming nuptials before the people. I will appear before them for the first time." He nodded. "Yes. This is the way. It will be an excellent first appearance."

"You should get a haircut," said Cairo.

"No. There are certain things about my experience that I cannot erase," he said, gesturing to the scars on his face. "And there are certain things that I choose to keep. I will never be the king that our father was. After what I've been through, it's impossible. But I will work to win back every single year that I lost. Every single year we all lost. I will be the ruler this country needs. On that you can trust me. Now. There are apartments set aside for you and your wife. Apartments fitting the new head of the military. We all have our responsibilities."

Ariel was still sitting in the room with Brianna when Cairo appeared. "Good news. We're not being thrown in the dungeon."

"That is good news," she said softly.

He extended his hand. "There are apartments set aside for us. And I have been given a new position. I'm to be head of the military. And we are to be presented as husband and wife tomorrow before the nation. It is when it will be announced that we have reclaimed the country."

Her heart kicked into gear. "You mean… Everyone will know. That you're back? That he's back?"

"Yes." It was scary, actually. Knowing that it would create a political shift in the world to have their identities revealed. Knowing that it would change… Everything.

And she and Cairo were simply… Married. They were married. It was something she could not yet wrap her mind around.

He nodded at Brianna, and then took Ariel's hand and led her from the room. "She's afraid," said Ariel.

"Just because she slept with Riyaz does not mean that she wants to marry him."

"I'm sorry. I think these are the consequences for her actions and she has to deal with them."

"She's your friend."

"I know. And if… If I feel like Riyaz is being unreasonable, I will intervene. But I actually think he cares for her. He will not hurt her."

"Cairo," she said slowly. "I'm only going to ask you this once. Are you… Giving your friend to your brother because you feel guilty about what we did?"

"It isn't guilt. But I will not oppose what my brother wants. I understand that you wish… You wish for me to be more civilized. I lived in your world for all this time, after all. I understand that you wish to believe that our marriage indicates that I am something that I am not. The truth is, I am from this land. I am the second son of the royal family. And my duty is to my brother. My king. My duty is to the people here. I do not have a concern for anyone's feelings. Brianna will not be harmed. She will be sheikha. She will be well treated. I have no need to intervene."

"She said she doesn't want to stay."

"It is a shame. But always was a possibility…"

"You said you rescued her. You said you rescued her and now you're willing to sacrifice her for this? What was the point of rescuing her at all?"

"Believe me when I tell you, she will be treated better by Riyaz than she ever would have been where she was headed. But it is not my story to tell."

"Do you love her?"

She hated herself for asking the question. His dark

eyes went flinty. Hard. "Love is not a factor for me. For anything."

It wasn't a denial. "Do you love her?" she repeated.

He shook his head. "I can't love. Not in the way that you mean. I'm sorry. If that sounds hard to you…"

"No. It's exactly what I would expect. And I received that better than hearing that you love another woman, actually. So thank you."

"I told you. I told you what my priorities were. You didn't believe me."

"I just thought at some point the human element would matter. Me. Brianna."

"My brother spent sixteen years in a dungeon. He is the human element for me. I…"

She saw something tortured in his eyes then. Dark and pained. "I might have devoted my life to freeing the country. But he had no life. None at all. He didn't even have the honor of being the one to free the country. It is… It is not something that I can ignore. It is not something that I can simply let go. I owe my brother years that he cannot get back."

"You didn't hold him in captivity."

His gaze became bleak. "You don't know what I carry. And it is of no consequence. For I must now support the throne. I must now support Riyaz. If he wants Brianna, he can have her. For my part, I have you."

He turned and began to walk down the corridor. The palace was as she remembered it. Golden stone inlay on the walls and the floors. The ceilings. It was familiar and yet somehow alien all at once.

And they were to be living here. Somehow, she had ended up in this palace anyway.

And she realized on some level that… That he had

chosen her over Riyaz. For all that he professed to have no feeling. For all that he professed Riyaz to be the most important thing… He had chosen her.

And he simply wouldn't take something from his brother again.

Did that indicate that he didn't care for her?

He pushed open the door, and she followed him. It was a sitting room, luxuriously appointed. "My chambers there," he said, gesturing to the left. "Yours are there."

"We're to have separate rooms?"

"It is how things are done."

It was not how they had done things last night. They had slept wrapped around each other. In that bed in the desert. But it was as if everything had changed. Between then and now.

"You must be tired. You should sleep."

"I'm not tired…"

"Then perhaps I am. In the next couple of days a great many things will unfold. You must have your strength saved up. For we will go public. As a restored royal family. And as husband and wife."

"Well. I guess… That will take some strength."

"And I did promise you a computer and a phone. You will be given those things. You may return to work."

She knew that should make her feel something. Happy. Excited.

She didn't. Instead, she went to bed alone. And while that should have been normal, it already felt wrong. And even though she knew she was with the right man, everything else felt wrong. And she didn't know what to do about it.

CHAPTER FOURTEEN

IT WAS LATE. He had helped Ariel sneak back into the palace. They should never have been out like they were. There would be hell to pay if they were discovered. His father would lecture him soundly on risking Ariel's reputation.

They were not children anymore. At fourteen, they would be held accountable for their actions. And people would be suspicious that their behavior had been inappropriate.

A smile curved his lips. He looked up at the desert sky.

"Ariel."

He had wanted to behave inappropriately with her. But he hadn't. Mostly because he would not subject her to any sort of censure. He cared for her so deeply. She was... The moon. That guiding light in the darkness.

He turned and began to walk back toward the palace. There was a door that could always be opened no matter the time of night. A way that he could sneak in. Undetected. It was the way that he had sent Ariel earlier.

"Cairo?"

He turned sharply to see Ariel's father standing there.

"Mr. Hart."

"Your Highness. I'm sorry to startle you. It's only that... I have not seen Ariel."

Ariel should have been back safely in bed by now. But it was possible her father had missed her.

"I... I saw her out here, sir. We had gone for a walk. But I saw her safely back inside the palace."

"I see," her dad said, his eyes taking on a suspicious light. "You know... It could be taken the wrong way. The two of you out here walking together. She is supposed to marry Riyaz..."

"She's my friend," said Cairo. "There's nothing more to it."

"I will take you at your word. Of course. You are part of the royal family after all. Known for their integrity."

He nodded, feeling relieved. "I'm being honest. You don't... You won't tell my father?"

"No. There's no need to speak to your father. Though... I cannot figure out how to get back into the palace. I left to find Ariel. And now... I do not wish to wake the staff trying to gain entrance. I assume there's a way?"

"There's a passage. Through the garden. I can show you how I get in."

Cairo woke up in a cold sweat. The memory that had played through his subconscious was one that he had done his best to banish.

He knew well how they had gotten into the palace. The enemies of his father. A word from Ariel's.

But where had Ariel's father gotten his intel? From Cairo. It was Cairo who had destroyed his family. Cairo who had dishonored them so. In his weakness for Ariel, and in his desire to stay out of trouble he had been the one that had caused all of this.

And yet again Ariel had been his weakness. It was... Unacceptable.

It's your fault.

Yes. But nobody ever had to know. It would help no one. It would fix nothing. He didn't even like himself to know. He had spent all these years trying to fix it. All these years trying to make it right.

It was being back here that had brought it all up again.

He despised it.

And yet here he was, to live with the woman who tested his every weakness.

But love? He did not possess the ability for that. Not anymore. And nothing else mattered but what happened next. He had not been right. He had not been what his brother needed, but he would be now. He would give Riyaz whatever he needed. He would... He would fight. He would give up his life for his country. For his brother.

And yet you took Ariel. And you managed very neatly not to think about how when given the chance to betray Riyaz again you did.

It was done now. It was done, and Riyaz lusted after another woman anyway. What did it matter?

He thought of going to Ariel. Burying his sorrow in his desire for her.

But he would not allow himself that. Would not allow himself that escape.

Ariel threw herself into work. She had been sad last night that Cairo hadn't come to her bed, but she couldn't wallow in that. She needed to get on with it. She had gotten on her email for the first time in a few weeks, and had begun to go through everything that she had missed. Made sure everybody knew that she wasn't dead. She had spun a story about reuniting with an old boyfriend. And how they'd had a whirlwind romance and marriage.

She was pretty proud of herself. PR wasn't necessarily her thing, but this was definitely a stunning example of some pretty genius PR.

But she wished that the story were true. She realized that for her it was. That she had reunited with the single most important man in her life, and it had seemed the most clear and obvious thing in the world to fall into his arms. To fall into his bed. To speak vows to him.

And she didn't know what he was thinking at all. She had thought that maybe they were on the same page. She had thought that perhaps they wanted the same things. She didn't know now.

You know that you don't want the same things. Because you care for him in a way that he has said he will never care for you. That was true. And it hurt to acknowledge it herself. But she wasn't going to lie to herself about it either. She wasn't half so fragile. She had already lived more than one life. A life where she had been certain she would end up living in this palace married to the sheikh. A life where she had fallen in love with the boy that she wasn't meant to love. Yes. She had already lived more than one reality.

She had been free in Paris. And yet, she had never come into this sort of freedom. She had been free in Paris, and yet it still hadn't felt like her life.

This felt much closer.

But still…

He didn't come to her bed again that night. Or in the days following. In the interim, she was subjected to married beauty treatments. Prepared for her public unveil as Cairo's wife. But it was more than that. They were revealing to Nazul for the first time that Cairo and Riyaz lived.

And that they were back in power.

She had thought that perhaps Brianna was being prepared for an unveil as well, but on the day, when she had been wrapped in sensuous silks, her hair done, her makeup applied to perfection, and she saw Brianna wearing her sweats, she knew that that was not actually the plan.

"You are not making your debut with Riyaz?"

"No. I believe that he will be waiting until the wedding that I have not yet agreed to."

"What do you have to go back to? I mean, what life is he asking you to leave behind?"

Her face went distant. "I… I don't have much. I have my business. I had… Cairo. As my friend. And I suppose that he is here now."

"It's the principle," said Ariel, hoping that she sounded like she was on the other woman's team. It would do no good to have there be division between them. When she walked back into the apartment, her heart stopped. For there was Cairo, standing there in full military uniform. A navy blue high collared jacket, a scabbard at his waist. He looked fearsome and glorious. And she wanted to cling to him and let the entire world know that this man, this dangerous looking man belonged to her. She marveled at the impulse. At the way that he made her feel.

It was the most brilliantly absurd thing.

She had never thought herself drawn to dangerous men. And yet…

Perhaps it was because she knew of the danger and destruction that had occurred here. But it made her feel… Good. Good to know that he could protect her if need be. Good to know that he would be the one looking out for her.

She was dressed in white. And she knew why now. Because they would make a beautiful contrasting picture standing together. And the idea had been to make her look somewhat bridal.

"Are you ready?"

"Yes," he said. "I've been ready for this moment for the last sixteen years. The question is… Are you?"

"I think we both know that the question is… Is Riyaz?"

A knowing look passed between them, and for a moment, she felt like they were a couple again. Like they were in some kind of unity.

She walked over to him and took his arm. And they walked from the room together. She wanted to melt into him. Into this moment.

"We will be standing on the balcony, where Riyaz will make a speech. As will I. You will stand to my right."

She nodded.

"I don't have to speak, do I?"

"No. You don't."

"That's good."

Though, she had the vague idea that she should ask if she was even allowed to speak. She wondered if she would like his answer to that question. She imagined not. They stepped out onto the corridor, and there was Riyaz. Standing there alone. He was wearing a loose white tunic, and white pants. His dark hair was long and loose. He still had a full beard, scars that spoke of immeasurable cruelties that he suffered at the hands of the guards here.

"Riyaz," she said.

"Ariel," he said.

They had not spoken directly since she had come back to the palace.

"I hope that you know," she said, "you have my loyalty."

"Yes. I do know. But my brother has you."

"Yes. He does. But he… He always has, Riyaz. I don't know if you know that."

He looked between the two of them, his gaze sharp. "Has he?"

"We will discuss it later," said Cairo. "For now we have a kingdom to reclaim."

They were the same height, and Cairo had lean muscle. She knew he was fast and agile.

Riyaz looked like a weapon in the form of a man. He did not have a sword at his waist, and yet, she had the sense that he did not need one. That he would be more than happy to take on any enemies with his bare hands. And that he would prefer it that way.

He was built like a beast.

And she had the feeling that between the two of them, a beleaguered nation would feel comforted knowing they had two kinds of lethal men at the helm.

They stepped out onto the balcony, and a ripple went through the crowd. She wondered how many of them had heard through rumor that this would happen. She knew that of course Cairo's people already knew. So there must have been some rumors that had made their way back over the border.

Whispers. But of course it would be hard to believe if you didn't see it with your own eyes.

"The al Hadid family is back on the throne," said Riyaz, his voice strong and clear.

Ariel turned and looked behind her just briefly. And she saw Brianna looking out from the shadows. She looked nervous. Then she looked very much like she cared how well Riyaz fared.

She did love him. Not Cairo. But Riyaz.

That made Ariel feel much better.

Whatever was happening between the two of them might be complicated, but it was not insurmountable.

And it was clear that Riyaz was the man that Brianna wanted.

"You will remember that years ago my family was betrayed. By a militia that rose up here, but also by the betrayal of the Hart family."

The words slammed into Ariel's chest. She had not been prepared for him to mention her family.

"Ariel Hart was promised to be my bride at the time, and her father took money to betray my parents. But we have done work to restore that which was destroyed. We will not live in the past. We will not live for revenge. My brother, Sheikh Cairo al Hadid, has taken her as his wife. I myself will take a bride in the coming weeks. But that will be a separate announcement for a separate time. You are free. And the indignities that you have suffered these long years will not go on. We will move forward. Strong and united. With my brother at the head of the military, we will also be undefeated. We will be victorious."

And now it was Cairo's turn.

"My brother addressed the betrayal of the Hart family. And we want to make sure that you know that we stand with you. We do not forget the indignity that you have suffered. Riyaz himself was chained up in a dungeon the last sixteen years. But he survived. For the sake of this country. So it is not lightly that we reconcile in this moment. But it is essential that we do so. But we cannot live in the past. Here in the darkness. My marriage to Ariel is a representation of all that we can be. All that we will overcome." He kissed her hand. Right there in front of the crowd, and it sent her heart soaring. The people cheered, and the royal family left the balcony. And she knew that this would be a day that would live in the history of this country forever.

This was the light at the end of a very dark tunnel. And she felt nothing but pride at the way that Cairo had made this happen.

It was so easy to get bound up in the personal component of the past. What her father had done.

And it was easy to not fully give credit to the work that Cairo had done to heal it. To heal all of this.

He had been tireless. But he had made this moment happen. He had.

And she…

She chose him. She chose this life. This life that this man had fought so hard for. These people that he had never forgotten. His brother that he would never abandon.

She admired all of it so. She… She loved him.

The simple truth was she had a life made of freedom.

All of the freedom that she could possibly desire. Her father hadn't been in her life anymore, and her mother hadn't really either. It had been up to her to do whatever she wanted. And she had… She had never fully moved on from Cairo. She couldn't have him. She didn't want anybody. And as she looked at her husband's profile, she dimly wondered if he had done similar, just opposite. If he couldn't have her he would have everybody. And maybe that was aggrandizing her a bit, but she couldn't let go of the fact that consistently, she was his weakness. Consistently, she was the area where he did not put his brother before everything else.

It made her smile. Even if just slightly.

And it made her certain. That no matter what he had said… No matter what he claimed about loving her…

She loved him. She loved him with all that she was. And she wanted… She wanted him.

Forever.

This wasn't Stockholm syndrome. She had fallen in love with him when they were children. They were fated. And so many people had stepped in the way to try and keep them from happening. To keep their love from being fully realized. But they didn't allow it.

She wouldn't allow it.

Circumstances might have made him hard and dark. Circumstances might have made it difficult for him to know what love was, but that did not mean that she should lose hope. Because for sixteen years, she had carried a candle for him. For sixteen years he had been the only thing. And if a separation, the presumption of death couldn't banish that, she wouldn't let anything else destroy it either.

She felt dizzy. Like she had made vows yet again.

Like this was a renewal in her soul. Something that she hadn't anticipated. She had loved him. Of course she had. For all these years. From the time she was a girl she had loved him. She had loved him with all that she was.

But this was… Admitting it. Claiming it. And owning her piece of it. Even if she could leave now, she wouldn't. She was not a prisoner, because she was deciding she wasn't a prisoner, not because of what Cairo had given her. Not because of anything other than her own choice.

She was choosing this. Choosing him.

But when it was time for them to go to bed again that night, he did not come to her room. And when she went to his… He wasn't there.

CHAPTER FIFTEEN

CAIRO HAD TAKEN to pacing the halls at night. He was in no fit state to go to Ariel's bed, and he knew it. And yet he craved her. With all that he was.

Tonight, as he roamed around sleepless, he heard footsteps. They were not hers. They were hard and heavy. Decisive.

"Riyaz?"

His brother seemed to appear from the shadows. "Yes."

"You don't sleep either?"

"Not conventionally."

His brother offered no explanation for that cryptic statement, and so Cairo did not ask.

"Perhaps it is this place," Cairo said. "Perhaps there are too many ghosts here."

"This is the only place I've been, for sixteen years. This is the only place I have been. And it is the only place I will ever be. For now I am the sheikh. So where will I go?"

Guilt assaulted Cairo. "I'm sorry," he said.

"For what?"

"It feels wrong. That I spent all those years out there. And you spent them in here."

"It's not as if you chose it, any more than I did."

"Still…"

"Do not play the part of regretful younger brother now. You were happy to make the decision to marry Ariel."

"You don't want her."

"No. I don't."

"Then why bring it up?"

"We've been separated for sixteen years. And I've been alone in a dungeon. I had no one to tease."

He looked at his brother. "Are you teasing me?"

"I think so. I spent a great many years not able to smile or laugh. But sometimes now I do. It is interesting."

And he knew then that what he really wanted for Riyaz was for him to leave all those years behind. He also knew that it was probably functionally impossible for his brother to do so. There had been so much pain. So much abuse.

So much solitude. And yet, he was speaking better now.

"I heard that you did not sleep in a bed. Have you now?"

And there was a slight grin on his brother's face.

"Yes. I have."

"But do you. Routinely?" It was clear by the look on his brother's face that when he was in a bed he was not alone.

"Sleep? No. But I have not learned to enjoy softness. I don't know that I ever will…fully be comfortable in it though."

"We should have traded places," he said, his voice rough.

Regret rose up inside of him. If he hadn't have told Ariel's father where that door was…

"It was not a question of should. Or a question of what we wanted. It's what happened. Carry your demons. I'll carry mine. We do not need to shoulder one another's."

And on that note, his brother turned and began to walk away from him. "You have a woman in your bed," he said. "So do I. Why are we in hallways?"

"I don't know."

Except he did know. He was staying away from her because… Because things had begun to feel complicated. Here. In this place. Where he could not ignore the truth of what he had done.

Of what he deserved.

He had taken her. And he had no right to do so. And it was only a happy accident that Riyaz had found a woman that he preferred. Otherwise…

He gritted his teeth and turned abruptly, going back to his apartment, to his room.

And when he pushed open the door, she was there.

She was sitting on the edge of the bed, naked, her sheet barely obscuring her glorious curves. "What are you doing in here?"

"Waiting for you," she said.

She shifted, and the sheet fell just between her thighs, covering the triangle of curls there. But her hips were exposed. She only just had her breasts covered with the edge of the white fabric.

And a kick of lust overtook him. Except… There was something more. Something deeper. And he rejected it. Wholly.

"I'm not in the mood."

"Everything about you suggests otherwise," she said, dropping the sheet and letting it slither down her curves.

For all that she had been a virgin when he had first laid with her, she had never had any sort of embarrassment about her body. Which he appreciated. She was beautiful, and she had nothing to be ashamed of, but he could certainly use a little bit of it right now. Because this… This restless display of all her glory was pushing against things he could not afford to have challenged.

He was too much on edge.

This was supposed to be his redemption arc. And had he not destroyed it already by taking her as his wife? Certainly, he could rewrite the story, certainly, things had worked out better than he could have anticipated, because of the fact that Riyaz clearly had an attachment to Brianna. But he had not known that.

He could not be redeemed. That was the problem.

And yet… There she was. Looking like temptation personified. Like everything he wanted.

And he did not think that he could turn away. Why?

He had proven that there was no redemption in sight for him. No change. The best that he could hope for was to fling himself on the altar of service to his brother. Because as far as his soul went? It was selfish. It always had been. It was selfishness that had driven him to give her father that information out in the courtyard. It was selfishness and the need to stay out of trouble. It was selfishness that had him out in the desert with Ariel in the first place.

Because the gravest sin had been what she had been about even before her father had approached him. When he had taken her into the room with the jewels. When he had let himself fantasize about making her his wife. And then what had he done? Years and years and years of working to reclaim the throne, to get Riyaz what he wanted, and instead, he had claimed her for himself.

His soul was hollow. It was corrupt. And there was nothing else that he could ever be. Nothing. The idea that he could be...

It was nothing more than a vague fantasy. But she was not a vague fantasy. She was here. In the flesh. Smooth and tempting and lovely and everything that he wanted.

And so he would have her. He would have her now. In his bed, because had he not already committed the unpardonable sins?

Yes, he had. Already he'd taken her. Already, his actions had seen his brother in prison for sixteen years. Already his weakness had seen his mother slaughtered on the tile floor of the throne room. Already his cowardice had caused the death of his father. His father who had fought until the end, while he had run away.

He was already these things.

And if he was going to be a sinner, then he might as well revel in it. Might as well glory in the iniquity. For what else was to be done?

He had sought to become better. Sought to become more honorable, but even in his pursuit of bringing back the power to the throne, he had been nothing but a hedonistic playboy. He could tell himself all manner of stories about why he had done these things, but some of it had been to glory in the freedom of being away from the soul. Some of it had been to glory in the fact that he was not in his traditional country where his moves would be watched. Some of it was reveling in the fact that he was alive. And the fact that he was not in chains.

What a grave sin it was.

There was no coming back from it.

The idea that he'd ever thought he could was laughable. And so why?

He knelt down in front of the bed and growled, forcing her legs apart, moving the sheet to the side and exposing the glistening heart of her to his gaze.

She was glorious. Pink and glistening and lovely. And he wanted to taste her. Dive deep into all that she was to satisfy his need.

He reached around and grabbed her buttocks, pulling her toward his mouth and licking her like he was a starving man. She gasped, and he pressed two fingers inside of her, loving the way she quivered beneath his touch.

She rocked against him and he tasted her, deep and long, curving his fingers as they thrust in and out of her, taking every cry of pleasure and bringing out yet more.

She was his. His to pleasure. His to corrupt. She had done this to him. Her. She was why. She was part of it. She was not innocent in this. She had known what she was doing to him. Always. She had tempted him. She was the one who had taken her clothing off back at his house. She had wanted it as much as he did. And she should suffer here in the depths with him.

If they were both to die of pleasure, then it would be no less than they deserved.

But it was a hell he would gladly burn in.

She cried out, pulsing, her orgasm making her shake.

He withdrew his fingers and lifted her up onto the bed, putting her on all fours, smoothing his hands down the elegant line of her spine, bringing one down to cup her rear before slapping her once, making her gasp.

"I wonder how many years it will take for me to cease to be able to shock you," he said. "I quite enjoy it. Your innocence is a novelty."

She looked over her shoulder at him, aqua eyes reaching down into his soul. "A novelty?"

"Yes. I wonder how long it will last."

He slapped her again, this time on the other side, and she yelped. Then he pushed two fingers into her from behind, testing her readiness at this angle.

He gripped her hips and pressed himself forward before he thrust hard.

Then with one hand he pressed between her shoulder blades, pushing her head down so that she could not look at him. He didn't wish to see her face.

How many times had he had sex like this? In this position?

Countless.

She could be anyone. She didn't matter. It was just more sex. Just more sin. And what was a little bit more? What was a little bit more when you were already hell bound?

He thrust into her blindly, chasing at the pleasure that he craved. The peak. The oblivion. This had been his life for sixteen years. Oblivion. Anything to block out the truth of it. Then he could pretend that he was on a mission. A benevolent one. With breaks for pleasure in between. But the reality was, he knew that he was the center. He knew that he was the murderer. The weak one. The straw that had broken the entire camel's back. He was the one that had caused all of this. It was his duty to try and make up for it. As much as he never could.

It was his calling.

The thing that he had to strive for.

Because it had all been his fault.

His mother's blood. His father's cries of agony as he had tried to avenge her, tried to protect them all.

And worst of all—yes, *worst*, because at least his parents had the benefit of being in the afterlife—had been Riyaz.

In chains.

Yes. He had tried to block these things out. He had tried to pretend that these things were not down to him.

Oblivion. He just needed oblivion. Except he could not get it.

Not without picturing her. Not without it being her.

She tossed her hair back, that pale, distinct hair, and squeezed him tight, and he knew.

"Ariel," he growled.

And he felt her shudder as he said her name. He felt his entire body arrive in spasms of pleasure. And he had done her a disservice, for he had not yet made her come.

He pushed his hand down between her thighs and thrust hard into her as his orgasm overtook him completely. He roared, and just as he did, he felt her pulse around him. Felt her climax.

And then she collapsed onto the bed, breathing hard.

His wife.

His beautiful wife. It could not be denied and neither could she.

It was Ariel. Only Ariel. His downfall. His muse. His everything.

"Cairo," she whispered. "Cairo, I love you."

And everything inside of him went dark.

CHAPTER SIXTEEN

THERE WAS SOMETHING possessed inside of her husband, and Ariel had no idea what it was. But he wasn't himself.

What even was himself? She didn't know. She thought that she knew him, but ever since they had returned here… He had been a stranger to her. Not coming to her bed, and then tonight… It was like he was running from demons. And she didn't know why. She didn't know what was hurting him so badly. Didn't know why he was distant, and yet intense all at once. It was like he wanted to draw nearer to her and also pull away forever all at the same time.

She simply couldn't understand.

"Tell me," she said. "Tell me what's wrong."

But he had still said nothing since she had said that she loved him. He wasn't speaking at all. He was just sitting there, his breath rising and falling harshly.

"Cairo," she whispered.

"No," he denied viciously.

"Cairo, I just want… I love you."

"You don't know what you're speaking of. You know nothing of love. Your father betrayed my family. He would have sold you as well if it suited him. He practically did. He didn't care what you thought of it, didn't care what your mother thought. How long would it have taken for him to sell you to the next highest bidder? He did so when he brought you to be engaged to my brother, did he not? What do you know of love? Has anyone in your life ever loved you?"

He spoke to wound. And his words hit their mark.

No, her father had been selfish. Her mother had been passive.

Even though her mother may have loved her, it wasn't an active sort of love.

It wasn't a love that helped or healed.

"You say that as if I've never thought of it. But of course I have. Of course I've wondered if my father ever loved me. Of course I've wondered why the bond between myself and my mother was so easily broken. Of course I have. But I do know what love is, Cairo. I have known. Since I was a girl of twelve. Maybe even younger. I have known that it was you. And when you were gone… Well, I couldn't love anyone else. I tried. I hoped. I was open to it, but it never happened. It never happened because I couldn't want anybody but you. And it never happened because you formed my concept of what desire was."

"And that is all it is," he said. "It's just sex. Good sex, but sex, nonetheless. It isn't love, my moon, and it never will be."

"Why? Because you don't believe in it? And why is that? What is love if not a sixteen-year pursuit to free your brother? That is love."

"That is atonement," he said, the words sounding torn from him.

"What?"

"You heard what I said, do not question it. You require no explanation. You are bound to me, and we do not need to come to an agreement on these things. But you do not need to tell me that you love me. Never again."

She sat there, her heart thundering hard. She thought that it would break into a thousand pieces.

Shatter.

And maybe she would shatter along with it.

She knew her father had died of a heart attack, and it had nothing to do with emotions. But what if it had?

Was it his guilt? Thundering around inside of his chest? Was she going to suffer the same fate?

It certainly felt like it. At least right now. As badly as it all hurt.

Except… No. Because what he was saying didn't make any sense. "Why bar me from saying it? I'm not asking you to say it in return. In fact, I'm asking nothing from you. All I'm asking is what you have already given. I am offering love. I love you. And I always have."

"No," he responded. "This is not negotiable. It is not sensible. You are acting foolish."

"Why? Because, actually, the thing is you've identified the problem with my father. He didn't love anyone but himself. He didn't love anyone but money. So why would you reject the idea of love? Love is what prevents these things from happening."

"No," he said, gripping her arms. "Love creates these situations. You know I fancied myself in love with you when I was a boy. A boy of fourteen. I wanted… Everything. With you. To kiss you, to lose myself inside of you. I wanted to learn what passion was with you. I wanted to steal you from my brother. I wanted you to be mine. All mine.

"I wanted it more than anything else in the world, and I risked your reputation running around the palace with you as I did. Running around out in the desert as we did."

"My reputation was never compromised."

"Nearly was. Or at least, I thought so. That last night, out in the desert, when you begged me to show you… That last night I met your father there. He knew. He knew that we had been out together. He couldn't find you and he questioned me on it."

"I didn't… I never knew. I had no idea that he had checked in on me…" She was confused. Because it was difficult to remember anything about that night except for being out with Cairo. Certainly not any interaction she might've had with her father.

"He met me outside in the dark. He made it very clear that he knew we were together. And he forced me to confess it besides. He also made it very clear that it would be bad if anyone found out. And then he asked me… He asked me to show him a way into the palace. One where he wouldn't have to disturb the staff. I agreed."

"Cairo…"

"That is how the invaders ended up getting into the castle. That is how my family was murdered. Your father gave them that information. It was his power. His leverage. He got it from me. Why? Because you and I were sneaking around together. Because even though we didn't kiss, even though we didn't make love, we might as well have. We compromised everything. I compromised everything. Because I was afraid. Afraid of getting in trouble. Afraid of losing time with you. Don't you see? It was that weakness that got everyone killed."

"No," she said. "It wasn't. It wasn't you. It was my father. It was his willingness to manipulate a boy and his feelings. He was willing to get you to give that information knowing that it would get you killed. Knowing it would cost your entire family their lives. Believe me, he did not care about the consequences. And he likely thought that you would be dead as well and there would be no regret for you because you would be in the ground. It is by luck and good fortune that you escaped. But you didn't cause it. He did. He betrayed you."

"No," he said. "He did not. I betrayed us all."

"That is ridiculous."

"It is a heaviness that I have lived with all these years. And I… I will never love you. I will never love anything. Because it could cost the safety of this nation. Already I allowed my desire for you to cloud my judgment. That is how we arrived here. You were meant for Riyaz."

"No," she said. "I was never for Riyaz." She shook her head again. "It was you. Only you. Always you. Do you not know?" She stepped forward and touched his face, his beautiful face. "Do you not know?"

He closed his eyes. "Riyaz was in captivity all this time…"

"You have been in captivity. You're enslaved to this. To this guilt that you feel, but you didn't do this."

He wrapped his hands around her wrists and pulled her hands away from his face. And then he stepped away from her. "You pity the wrong person."

And then he walked out of the room and left her alone there.

Left her alone with her heartbreak.

And she knew that it was up to her. Whether she would allow it to destroy her, or whether she would find a way to be strong.

CHAPTER SEVENTEEN

HE RODE OUT in the darkness, his horse's hooves kicking up sand, the echo of the hoofbeats sounding in his soul.

She'd looked at him and she'd pitied him. Felt sorry for him. Wouldn't allow him to accept his guilt.

And she…

She thought that he was a prisoner.

But no. She was.

I love you.

How could she love him? Not only did she not truly know who he was, not only did she not truly know the perils of his character… But…

You have failed again. You have failed in a way you haven't seen. For it was not just Riyaz… It was her.

He had taken away her freedom.

She had begged him not to make her prisoner, and he had done so anyway. And he had told himself that allowing her access to a computer made her free?

And now she said she loved him. What insanity was this? Would he ever not be a monster? Would anything about him ever be right?

There, deep in the desert with nothing around him, he let out a primal growl that seemed to vibrate the earth around him.

It was grief, and it was regret. For all the damage he had caused. For all that he could not put back together.

Except you can. You can set her free.

Because whose atonement had she ever been? Certainly not the country's. And not Riyaz's. He had wanted her, and he had brought her back here.

At first, it had been to prove himself to his brother, a salve for his guilt. And a way to punish himself.

But then… Then it had been about having her. Possessing her. Regardless of what she wanted.

And he might be a monster beyond redemption.

For he had proven his own selfishness at every turn. He would never be able to restore the sixteen years of Riyaz's life that had been lost. He could not bring his parents back from the dead.

He could not allow himself to love Ariel.

Or rather…

He did love her. But he needed her to not be near him. And if he really wanted to do the right thing, he needed to allow her freedom.

He had to send her away.

He rode, far and hard away from the palace, and by the time he returned, the sun was rising. He had not slept.

He didn't need to.

He was resolved.

He dismounted the horse, and a servant came to relieve him of the animal.

Then he pushed open the double doors to the palace and began to walk toward his and Ariel's apartment.

He opened the door, and then saw her there, sitting on the couch, in a robe. Looking as if she had sat there all night.

"Get dressed," he said.

She looked up at him, her eyes red.

"I'm quite enjoying a slow morning," she said.

"You must prepare yourself."

"What's happening?"

"You are going back to Paris."

"What?"

"You're going back."

"I didn't ask to go back," she said.

"And I did not ask you what you wanted. I will not hold you here. I will no longer tie you to this family. Or to a past that… Was not your fault."

"I know it isn't my fault," she said. "But you don't. You don't know it isn't your fault. And now what are you doing? Punishing yourself?"

"I am making things right. This is the only thing that I can set to rights."

"I chose you," she said. "Don't you understand? I chose you, Cairo. If I hadn't… Don't you think I would've had a lover in these last sixteen years? But it was always you. I had freedom. I had freedom to be with whoever I wanted, and I didn't want to. Because I could never get you out of my heart. I had a choice. And now… Kidnapped or not, you are my clear choice."

"No," he said. "You will not be another in my long list of sins, Ariel."

"And you think that sending me away and acting like none of this ever happened will… Absolve you? You're just afraid. You're afraid of what you feel for me. And you're making it about me… It isn't fair."

"I will carry you out to the private jet myself."

"A reverse coup and a reverse kidnapping. You really have had a busy few weeks."

"You think I'm kidding."

And he could see something change in her face. Some kind of acceptance. Some kind of resolve. "You need me to do this."

"No. You need to do this."

"No. You need me to. And so I will. I will prove to you that I love you."

"Didn't you hear what I told you about what happened?"

"Is that why you're telling me? To prove to me that you don't deserve to be loved? It's too bad for you, because I think that you are. Because I care about you. I like you, and I love you. And I always have. What an inconvenience for you." She stood up. "But I'm going to get dressed. I'm going to get on the plane. And in two days I'm going to come back. I'm going to buy a plane ticket, and I'm going to show up at the palace. Unless you want to come find me beforehand. To ask me to stay with you. Not kidnap me. Not make demands. You know where I live."

And she began to collect her things. And he simply watched.

And then, in only an hour, she was gone. In the air, headed back to Paris.

And he found himself walking, stumbling, out of the apartment. And down into the dungeon.

She was broken. Possibly irrevocably. Possibly forever.

By the time the plane landed in Paris, and she got in the car that took her back to her apartment, the apartment that she had been so sorry to leave just weeks before, she felt like she was so brittle she might fall apart.

He didn't love her. So maybe it was a foolish thing, to think of buying a plane ticket and going back.

But she didn't know how else to show him. To make him believe that she was choosing him.

But what she wanted… What she really wanted was for him to choose her. What she really wanted was for him to understand.

Yes, he had given her father information that her father had misused, but it wasn't his fault that her father had betrayed them.

But she didn't really think that was the problem either. She just thought it was fear. A feeling of not being enough. And she knew what that felt like. Because she… She had always felt like that. Her father had used her to maneuver politically, and her mother had sort of dropped out of her life.

She knew what that was like.

But being with him, experiencing the intensity of their connection, it made her feel more than enough. She was so brave when she was with him. So much more herself than she'd ever been.

She craved it. She wanted it back. She wanted to be with him.

But at the same time she knew that she would always take that forward with her. Wherever she went.

She might not be with him. But she would always be with him.

But she hoped. She truly hoped that he would come for her.

He had told her once that it took hope to save Riyaz.

And she needed hope now.

Badly.

The dungeon was where his brother found him. Laid out like a sacrifice to enemies who were no longer there.

"What the hell are you doing?"

He looked up into the darkness. "I am seeing what it was like for you."

"Well. I still sleep down here. So you might ask before you enter."

"Why do you sleep down here?"

"Because you don't change immediately," said Riyaz. "I hate it here. And yet for many years it was the only place I saw. There is a safety to it. But it is captivity." He could hear his brother move toward him, sit down on the bench beside him. "But then. Everything is a cage of some kind. None of us are truly free."

"No," he said.

"I know that Ariel left. Why?"

"Because I told her to."

"I see. And why would you do that? You want to keep her."

"Look at where we are, Riyaz. We are in a dungeon. Do you really think it appropriate to keep a woman in the palace against her will? Even if it is in my bed and not a dungeon?"

"Did she say she didn't want to be with you?"

"No. But, she didn't have the choice to come here in the first place. Not now, and not all those years ago. She doesn't even know what she wants."

Riyaz laughed. "Is it her that doesn't know what she wants? Or is it you?"

"And what about you? You are keeping a woman prisoner as well."

"Have I expressed a moral difficulty with this?"

"I would think that you of all people would."

"Why?"

He had nothing to say to that. His brother didn't simply know... What was there to be said?

"Do you want her?" Riyaz asked him.

"Ariel? Of course. I have upended everything to have her. I betrayed you. Again."

"What do you mean again?"

"You said that we should keep our demons to ourselves, Riyaz. But I think you should know about mine. I was in love with Ariel when we were children. And I used to sneak out with her. When we were fourteen we went out into the desert. And we were caught. I was. By her father. And he asked me a question... And I answered it. To keep myself from being in trouble. I gave him an easier way to get into the palace. I did not feel as if I could tell him no. He would... He would reveal what happened between myself and Ariel."

"So you're the reason they came into the palace."

"Yes," he said.

"That was a very stupid thing to do," said Riyaz.

He didn't deny Cairo's fault the way that Ariel had.

"It was," Cairo agreed.

"Fourteen-year-old boys are stupid."

"Yes. And you were sixteen. And suffered greatly for my stupidity."

"They were intent on killing the royal family, they would've done it somehow. Even if it'd been exploding a motorcade. It would've occurred. This was a neat and clean way to do it, but... They would've found a way."

"Are you trying to absolve me?"

"No. Your actions led to that event. But you cannot control the intent of others. So, yes, something that you did played a part in the way they were able to kill our parents and take me prisoner. But... I believe it would've happened either way. And perhaps we would've been blown up."

"You can't know that."

"No. But you can't know otherwise."

"I don't understand," Cairo said. "Are you blaming me? Forgiving me?"

"I can't do either. Here is one thing you learn with only yourself for company for a great number of years. The world turns regardless of your involvement in it. In the dark of night, you have only yourself. And the only way you can be rescued is if there is someone out there who cares enough to do it. I can't absolve you. You have to absolve yourself. But you are the person who came for me. Whether you are blameless or not… That is something."

It wasn't a rousing speech of forgiveness. It was something deeper than that. It was something that Cairo could actually…accept.

Neither of them were perfect. But they were here together in the dark. He had come for Riyaz when Riyaz needed him. And now Riyaz had come for him. And perhaps they could never make fair the things that were unfair. And perhaps they could never make whole the things that were broken.

And perhaps he could never be redeemed.

But maybe… Maybe he could be loved. Just as he was anyway. Because wasn't that what Riyaz was giving him? Not absolution, and not blame. Just acceptance.

"I have to go to her," he said.

"Of course you do," said Riyaz.

"I'm not taking her prisoner."

"I wouldn't care if you were."

"Yes. I know." And he decided that he would not

challenge his brother on that. That was for him and Brianna to work out, and he had a feeling they would. At least eventually.

But Riyaz's woman was not his problem. He had to go and get his own.

CHAPTER EIGHTEEN

SHE HAD BOUGHT the tickets. She was leaving tomorrow. If he didn't come…

If he didn't come she would be devastated. But she would go to him. She would show him.

She would show him what she had chosen.

She went to the window and looked out at the Parisian skyline. And that was when she saw him.

Run.

The word echoed in her soul. She flung the door to the apartment open and began to run down the stairs, all the way down to the street, and by the time she got there, he was just about to approach the door.

"Cairo," she said.

"Ariel."

And she found herself in his arms. Kissing him.

When he pulled away, his breathing was ragged. "Ariel," he said. "I've come for you. My brother did not magically forgive me. And I am not immediately redeemed. I am not a different man than the one that you left behind. But I am… Willing. I am willing to accept what you have offered me. You came to me while I was in the dark. You came to rescue me. To lift me out. And I want it. I want your love. And I want to reach out and take your hand and give you my love in return. I was afraid… Because… Of what I felt loving you had cost before. But really, it wasn't that. It was just knowing what it feels like to lose you. And wanting to never lose you again. And so… I cut you off myself. As if that made it better. But the problem is… I don't know what makes things better. I know how to fight. And I know how to embrace oblivion. But you… You are peace. And you are sharp and clear. And you are quite different from anything that I have ever had. I'm not sure I know how to love. But I want to."

"Oh, my sun," she said. "Don't you know that you burned so bright? Don't you know that you've known how to love me since you were a boy? It's as natural as breathing to us. We couldn't stop if we tried."

"You're right," he said, as if it was the most wondrous thing. A revelation.

Her heart hurt. With joy. With pain for him.

With hope.

"We never need to be shown. Not by anyone. It was simply part of us."

"Fate," he said.

"Fate we had to choose," she said, stepping toward him and taking his hand in hers. "I want to go home now. To Nazul. Take me to the desert."

EPILOGUE

It took a number of years for Cairo to feel as if he had fully forgiven himself for the mistakes of the past. It was different to face those feelings, rather than simply running from them. And once he did begin to look at them critically… It had been hard.

But Ariel had been there for him every step of the way.

And things changed radically when she gave birth to their first child.

A daughter.

And it shifted the landscape of his soul.

In much the way Ariel had done the first time he had seen her.

Undeniable love. A love that felt fated in ways he did not ever think he would understand.

But it was actually that love that changed everything for him. That made him fully understand.

A person was never worthy of the love they were given. A person simply had to accept it as a gift, and work to be the best they could.

"She looks so much like you," Ariel said, brushing the top of their daughter's dark downy head with her forefinger.

"And yet, she is her mother's daughter. For she has my heart. Without question. Always."

And then from behind his back he took out the gift that he had brought for her earlier. Not diamonds. Not gold. An orange.

He handed the orange to his wife, and she smiled. "I love you," she said.

"I love you, *ya amar.*"

* * * * *

THE CHRISTMAS
HE CLAIMED
THE SECRETARY

CAITLIN CREWS

MILLS & BOON

CHAPTER ONE

IT WAS NOT the first time in Tiziano Accardi's admittedly splendid life that a woman had fallen at his feet.

The notable difference on this occasion was that the woman in question had not been gazing upon him as she tumbled, tossed to the ground at the very sight of his much-remarked-upon male beauty.

How delightfully novel.

Tiziano, never in much of a hurry at the best of times, was particularly unhurried today. His humorless and deeply boring brother—who was, unfortunately, the stalwart and responsible CEO of Accardi Industries, the keeper of the family purse strings, and, worst of all, distressingly immune to his younger brother's much-vaunted charm no matter how Tiziano tried to win him round—had demanded that Tiziano present himself for his biweekly dressing-down. It would have been a daily occurrence, if Ago had his way, but Tiziano could not always be asked to make an appearance in the office. Not when there were far more interesting places to be. A beach in Rio or the Philippines, for example. Any of the world's glamorous cities, from Milan to Tokyo and back. Or, really, any other place where beautiful women gathered.

He was something of a connoisseur.

But here in the dreary office he was today, against his better judgment. And will. He had woken up in London for the first time in some weeks this dreary fall, and thanks to the perfidy of his household staff, working in concert with his brother's fearsome executive assistant, Ago knew it.

The thunderous summons had been delivered at top volume, down the phone Tiziano would never have answered had it come from his brother's line.

It was not that Tiziano disliked his role as the company's chief marketing executive—his official title, for his sins. On the contrary, he not only enjoyed the job, he was also—to everyone's great surprise, apparently, given how often it was mentioned in tones of nearly insulting wonder—quite good at it.

A reality that he knew drove his brother rather round the bend.

Because it would be easier to dismiss Tiziano if the younger Accardi brother was nothing more than the empty-headed man-whore the tabloids made him out to be.

It was also true he gave said tabloids ammunition, but he was only a man, after all, and therefore tragically imperfect. He was always the first to say so. Was it his fault that so many beautiful women found him irresistible? Or that because he enjoyed a lively evening out, it was assumed that he was as vapid and fatuous as a great many of the people who tended to take part in those evenings?

The real scandal, Tiziano knew, was that he had actually participated in his brother's bid to make the family company—the one their grandfather had started in

Italy and their father had expanded into foreign markets—into the multinational corporation it was today. Complete with its own shiny, glossy headquarters in giddy London, far away from the ancient family heap outside Firenze, awash in wisteria and regret.

Not that such inconvenient facts got in his brother's way when he wanted to deliver a stinging lecture or five. When Ago took it upon himself to roar on, stern and uncompromising and with much talk of *family legacies* and *what is owed to the Accardi name*, neither God nor man could stop him.

Tiziano, who considered himself a bit of both, if he was honest, was well used to the storm and drama of it all.

He even found it all a bit entertaining, usually. Ago *did* like to go on and on and Tiziano quite liked lounging about, acting as if he was as useless as most believed he was. It was a game they played. It reminded him of when they were heedless children, chasing each other across the rolling hills of Tuscany and dodging cypress trees as they ran. How could he not enjoy the adult version of that?

Especially because his brother clearly did not, growing ever more grim and disapproving in response to Tiziano's indolence. Tiziano had imagined that at some point in the not-so-distant future, he would *actually* find himself sprawled out on the floor of Ago's office, pretending to nap whilst his brother delivered his favorite lecture about *optics*.

In truth, he'd been looking forward to it.

Sadly this fall, the lectures had turned to distressing orders to take up the old ball and chain, a dismal enterprise that Tiziano had intended to happily avoid for the rest of his life. After all, he was the spare to the Accardi fortune, thank you. Not the heir. What did it matter how he entertained himself? Empires hung from his brother's stern, uncompromising fingers, not his.

A point Ago did not seem to think mitigated what he believed to be Tiziano's responsibilities.

So it was possible that the sight of the woman before him—who'd been scowling down at the heap of file folders in her arms as she charged down the stairs that he'd been climbing in as desultory a fashion as possible—was far more intriguing to him than she might normally have been. Particularly when she went down on the landing as they both reached it, falling over what appeared to be her own serviceable pump, then hitting the ground. In an explosion of documents that rained down all around her, she came to a stop a scant centimeter from his big toe.

Clad in hand-tooled leather by the finest artisans in Rome, *naturalmente*.

"I'm well aware of the effect I have on women," Tiziano assured her when she came to a complete stop, and the last of the documents finished its snowy descent to lie on the landing beside her. "But I must give you points for effort, *cara*. Making it rain with a shower of corporate documentation is a lovely touch. Truly."

And on any other day, at any other time, he might have left it at that. He might have nimbly stepped over yet another woman prostrate at his feet and carried on taking the longest route possible to his brother's vast executive suite at the penthouse level of this gleaming tower in the City. On any other day, he would have forgotten her before he made it to the next landing.

But then, this was not any other day.

Because Ago had declared that not only was Tiziano to marry, a horror in and of itself. But more, he was expected to marry the tediously virtuous bride of Ago's choosing. Tiziano knew of the girl in question. Had even met her on several tiresome occasions drenched in respectability and its dire twin, responsibility. She was a nun-like virgin, according to all accounts as well as his own observation, who happened to also be the beloved daughter of one of Accardi Industries' best clients.

Though perhaps *beloved* was not the right word. What was indisputable was that Victoria Cameron was her loathsome father's only daughter. As far as Tiziano could see, the man's fervent desire to control his daughter's matrimonial choices, while making certain they benefited him, was nothing short of medieval. Tiziano would be very much surprised if poor, boring Victoria had ever known the touch of a man. Or had ever spent more than three seconds in the presence of one without her father looking on and jealously guarding over her.

As if an untried convent-bred girl was such a lure in these depraved times that men needed to be restrained in her presence or they might go mad with lust and longing.

It was laughable.

When Tiziano had suggested to his brother that prissy, pearl-clutching moralist Everard Cameron dispense with the theatrics and simply mount a virginity auction the way he clearly wished to do—though without calling it what it was—Ago had only glared at him in that way he did, all steel and disappointment.

That hadn't changed the facts.

Ago intended that Tiziano should be the highest and best bidder for a prize Tiziano did not esteem in the least. What was required of Tiziano was very simple in this case, according to his brother in all his consequence and condescension, handing down dictates from on high. Tiziano need only restrain himself from the worst of his excesses and then, once married and settled and domesticated entirely, confine said excesses to the sacrament of marriage.

Given that Accardis did not divorce, because why divide up properties and assets when it was easy enough to live separate lives on said far-flung estates, his brother was delivering nothing less than a life sentence.

Tiziano liked his life as it was. He was in no particular rush to usher himself into his own cell.

That was why he was still standing there, looking down at the heap of hapless female and corporate documentation at his feet. And that was why he was there to receive the full force of the woman's scowl when she lifted up her head, shoved back a bit of the red hair that had fallen into her eyes, and made it clear that her scowl was no mistake.

By deepening it as she beheld him.

"I can't say it's surprising to discover that a man dressed like you is a waste of space," she said, incredibly. She pushed herself up and looked around, as if taking in what had become of her file folders for the first time. "How chivalrous. By all means, please keep doing whatever it is you were doing. I'm sure it's more important than helping a woman as she *falls down the stairs.*"

Unused to that tone of voice when delivered by a female instead of his brother's deep growl, it took Tiziano a moment to realize that she was *scolding* him.

And then, as if the scowling wasn't enough, the woman simply…ignored him. She set about collecting all her papers, crawling about on the floor before him on her hands and knees. He might have assumed that was another bid for his attention. After all, it did give him quite a view. He had never seen the woman before, but it was clear at a glance that she was one of the innumerable faceless minions who worked here. Probably a secretary, he would wager, or something of that ilk. The pumps she had tripped over were cheap, with scuffed heels, and the undersides were worn away. The pencil skirt she wore was a shade of muddy brown that he doubted anyone would consider fashionable. And as she scuttled about on her hands and knees before him, the cream-colored blouse she had tucked into her skirt pulled up, showing him an intriguing glimpse of shocking pink lace.

He was no callow youth and still, there was something about her that captivated him. Perhaps the way her hips moved this way and that, forcing him to contemplate the span of her waist, and how it might feel to measure her curves with his hands.

It was tempting to assume she was crawling before him for precisely this purpose. To tempt him in just this manner.

But perhaps what really intrigued him was how unselfconscious she seemed. And, more surprising by far, as if she truly could not give a toss whether he stood watching her gather up her papers or not.

It was not a sensation he had ever felt before.

He was Tiziano Accardi. He was not ignored. He could not recall a single moment in his life when he had not received as much attention as possible from everyone and anyone in his vicinity.

And he could not say that he was filled with *excite-*

ment, precisely, that it was occurring now. What he discovered—as one lowering moment followed another while she continued to crawl around the landing, muttering to herself as she stacked up her documents and shoved them back into the folders they'd come from, as if she'd entirely forgotten that she wasn't alone—was that a lifelong question had finally been answered. Here, on an ignominious stairwell landing, on a gray and unremarkable Tuesday in the midst of a gloomy autumn.

He liked to say, and often did say, that it was not *his* fault that he was so magnetic that no one who encountered him could help but make him their focal point in all things. How could they resist? Yet now he discovered that he really did prefer the comfort of forever knowing himself to be the center of everyone's thoughts.

All thanks to this nameless woman who, if he was not mistaken, had actually *dismissed* him.

He told himself that it was in the spirit of discovery, nothing more—certainly not a childish wish to refocus attention where it clearly belonged—that he squatted down before her, relieved her of the file folder she held, then scooped up a huge pile of the remaining papers and tossed them inside.

"That's not actually helpful," she told him. Not quite the sweet thanks he'd expected. She pushed back from all fours so that she was kneeling before him and fixed him with a baleful glare. Another expression he had never before seen on a female face when it was pointed in his direction. Much less from her current position. "You do realize that I have to put them in order, don't you?" But then she let out a laugh. "Who am I kidding? I doubt very much you have the slightest idea what people do with the documents that keep your company chugging along, do you?"

"So you do know who I am." Tiziano smiled. "That is a comfort. For a terrifying moment there I could have sworn that I had become unremarkable."

"And who, may I ask, could possibly avoid knowing you even if they wished it?" Her accent was filled with hints of the north, meaning that where she came from in this cold country was even more frigid and inhospitable than London in the dark of a late, wet autumn—though her cheeks were rosy. He found himself contemplating them with interest. "I was under the impression you dedicated yourself to becoming as ubiquitous as possible before the age of sixteen."

"I'm delighted you noticed," Tiziano drawled, wrenching his attention away from her *cheeks*. "But, *cara*, surely you know that as delightful as all this flirtation is to me, it is in no way wise. You must not need your job overmuch if you are willing to risk it for the chance to sharpen your claws on a man of my stature."

As he watched, more fascinated than he cared to process at the minute, her eyes—a surprising shade of gray that put him in mind of the foggy, moody mornings that were the parts of London he loved best—looked very nearly murderous. She flushed slightly, making her cheeks all the rosier. And while in most women he would assume that was an involuntary, biological response to a perfect specimen such as himself, he rather thought that when it came to this creature, it was all temper.

How extraordinary.

And then she didn't give in to it, which was even more impressive.

Instead, she produced a tight smile. "I must have hit my head when I fell," she said, though Tiziano thought they both knew quite well she had done no such thing. "My apologies. As a matter of fact, I do quite need this job. Thank you for reminding me."

"It is forgotten," Tiziano said with a magnanimous wave of his hand. "But tell me, *cara*, what is it you do here?" He looked down at the file folder in his hand. "A bit of filing, is it?"

"A bit of filing and a bit of typing," she replied, and not in the tones of a woman who revered either of those tasks. But then, neither would he. "They don't call it the secretarial pool these days. But effectively, that's what it is."

"You're a secretary?"

"I am indeed." She cleared her throat, perhaps hearing herself echo back from the walls of the stairwell, because when she looked around again she seemed significantly more flustered than she had before. "My supervisor will not be pleased that it's taking me so long to come back with these files. And that they'll have to be put back in order."

"How long have you worked here?"

She took her time looking back at him, and though she was still attempting that tight smile, her gray gaze had gone suspicious. "A year," she said. "Well. Nearly."

"A year." He tilted his head slightly to one side. "How odd. And yet I'm certain I have never seen you before."

Then, to his amusement, he watched any number of sharp replies rise and fall in that gray gaze of hers. He had to assume each was more acid than the last.

He was oddly disappointed when she did not gift him with any of them. Instead, she smiled wider, though he was certain, somehow, that it did not come easy to her. "Every moment has been a joy."

Tiziano laughed. "I rather doubt that. Whether they call it a secretarial pool or not, it sounds unpleasant. I can't imagine I would enjoy it myself."

But she was not drawn in, another first. "I apologize for my potentially concussed outburst before, sir," she said, and it was all sweet enough. Trouble was, he didn't believe her.

She made as if to rise but he beat her to it, getting to his feet and then reaching down to take her by the elbow and pull her up.

And there was nothing to it, the way he gripped her arm and drew her from the floor. She could have been a grandmother. A child. But he was entirely too aware that she was neither of those things. She was a woman.

More important, she was nothing at all like the exceedingly dull Victoria Cameron.

As far as Tiziano could tell, Victoria had been raised to be, at best, a particular kind of adornment. Her father came from a long line of overbred aristocrats, with various titles knocking about his closet. His daughter had been engineered since birth to appeal to the only sort of man Everard Cameron truly esteemed—that being a man like himself.

His daughter was thus innocent and untouched to suit the dynastic aspirations of a man who needed heirs. And more, wished to go about the making of them with confidence that the sons and daughters who bore his name could come only from his loins. Tiziano had no doubt that Victoria was equally capable of overseeing a variety of stately homes, staffs, and all the rest of the nonsense that went along with a certain degree of consequence in some circles. She would go about it with blameless efficiency and a minimum of fuss, selecting the appropriate friends, activities, and boarding schools for whatever heirs she produced and then taking herself off to breed corgis or *take an interest* in the stables.

She was most assuredly not the sort who would take up with a string of lovers once her childbearing duties were dispatched. Not Victoria. She would dedicate herself to tedious charities and saintly volunteer opportunities, piously giving back while *setting an example* as best she could. She was a paragon, raised to neither expect nor demand anything of the men in her life, while making a quiet sort of mark upon the world that would be remarked upon only in her obituary.

Even thinking about shackling himself to such a relentlessly irreproachable creature just about put Tiziano into a stupor.

Meanwhile, he knew a great many things about *this* woman who he still held in his grip, entirely too aware of the warmth of her skin against his palm.

"Did I ask you your name?" He knew he had not. "I'm certain I meant to."

She swallowed, then lifted her chin. And he took her in, the red hair curling so wildly that it defied the clips she'd attempted to use to tame it. Those gray, expressive eyes that marked her not as a paragon, but a woman of decided tempers.

Passion, something in him whispered.

"Annie," she said, with obvious reluctance. "My name is Annie Meeks. Sir. I take it you mean to report me?"

"I'm not going to report you," he assured her. And

then, indulging an urge he could not have named, he tested her name on his tongue. "Annie."

This time, when she flushed, he knew it wasn't temper. And more, that it wasn't the sight of him that made her react that way. That it was this—her name in his mouth. Something personal to her. Something that wasn't intimate, by any means, but also wasn't the same, run-of-the-mill attraction every woman who crossed his path felt at the sight of him.

Tiziano fancied he felt something like it, too. And he was pleased it existed, he told himself. And better yet, that it was manageable.

Because Annie Meeks, run-of-the-mill secretary in the bowels of Accardi Industries, was in every possible way inappropriate. She was no gently bred aristocratic miss. Her broad vowels were coarse, and marked her as beneath him even if the obvious differences in their attire had not already done so. He suspected that one of his shoes could have bought her entire outfit. And whatever wardrobe went with it. Twenty times over.

"Thank you." Annie's tone was guarded. Her gray gaze searched his. "I wouldn't blame you if you did report me. I'd like to assure you that I hold both you and the company in the utmost respect—"

"That is enough now," Tiziano said with a dismissive laugh. "I'm not my brother. He is far more concerned with appearances. What is appropriate, what is not. If I were to claim that I was suddenly worried about such things that would mark me hypocrite, I fear."

She made a neutral sort of sound, still holding herself too still. Though he could feel a slight quiver within her, there beneath his hand.

He let his gaze move over her, remembering the hint

of pink lace, the indentation at her waist. The echo of that liveliness in the temper he'd seen crack like lightning through the gray of her gaze. The rosy cheeks. The spray of freckles above her nose.

She would do.

In fact, she would do quite nicely, especially if she really did need her job. Or any job, really, which Tiziano supposed applied to most secretaries and all such people who were forced to work for their living. That meant she had a price. And, happily, he was nothing if not capable of paying it.

He could pay her far more handsomely than anything she was likely to get by filing tedious documents and answering to the phalanx of beige middle managers in this place.

Because he had an idea. The kind of idea that made him a marketing genius, if he said so himself. Only in this case, it was not the company that he would be marketing. But his own private life.

"I have a proposition for you," he said.

Her gray eyes narrowed. Once more, not quite the hosannas from on high he might have expected from another woman. But he liked the unfamiliar sting of it. "I'm honored," she said, and he could see that this was clearly a lie. She swallowed, then forced a smile that did not reach the outrage in her gaze. "But I must immediately decline any propositions. Mr. Accardi. Sir."

Tiziano let go of her elbow and stepped back, so he could lean against the wall and study her. And the more he looked at her, the more he was certain he'd found the answer to all of his problems. Particularly when she had her temper working. If he took her at face value, scuffed shoes and ill-fitting attempt to follow the corporate dress code, he could see her as one of these working girls who seemed to fill all the cities of the world—one indistinguishable from the next. There were veritable hordes of them traipsing about the Big Smoke, dreaming of getting on the property ladder, squeezing out a few whelps with some milksop lover, and then ascending to the dizzying heights of a semidetached in one of those indistinct English towns made mostly of cheerless bricks and the faint praise of middle-class ambitions. But if he squinted, he could see something else.

What he could make of her.

"What do you dream about, Annie Meeks?" he asked.

She blinked, her expression suspiciously bland. "A time machine. So I could go back and take the lift."

A beat, and then he laughed, and this time in sheer delight. "But you do not understand, *cara*. I must congratulate you, for your life has just changed." He paused, but she only continued to gaze at him balefully. He inclined his head. "It cannot possibly be your wish to toil away, unnoticed and unappreciated, forever. And indeed, you do not have to. Tell me what it is you dream of and I will make it happen. This I promise you."

"I really must have a concussion," she murmured. Nothing about the way she looked at him softened. Surely he should not have found that compelling. "Because I might not be as sophisticated as some, but I hope I'm not foolish enough to imagine that something that appears too good to be true is anything but."

"For all you know this is an expression of my many eccentricities. Perhaps I trawl the abandoned halls and back stairs of Accardi Industries, bestowing goodwill upon whomever I pass."

"If you'll forgive me, I think we all know you do no such thing."

He laughed again, because she'd said that so sweetly, and yet he could see the truth of her feelings in her gaze. "I'm starting today."

"And what will you do with my dreams if I share them with you?" she asked, in a tone he could only call *challenging*. "Assuming I can remember any of them, that is. Fickle things, dreams. It's mostly those who can afford to indulge them who ponce about, worrying over them in the first place. The rest of us have work to do."

"What if I made it so you could afford to ponce about at will?" he countered. "Or anything else you like, for that matter?"

"And maybe tomorrow morning I'll wake up to find myself the Queen of England," she replied briskly. "But either way, that won't get these files sorted or my rent paid. So if you will please excuse me—"

"Annie," he said, liking the name more and more, each time he said it, "I want you to be my mistress."

He thought she might collapse, perhaps. Or smile knowingly. Maybe he expected her to do as another woman might and feign a great and theatric dismay. What he did not expect was the way her brows drew together, treating him once again to that ferocious scowl.

Tiziano liked it even better this time around.

She flushed once more, and he understood that he was seeing her temper again. A bright hot flare of it, unmistakable.

He liked that even more.

"Or you'll have me fired, is that it?" She laughed then, though it was a sharp sound and bitter besides.

"No need, Mr. Accardi. I'll save you the trouble and quit."

Then she took the files she held and threw them on the floor. This time they didn't go up in a plume of fluttering papers. This time they made a loud bang, and even so, it was less furious than the way she looked at him.

She took a deep breath, and something gleamed in her gray eyes, putting him in mind of a set of talons. "And having quit, let me be clear. I think you are the most—"

"You mistake the matter, I think, *cara mia*," he interrupted, silkily. "You will be my mistress in name only, *chiaramente*. Or did you imagine that I, Tiziano Accardi, who is often seen in the adoring company of princesses and international superstars, would lower myself to propositioning women for sex in sad office stairwells?"

CHAPTER TWO

ANNIE MEEKS HAD never been this close to a real, live billionaire before. Or really any powerful being, so drenched in privilege that he was *languid* about it.

But she had been to a zoo or two in her time and really, this was no different from standing at one of the big cat enclosures, watching a creature who should have been impossible slink about before her, all sleek and mesmerizing, as if to distract the unwary from the fangs.

She knew that was fanciful, at best. The reality was that Tiziano Accardi was no otherworldly jaguar, prowling about London, a creature of myth and legend.

He was a man. A man who was wearing hundreds of thousands of pounds worth of bespoke attire, which, like everything about him, was so obviously expensive that he could get away with wearing it all so carelessly. But he was a man despite all this.

He was also astonishing.

Annie had seen his face on a thousand tabloids, like everyone else who drew breath. In pictures, the ethereal quality of his beauty was what came through. The operatic cheekbones. The sensual mouth. The contrast between all that and thick, dark hair that tousled about over moody blue eyes.

In person, however, there was that voice of his, like sin distilled into wonder. More worrying, there was a kind of brooding masculinity that poured off him, making her think less about the things that made him beautiful and more about those things that made him a man.

She had to remind herself, sharply, that gifted as he might have been in physical attributes, it was the gift of his particular genealogy that truly made him who and what he was. Generations of wealth and importance, handed down from parents to child again and again, so that it was no wonder he thought he was God's gift.

There was not a single thing in his life to indicate otherwise.

But that didn't explain what was happening here. Or the staggering thing he'd just said.

"I don't know what you normally do in stairwells," Annie found herself saying, which wasn't wise. Particularly in that tone of voice.

Then again, she'd quit her boring and yet stressful job here at Accardi Industries. And she would have to deal with that later and all the ramifications of it, she knew that. Truth was, she already regretted it. Annie was tempted to simply set off down the stairs and go right back to work, assuming—correctly, she was sure—that Tiziano Accardi could no more pick one secretary out of a pack than he could do his own washing up. He'd never worked a day in a job that wasn't granted to him by virtue of his surname. She doubted he even knew how to locate the lower levels of the building where the common folk toiled away.

But she'd given him her name, hadn't she?

She could feel the panic creep in, because scruples were all well and good, but they wouldn't do a thing to pay her debts. And well did she know it. Because if being honest and having scruples in the first place got a person ahead in this life, she'd be at Goldsmith's even now, studying for her art history degree. The way she'd been doing before her thoughtless, selfish sister had taken out all that credit in her name.

But she couldn't let herself think about Roxy. Not now. Not here in this very stairwell where she'd made a right mess of the lifeline she'd arranged to climb out of the hole her sister had put her in.

"It is true that I'm very versatile," Tiziano drawled, in an alarming manner. *Alarming* because she couldn't simply *hear* the man. She could *feel* that voice of his all over her, low and silken. "But alas, *cara*, ours must be a business arrangement."

Annie didn't know what was worse. The way he said that empty endearment, so *Italian* and so careless. Or the way he'd said her actual name before, which had made everything inside her…shiver.

She was still shivering, a fact that made her temper kick in.

"I don't understand this conversation and I don't want to," she said flatly, because she, by God, would *act* as if she was made of sterner stuff no matter what was quivering about inside her. "Here's what I do know. You are literally famous for being able to step into the street and have women attach themselves to your trouser leg before you've taken a step. There's no reason for you to be talking to me. About any kind of arrangement. Ever."

His surprising blue eyes—because surely a man so

utterly Italian should have eyes like bitter coffee or melting chocolate or tiramisu of some kind—gleamed in a way she also felt *all over*. "But you see, that's why you're perfect."

There was something about the way he lounged there against the wall, as if his very spine was too lazy to support him otherwise. She knew that was the general take on Tiziano Accardi in all things—that he was only ever upright, and clothed rather than cavorting about in sensual undress, under protest.

But the look in those stormy blue eyes of his made her suspect that wasn't quite true.

"Perfect," Annie repeated flatly, ordering herself to ignore the man's *eyes*. He was an Accardi. An Accardi soul had no windows, unless they offered the most expensive view in any given city. "Why do I think that even if that's true, it's not a compliment?"

He lifted an indolent shoulder. "It appears you are remarkably suspicious, *cara*."

That endearment again. She couldn't say she cared for it. But that was the least of her concerns.

Annie knew exactly what she needed to do. It was glaringly obvious. All that was required of her was that she excuse herself, politely. Pick up the file folders once more, then march herself off to her supervisor's office. It wasn't ideal that Tiziano knew her name, certainly, but why did she imagine that he would remember it? Surely men like him saw a woman and had instant amnesia that any others existed or ever had.

That was likely to happen even more quickly in a case like this, surely, when it wasn't as if he'd noticed her. As a woman, that was. Instead of…whatever it was he was proposing.

She didn't have to know exactly what a man like him was proposing to her to know it was unflattering. Their relative positions in the world told her that without either one of them having to say a word.

There was no question about what she needed to do, and yet…

Deep inside her, she felt a long-dormant curiosity shake itself off. She'd packed it away with all the rest of the things that she'd so foolishly thought were hers, until Roxy had taken them from her, one by one. Dreams. Curiosity. An interest in the world around her. She'd put all such childish things behind her when she'd accepted reality, courtesy of her faceless bank and the notification of insufficient funds that had made no sense to her.

Until it had.

These days Annie kept her head down and her mind empty and told herself that was better. Much better, because the kind of person she was now, who budgeted down to her every penny, and would do so for the next three decades at least, didn't waste time dreaming herself silly.

These days she was practical. Distressingly so.

But there was a jaguar in the shape of a man lounging there before her in a bloody stairwell and there was that twisting, quivering sensation deep in her belly. And before she could talk herself out of it, or remind herself what was at stake here, she found herself tilting her head to one side in consideration. And even crossing her arms as she regarded him.

As if she had nothing to lose.

"Explain to me what you mean," she told him, less an invitation than a command, and she could see he found that amusing. Those moody eyes of his gleamed.

"My brother has taken it upon himself to rehabilitate my tattered reputation," Tiziano said in that *voice* of his that no tabloid photo could have prepared her for. Expensive silk with a hint of some rougher edge that made her...too warm.

"A doomed enterprise, I would've thought," she retorted. Tartly.

The gleam in his eyes intensified. "Just so. But perhaps you have heard of my brother as well, and so realize that he cannot be told anything when he has made up his mind. Mountains are more malleable. And infinitely more pleasant."

"I can't say I'm familiar with either," Annie said with a sniff. "Not a typical feature of the lowly work I do, as it happens. No mountains or billionaire bosses lurking about. Just secretarial work, on command."

"What I notice, Annie, is that you sound as transported by your profession as I am by my brother's plans for me." He almost sounded like he meant that. That anything about them was at all similar. It didn't make sense. Especially when he smiled. "Surely if we join forces, we can help each other."

"There's no question that you could help me, if you deigned to do so," Annie pointed out with what her sister had once called her *relentless and unnecessary honesty*. Not that they talked any longer. "Just as there's no question that such help would inevitably come with strings. Nooses, I reckon."

"Nooses are little more than a necktie, unless you tighten them," Tiziano replied. "Though there are some who crave such things, of course. To each their own. Life is meant to be a banquet."

Annie ignored that, and not only because, in her experience, life was less a banquet and more a bit of cold, dry toast no amount of jam could disguise. "The real question is, what help do you imagine I could give you, and why do you imagine I would wish to give it?" She shook her head with more resolve than she felt, which should have scared her. "There are words for women who sell their services to men like you. But I expect you know that."

What she expected, really, was for him to take offense at that suggestion.

"You're thinking of words that are applied to lesser men, surely," Tiziano told her, those dark eyes dancing, clearly not the least bit offended. "When a man such as myself partakes of transactional relationships, an entirely different vocabulary is brought to bear. Many such women are known as *wives* to a man with a fortune, I think you'll find."

"To clarify," Annie said dryly, after a moment, "as romantic as this conversation is, you are not proposing marriage."

"Certainly not." There was a flash of that smile of his that she was distressed to discover affected her, no matter how many times she'd seen it splashed across the tabloid newspapers. Or even flashed about this very stairwell. "Though matrimony is at the heart of my current dilemma, it is not what I require of you."

"I see it's become a requirement. That's a bit fast, don't you think? Moments ago you were begging me for a favor. But not for sex in the stairwell, because you are you, the great and vainglorious Tiziano. I beg your pardon. I meant *glorious*, of course."

"*Certo.* Of course you did."

And then, for a moment, everything seemed to collapse into that gleaming gaze of his and the way he looked at her, as if he, too, couldn't quite understand what it was he did here.

Annie was no expert on the man, or any man, but it almost looked to her as if he…caught himself up. He had the look of a man emerging from a dark interior into a sunny day. As if he didn't quite know what he was about.

She waited for him to make his excuses and swan off, back into his glittering life, but he didn't. He crossed his own arms, so they were facing each other now, mirroring each other's body language.

And Annie couldn't think of a single reason in all the world that she should feel something rather like *hot*, when it was the middle of a blustery November.

Tiziano considered her. "My brother feels that the rehabilitation he seeks for me can best be achieved by playing the sort of futile games our ancestors so enjoyed."

"Land acquisition? The callous disregard for serfs and slaves?"

His eyes gleamed again and he nodded faintly, as if to say, *point to you*. "Along those lines, yes. It's a tale as old as time. Find the most virtuous girl in all the land, renowned for her saintly works and unblemished innocence, and hand her over to a dissolute rake such as myself so that she might cure him. We've all heard that story before. We all know how it ends."

Annie sniffed. "Syphilis?"

He laughed, and she had the sense that he was as shocked by the sound as she was, as if it was no affectation on his part this time but an honest reaction. And again, there was no reason she should react to the things

he said or did. He was nothing to her. Just an odd inter-
lude with no bearing on the rest of her life.

"I assure you that my dissolution does not run quite
so deep," he told her, his gaze and voice still ripe with
that unsettling laughter. "Nonetheless, I find myself
less than amenable to the idea of shackling myself to a
paragon of virtue that my brother feels I should."

"Perhaps he should marry her," Annie said with a
shrug. "If he's so taken with her."

"I have suggested the very same thing," Tiziano said.
"Alas, no greater martyr has ever walked the planet
than Ago Accardi. So despite the fact that the poor girl
ticks every last box on my brother's wish list for a perfect bride, he has declared that she is for me. His un-
worthy younger brother, who can only be elevated by
such a connection."

"Look," Annie said. "If I know anything in this life,
it's that families are complicated." She knew better than
to think of Roxy at a time like this. Or at all. Her sister made her far too upset, even now. She cleared her
throat. "But no matter how tempting it might be, surely
honesty is the best course."

"You do not know my brother." Tiziano sighed. "It is
not that I don't understand him. I do. He had to grow up
too fast when our father died. His whole life has been
consumed with what he sees as his duty to the family legacy. I am the only stain upon his record, and he
wishes to wash the record clean."

Annie blinked. "I didn't expect psychology from you,
I have to say."

"I'm very complicated, *cara*," he said, with a grin
that encouraged her to think he was lying. When she
found it did the exact opposite. "But just because I un-

derstand my brother doesn't mean I wish to live my life with his foot upon my neck. Much less married to a woman who bores me silly. It's not her fault. She's lovely. Blameless in every way. And yet."

Annie told herself that was all catching up with her, careening into him, shooting off her mouth, and quitting the job she couldn't afford to lose. That was why she suddenly felt so…itchy. It had nothing to do with him waxing rhapsodic about a woman she didn't know and *he* clearly didn't even like.

"But meeting you has given me the key to this mess," he told her. He managed to give the impression of great flourish when all he did was *look* at her. "A mistress."

It was an archaic word. Annie told herself that was why it seemed to wind its way through her, like sensation. She made a show of impatience. "Again, surely you already have a battalion of women who could fill that position."

"I do," he agreed. "But we are not discussing what I might look for in a woman I wish to actually have such an arrangement with." One of his brows rose. "You see, do you not, the words we use when we speak of these arrangements. Far more civilized than what you were suggesting, I think."

"Wealth is always civilized," she agreed. "Because if you have the wealth you get to decide who's civilized and who's not. It's a snake eating its own tail kind of a thing."

"What I need is a woman wholly inappropriate for me," he said, and there was something so smooth, so silken about his delivery that it took Annie a moment to realize he was insulting her. And ignoring what she'd said. "A woman beneath my notice."

"Would that I was beneath your notice," she replied, and she could hear the edge in her voice. "I could even now be free of this conversation."

His mouth curved. "I'm not trying to insult you. I'm speaking only of how others will see such a connection."

"Because you are blind to class differences, I'm sure." She reminded herself that there was absolutely no need to fence words with this man. That could only prolong this interaction. "And I don't see how this would help you, anyway. So you date a secretary. Why on earth would anyone care? You date anything that moves."

"We will not be selling me *dating*," he replied, looking and sounding so unruffled he might as well have been half-asleep. It was maddening, she found. "We will be selling a mad, passionate love affair that I will, of course, refuse to give up even should I agree to marry on command."

Something inside her jolted at that, in ways Annie did not care to excavate, but all she allowed herself was a sigh. "I would've said you were incapable of such a thing."

"That is my point."

And if she wasn't mistaken, the famously easygoing Tiziano had a temper, after all. She could see the flash of it in his blue eyes. If she was at all wise, she would beat a hasty retreat—but she didn't move. It was as if she'd forgotten how.

He went on. "If I were to come before my brother and declare that I'd fallen head over heels with one of the numerous interchangeable supermodels who follow me about from one party to the next, he would dismiss it. And carry right on with his plans. But if I present

him with a woman like you, a woman entirely different from all who have come before, that will give him
pause. It will be tempting to believe that the only reason I could make such a choice is the reason anyone
acts so far out of character." When she only gazed back
at him, he sighed. "Only the deepest, most passionate
love, Annie."

"Sounds to me that you've been reading far too much
Mills and Boon," Annie said dryly. "It's made you silly
in the head."

His eyes were gleaming with amusement again, and
she preferred that.

She opted not to ask herself why she was tallying up
preferences concerning the *jaguar* she was currently
cooped up with. *Only no one is* cooping you up, she told
herself sternly. *You can literally walk away at any time.*

Yet here she stood.

"It won't be a lifetime commitment," he continued in
a dampening tone. "I imagine it will take no more than
a week or two. Everyone wishes to announce the engagement at Christmas. I imagined that if I start banging on about how I refuse to give up the brand-new
love of my life, my saintly intended will call it off before then. Or rather, her bulldog of a father will do the
honors. We should both be back to our lives in short
order." This time both brows rose, in an expression of
breathtaking arrogance that, somehow, suited him. "Although if you agree, your life will be vastly and incal-
culably improved."

Annie frowned at him, because that shouldn't have
been appealing, gift horses being what they were. And
yet. "You don't know the first thing about my life."

"I know that if you were a woman of means, you would not be toiling away as a secretary."

Annie opened her mouth, prepared to mount an argument when she wasn't sure why she felt so compelled to argue in the first place, but he lifted an indolent hand.

"Think," he urged her quietly. Intently. Not without that arrogance, but with a kind of seriousness besides. "What do you have to lose?"

And despite herself, Annie did think.

There was a part of her that wanted to rail at him. To point out that for all he knew, she had a partner she adored and twelve lovely children waiting for her at home. But then, if she did, would she have lingered this long in a stairwell with a stranger?

The fact was, she had neither. Annie lived in a grotty bedsit in a questionable neighborhood, twenty minutes' brisk walk from the nearest Tube. Not that she bothered to walk to the Underground anyway, because saving every penny she could meant walking to work, though it took the better part of ninety minutes. In all weather. She ate tinned beans on toast more nights than not, washed her things in the sink, and rationed out her teabags.

She'd been scrimping and saving like this for a year now, and what did she have to show for it? Precious little movement on her debt, that's what.

And meanwhile Roxy had fled to Australia, where she could text her insincere apologies every now and again and carry on living as she pleased. Quite as if she hadn't ruined Annie's life.

It hardly seemed fair.

Also unfair was the simple truth that Annie had spent her whole life doing the *right* thing, not necessarily the easy thing or even the pleasurable thing. She'd gotten stellar marks at school. She'd worked hard for her place at university. She'd never given her poor aunt a single moment of worry, because surely the poor woman had enough on her plate, raising her dead sister's kids as her own. Annie had followed every rule. It had never occurred to her to act like her sister, so reckless, so ungrateful.

And what did she have to show for it? Roxy was living merrily Down Under, splitting her time between Sydney and Melbourne, or sunning herself on the beaches of Brisvegas. Annie was here. But even if Roxy hadn't helped herself to Annie's credit cards, Annie wouldn't be living *merrily*, would she?

She would be working toward her degree, congratulating herself for pursuing art history, which could be put to sensible use later. Rather than what she truly wanted to do in this life—because she'd decided long ago that it was irresponsible to risk throwing herself into her painting. Painting was almost certainly not going to pay any bills.

But if she took Tiziano up on this offer, she wouldn't have to worry about bills for a long time. Possibly not ever again. She could do what she liked. She could turn her grandmother's old cottage, locked up tight and neglected these last few years, into a studio and lose herself in oils and colors, canvas and daydreams…

Annie knew one thing without question. Her sister wouldn't have waited this long to say yes, as loudly as possible.

So what was holding her back?

Where had following the rules gotten her? She could decline this offer, but what would she have to show for it? It would take her years to dig her way out of the hole Roxy had left her in. Years upon years, just to get herself back to zero. At which point, there'd be nothing to do but start all over again.

Just once, she thought now, she should take the easy way and see what *that* was like. Just once, what if she threw caution to the wind like everyone else seemed to do with little to no repercussions?

She wouldn't be the first woman in the world to find a *transactional relationship*, as Tiziano had called it, appealing. There was a reason it was called the oldest profession, and if he meant what he said, he didn't even want the traditional form of payment.

Tiziano could have pressed his case, but he didn't. He stayed where he was, lounging before her, looking supremely unconcerned as she grappled with her conscience. And a few things that had nothing at all to do with her conscience, but should have.

She thought of her sister's last text, all *Xs* and *Os* and a picture of a sandy beach, as if that was supposed to stand in as some kind of consolation prize. And then:

It just got away from me. I didn't mean anything by it. Wish you were here.

Wish you were here, indeed.

The words seemed to echo inside her, growing heavy spikes and sticking in deep.

Maybe, just maybe, this was all a huge message from above that what Annie needed to do was change, well, everything.

And there was no time like the present.

After all, how likely was it that a jaguar would escape from the zoo once—much less again, when she'd had more space and time to think through what he was offering?

"Very well, then," she told him, sounding dour and formal to her own ears, but he might as well know up front that she wasn't like the women he was normally draped in. That was meant to be the whole point. "I'll do it. But there will have to be rules. Boundaries. And penalties if those things are compromised."

She expected him to balk at that. Because surely he was used to the world turning to his specifications. And she had no idea what boundaries she ought to demand or what penalties she should require if he broke them, only that she couldn't simply *acquiesce*. Not without *some* backbone.

But Tiziano Accardi, who still reminded her far too much of an exotic and oversize cat, which wasn't good for her and was no way to begin a business proposition, only smiled.

CHAPTER THREE

IT WAS THE strangest moment of her life, including the terrible moment when she'd finally discovered what Roxy had been up to. Just like then, Annie stood still while the sense that everything was changing—might, in fact, already have changed—hurtled toward her at breakneck speed. And with no way out.

Only this time she was still standing in an Accardi Industries stairwell.

Whether that was better or worse than standing in an impersonal corporate bank location, facing the grim reality of skyrocketing debt she hadn't acquired yet was responsible for, she couldn't say.

Yet.

Tiziano smiled at her for what seemed like a very long time after she agreed to his proposition, making her instantly regret her choice. But not enough, somehow, to open her mouth and tell him she'd changed her mind. Not enough to do what she should have done from the start and just…keep walking down the stairs.

Eventually, he pulled his mobile from his pocket, typed something in, and then returned the full force of his sultry attention to her.

"Molto bene," he murmured. "My assistant will

meet you and take down your many particulars. I will meet with my brother and begin making noises about the heart wanting what it wants and so on. That is the phrase, no?"

"It is *a* phrase," Annie said, surprised that she could speak when she couldn't seem to do anything else. Like leave. Or stop this thing even as she stood here watching it hurtle out of control. It was as if she'd hiked herself over a fence and taken a dive straight into one of the big cat enclosures at the zoo. Now it wasn't a question of *if* she would get eaten alive, only *when*. She cleared her throat and straightened out her spine. "If you're really trying to sell the idea that you've fallen suddenly and improbably in love, I might suggest that you look a little less cynical while you're about it."

Annie expected some fangs at that, but Tiziano only laughed, which did nothing for her composure. As she was contemplating that laughter, and the way light seemed to appear from nowhere and cascade all over his beautiful face while he did it, she heard the door on the landing above them open.

And maybe it wasn't a surprise that her first reaction was relief. Surely whoever turned up would restore some much-needed reality to…whatever this was. Annie would limp off back to her supervisor's office with the bruises she was surely developing, and by the time she settled in with her tinned beans this evening in front of her laptop, streaming programs so as not to pay the television license, she would think this had all been a bad dream.

Then again, she thought as he sobered, his face growing no less beautiful as his laughter faded, *perhaps not a* bad *dream, necessarily.*

There was the sound of heels against the steps and then a woman of indeterminate age appeared before them. She could have been anywhere between thirty and seventy, built sharp and slender, with the sort of long face and aggressively nondescript white-blond hair that—even ruthlessly contained in a sharp bun—made her resemble nothing so much as an Afghan hound. She marched down the steps, gimlet-eyed, until she stood beside Tiziano.

"This is Catriona," Tiziano announced, back to sounding lazy. "She handles my personal affairs, insofar as they require handling. I will leave you in her capable hands."

"Right," Annie said. "Because there are so many affairs, they really do need a manager."

Tiziano only laughed again. The woman beside him did not. Undeterred, Tiziano treated Annie to a sweeping, comprehensive study, from her head to her feet. So intent was he that she found herself flushing in response, as if he was actually reaching across the landing and putting his elegant hands on her.

Or maybe it was the rapid-fire Italian he launched into, the lyrical language seeming to wind its way all over and even *into* Annie while Catriona nodded her sculpted blond head, typed busily away into her mobile, and murmured the occasional, *"Si, si...pronto."*

After what felt to Annie like a lifetime or three, Tiziano straightened from the wall. And when he looked at her then, those blue eyes of his seemed as unnaturally bright as the rest of him, and pierced straight through her. She felt pinned to the wall.

"Arrivederci, cara," he said, though it sounded less

like a goodbye and more like a threat. "*Ci vediamo presto.* I will see you soon."

That was almost certainly a threat, or anyway, that was how her body reacted to it. She flushed from her hair to her toes, and the embarrassment of it made her blush even brighter, until she was fairly sure her skin matched her hair.

Tiziano only smiled again, this time in a way that made Annie's breath seem to…stop. A condition that did not improve when he turned and headed up the stairs in all his state, leaving her in his wake without the faintest idea how she'd let this all happen.

It was a lot how she imagined people must feel when they woke up blindly hungover with the attendant splitting headache and evidence of a night ill spent, a rite of passage she had managed to avoid thus far.

She swallowed hard, then turned to find Tiziano's assistant watching her, very closely, with absolutely no expression on her face.

This was Annie's chance to escape, now that Tiziano had taken himself off. His attention was like a tractor beam—she could admit that to herself, now he'd left—and it was time she did what she could to repair this situation. Meaning leave this building immediately and worry about her debt later, when—

"If you'll follow me," Catriona said, in a smooth, honey-toned accent that flirted with Received Pronunciation without actually making her sound *too much* like a BBC announcer. Though it was a close call. The BBC by way of Essex, to Annie's ear.

"Well," Annie said, as if she was hedging. As if she didn't know what she wanted to do. As if this was a debate. "I really shouldn't."

Catriona merely held out a slender arm and inclined her head toward the stairs, indicating that Annie should precede her.

Later, Annie was sure, she would think back to this moment and recognize it as the point of no return. After all, no matter how sleek, it was highly unlikely Tiziano's *assistant* was also a billionaire in her own right. Or any kind of uncaged predator, roaming the stairwells of London to scoop up the unwary.

Not that Annie was one of *the unwary*. What she was, she reminded herself then, was eternally neck-deep in the quicksand of Roxy's debt—and sinking. Unless she took this opportunity. Unless she acted completely out of character.

But then, what had acting *in* character done for her so far?

And then, before she knew it, she was walking up the stairs.

Catriona quickly proved herself to be an unstoppable force all her own. First she swept up the stairs just slightly behind Annie—not unlike a proper herding dog, Annie thought dryly—and ushered her into an office on the floor just below the executive level. She bid Annie take a seat in her office, which was all done up in elegant pastels, and then she proceeded to interrogate Annie. Over every last detail of her life.

Catriona left no stone unturned. She cracked open a laptop, input all of Annie's answers, and was not the least afraid to ask for further clarification. When she was done, Annie sat there on the dove gray settee, feeling rather like she was cracked wide open. Like a hopeless egg that could never be repaired.

Meanwhile, Catriona ignored her entirely and

launched herself into a flurry of activity, sending out a barrage of emails and then making rounds upon rounds of calls. This meant that there was no opportunity for Annie to talk about second thoughts. Or even, really, to have them.

Later, after Annie signed stacks upon stacks of legal documents, Catriona led her out of the office without once looking up from her mobile phone as she typed out more messages, sprinting along in her high heels as if they were a cozy pair of trainers.

Annie had trouble keeping up and she was well aware that *she* wasn't the one with her face in a device.

"Mr. Accardi will have all your debts settled by the close of business and an initial sum transferred into your bank account as a gesture of good faith," Catriona told her coolly as she strode along. "The contents of your flat will be boxed and transported and should be at your disposal by morning. Does that meet with your approval?"

Annie had been grateful that they were moving, charging down a hushed corridor as Catriona asked these questions and rattled off this information as if it was…something less than life-altering.

She felt something intense wash through her, so full-on that it nearly knocked her off her feet. This was all it took, in the end. All the struggle, all her work, all she'd given up—none of that mattered. Tiziano need only belt out a few instructions, this fearsomely poised woman had only to carry them out, and *poof*. Annie's worries were gone as if they had never been.

The whole thing, from falling on the landing to now, had taken less than an hour.

Less than sixty minutes to become a completely different person with a brand-new life, and she hadn't even gotten to the *mistress* part yet.

At the bank of lifts, Catriona paused and lifted a brow. Annie remembered that she needed to actually speak. That her *approval* was required. She managed to clear her throat.

"Yes," she said, aiming for sounding placid though her lips were numb. "That's fine."

And she must have lapsed into a kind of walking, debt-free coma then, because later she would have no memory of exiting the building, or climbing in whatever vehicle was waiting for them. Annie only knew what was happening again when they arrived at what looked like a small museum in Hampstead, notable for its size, its odd crescent shape, its gleaming white exterior, and also the fact that it sat off the main road on its own acreage. Complete with a tennis court, a pool, enough glass to suggest the builder had meant to build the whole thing in a place like Mallorca to let in the kind of sun England lacked, and a sprawling sort of forecourt where cars—plural—could park.

Indeed, there were several obnoxiously sparkling sports cars of obvious pedigree sitting there already, parked *just so*, and beaming expensively in what little light remained of the mid-November afternoon.

"I would have imagined Tiziano as the sort for a flash flat in Central London," Annie observed before she had time to think better of it.

Catriona betrayed nothing on her smooth, unreadable face. "Mr. Accardi has several London properties."

Annie assumed that meant he *also* had a flash bachelor flat for his debauched purposes. She told herself it was a relief that he did, and that he hadn't had her brought there. For that likely meant he intended to go off and carry on with his usual behavior where she wouldn't have to see it, and wasn't that nice?

But it didn't feel nice, she discovered, as she thought about it while the car they were in took its place in the shiny lineup. It didn't feel nice at all, and she couldn't have said why.

Catriona marched into the house—because it was, indeed, a house and not a museum. A house much bigger than the one where her bedsit was located, in fact. It was more the size of the whole block. Annie trailed along behind Tiziano's assistant, grateful that she could gape around at all the wealth on careless display rather than interrogate her feelings. About anything.

Inside, they were greeted by more staff, and everything became a whirl of directions, orders, and then, with an impatient jerk of her head, Catriona charged up the curved stairway that hugged one of walls that seemed to float about the place, giving way to the glass walls. Clearly Annie was meant to follow, and so she did, feeling more and more like the most egregious country mouse with every step.

Especially when she was marched down a hall into what was apparently its own *wing*, then shown into what was very clearly nothing more than one guest suite among many in this sprawling place. Still, it could easily fit her entire bedsit, times ten. She stopped walking as soon as she realized this, standing in what she thought was the main part of the suite, though it was hard to tell with all the posh glass and views over the Heath.

Annie suddenly realized she didn't know what to do with her hands. It seemed an odd thing to notice, but for a breath or two it was the only thing she could concentrate on.

"Welcome home," Catriona said in her unruffled way, managing to indicate that she noticed how ill at ease Annie was without *harping* on it, somehow. "Please take the rest of the day to settle in. A light tea will be brought up within the hour. If you'd like a supper later, all you need do is ring." She said that as if Annie should know what that meant, when all she actually knew was the sort of *ringing for servants* characters on period dramas did, but Annie nodded knowingly anyway. "Don't hesitate to ask for anything you might need."

Though Annie thought, when the door shut soundlessly and expensively behind her, leaving Annie alone in her *rooms* in bloody *Hampstead*, that the other woman rather hoped she *would* hesitate.

Not that there was any need to test the theory, because the *light tea* that was wheeled into her later would pass for an indulgent cream tea or two anywhere else. She had no need to *ring* for anything. The suite was equipped with three separate large-screen televisions set into walls and made to look like art installations. It had its own gym, a sauna, and balcony. There was an office, a study, and another room for no apparent reason. There were also shelves full of books in all these rooms—clever nonfiction, tedious business treatises, and quite a bit of fiction, too. Better still, there was a lake-sized bathtub with its own view across the Heath, and that was where Annie spent her first night as a very rich man's supposed mistress. Lounging about in a glorious bath, outfitted with every possible indulgence, reading thick novels while she stuffed herself on fin-

ger sandwiches, petit fours, and decadent chocolates.
Before taking herself off to a gloriously soft platform
bed where she slept like a queen.

She rather thought she could get used to such luxu-
rious splendor.

And yet the following week passed in far less indolence than that first night might have led her to expect.

Assuming that a person could really have any *expectations* about being swept up in the whirlwind that was
the Tiziano Accardi experience, for which, apparently,
he didn't even need to be present. That was just as well.
If asked, Annie would have said that a man like Tiziano
did very little at the best of times. Lounged about on this
or that chaise, perhaps, forever awaiting the proverbial
peeled grape, a nubile young woman, or ideally both.

But there were no nubile young women to be found in
his overtly modern mansion in Hampstead. The house
was filled with staff, none of whom seemed to be ro-
mantically inclined toward him, though all appeared
rather unduly dedicated to the man. Many of them, she
found as the days passed, had been with him since he
was a child.

Some had even been with the family since his father was a child.

Annie had imagined she'd find a man like Tiziano
surrounded by cynical staff, all champing at the bit to
get out from service and away from their boss's antics.
She found instead a vast house stuffed full of the sort of
loyal family retainers she'd always personally believed
were the province of a certain type of self-referential
British fiction.

But it really did seem that none of the people who

worked here were the least bit interested in changing their situation.

Maybe it wasn't that she found it surprising so much as she resented it. Because since she couldn't whip herself into a lather about the treatment of his underlings, she had no choice but to concentrate on the ways that *she* was expected to change. This was what Tiziano had bought when he'd thrown all that money her way. This was the transaction.

The first day or so were spent going through her meager belongings, which she was not permitted to do alone.

"Don't be silly," Catriona said when she arrived that first morning with the contents of Annie's bedsit in tow, then made it clear she intended to remain in all her faintly disapproving state. "I am trained to do these things."

What that meant, Annie discovered, was that Catriona ruthlessly divided Annie's possessions into two piles. One was of items that were to be packed away until her arrangement with Tiziano was over. That was the bulk of what little she had. The rest she was allowed to keep with her, though there were precious few of those and all of them personal keepsakes.

Her clothes were unacceptable, Catriona made clear. In every respect.

By this point, she'd slept in this house three times. The first night, the glory of the bath and the small fact that her debts were cleared had sent her off into a sound sleep. On the second, however, the silence kept waking her up. Jolting her to heart-pounding alertness as she kept sitting up in a panic, looking around to see why it was the London that ought to be carrying on outside had gone so preternaturally quiet.

The bed was too soft, that second night. The down in the pillows was too pokey.

Yesterday, she'd had two full days of having trays of food delivered to her whether she was hungry or not, endless cups of tea placed at her elbow, and Catriona's matter-of-fact approach to dividing her things. If that wasn't enough, Tiziano's blade of an assistant had then sat her down for a brisk recitation of debts cleared, monies allocated, and an overview of what had been sketched out for the trust Tiziano intended she use to follow those dreams he'd been banging on about in that stairwell. Plus more stacks of documents requiring her signature. It was all bloodless and overwhelming and she'd slept like a log.

So deep and so hard that when she'd woken up this morning, she'd had a dizzying moment of failing to recall precisely who she was. Much less *where* she was.

It stayed with her all morning, that feeling.

And it was not improved now. Catriona had herded her into a car after lunch, announcing that it was time to see to her woefully deficient wardrobe at last.

"I thought the point of all of this was that I was supposed to seem completely outside the normal realm of the kind of woman that man dates," Annie argued, perhaps a bit snappishly. "Wardrobe and all."

"There's a difference between the reality of a secretary and the public's Cinderella fantasies involving a secretary," Catriona informed her coolly as they were whisked off down the private lane. "We are going for the latter, Miss Meeks."

Annie had wanted nothing so much as to argue that,

but she found herself curiously unable to say anything at all. She wanted to scream out that she hadn't signed up for any *Cinderella* stories, for God's sake. She wasn't the sort of person who believed in such tosh—not after the crash course in reality she'd had this last year. Besides, this was no fairy tale. This was all sleight of hand. All she had to do was loaf about looking mistressy and inappropriately northern, biding her time until Tiziano and his brother came to terms. She couldn't see how that should involve any particular effort on her part at all.

But Catriona was merely doing her job, and no matter if her manner was chillier than that of the average great white shark. There was no point arguing with her. Catriona was tasked with carrying out Tiziano's vision and Annie felt sure that somewhere in all the papers she'd signed, she'd agreed to go along with it, too.

And so, for the next few days, Annie simply…surrendered.

As much to the lashings of cream teas on command as Catriona's ruthless approach to shopping at what appeared to be every exclusive boutique in every upscale neighborhood in London. She subjected herself to climbing in and out of an endless array of clothes while Catriona wielded the credit card, and more, made the final decisions.

Nor was shopping all that was in store. Long after Annie had become numb to the astronomical prices, the casual condescension of the shop girls, and Catriona's blunt responses to outfits she didn't like, Catriona towed her off to a spa so exclusive that the staff all knew her name the moment she arrived. As if she was an old, dear friend.

"Welcome, Annie," they all said, in matching tones

of obsequious delight, as if they'd known her from the cradle. "How lovely of you to drop in."

There was no checkout counter or product display in this spa, located in one of London's poshest neighborhoods, where Annie had never ventured. Nor had she ever found herself in a place like this, where there was no opportunity to so much as inquire after the price of anything. Why bother, when bottomless wealth was assumed?

The first day she was massaged and steamed, wrapped and packed in mud, which one attendant chirpily remarked was "getting London off your body."

What could Annie do but freefall into it?

And if she daydreamed a bit about stormy blue eyes in the face of a fallen angel, that was her business.

The next day, she was led straight back into the spa, but this time it was very plainly not about relaxation. This time, it was all about beautification.

She apparently needed a total overhaul, and her feelings on this were not taken into account. Her pride was not consulted at all. Her attendants smiled when she grumbled, but they had their orders.

Like Annie, they answered to the coldly efficient Catriona in all things.

Her hands and feet were tended to, nails buffed and polished. Hair she didn't even know was growing on her body was waxed away and/or shaped. And after a facial that had involved hot peels and exfoliants galore, her lashes and brows were tinted, with a bit of a lift to the lashes as well.

More procedures than she'd ever heard of were practiced all over her, and when they were all done, her hair was cut and quietly colored to enhance its natural shade, then blown out and styled to perfection. Instead of her usual mess of red curls, she now had a deeper copper gleam and suggestion of wildness, carefully arranged into sophisticated disarray.

Only when her hair was deemed suitable was she bustled into yet another part of the spa, where a host of technicians dressed all in black swirled around her, applying makeup with what seemed like trowels. She braced herself. Because sooner or later she was going to have to look at their work and try her best not to recoil.

But when they all stepped away and presented her to herself in a room of mirrors, Annie was a bit disappointed—in herself—that she felt so…awed.

Because she saw at once what Catriona had meant about the public's fantasy of a Cinderella secretary and what they'd done here to realize it. Annie looked like *herself*. It wasn't as if anyone who'd known her for her whole life would no longer recognize her. And yet, at the same time, it was as if every part of her *glowed*.

As if the work they did at this spa was inside out.

Annie couldn't get over it. It was as if her own private sun shined down upon her, bathing her in the sparkle of her very own gold. The way a similar light had found Tiziano in that stairwell, transforming him into something far more dangerous than just a man.

She studied her reflection, trying to figure out what the shift was. The many treatments, sure, but she thought she ought to be able to tell exactly what was different. When she was wearing the sort of outfit she'd worn as a uniform at Accardi Industries. A pencil skirt. A blouse. Heels.

But though Annie would have said that she hadn't the faintest idea how to tell the difference between one item of clothing and the next, even she could tell that the clothes she wore now bore no resemblance to the ones Catriona had ordered packed off into boxes to be stored in some attic. It was the quiet, stately elegance of the fabrics, perhaps. It was the way they whispered against her skin, and the way the shoes, though high and surely structurally unsound, felt instead as if she were standing there in cozy bedroom slippers.

There was the hint of gold at her neck, the kiss of pearls at her ears.

She saw exactly what Catriona—and, she supposed, Tiziano—was going for. She looked fresh-faced, bright, and as filled with understated elegance as the clothes she wore. A modern-day working girl's Cinderella, in other words.

A masterpiece by any measure.

Damn it all.

Annie turned to face the other woman, who stood in the corner, her arms crossed, looking—it had to be said—unduly pleased with her handiwork. It was the most expressive she'd ever been in Annie's presence, and Annie couldn't help feeling as if that were a bit personal.

"I thought you were mad," Annie said quietly. "But even I can see the miracles you worked here."

The other woman inclined her head in her typically cool fashion, but there was the faintest hint of a flush of pleasure on her face. "No miracles required," she replied in her usual smooth way. "But I do take pride in realizing Mr. Accardi's vision."

And though there was no further personal talk, if that even counted as personal talk in the first place, Annie

felt buoyed by the conversation. It was as if she and Catriona had come to a meeting of the minds.

She had almost forgotten that the point of all of this
was not Catriona at all.

The point was the man all of this was for.

Annie had gone out of her way not to think about
him over these last few days. Despite sleeping in his
house, dreaming of him, and waking in a bed he owned.
Then spending days preparing herself. For his pleasure.

Like some barbaric virgin sacrifice, after all.

She told herself, briskly, not to be dramatic. After
all, hadn't he made it clear that he wanted no part of
her body? Not in that way?

You know he did, she told herself tartly, once Catriona dropped her off that evening. Leaving her to walk,
unattended and better dressed than she'd ever been before, to walk down a winding, cobbled street toward the
restaurant where she was to meet up with Tiziano at last.

She told herself that she was glad he'd made himself
so clear the day they'd met. That she was *delighted* a
man like him wanted nothing to do with her, not really.
And that as they played this elaborate game of pretend,
she would have the opportunity to know, up close and
personal, that men like him were exactly as vile as she'd
always supposed.

Annie kept telling herself that with every click of her
heels against the hushed, expensive street, where she
never would have come of her own volition. She hadn't
even known there was a restaurant here, she thought,
not that she spent her time cataloging swank restaurants
in posh Central London neighborhoods.

But then, that was because the likes of her weren't
meant to know there was a restaurant here. There was

no mark upon the door. It was merely an address to what looked like a converted old Georgian house. She half expected that when the door opened at her arrival, it would be Tiziano standing there, welcoming her into one of his numerous London properties.

Instead, she found herself ushered swiftly through the lushly appointed house to a private room. The smiling, yet distant, butler—or that was what she assumed the man was—swung open the door and waved her in.

And finally, Annie saw him again.

Tiziano Accardi, who was not a figment of her imagination, bolstered into something impossible over the past week because she'd been immersed in *preparing herself* for him. To be his mistress, if only in name.

If anything, he was *more* astonishingly beautiful, seductively masculine, than she remembered.

He stood by a set of French doors that opened to the garden below, looking out. Though she knew in an instant that he was fully aware of her presence, he waited for the door to close before he turned.

His gaze found hers, the blue of whole seas Annie had never seen with her own eyes.

But she could see him.

And she could feel the immensity of him fill the room they stood in, making her feel small—but in a way that only made her want to marvel at him. To celebrate the difference in their positions.

It was in that moment that Annie realized, with a certain sinking sensation, that she had completely underestimated the situation she found herself in.

CHAPTER FOUR

TIZIANO WAS PREPARED for Annie to look well. To look irresistible, yet unexpected. That was what his assistant had been told to achieve and he already knew that Catriona had spared no expense.

But *looking well* in no way described the woman who stood before him.

The woman he'd met in that stairwell, red-haired and gray-eyed, had been pretty enough, in her way. He could admit to himself that had she not been, he would never have propositioned her as he had. He was who he was, after all.

Yet the woman before him tonight made something deep within him still.

She was luminous. She looked almost ethereal, and it took almost everything he had to stay over by the windows when everything in him demanded he cross to her. And better yet, sink his hands into all that thick, red-gold hair. He wanted to wrap it around his fists, then hold her so he could plunder that wide, generous mouth at will.

He wanted to trail his way down the length of her body, dressed to perfection in a body-hugging skirt that made her curves nothing short of a national treasure.

He wanted to press his mouth to the pale honey of her skin until he'd tasted every inch.

God help him but his sex was heavy, and the need for her so intense, that he had a moment of something far too close to panic as he wondered whether he would be *able* to keep his hands to himself.

As if he was no more than some heedless boy, hopped up on hormones.

The silence dragged out between them, and he knew that it was happening. But he seemed to have no access whatsoever to the charm that had always served him so well until now.

He rather felt as if someone had dealt him a stinging blow to the head. There was a ringing in his ears and his heart pounded, only making the need in him wind tighter and tighter.

"I'm sorry if the dress-up doll you ordered is not to your taste," Annie said tartly then, with that broad hint of the north shaping her words. And his weakness had always been beauty, packaged to drive men wild. He hadn't realized that all of his experiences had been lacking *this*. This kick. This tartness that made his mouth water.

Her.

"You'll do," he replied.

And realized only after he'd said it that he'd done it just to make her eyes flash like that. Because he basked in it. He wanted to do it again and again.

Instead, he crossed to her, taking her arm solicitously and leading her to the table. He seated her before the fire with great formality, then took the chair opposite.

Annie looked around, taking in the quiet, unobtrusive elegance of their surroundings. "I can't tell if this is a private house or restaurant."

"A little of both, I suppose," Tiziano replied, absurdly let down that she wished to discuss…the *place*. "It's more a kind of club. Where gentlemen of certain social strata have been entertaining women for centuries."

She seemed almost to relax at that, though her eyes glittered. "Mistresses. You mean mistresses, don't you? Not wives. Or any women auditioning for a ring, for that matter."

"Certainly not," Tiziano agreed, and was pleased to note he'd located his grin again. At last. "This is England. In Italy, these things were more fluid. They still are, because expectations are different. But in London, clubs like this exist so that men of a particular station might leave their duty at the door and cater to their true wants and needs within."

"I wouldn't have thought you cared about privacy."

"The point of this evening, Annie, is not the privacy. It is not what goes on here. It is what will happen when we leave."

"Will I be chased down an alleyway by a pack of baying paparazzi, then?" She wrinkled her nose, as if imagining such a scene. As if Tiziano was the starlet du jour, who could expect such treatment during her fifteen minutes of fame. "That's one of the perks of your existence, by all accounts. I can't say it holds any appeal."

"There will be no packs and no chases in alleys." Tiziano leaned back in his chair. "This is not that sort of establishment, because the paparazzi know that if they take pictures of those who frequent this place, they will not get the other pictures they truly want that will sell their tabloids. Still, there are those who lurk in the shadows and make note of who comes and who goes anyway. They might not take a photograph, but they like to know who's in play." He inclined his head. "You can consider it a soft opening for your new position."

Then he sat back, enjoying himself far more than he should have as the staff came in with their meal, when this should have been no more than another tedious business meeting. Annie was far more captivating than she had any right to be.

He took pleasure in her artlessness. Her reaction to the presentation of the meal, and then, as if that were not mesmerizing enough, her clear delight in every bite of the food, which he knew to be reliably excellent. But he had never been here with a woman who acted as if each and every bite was a revelation.

As if she thought the point of being here was the food, not the company.

Perhaps that was truly why he was captivated, he found himself thinking later, as their rich, decadent dessert was cleared away and they were left with tiny cups of strong coffee.

He was not sure he had ever made it through an entire meal here before. Normally, he would expect to be deep inside his companion by now, food forgotten, as they both took their pleasure as they could.

Tiziano did not know how to process the strange notion that he found a different kind of pleasure in this woman. In how fully she threw herself into every bite she took or gave herself over to every sip.

He couldn't tell if he had never known, or if he had only forgotten, that pleasures could be so uncomplicated. That there was a beauty in the simplicity of joy. And he found himself fascinated by this woman who had seemed so bristling, so armored, when he'd met her. Yet now appeared to think nothing of showing him her every last reaction to the delights of a fine meal.

Stranger by far was how deeply he enjoyed her reactions.

So unstudied. So *real*. It made him wonder when he had last experienced anything quite so authentic.

If he ever had—or if that, too, was something that had died in his childhood.

But he did not like to think of such things.

"I trust you are enjoying the house in Hampstead," he found himself saying into the silence, because another thing that set Annie apart was that she made no effort whatsoever to draw him out. She did not *attempt* to captivate him in any way.

Left to her own devices, he was forced to conclude, she would sit in perfect silence here. She would enjoy her food, not caring in the slightest if a single word was ever spoken between them.

It was not that he found this *refreshing*. That was not the right word. But it was a novelty, and he found himself longing to explore it. To explore her. He hadn't been thinking of such things this whole week. He'd been laying the groundwork with his brother and preparing to wage his little war before Ago acted like a feudal lord and made declarations about Tiziano's future for all the world to hear.

He hadn't expected to be knocked sideways by the sight of his little secretary, all dressed up as his mistress.

But since the sort of exploration he craved was not advisable under these circumstances—for reasons he was certain he would recall in due course—he settled on making conversation.

"It's a lovely house, isn't it," she was saying, which he knew by now was not a question, coming from the English. "Lovely people working there, too. To be honest, I'm a bit surprised."

"That I own a house? I do not know how to tell you, *cara*, that my real estate portfolio is varied and vast."

"That you inspire loyalty," she retorted. And he saw it again then. The girl he'd first met in that stairwell, in a shower of documents. It was there in her eyes and the spark of it seemed to glow in him, too. "Not what you're known for, I would have said."

"I do hate to disappoint you."

"I wouldn't say it's a disappointment." But then, while he watched, interested despite himself, her cheeks reddened. "Right." She sat up straighter. "Tell me how you think this is going to go. This whole mistress game."

"I'm not going to tell you everything." He offered her a disarming smile, though he wasn't sure it worked the way it was meant to. Not on Annie. "Your natural reactions are part of the point."

"Because you want an overawed country mouse, I assume." And he was certain he could hear whole moors in her voice just then. The wuthering wind and all.

"Only some of the time," Tiziano assured her. "As for the rest, well. After tonight, we will endeavor to be caught out."

Her gray gaze was steady. "Caught out where?"

"There will be any number of tedious, interchangeable events," Tiziano said with a bored sort of shrug. "But this game of ours will rise and fall on how swept away we are by each other. How heedless we become in public. That sort of thing."

That gray stare did not so much as waver. "How heedless do you imagine we will become?"

"Exceedingly heedless."

And then, following an urge that he should have quelled, he leaned in closer. Because she was not like the other women he knew, and the point of making her his mistress was not to treat her as if she was.

He knew that. Truly he did.

He knew it, but he couldn't seem to make himself behave.

"Shall we practice?" he found himself asking, even though he knew he shouldn't.

Tiziano expected her to draw back. To haul off and hit him, or even storm from the room. Because this was most certainly not what they'd agreed upon. Or maybe it was, because he did like to put on a good show, but he'd intended to ease into that part.

But she did none of the things he expected her to do. Instead, she propped her elbows on the table and rested her chin on her hands. Her head canted slightly to the right as she regarded him.

"If you mean a kiss," she said, as if she'd given the matter a great deal of thought, and Tiziano was not prepared for the way that notion rebounded in his sex, "then I suppose we'd better."

Once again, he found he had to remind himself that he was no green, spot-faced whelp. Nor ever had been.

The way his body reacted to her statement, anyone might have been forgiven for confusing the issue. He took a moment to study her, to calculate the best way forward when he couldn't quite trust his own reactions.

He knew a great deal about Annie Meeks by now. The exhaustive questionnaire that his assistant had administered covered all possible areas, doing away with the necessity of any sort of question and answer between them.

It was not necessary for him to ask her where she came from, for he knew. She had been raised in the north, in one of those Yorkshire towns that had once been little more than a textile mill, all dark bricks and gloom. Her parents had been killed in a boating accident when she and her sister were young, leaving them in the care of an aunt. There had been a grandmother, doting by all accounts, but she had died some years back. The sister, three years younger than Annie, had decamped to Australia some eighteen months ago, after what appeared to be extreme dedication to partying. Annie, by contrast, had spent her gap year interning at an art museum in Leeds while working as a waitress on the side. She'd spent her fresher year at a college here in London in an art history program, but had quit her education to take up her secretarial job at Accardi Industries.

But he knew more than that. He knew that her sister had stolen at least one credit card and Annie's identity, too. He knew she'd racked up enormous debt in Annie's name. Or rather, the sort of debt a woman like Annie would consider enormous. That was what he'd paid off this week.

Beyond all these facts, he knew her romantic history as well. Such as it was.

He studied the picture she made before him now, glowing softly in the candlelight. She was even more beautiful than he could have imagined, and he could admit that after he'd seen her crawling around on the floor before him, he'd done some imagining. Tonight she looked far more sophisticated than she had then, yet there was also an air of innocence about her no one who saw her would be able to resist.

Tiziano was banking on it.

What he had not expected was that he would fall prey to it, too.

He'd expected the report from Catriona to come back with the expected teenage boyfriend or two. Then a bit of experimentation, for wasn't that the purpose of university? He had greatly enjoyed the women of Cambridge in his years there. The report, however, had indicated that this woman who was to act as mistress to one of the most dissolute men in Europe, by his own reckoning, was innocent.

Almost entirely.

Save for a few kisses, Annie Meeks was largely untouched.

Tonight, gazing at her beauty before him, he found this unfathomable.

Not least because it meant that he couldn't haul her up against him, hold her to the wall, and ease that ache in his sex the way he'd like to do.

And he really couldn't recall the last time he'd felt the slightest inclination to practice *restraint*.

"Or maybe we shouldn't practice kissing," Annie said, which made him realize he'd been gazing at her for some time, letting the silence between them stretch out. "Though I will say, I was under the impression there was scarcely a lass in five continents who you *wouldn't* get off with, given the slightest provocation."

"I do have some standards," Tiziano replied, with a laugh, though he couldn't decide if he wasn't the smallest bit offended. He, who took offense to nothing. "Some would say I have the highest standards imaginable."

Her smile was placating. "Did someone actually say that to you? Out loud?"

Tiziano stood, smoothing his hand down the front of the suit he wore. He was aware it wasn't a necessary gesture. Unless his aim was to direct the attention of his companion to an abdomen that he knew, quite objectively, was stupendous.

Maybe he was *preening* for this woman.

Annie followed the movement of his hand, then raised her gaze back to his. "I'd have thought that a man as comfortable putting yourself about as you are wouldn't be afraid of a little kiss."

The dossiers he had his assistant prepare had always seemed sufficient, before. But Annie was different. He didn't care about the facts of her life, not when what he really wished was that he could read her. Because he couldn't. Her gray eyes might as well have been a bank of thick fog for all he could see through them. He had no idea what she might be thinking.

And when had he ever been in the slightest doubt about what went through the female head in his vicinity?

But not this female.

Not Annie.

"I was under the impression that you hadn't done enough kissing to call yourself an expert," he said, mildly enough.

He wasn't sure what reaction he expected, but it wasn't the way she laughed, and not the way the women he knew usually did. Not that tinkling bit of laughter, as if they were trying to sound like bells gently ringing. This was a bawdy laugh. The kind of laugh that would turn heads in a restaurant, causing those who heard it to find it either shocking or infectious.

Tiziano found it a bit of both.

Because it lit him up. It seemed to move inside him, as if the sound of her laughter was kicking down doors he hadn't known were closed within him.

He felt something like…dazed. Or possibly intoxicated.

"I've seen pictures of you," she told him. "I couldn't have avoided them if I wanted to. Sometimes there's kissing and sometimes there's not, but the last thing I want is to look like is a fool in photographs the whole world will be looking at. Better safe than sorry, I always say."

"Not always," he found himself replying, with something less than his usual careless ease. "Or I doubt you would be here."

Annie laughed again, but she was pushing back her chair and rising to her feet. And he had miscalculated, because as entranced as he might have been by the curves he'd seen in that stairwell, and that bit of pink lace he still carried around in his head, he hadn't been adequately prepared for the sight of those curves in clothes cut to flatter them. Eating a meal with her had lulled him a bit, it seemed. It had made him forget.

She was…lush. There was no other word that fit. Annie had the sort of proportions that made men silly. Across the ages, across cultures, an hourglass shape such as the one before him now inspired the male of the species to go a little light-headed. Their hands itched to carve out that shape in the air between them, to see if the curves before them matched.

It was past time, Tiziano told himself sternly, that he attempted to get hold of this *hunger* that was making him so restless. Clearly, it was a function of his having announced he didn't intend to bed her. He was so unused to restriction that the very hint of it drove him to distraction.

He lifted his hand, then beckoned her close with two fingers.

Languidly.

And told himself that his low, intense heartbeat then was merely his body's way of congratulating him on a job well done in choosing a woman so unlike his usual fare. A woman who was certain to captivate the world, if only because she was so unexpected. Not at all who people expected to see on his arm. They wouldn't be able to look away from her. They would believe, almost without meaning to, that he'd fallen head over heels in love with her on sight—for who could not?

He was not considered a marketing genius for nothing.

Annie moved closer. Then she stood there, gazing up at him, and it was only then that he could see some hint of what might be going on beneath her surface. The tinge of pink on her cheeks, the faint widening of those gray eyes.

It roared in him like triumph.

"One kiss," he said, and he meant to sound sophisticated and possibly even bored, so he could not have said why it was his voice came out so…raspy. "For practice, that is all."

It did not help when she shivered, delicately, and then

tried to hide it. Possibly failing to realize that he could see the way her nipples tightened behind her soft blouse.

Tiziano gritted his teeth. Then he stopped, and made himself smile.

"Come closer," he told her. Gruffly.

"Said the spider to the fly," she replied. She laughed again, only this time it was less that surprisingly full-throated expression of joy. This time it was much more uncertain.

It was a good reminder, and Tiziano took it. He reminded himself that while he surely was no one's idea of a saint, that didn't mean he couldn't attempt to play the part. Since it suited his plan here. Besides, being careful with her was certain to infuse their public outings with a lovely sense of him *doting* upon her in a way he never had before. Not with any of his other women.

And it would make them seem even more convincing.

He reached over and slid his hands to her face, cupping it between his palms. She was wearing much higher shoes than she had been when they'd met, and he liked, very much, the height they gave her. They put her at just the right angle so that he only needed to bend down a reasonable amount to put his face near hers.

And then, aware that she was regarding him solemnly with those rain-soaked eyes of hers, Tiziano pressed his mouth to hers.

Rather formally, really.

He was certain he had never kissed a woman so *delicately* before in all his days. But Annie was not just any woman, and this kiss was not about him. Therefore, he did not indulge that darker, beating thing within him that wanted only to pull her closer. To wrap his arms around her and press her lushness against him. He did not deepen the kiss the way he would have at any other time, to get a taste of her and drive them both wild.

Instead, he kept it *saintly*. Chaste and easy.

The kind of kiss that would look lovely when it was splashed across a front page somewhere.

But what Tiziano was not prepared for was the *ache*.

The kick of a kind of eroticism he was wholly unfamiliar with. For he was not indulging it. He was not chasing it. It was the simple fact of their lips, pressed together. It was the warmth and the feel of her.

To his astonishment, his body responded as if he was already deep inside her.

Tiziano kissed her like that a moment more, then pulled back. He was shocked to find his heart still beating wildly, that ache inside him so heavy and intense it was a wonder he could see straight.

He dropped his hands and smiled at her. He thought to himself, *extremis malis, extrema remedia*. Because in this case, the game he played was worth this attempt to make himself into some kind of martyr.

Why not smile while he was at it?

Tiziano was therefore completely unprepared when all she did was blink a few times. She pressed her lips together, as if tasting them, which should have been sultry...save for the expression on her face.

It took him some moments to comprehend that Annie Meeks, of late a secretary, really was looking at him as if she had just had...a less than ideal experience.

A less than *transformative* moment in his arms.

"Well," she said, in the bright sort of tone that one uses when trying to make the best of a bad situation, "that's a bit of a letdown, isn't it?"

"I beg your pardon."

It was not a question. He was not begging. He was… flabbergasted. A *letdown*?

"I've been kissed before, of course," she told him, in a confidential sort of manner that made him want to throw the table they'd sat at out the window. As if he was a common brawler. "It was all very much the same old thing. You know, very run-of-the-mill. Lips upon lips, and if you think about that—about what it *is*—it's not very appealing, is it? But I did hope…" She flapped a hand at him. The way he had once seen a woman in the country flap a hand at her *chickens*. "What with all the hue and cry about Tiziano Accardi, the greatest lover of his generation—"

"I see you have read widely, indeed."

"It's just that I thought it would be *exciting*," she said.

And the mad part was that she sounded almost philosophical. As if she'd given it a try, and she appreciated him doing his best, bless him, but in the end was disappointed.

Disappointed, by God.

It was unsupportable.

Tiziano acted without thought. He moved toward her again, hooking his hand around the nape of her neck and hauling her toward him. And he took a great pleasure in the way her body thudded into his, all of her lushness suddenly *right there*.

He anchored her against him with his hand in the small of her back, pressing her where he wanted her and enjoying too well the high-pitched little sound she made in the back of her throat.

Without worrying about his impending sainthood or

tabloid photography or any social niceties of any kind, he bent and claimed her mouth.

The way he'd wanted to all along.

And this kiss was pure fire.

Tiziano licked his way into her mouth. He angled his head, drawing her closer, so that he could taste her and tease her, tempt her and beguile her, every time his tongue slid against hers.

He kissed her again and again, shifting position so he could sink his hands into all that red-gold hair at last. And still he kissed her, until that beating thing in him was so loud he was certain that she could hear it, too. That all of London could hear it. He kissed her until she was quivering in his arms, her body soft against his, her breath coming hard and high.

Tiziano kissed her until she was weak in his arms and then he kissed her more, until he thought it was possible that they would both taste nothing but each other for days to come.

Months, even.

And only when he was on the very brink of throwing her down to the floor and coming down after her, wild and greedy to fully claim her as *his*, did he stop.

Though it cost him.

He set her away from him, and his self-control— which some might have thought no more than a myth— had never before been so tested.

It hung by the barest thread.

But he held her upright until she looked around, flushed and flustered. She swallowed hard, seeming to struggle to find her balance. Only then did she step away, putting the necessary distance between them— not that it did any good.

Her taste was in his mouth. And the need for her was in his sex, like a shout.

Annie stared at him, but despite the clamor inside him, he took it as a victory. Because this time, she seemed to have no commentary whatsoever. Her eyes were huge—and he could read them clear enough.

Especially when she lifted a trembling hand, pressing the pads of her fingers to her own lips.

If he was a better man, a saint or a martyr, he might not have taken such satisfaction in this.

Luckily, Tiziano had never *truly* pretended to be anything of the kind for more than a few moments. Right here in this room.

He made himself smile, though he had never felt less like smiling in his life. But he had been playing his role for a long, long time, so he trotted it out, forcing himself to relax. Languid and unconcerned, because that was who Tiziano Accardi was and always would be.

It was critical that this woman, above all others, know it well.

Because, whispered a little voice inside him, *this woman is the first you have ever met who might threaten it.*

He shoved that thought aside.

"Tiziano…" she whispered, but barely. As if his name was a curse. Or perhaps, more tempting still, some kind of prayer.

He did not wish to be tempted. Not by this woman. It was an outrage.

But all he did was incline his head. "I trust you have no further concerns about my ability to sell a decent kiss, Annie."

The hand at her mouth dropped to her side and her

gaze followed, and Tiziano had no earthly idea why he should feel those things like some kind of loss. As if she'd taken them from him. When she lifted her gaze again, that unreadable mask of hers was back and he could not help but resent it.

Though it was clear to him that he should not. That he should not care in the slightest.

"I think it should be perfectly adequate," she told him. "For our purposes."

Adequate. The *insult* of it all.

Her voice was bland. Her gaze, even more so.

Tiziano did not for one second mistake that for the challenge it really was.

"I'm delighted you approve," he murmured.

And it took far more effort than it should have to make himself appear as unbothered as he usually was—and about everything. He took against it. And her.

Hard.

Tiziano's smile then was languid, but the way Annie stood straighter, he was sure she could see the light of battle in his gaze. He did little to hide it. "And do not worry, *cara.* I doubt your need for practice shows. Much."

CHAPTER FIVE

KISSING TIZIANO WAS a terrible mistake.

And not because he had clearly agreed that she needed practice—something she should never have said to him. Annie knew immediately that she shouldn't have taunted the man. She didn't know why she had. That simple kiss had been bad enough. She'd no idea what devil it was that had wormed its way inside her, making her challenge him the way she did.

It hadn't been a wildly passionate initial kiss, even she could tell that. But still, a press of Tiziano's lips to hers had wiped out any memories she might have had of her teenage years, where she'd gotten a kiss here or there. Never anything serious.

Yet it had all been embarrassing in comparison to the simple mastery of Tiziano's mouth on hers.

And the thing was, she really had done a lot of reading. There was no reading about Tiziano Accardi, tabloid darling, without all those *pictures*. And so she'd seen him nuzzling up to countless stunning women, looking lazy and satisfied, like a smug cat. All of those pictures had seemed to her far more tempting and treacherous and *serious* than that first kiss he'd bestowed upon her tonight.

Which wasn't to say she hadn't felt it.

She'd felt it *everywhere*, that firm mouth pressed against hers. And maybe because of that, because she could tell it was a simple little kiss when she knew he was capable of so much more, it was as if she couldn't help herself. She'd been forced—*compelled*, even—to push him.

Three days later, she was still reeling.

That night had ended shortly after their kiss, which was a great blessing, to her mind. She was surprised that she was capable of speech. Or thought. Or any motor function at all, come to that. He'd ushered her out of the little house, then bundled her into one of his sleek sports cars, all while seeming to hang on her—acting more attentive than she'd ever seen him.

Tiziano playing the besotted lover, she assumed. And even though she knew full well it was an act, it was shockingly effective. Her breath caught. His intent focus made her…melt.

That was a maddening thing about this man. Everything he did was effective, when he presented himself as anything but.

"Were we spotted as you hoped?" she asked with excessive politeness as he drove them through London, controlling the powerful car as easily as he controlled her. A thought that made something in her seem to shake apart.

"I'm certain we were seen, yes," he replied, in a manner that made her wonder if he'd seen to it himself. He slid a look her way at a traffic light, then returned his attention to the road. *This was a good start.*

And he hadn't spoken the rest of the drive to Hampstead. Once there, he escorted her to the door of his own house and executed a sort of half bow that should have looked absurd in this modern age—but, somehow, did not, because of the *Tiziano* of it all. Then he turned and strode back to the gleaming car and drove away.

No doubt off to entertain himself in his usual fashion, she had told herself stoutly. And wasn't it a delight that she was not cooped up in some flat with him while he entertained his many women?

Yet she couldn't even work up any temper over it, and not because it wasn't her place. But because the only thing she could think about was that kiss.

The *real* kiss. The kiss that had been any number of kisses, one after the next, hot and breathless and impossibly wild.

She thought of little else for days.

Three days, in fact, night and day alike, until she found herself waiting for him in the excruciatingly spartan foyer of what she assumed was the very bachelor flat she had been glad to avoid. Catriona had handed her off to a set of attendants who, the other woman said, would be responsible for all of Annie's *evening looks* from here on out. Given that it had not been evening at the time, Annie had been confused.

But it had taken the women who'd set up shop in her suite whole hours to prepare her for the dress she wore, an inky blue that hugged her shoulders and drooped just slightly in front—then swept down to expose the whole of her back.

If she exhaled too hard, Annie was fairly certain she might show her arse.

Then don't exhale, pet, retorted one of her attendants, with the sound of Hull in her voice. It made Annie feel a bit homesick, but in a good way.

It helped her remember who she was, and she needed that, because she saw no sign of herself in this creation her attendants had made. There was the impossible dream of a dress. But her hair was twisted up into something breathtakingly complicated, too, a mess of braids and twists that somehow all smoothed together to give the impression of a sort of bohemian sophistication that should not have been possible. Her eyes were smoky and mysterious, something she could see in the giant mirror across from her in this minimalistic foyer, where, if she wasn't careful, she would forget who she was looking at and surprise herself anew.

Annie blew out a breath and ordered herself to stop thinking about his open mouth on hers, the way his tongue had taunted her, drawing her out, sending all of that delirious heat crawling around and around inside her—

A faint noise made her jolt and her head whipped around.

And it was as if she'd conjured him out of the air.

Tiziano stood there, everything about him brooding and dark, save that blue gaze.

She dreamed about that color blue. That specific shade. It was as if it haunted her.

"What on earth are you doing in my foyer?" he asked in that haughty sort of amazement that he wielded far too easily. And too well.

"Waiting for you." And though all kinds of butterflies were wheeling around inside her, she was pleased that she sounded calm. Or calm enough.

"You're playing the role of my mistress, not my maid." There was that glittering thing in his gaze again then. And a kind of tightness in the air between them that made her belly feel hollow. "Mistresses do not lurk about in foyers like the help, *cara*. I thought perhaps you'd been struck down in traffic, only to discover you were dropped off a quarter of an hour ago."

"I wouldn't call it *dropped off*," she argued. "They had to smuggle me in. It was like a kidnapping. They flung coats over my head and hustled me in through the service entrance."

"Does the glamorous life not suit you?" His voice was a smooth weapon. "A pity. It is considered the height of fashion to sneak in and out of buildings, concealing your identity and keeping your whereabouts mysterious."

"Is this because of the tabloids?" Annie made a face. "It seems a bit odd, doesn't it, that for all your money and all your power you're still at the mercy of a scrum of men who hang about in the street."

He gazed at her. "My company is generally held to be more than enough recompense for any indignities suffered in the service entrance."

Annie wished then that she hadn't stayed seated when she'd caught sight of him. She felt like a schoolgirl. But she thought that if she leaped up now, she would look even more foolish. Instead, she folded her hands in her lap and smiled at him.

Perhaps a little patronizingly, if she was honest. Because he'd earned it. "I'm sure your company is a tremendous lure," she said in an encouraging way that suggested she thought no such thing. It was worth it for the way his astonished blue eyes widened. "It's just that you could buy yourself the lot of them, couldn't you? I have to wonder why you don't."

He only stared at her as if he wasn't quite certain

what shape she'd taken, right here before his eyes, and she took that as encouragement.

"It's one thing if you're an actor or some such. You need the publicity. But you are an Accardi. You already have everything you could possibly need, and then some. So I can only assume you enjoy the silly games of hide-and-seek, or surely you could just go ahead and buy yourself whatever agency hires these people. And fire them."

He blinked, more than once. That was all the reaction she got, but she congratulated herself all the same.

"You have already spent more time these past few moments thinking about the paparazzi than I ever have," he told her, back to sounding something indolent and authoritative at once. "It is not necessary to always sneak in and out of service entrances. I only do so when I wish to control the narrative." His brows rose, and he seemed to look down upon her from a far greater height than his six feet and then some. "Because it is my narrative, *cara*. This you must know above all else. It is my story, and it will always be told the way I wish it to be."

"Right," she said briskly. "You are a master storyteller. Noted."

She thought that there was something heavy, there in the air between them, but in the next moment he laughed, and it was gone.

Though, for the first time, Annie wondered what story his laughter was meant to tell.

"Come," he said, sounding as lazy as he ever did. As if she had made all of this up, the tension and the *storytelling* and even the layers she'd thought she'd seen in him here, for a moment. "This time we will exit through the front door. There will no doubt be a gauntlet of flashbulbs for you to navigate. The trick is never to look at anyone directly, no matter what they might say, or how they call your name. Or you will find yourself blinded and confused, and they will pounce."

"This gets better and better," Annie said brightly. She stood up then, and found herself smoothing down her gown, though it didn't need the attention. When she looked up again, Tiziano looked almost…stricken.

But she must have been mistaken. This was Tiziano Accardi, the man of a thousand lovers, and in any case, she was no more than an employee. Something she would do well to remember, she told herself sternly, when he put a hand to her back and guided her from his flat.

This is not a date. He is not treating me in this fashion because he has any designs on me whatsoever. Annie kept repeating that to herself, especially when the private elevator delivered them to the lobby. That, too, was kitted out in enough glass that all she could see was the jostling throng of people already waiting outside.

"'Once more unto the breach,'" Tiziano murmured, but all Annie could concentrate on was the feel of his palm in the small of her back. His flesh against hers. The heat of his palm, and the shivery sensation that radiated from that point of contact, until even her knees felt weak.

But there was no time to indulge *sensation*, of all things. Instead, she had to walk out into that baying crowd at Tiziano's side, doing her best not to fall off the skyscraper high heels she wore or betray too much anxiety to the watching horde outside.

She didn't realize how much the thick glass doors

were muffling the intensity of the crowd until the doorman opened them wide and Tiziano led her into the thick of it.

It was chaos. It was terrifying. If Tiziano hadn't kept hold of her, Annie would have stopped dead as the wall of noise hit her and then turned to run back inside. She wouldn't have thought twice. It felt animalistic, the wild urge to put as much distance between her and all these harsh voices as possible.

And the voices were secondary to the lights. The *pop-pop-pop* of the lights, like weapons. It took her long, spinning moments to remember what Tiziano had told her. Not to look at them directly. To keep her gaze away from those constant flashes of lights.

It was too late, of course. Annie felt blinded and fractured and had no choice but to rely entirely on the man who guided her smoothly enough to the car that waited for them at the curb.

She slid inside and then realized in a panic that Tiziano was sliding in right behind her, so she had to heave herself across the leather seat toward the far side of the vehicle. All that noise was cut off, abruptly, by the slamming of the door, but then they started batting at the windows and the sides of the car.

It took her a long while to even notice she was holding her breath.

The car pulled out from the curb, slowly, but Annie was unable to move, or breathe, or even process what had just occurred. She thought, then, in that same spinning sort of panic, about all the tabloid magazines she'd seen in her lifetime. All those pictures. Had they all been taken like this? People hunted down in this way? It was nothing short of horrifying.

"Indeed," Tiziano rumbled from beside her, and it wasn't as if she'd forgotten he was there. He was not forgettable in any way. But she was startled to hear him all the same. It seemed to take an enormous amount of willpower to turn her head, and then to look at him. And even more to understand that she must have spoken out loud. "I have not paid these things much attention in a long while. I fear it is true that a person can get used to anything."

Annie swallowed, hard. Without meaning to, she lifted her hand and placed it over her heart, not surprised to feel the drumbeat there, a panicked staccato. "What I can't imagine is courting that kind of attention. It seems nightmarish to me."

Tiziano's dark expression was lightened in no way at all by the blue of his eyes. "Attention is currency, *cara*. My family is wealthy, *sicuramente*. But the perception of the Accardi wealth far outstrips our actual holdings." His mouth curved. "For surely there could be no playboy so disreputable as I, unless there was a vast fortune behind it."

"You could also be above such games." But even as she spoke, Annie could feel her whole body flooding with a kind of relief. As if she really had been under attack and was only now processing the fact that she'd survived. "Not every rich person appears in the tabloids."

"There are arguments for and against. My brother would prefer that the Accardi name never appear in print, unless that print is on the next round of contracts. But then, many of the contracts we enjoy have come to us because of the very profile I maintain that he so detests."

Tiziano shrugged all of that away, as if it was nothing.

Annie wanted nothing so much as to delve into the Accardi family dynamics. But that seemed a risky endeavor at best. For one thing, she couldn't really see this man opening up in any real way. And did she really want him to? She wasn't doing this because she wanted to make him a friend. She was doing this because it was as if she'd somehow won the National Lottery. For once, she intended to bask in her good fortune. If it involved flashbulbs in the face and three long hours to get ready to go out, that seemed a very small price to pay.

She smiled at him. As professionally as she could, given the circumstances. "I was told we were going to some kind of premiere."

He waved a hand. "Some film," he said carelessly. "When you invest in cinema, they do not call you a shareholder, you understand. They call you a producer and the honor of seeing your name on the screen is considered more than enough payment for some. Depending on the investment, of course. I am, obviously, a great patron of the arts—"

"In that you like to date actresses?"

His eyes gleamed. "Just so. They invite me to the premieres. As an investment opportunity or because they think my ego demands it, who can say?"

"Does that mean…?"

"There will be all manner of famous people about tonight?" He laughed, that warm, rich sound that filled the car and made her remember, too vividly, the feel of his palm against the flesh of her back. "I did not think you cared about such things. I should warn you now that you will lose any wonder you might hold for famous people before we're done."

"Including you?" she dared to ask.

And her reward was the way his mouth curved into a ghost of a smile. "Me most of all."

"I was a little more concerned about walking a red carpet," she said after a breathless moment and too much deep blue in her head. "I've never been all that interested in famous people."

"Aside from me, of course. Of whom you have read so much and so widely."

Annie sniffed. "I thought that was a job requirement."

And later, when she lay in her bed on its high platform, there in her room of glass, what she remembered was not the paparazzi. Nor even the supposedly more legitimate press corps who shouted Tiziano's name as he walked her down the carpet, which was indeed bright red. It was not the film they watched. She couldn't recall a single scene, because all she could seem to focus on was the man sitting beside her and the brooding intensity of him in the dark. It was not even the party they'd gone to afterward, where every face before her was one she recognized from her telly or the supermarket checkout line.

All of that she filed away, but what she remembered most was the two of them cocooned in that car, gliding through the London streets, his laughter all over her like heat.

It kept her awake well into the night.

The good news was that the job of pretending she was Tiziano Accardi's mistress took place at night. No matter how late they stayed out, very often past dawn, nothing was expected of her until the next afternoon.

"I don't think I fully understood that what famous

people are, really, are vampires," she said one night as she sat wrapped up in a dream of a cashmere scarf turned elegant blanket in the car, so delirious that she couldn't tell if she was falling asleep or perhaps already lost to dreamland.

Tiziano's voice hinted at all that dark laughter that lived in him, and she could feel it inside her, too. "In more ways than you know."

The job itself did not include the more physical duties a typical mistress might expect to undertake. That meant Annie could have been as lazy as she wished. For the first week or so, she was. But after only that single week of excessive luxury, with cream teas wheeled to her at the snap of her fingers, it became clear that she needed to take better care of herself. Not only because she otherwise might need a new outrageously overpriced wardrobe, but because all that laziness made her peevish and strange.

If she couldn't work or study or paint the way she had once upon time, she could at least *move*. There were various rooms throughout the sprawling house, outfitted with various kinds of exercise equipment. One of those trendy stationary bikes. Various rowers, one shaped like a wooden bow and others stripped down to so many efficient parts. There was a weight room equipped with intimidating machines and racks of hand weights, all gleaming invitingly. There were treadmills on every floor and the gardens outside should the British late November ease its cold, grim grip.

But Annie found she liked the pool best. Because there were no mirrors or staff about to watch her. Because she could dive beneath the water, always kept precisely at the most perfect temperature, and simply swim.

And because swimming made her think, not of Tiziano Accardi for once, but trips to the seaside she and Roxy had taken when they were small. When their parents were still alive. When they would hire a caravan, eat tinned meat sandwiches on cold beaches, and shiver in the inevitable summer rain. Both girls had learned how to swim at one of their parents' favorite holiday parks.

While she was swimming, it was easy to remember only the good things. She and Roxy tucked into bunk beds, giggling late into the summer night. Chasing each other up and down the stretch of gray beach, pretending they might at any moment swim for Denmark. Their grandmother coming for a few nights to tell them stories about mermaids singing to the boats in the North Sea and selkies sunning themselves on the rocks.

Annie could remember, almost, her mother's calm voice as she read to them on the little sofa in the long summer evenings. She and Roxy would take a place on either side of her, a shoulder each, while their eyes grew heavy and their sticky fingers seemed to adhere to their own cheeks.

She remembered her father teaching his girls to dance, propping each of them on his feet as he moved around what little space there was inside the caravan while Mum fried up the sausages and the wireless played happy songs.

Annie still knew all the words.

And she sang them to herself as she swam in that pool, with the late November weather sometimes bucketing down against the glass outside. Her heart would leap happily inside her chest as she cut through the water, swimming end to end, over and over. And once she'd sung herself everything she knew, she started over again, until she found her way back to calm.

Because that serenity was what she prized, she realized. It was what made the difference.

Her input was not required in any of the other things she was called upon to do. Her outfits were chosen for her. Her *looks* were decided on by her team of attendants, and her thoughts on them were never requested. Sometimes it all made her feel a bit claustrophobic, stuck in a chair with so many people buzzing around her as if she were nothing more than a mannequin. But the more she swam, the calmer she felt in the pool as well as in the chair, and the better she could enjoy her afternoons being transformed into the perfect Accardi mistress. Because those afternoons were the calm before the storm.

The storm was Tiziano, thunder and heat.

And his plan was working just the way he'd intended it should.

At first, the pictures were of him—and her elbow, perhaps. Sometimes with a throwaway reference to his "friend." Or his "female companion," if they were feeling saucy. No one asked her name, and although there were always shouting matches beneath the bright lights, Tiziano did not furnish it.

But as the two weeks he'd expected rolled into three, and November gave way to December, he started taking her out to restaurants. All of them extraordinary, exclusive, and different from the club where they'd met that first night only in that there were other people in attendance. Or other people she could *see*, anyway.

That week, the tabloids were filled with pictures of the two of them looking intimate by candlelight, or walking out of exclusive restaurants in London neighborhoods she had never dared set foot in on her own, for surely there was an income prerequisite for breathing such rarefied air.

Who is Tiziano's mystery woman? the papers demanded.

Wild theories abounded online. But it wasn't until an art opening that first week in December that she began to understand exactly what Tiziano was doing.

The night started the way all her nights did. She presented herself to her attendants in the chair that now occupied that bonus room in her guest suite, that was, itself, now a mere extension of her newly vast wardrobe. By now she knew to appear in a shirt that buttoned down the front, and a pair of easy tracksuit bottoms. Not that either of those items were any less exquisite than everything else in her wardrobe, courtesy of Catriona. She was styled to an inch of her life, packaged in the gown du jour, and then swept off in a car to be delivered to Tiziano.

This particular night, the car had pulled up outside Accardi Industries. She'd spent a few moments wondering if she would have to parade into the office where she'd worked as a secretary dressed up like the belle of the ball.

Though even as she thought such a thing, she laughed at herself. Because who would recognize her? Her supervisor had never looked north of her chest. And none of the other secretaries she'd encountered would look twice at a woman dressed as she was now. It would never occur to them that they could know her.

But she didn't have to put that to the test because Tiziano slid into the car, flashing her a grin that seemed to take in the whole of the sleek gown she wore and every inch of her exposed skin. As if his fingers moved all over her.

She sometimes wished they would.

Annie felt herself flush, and worse, felt the blue of his gaze, as if he knew exactly the sort of thoughts that had been plaguing her more and more lately.

If so, he said nothing. Sometimes, they would sit together in these vehicles of his and he would indulge himself in what she liked to consider his teasing. He would ask her questions designed to embarrass her. They were always probing. And inappropriate. At first, she'd taken great offense—until she realized that he meant her to.

But he wasn't the only one who could play games, and so once she made that determination, Annie made it her solemn duty to respond to each and every query of his with the same equanimity.

"Is it embarrassing to have that accent?" he might ask, lazily.

She would smile in return. "No more embarrassing than having more money than sense, I wager."

Most of the time, when they arrived at these events, they were both a little wound up from the battle that had just occurred in the car. She could see it on their faces in the pictures that turned up each morning. In what appeared to be every tabloid in every country across the globe.

Though it took her longer than she wanted to admit to figure out that the point of it was the pictures. Because it made them look like they'd engaged in a far different battle in the car.

Tonight, he took her to dinner and then to an art gallery, where he tucked her arm into his, and leaned too close as he led her from one piece to the next. He murmured for her ears only, his mouth so near to her she felt electrified by his breath against the side of her face.

And she knew it was for show. She knew that Tiziano was only playing a part. But it was hard to remember that it was all the same bit of theater when he was so good at it.

"Don't react," he told her while standing before a painting of a great, oblong object that shot from the earth to pierce the sky. "But I know the artist and I am quite certain that is a *highly* exaggerated rendering of his most prized possession." He looked down at her, his blue eyes gleaming too bright. "*Excessively* exaggerated, according to all accounts."

And Annie wasn't pretending to laugh when he was outrageous, she was really laughing. Just like she didn't need to pretend to be interested in all the rest of the things he said to her, because she truly was. He knew a shocking amount, not only about the artists' private lives and their favored appendages, but about their work. About art in general and how it mattered more than ever these days.

More astonishing still was that he actually listened when she told him her own thoughts and opinions.

He listened the way other men made love, Annie found herself thinking. And it followed, then, that he must make love the way other men made art—

But she couldn't indulge that line of thinking. Not here. Not with so many eyes upon them and her tendency toward a blush at the least convenient moments.

They'd been going round and round for some minutes now, standing before a canvas they disagreed on.

He thought it was trite, she thought it was subversive, and Annie only gradually became aware of someone else standing in her peripheral vision as they argued the point.

She turned automatically—and found herself caught immediately in a stormy blue gaze she recognized.

Except this was not Tiziano, wreathed in easy grins and oozing languid insolence. She knew at once that this could only be his intimidating brother, the stern and disapproving Ago.

And tonight, it appeared he intended to share that disapproval equally between his younger brother…and her.

"What is the meaning of this?" he demanded.

Tiziano pulled Annie close into his side, and though he laughed as he looked down at her, there was a certain coldness in his gaze that hadn't been there before.

"My brother wishes to chastise me," he told her, and she understood that he was not speaking to her, though he appeared to address her. "But if that was all he wished, he would do it in Italian. That he is speaking in English, you understand, is a way to signal to you that you ought to feel shame in my presence."

"Doesn't every woman feel shame in your presence?" Annie asked, without thinking. "I thought that was the entire point of you."

Ago shifted position and frowned as if Annie had managed to surprise him. What she couldn't tell was whether it was her accent or her irreverence.

But Tiziano smiled, and it reached his eyes. "Afterward, perhaps," he murmured. "Not usually *during*."

His brother swept to look up and down the pair of

them, and focused his attention on Tiziano. "You know that your fiancée is here, I trust," he said coldly.

It wasn't as if Tiziano had hidden anything from her. Annie knew that the purpose of the game they played here was to save him from the altar. He'd told her all about the worthy creature his brother had chosen to domesticate him. She'd looked Victoria Cameron up herself. But it had never really occurred to her before now that Victoria was a living, breathing woman who might, for all Annie knew, have a host of feelings about Tiziano. Why else would she have agreed to marry him?

How had that not occurred to her before now?

"I do not recall proposing to anyone," Tiziano was saying, mildly enough.

But looking back and forth between the brothers— both of them so tall, so dark, so elegantly ferocious, each in his different way—Annie had no trouble seeing that Tiziano was not in any way as languid as he was acting.

If anything, he looked more furious than Ago did.

Not outwardly. Never *outwardly*. But surely his own brother should have been able to see it, too.

If he did, Ago gave no sign. "All the arrangements have been made with her father. As you know well." He shifted his cold gaze to Annie and inclined his head, but slightly. "If this is news to you, I regret it."

"I don't think that you do," Tiziano replied, almost cheerfully.

Yet Annie could see he was anything but cheerful.

"I told you not three hours ago that tonight was to be the first glimpse of you and Miss Cameron in public," Ago bit off. "Was I unclear?"

"And I told you, not three hours ago, that I have no

intention whatsoever of playing this game of yours," Tiziano returned.

Once again, Ago looked directly at Annie. "My brother is using you," he told her coldly. "He uses every woman he comes across, I fear, but it is you he is using most egregiously. For he knows well that it is time he did his duty. And that is not you, Miss Meeks. I fear it will never be you. I hope he has not told you otherwise."

Annie wished that she had prepared for this. That she had some sort of script that she could fall back on, because all she could do in the face of Ago Accardi's obvious fury was gape at him.

Beside her, she could feel Tiziano coil, as if he was *only just* holding himself back from swinging on his brother. Right here in the middle of a posh, absurdly upmarket art gallery that seemed to be filled with even more famous people than that film premiere.

But Tiziano did not get violent. Instead, he pulled Annie even closer to his side, almost as if he meant to shield her. "If you have something to say, brother, you say it to me. I told you already. Annie is nonnegotiable."

At that, Ago scowled. He turned that scowl on Annie, but only briefly, before aiming it back at Tiziano.

"I told you," Tiziano said, his voice low, as if that scowl was a shout. "Again and again, I have told you. I will not give her up. This is not up for discussion. Yet the great and powerful Ago Accardi hears only what he wants to hear. And has a magical deafness when it comes to anything I might say. I am used to it." And the way he glared at his brother should have turned Ago to stone. "But I will not have you vent your spleen on the woman I love."

And Annie knew that he was playing his role. *She*

knew it. She had signed all those contracts. She had walked out of her life and straight onto this stage.

But knowing that didn't help. It did nothing at all to keep that electric bolt of sensation from coursing through her, a wildfire of need and longing, at the sound of Tiziano Accardi saying he loved her.

No matter how little he meant it.

Well, she thought then. *That's not good.*

CHAPTER SIX

TIZIANO FELT THE jolt go through Annie, and he wanted nothing more than to explore it, chase after it—but not with his brother looking on.

He had planned for this moment. He had known it would happen tonight. He'd sat in his brother's office earlier, subjecting himself to one of the lectures that had been increasing in frequency and *sturm und drang* of late, knowing that this art opening would offer the best opportunity to flaunt his mistress directly at Ago and the Camerons. No more containing his behavior to the tabloids, and Ago could take it up with Everard Cameron himself if the old man had a problem with it.

As Tiziano very much hoped he would.

But now it was happening, and it was different from how he had imagined it.

Because he didn't much care what Ago thought or what Everard Cameron was doing. All he found he could think about was protecting Annie.

Tiziano didn't know when *that* had started. He was not, by nature, a protective man. Not for him the doting on others that seemed to occupy so much of some people's time.

He and his brother had been taught to consider these

things a weakness. Why dote on anyone? What mattered was duty.

But even if he hadn't been raised to acknowledge and flout his own duty, he could not comprehend why he had such urges toward a woman he employed. Perhaps he did not pay her a salary, but then, he had always been significantly more old-school than people tended to believe, given how flamboyantly modern he made himself out to be when it suited him. The bottom line was that it made far more sense to him to house her and dress her and call her his mistress than to simply pay rent on a flat, as he knew some men did, and move various women in and out as his ardor cooled.

Possibly, having never done either before, he was treating Annie less like a run-of-the-mill mistress and more like a favorite. The way a notorious ancestor of his had treated an opera singer of some notoriety back in Venice in the 1800s, happy to leave his wife and children to rusticate in the country until he was forced to make appearances. Always against his will.

Tiziano found he understood.

Because everything would be going swimmingly if it weren't for these *feelings* inside him that he could hardly make any sense of. If it weren't for the way her shoulders fit so neatly in the curve of his arm, so that he was assaulted by her delicate scent each time he inhaled.

It made him wish he was a different man. The man he was pretending to be, in fact. It made him want to *do things*. And not the things he was normally associated with.

He was not surprised when his brother let out a short laugh.

He was equally stunned.

"'In love?'" Ago repeated, in tones of disbelief. "You. Tiziano. *In love?* I doubt very much you know the meaning of the word."

"Come now, brother," Tiziano said, sounding lazy out of habit when the truth was, he was far more focused on that faint shivering thing he could still feel running through Annie's lush little body. "Surely you do not wish to put your own ignorance of emotion on display like this. It hardly speaks well of you."

And then, before Ago could respond as he surely would, Tiziano stepped away. He steered Annie away from his brother, away from this conversation, *away* from this danger he'd put her in. He headed into the crowd, where he could engage in easy, pointless society conversations that did not involve him making any kind of declarations whatsoever.

But he did not remove his arm around Annie's shoulders. He told himself it was all about maintaining this fantasy that he was selling. He of all people knew how important that was. This was his show, after all.

Eventually, they moved away from the main part of the gallery and found their way to one of the tall café tables that had been set about the glassed-in atrium, while delicate foods and all manner of drinks were passed regularly by out-of-work West End actors. There was no need to hold on to her at a table. Obviously he released her.

But Tiziano was forced to admit that he had a hard time losing that contact with her.

A much harder time than he wanted to admit, even to himself.

Even if there was something to be said about standing close beside her, angling his body so that it was as if they stood there all alone. He, who had always preferred the bright company of the many, discovered that he wished it really was only the two of them.

"Your brother is rather fearsome up close," Annie said softly, cupping her glass of wine in a manner Tiziano could only describe as grateful. As if she thought it was saving her from him.

There is no saving you, he wanted to tell her, and not because it was part of the role he played.

"He has cultivated his fearsomeness," Tiziano assured her. "When we were boys, he was perfectly normal. It is only over time that he has had every inch of humor drained from him, as if he sprung a leak."

Annie took a sip of her wine, and only then looked at him in her gray, steady way that made everything go still inside him. As if he were the one with those tremors moving deep within.

"What happened?" she asked. "To drain him?"

Tiziano was too caught up in her gaze for his usual deflections. "He became boring, as too many members of my family have done in their time," he said, offhandedly, though he didn't produce a smile the way he usually did when he said such things. "It is a terrible affliction. You will find it crops up everywhere."

She didn't laugh. Her gaze didn't even lighten. Instead, he saw the suggestion of a frown begin in that wrinkle between her brows. "What does he think happened?"

"Ah. Well."

And Tiziano knew that they were standing in the middle of a bustling art gallery. That Ago himself was likely watching them at this very moment. He knew that the glare of so much attention was no time or place for confidences. He couldn't recall the last time he'd had the occasion to share any personal details with anyone. Not real ones.

He only shared stories that made him look even more disreputable than he was.

But there was something about the way Annie looked at him. As if she was silently, almost hopefully, encouraging him to be...

Not different, but *better*.

It should have irritated him. Instead, it made Tiziano wish for things he knew too well were impossible. He had picked his role long ago. For Ago could only be the avenging angel when there was a convenient devil forever at hand.

"Ago is the eldest son," he found himself saying, simply enough. And though that was true, and as comprehensive a way to explain his brother as any, something about the way Annie waited pushed him to go on. When he never spoke of these things. "And in a family like ours, despite what he may have wished or wanted, Ago was required to have a head for the business from a very young age. The Accardi legacy, you understand, is all that matters. He was encouraged to take part in pursuits that were carefully arranged to suit the business, and his future. If it did not serve the legacy, it was not for him."

Memories Tiziano had not aired in years pressed in on him, but he pushed them away. He and Ago had not been young in a long while. And they had been permitted their freedom, their happiness, for so few years. What good was it to recall such things now?

"It might surprise you to learn when he was young, Ago fancied himself a bit of an artist, after a fashion,"

Tiziano heard himself tell her. When he had never told another soul such a thing. It was not that it was a secret, or even his, but that it was painful. For too soon had they both been hauled out of the sweetness of art and childhood and taught instead how to make money. The only thing any member of his family truly believed in.

"Is that why we're here tonight?" Annie asked. "This is his gallery, is it not?"

Tiziano smiled. "He owns it, but do not lapse off into any artistic daydreams, *cara*. Owning a gallery is not romantic. It is the opposite." He shook his head, and wished she was still snug beneath his arm. And since when was he a man of *wishes*? "The art and romance was quickly beaten out of my brother. All the hopes and dreams of the entire Accardi Empire were placed upon his shoulders and he, being dutiful and good, widened his shoulders. The better to hold them all. He is the heir. The legacy was in his hands."

Another woman might have rushed in to say something. Anything. To express outrage that a boy should be molded so young, perhaps. Or make some crack about how Tiziano had missed out on similar guidance.

Annie only eyed him a moment. "And what was put on your shoulders?"

For no reason at all that he could comprehend, Tiziano smiled. But it was a bitter thing. And it seemed connected to all those memories he refused to entertain.

"Nothing at all," he told her with a soft ferocity that sounded nothing like him. Or more like him than he allowed outside his own head. "Air, if that. I was abandoned to my own devices—and vices—and encouraged to stay out of everyone's way. I was the spare, you understand, but there was no real concern that I would ever be called upon to take Ago's place. And thank goodness, as it was quickly determined that I would be useless in such a role."

"And so you decided instead to be outrageous." And Tiziano found himself mesmerized by the way she ran her index finger around the rim of her glass. As if it was a precious instrument and if he leaned closer, he might hear it sing. "Because otherwise, you did not exist."

It was as if she knew.

That was the wild notion that raced through him then, as if she had been there throughout the lonely days of his childhood once Ago was removed from his "influence." Tiziano had not taken well to the loss of his only friend and companion, sequestered away in the Tuscan countryside for years before he was sent away to a cold boarding school in darkest Britain. He had dedicated himself to finding ways, every day, to come to the attention of his tutors, his parents, Ago himself, and even, while he lived, their forbidding grandfather.

And Tiziano had not cared much if that attention was positive or negative. Not so long as it proved he existed. That he was not forgotten.

That he would not *allow* them to forget him.

For he had lived in that great house, where ghosts did not walk the halls. They were fastened to the walls in interchangeable portraits, their names known to few and important to none, every one of them a lesson in what happened to an unsung Accardi son if he allowed them to shunt him away.

It was in school that Tiziano had discovered that outrageousness could be used as leverage, and that his understanding of how to claim a room and make even those who loathed him pay attention to him was an advantage. A talent, even.

He knew perfectly well that when he'd demanded a courtesy title from Ago after his brother had been made CEO, no one expected him to do anything with it. He'd taken a great deal of pleasure in proving them all wrong.

In his own inimitable way.

Though he had not allowed himself to think of such things in longer than he cared to recall. Possibly ever.

"What of you and your sister?" he asked Annie then, too aware that she was watching him closely. When he had the strangest notion that she just might be the one person alive who could read him. When everyone else he met took him at face value.

He *wanted* them all to take him at face value, he told himself. Annie included.

But then, there was that note in his own voice he hardly recognized. A roughness there that was nothing like him. Or perhaps it was simply that he did not sound as indolent as he usually did. Too caught was he, still, in all of that solemn gray.

And all it seemed to demand of him.

He cleared his throat. "And do not tell me the two of you did not have roles to play, for surely we all do."

"It's hard to say," Annie said, with a forthrightness that stunned him. He had spent time with her now and still, he could not get used to how frank she seemed to be in all things. He kept looking for the catch. "While my parents lived, everything seemed happy-go-lucky and easy, but it is possible I only remember it that way because I lost it. It seemed less as if we played roles, Roxy and I, and more as if we were a unit. But then everything changed after the accident." She shifted against the table, but did not move any closer to him. He resented it. "My grandmother wanted to take us, but she was too old and frail by then. So we went to my aunt's and we became different people."

"How?" he asked, when he shouldn't have cared. If she had questioned him, he would have laughed and told her he didn't. But she didn't ask.

Instead, she considered the question. "Roxy acted out. And I...disappeared. Maybe we were always destined to be that way, one sister bad and the other good. Or maybe the accident is what shaped us and made us who we are now." She lifted a shoulder, then dropped it. "But either way, none of it can be changed. She gave up trying to do the right thing, but then, I gave up art. And maybe, even if my parents had lived, this is who we'd have become anyway."

"You cannot change what happened," Tiziano agreed, again in a voice he did not recognize. "But you can always change who you are."

"Is it so easy, then?" she asked, and there was something different in her gaze. Some kind of bleak challenge that Tiziano did not wish to accept or even acknowledge. But he couldn't seem to look away. "You have the perfect opportunity before you, Tiziano. All you need to do to change, to become the man your brother wishes you to be, is marry that girl. She seems perfectly nice, by all accounts."

"How would you know?" Tiziano found himself asking. "I was under the impression she remained locked away in her convent, cursed to remain there until her father marries her off."

"She is involved with a great many charities," Annie said calmly. Too calmly. "And I think you know that.

Because I know it, and everything I know about her is widely available online."

Annie regarded him for what could only have been a moment or two. There was no reason it should have felt to him like a lifetime.

Or why he couldn't tell if he was relieved or…not when she continued.

"There's no reason at all you couldn't have a lovely little life," Annie said softly. "But instead you've chosen to concoct this whole scenario with a fake mistress and an entire production behind it, just to prove that you can never, ever be anything but what you are. So tell me. Do you really think change is so easy?"

There was the sudden sound of laughter, too loud and too close. Tiziano remembered himself with a start, and straightened. As if that could change how enthralled he'd been by Annie, and every word that crossed her lips. It was a funny thing to find himself too busy *actually* being captivated by her to make sure he was *acting* as if he was.

It made him feel…outside himself, somehow.

He took a moment, looking around, but the loud burst of laughter had come from a group standing around another table nearby. It had nothing to do with him. Or with Annie.

Was he relieved or irritated? Why couldn't he tell?

Tiziano scanned the atrium, then looked back into the gallery proper. He found his brother almost immediately. Ago was engaged in what appeared to be a deep conversation with an older man Tiziano knew, even from the back, was Everard Cameron. And the virtuous Victoria herself, the fiancée he refused to claim, stood at his brother's side.

Annie was right, of course. Tiziano accepted that as he looked across the crowd at her. Victoria Cameron was wholly unobjectionable. Quite pretty, really, but then she would have to be, if her father imagined that he could sell her off in this way.

It wasn't that he was afraid of change, he told himself as he gazed at her. Because he wasn't. He never had been. It was that marrying her was the same thing as crawling into one of those gilt-edged portraits in the family gallery. It was accepting the inevitability of becoming another family ghost.

Tiziano had no interest in fading off into obscurity, whether by becoming respectable or any other means.

The Accardi family had enough ghosts as it was.

"You could say you'd seen the error of your ways tonight," Annie said from beside him, as if she knew what he was thinking when she couldn't. Of course she couldn't. For one thing, he did not think in English.

And yet Tiziano could still hear that same thing he'd seen in her gaze. He could hear that same dark current and though he could not name it to save his life, it made something inside him seem to turn over. It made his blood heat while a kind of temper beat low and hard.

It made him remember things he preferred not to recall and, worse, want things he had long since decided he could not have.

Annie wasn't finished. "You could march right over there right now," she said. "You could smile at her in that practiced way of yours and be exactly the man your brother wants you to be. You could pretend to be that man as easily as you're pretending to be with me. It's only a little bit of change, after all. It should be easy."

It seemed to take him a lifetime to angle his gaze

back down to Annie. And something in him seemed to tip over, then scatter to the winds, because the gray in her gaze no longer seemed steady in the least.

All he could see in her was a storm.

And God knew there was nothing he liked better than a storm he could dance in.

He already wanted her. It was possible he'd wanted her from the moment she'd landed in a heap at his feet.

But just then, that wanting became a wildfire, and it set about burning him alive.

"I could do all of those things," he agreed, and though his voice was low, it was made of smoke and ash. He could see the way the heat got into her, too. "But between you and me, *cara mia*, I do not think my brother wants to be the man he is. So you will pardon me if I do not rush to become the man he thinks I ought to be, either."

He'd gotten too close to her as he spoke, so that their faces were nearly touching. And it was as if everything else fell away. He didn't think. He reached over and traced a pattern from her temple to her chin, as if he was sketching out all these odd and unknowable urges within him. And then, feeling intense in a way he could not have explained—as if his very life depended on it—he traced the shape of her lips, once. Then again.

And this time when he felt her shiver, he didn't pretend.

He knew exactly what it was.

The fire in him raged higher.

"You're really putting on a show," she whispered, though she didn't sound at all like herself. She did not sound calm and steady, and he took it as a victory. "It's more convincing by the day."

"Well, then," Tiziano said, his voice a low growl. "We really ought to make it good."

And he leaned in, kissing her softly, to start. Then he deepened the kiss, almost inexorably—just a taste, just a quick dip into the flames—before he pulled away.

He saw a quick glimpse of a shattered sort of expression on Annie's face, but she looked away quickly. And he had no time to follow it up, because he could feel the weight of Ago's fury from across the gallery.

And this was supposed to be a show.

So he straightened, letting his hand rest on the nape of Annie's neck, and met his brother's gaze with his own.

He did not look at his supposed intended. Because lovely as she might be, and blameless in this, it was not about her. Tiziano saw only Ago's stern expression, and did what he did best—he lifted an insouciant brow.

Daring his brother to do something about what he'd just seen.

Knowing all the while that Ago was not the sort to start a scene in public.

Tiziano told himself it was taking Ago on, instead of merely ignoring his suggestions as usual, that left him feeling so unsettled. He told himself that he was gearing up for battle, that was all.

And when he was approached by a set of high rollers who were clearly there to give Annie the once-over, he turned his smile up to its full wattage and took to his favorite stage. And a quick glance at Annie showed him she was back to her serene exterior, no hint of any *shattering* he might have imagined on her face.

But that unsettled feeling did not improve as the night wore on. When it was over, he and Annie were once again sitting together in the back of his car while London streaked by outside.

"You look unduly grim," she said, though she was looking out the window.

"I am devastated for you that you signed that non-disclosure agreement on your first day here," he murmured. "Think of the books you could sell about the truth behind the Tiziano Accardi show."

"I would never write that book." But lest he imagine she was somehow transported by sudden loyalty, she laughed. "Because it wouldn't sell. No one who's really happy and carefree spends as much time as you do *convincing* people that he's both of those things. Deep down, everyone must know it."

That landed hard. His laugh sounded hollow.

"Don't be silly," he told her. "Everyone thinks only of themselves. They take everyone else at face value."

He felt her gaze on him then, as if the gray of it was a touch. "Do they? Or do you?"

His mood did not improve when he walked her to the door of his house in Hampstead, an investment property he had never lived in and now never would, as it would always remind him of this woman and absurdly chivalrous urges like this one, to see her to the door. Tonight all of the house's modern lines seemed to gleam with particular malice against the deep December dark.

Her voice seemed to taunt him. *Does it? Or do you?*

Tiziano found himself standing there like a foolhardy suitor as the cold and damp pressed in against them. As Annie, his mistress in name only, gazed up at him as if this was the end of a date.

As if he was a man who *dated*.

"You don't have to look at me like that," she told him,

as the night seemed to spin off into mist and wonder around them. And Tiziano thought he could hear the same sort of turbulence in her voice as he felt inside. He thought he could see the echo of it in her gaze. Or maybe it was that he only wished he did. He *wished*.

"No one's watching."

And it was the challenge in her voice that called to him.

Or that was what he told himself, anyway, as he moved in close. He framed her face with his hands and took her mouth with his.

Not a show this time. Not an experiment.

This was a claiming. A wish made real.

Tiziano kissed her the way he wanted to, because he had to kiss her or die, and he chose not to analyze that certainty within him. He kissed her because he couldn't bear not kissing her. Because he wanted the taste of her in his mouth again.

Always.

He kissed her again and again, flinging them both into that wildfire that raged in him, the sheer madness of the things she stirred up in him, and the wanting.

The wanting that would not leave him be.

The wanting that would take him over and turn him into someone he did not recognize—

And Tiziano had learned this lesson a long time ago.

It was no good to want things. It was worse to want people. That only meant that they could all be taken away.

Better by far to want nothing.

No matter how wild the fire was, how high the flames, he knew better.

He set her back from him, but took a deep pleasure in the way her breath came then, a ragged truth she couldn't hide. And in the way her eyes went wide, slicked with sensation.

Despite himself, he took pleasure in it all.

"What…?" she swallowed, and shook her head, and for once sounded nothing even close to *calm*. "What was that?"

"I don't know," Tiziano gritted out. "I wish I did."

And then he made himself turn and leave her there, her panting breaths making clouds against the night.

Before he couldn't.

CHAPTER SEVEN

ANNIE DID HER best to put *kissing* out of her mind.

Because concentrating on it, she was certain, would only drive her mad.

And the last thing she needed was to be…*more* unhinged where Tiziano Accardi was concerned.

The day after the night of the kissing she wasn't thinking about and the art gallery talk of who could change and who couldn't that she couldn't stop remembering, Annie swam until she was exhausted. Lap after lap, until the motion of her arms against the water made her feel real again.

Made her feel like herself again.

Because she wasn't truly Tiziano's mistress. She needed to remind herself, apparently, that it was a role, nothing more. She could have been anyone. If he hadn't happened upon her in that stairwell, he would have chosen someone else for this and he would be behaving the exact same way. She would be looking at the very same pictures in the very same magazines. There was no point getting herself wound up about all those dark glances and what they might mean.

They meant nothing. Just because she sometimes thought she could see something in them didn't mean it was there. Or that it mattered if it *was* there, some-where. Nothing could come of it.

And meanwhile, she had a job to do. That was the price of the life she'd have any day now, debt-free and provided for, at last.

Now that it was December, Tiziano seemed to have nothing but holiday events. Every charity threw a ball. Every group he'd even smiled at one time apparently required a celebration at the end of the year, and his presence was demanded.

And at every single event, Tiziano went out of his way to appear even more besotted than he had at the art gallery. There were the longing stares. The absent toy-ing with her hair, a bracelet she might wear, the edge of her gown. If there was dancing he would draw her out onto the floor, then ignore the steps to every dance as he held her close—as if he could not wait to hold her the very same way in a bedroom.

Very often, Ago Accardi himself stood nearby, glow-ering. Sometimes the mean-looking older man she knew was Everard Cameron stood with him, clearly sharing his displeasure. But even if they weren't there, the tab-loids were, and all the papers overflowed with specu-lation and photographic evidence of Tiziano Accardi's new passion.

She really ought to have been congratulating herself at a game well played. But the longer this went on, the more there was another aspect to her masquerade that she hadn't been prepared for.

Maybe it was because a world filled with mistresses and tabloids was so far outside the scope of her regular life. Maybe she was naive. But it hadn't really crossed her mind that people she actually knew would read the tabloids she appeared in and come to the same conclusions about the show she and Tiziano were putting on. It was her fault. All she'd been able to think about was getting out from under all of that debt. That was the only consequence that had mattered to her.

"Aren't you a dark horse," her sister Roxy said, actually calling Annie directly for the first time since she'd left for Australia.

Annie, who'd taken the call in disbelief and had assumed it was an accidental dial, now found herself staring down at her mobile as if it turned into a snake in her own palm. "I don't think I'm any kind of horse, actually."

Roxy hooted with laughter. She sounded the way Roxy always sounded. Irrepressible. Merry. Offensively unaware of the wreckage she left behind her. "Here I am feeling wretched about that whole mess, and all the while you've been angling for a much bigger payday," she said. "I'll be honest, Annie. I didn't think you had it in you."

"You've been feeling wretched?" Annie asked, pinching the bridge of her nose, because it was that or melt down. "Really, Roxy? But not wretched enough to *do* anything, though. Is that what you mean?"

"I've seen the pictures," her sister replied with another laugh. Not exactly the sound of repentance. "Why don't you sell one of those great, honking necklaces you're always swanning about in? I don't think you'll have any more issues with the bank. You can pay everything off and buy a manor house or two, if it suits you."

"I am not—" Annie began, but then stopped herself. There in the window seat of her expansive bedroom in her guest suite in the wing of a sprawling mansion overlooking Hampstead bloody Heath.

Because what was she planning to say, exactly? That she needed her sister to cough up a few quid to pay a debt that was already paid? It seemed spiteful. Not that Roxy didn't deserve a little spite, but despite her deepest martyrish feelings, Annie understood why she'd done it. Even better, now.

Because wasn't she doing what she was doing for the same reasons? Because she'd had more than Roxy, and life was easier with more.

She started to tell her sister that she wasn't the gold digger the tabloids made her out to be, but stopped that, too. Because she might not be using the feminine wiles the world thought she was, but she was still getting the same result. And for the same reasons.

Because in a week or so, this would be over. Everard Cameron would call off the agreement he'd made with Ago, Tiziano would return to his normal life, and it would all be worth it, because Annie would be free to do as she liked. Forever.

Could she really carry on blaming her sister for causing the very situation that had led to this?

Well. Maybe not forever. But today wasn't forever, was it? "I can't believe that the first time you call me after you made me quit university is to act as if we're the same. *I* haven't stolen Tiziano Accardi's credit card."

But her sister only laughed, not sounding the least bit offended. "How are we the same? I'm lucky if a bloke buys me a drink, Annie. No one's showering me in jewels."

And though she rang off after that, and didn't pick

up when Annie called her back straight away, it seemed to start a kind of avalanche.

Because suddenly, Annie was aware of other people's opinions. Regular people's opinions. It felt as much like an assault as the paparazzi flashbulb gauntlets.

The world, as far as she could tell, didn't really like the idea of everybody's fantasy boyfriend actually falling for someone.

They took against it strongly, in fact.

There were the knowing glances from some of the women, in case she didn't know he had a history. And outright hateful glares from those who'd imagined they'd had a chance. Worse still were the speculative looks from the men, imagining her performing her *duties* while they stood about having genteel conversations about the weather and the monarch's health.

Ago's disapproval, when she faced it, was almost comforting in comparison, because all he seemed to see was her inappropriate station. Not what she might get up to in bed with his brother.

There was some part of her that thought she should have been delighted that the whole world believed her to be a scandalous woman of some kind. After a lifetime of being mocked for being the very opposite, she should have found it as amusing as everyone else she knew did.

Annie Meeks, *femme fatale*. Annie Meeks, *notorious mistress*. It was absurd.

But oddly enough, no one came forward to tell the world that the Annie they knew was the last woman alive anyone should imagine would end up with a man of Tiziano's appetites. The friends from up north and her year in university who got in contact with her—in ways that ran the gamut from admiring to gentle teasing, to obviously envious, and sometimes straight-up creepy—all seemed to believe it well enough.

Annie found that the longer it went on, the harder she found it. Because it wasn't just that the world thought she was scandalous now. She probably would find that amusing someday. It was more that they all thought that she was some kind of sex goddess.

So wildly, unconquerably sensual that Tiziano Accardi himself was besotted and obsessed with her.

And it seemed wildly unfair—some kind of cosmic joke—that not only had they done nothing but kiss, but she was still the same boring virgin she'd always been.

She had never thought virginity was particularly boring before. Annie had never felt it as a burden, the way she knew some did. She'd never been seized with the burning need to get rid of it and she hadn't been holding on to it as if it was sacred, either. It was what she'd told Tiziano that night in the art gallery. She'd disappeared after the accident. She lost her parents. Maybe she'd thought that she would lose her aunt, too, if she wasn't perfect, and then what would become of her and Roxy?

So she'd been perfect in the way she knew her Aunt Sharon would understand and appreciate. Perfect marks. Perfect behavior. Perfect everything, all the time, so there really wasn't any room to worry about boys or sex or the fact she was now in her twenties and still hadn't been fussed enough to set about losing her virginity. The way her friends and her sister had done when they were still teenagers.

Annie found she worried about it a lot, now.

It seemed almost twisted, somehow, that she was being crowned the queen of a kind of passion she'd never experienced. She found herself reading articles about her own so-called *white-hot* romance and wondering who that woman was. The captivating, sensual creature the whole world seemed to think was her.

They imbued her with all manner of bizarre powers. She was a natural seductress. She used her feminine wiles to entrap every man who laid eyes on her. Even though she knew from experience that she turned precisely zero heads when walking down a street, now that she'd supposedly turned Tiziano's, her supposed beauty was treated as a fact. Something objective instead of opinion that until now, no one else had ever shared.

Even the articles that were cruel set about their cruelty very specifically. They disparaged her physical attributes—by claiming she wasn't as pretty as she thought she was, which still meant she was considered pretty. Or they mocked the way she moved, claiming she slunk about, vamping it up wherever she went. When really she was just walking in shoes that were so high she had to slow down or she would trip again.

Given that she'd met Tiziano because she'd fallen off a pair of pumps that were barely an inch high, she knew better than to tempt fate.

But it was the same issue. She was as fascinated by an angry blog post about her course, common slapperish tendencies as she was by a glowing puff piece that made her sound like an angel. Because at the center of it, no matter how much she read or how many films she watched or how much information she gathered, one single truth remained.

Tiziano was an extraordinarily famous playboy.

And Annie didn't know how to play.

One night, she excused herself from another round of brotherly acrimony and made her way to the women's lounge, which was what some fancy venues liked to call their loo. This particular grand hotel ballroom had plush stalls, flattering lights, and an entire sitting area with attendants and a small salon.

When she walked in, all the women in the room stared at her and went silent.

Then began whispering.

Another brand-new experience Annie had never had before Tiziano. Because who would be interested in whispering behind their hands about *her*? She'd been a secretary, for God's sake. And not a high-powered one, like many who were often the true power behind the flashy CEOs everyone worshipped.

She wanted to turn around and leave, but she'd already walked in. And there was something in her that thought she would actually rather die than let these people see that they'd gotten to her. Surely a sex goddess such as herself wouldn't even notice situations like this.

Annie swept over to the huge bank of mirrors along one side of the room and placed the tiny, bejeweled purse she carried on the countertop like a declaration. Then she pretended to inspect herself the way she knew the rest of them were. Looking for flaws. Looking for chinks in her armor.

But as ever, Tiziano hired only the best. She looked flawless. Tonight, in this room, she took pleasure in that.

She snapped open her bag and fished out the lip color she'd been told to reapply at will, and did so, finding the instant glossiness almost comforting. Because this all felt like an out-of-body experience anyway. And the more she used things like gloppy lip color, the more she felt like she really might be on the stage.

And that made it easier when a woman she thought she vaguely recognized slid into place beside her at the counter.

"You must share your secrets," the woman murmured. "Who would have thought Tiziano Accardi himself could ever be brought to heel? It's an impressive feat."

"She's not impressed, in case that isn't obvious," came another voice, and Annie saw that another woman had come to stand on her other side. And though she was smiling, there was nothing friendly in her gaze. "She's jealous. The most she could get out of our Tiziano was a night."

Our Tiziano. The cheek.

"But what a night it was," purred the first woman.

"Ladies," Annie replied, and it wasn't until she saw the smile on her own face that she realized that quite without meaning to, she was essentially doing an impression of Tiziano. All lazy amusement, as if she couldn't fully rouse herself to have this confrontation. "I'm perfectly aware that Tiziano has a past filled with all kinds of adventures. But as you must know, if you know him at all, where he excels is in the present."

She did not say, *And his present is me*.

But then, she didn't have to. It was clear that they took her meaning, and more, were there to snap at each other more than at her. Annie tossed her lip gloss back in her bag and left them to it—a little too aware of the way the whispers followed her as she left the lounge.

Back out in the gala proper, the band played on and Tiziano held court his usual way. For a man who was always trying to convince everyone that he did nothing, he certainly seemed to be forever surrounded by all kinds of people who sought his advice.

The more time she spent with him, the more Annie realized that everything about him was a contradiction. Peel away one layer and ten more appeared, each one different from the last. It was hard, now, to remember how she'd felt about him when she'd met him that first day. Or how she really had thought this would all be easy, because it had never occurred to her that she could possibly fall beneath his spell.

But whatever half-formed thoughts she'd had about *men like him* back then, she'd come to realize over these weeks that in truth, there were no men like him. Whatever else he was, Tiziano Accardi was decidedly singular.

The lights in the ballroom were low because all the speeches and applause were over now. It was all about dancing and drinking, and everyone seemed to agree that was best done with as little clarifying light as possible. Annie liked it. She didn't feel as on display as she usually did.

For a moment, she was just one more woman in a pretty dress swirling around a ballroom filled with the same. She wound her way through the tables that edged the dance floor, keeping her eyes toward the front, where Tiziano stood in his pack of admirers. Annie hardly noticed them, because he still shined far too brightly, even in a darkened room.

She would have thought that spending time with him would make him somehow more unattractive to her. That it would dull the impact of all that male beauty, or at the very least, render her immune.

Instead, the opposite seemed to have happened.

She could feel it happening even now, sinking into her bones, changing her even as she moved across the ballroom floor.

It was as if he pulled her to him, but he wasn't even aware that she approached.

Annie could take in the fine cut of the dark suit he wore, tailored into a kind of love letter to his perfect form. She could let her heart do as it wished at the sight of that inky dark hair, always looking as if it was about to be tousled, or had only just been. As she drew even closer, she could let herself experience the sweet shock of his eyes that looked black in the distance, yet were blue up close.

But nothing compared to the way his gaze shifted, then found Annie in the dark.

And once he found her, his gaze grew intent.

There were still several tables between them, and Annie thought that for once, in the dark here with all the shifting lights over the dance floor, there was no harm in doing nothing at all to mask her reaction. To simply letting herself feel it.

It was as if his gaze alone set her alight. As if all that blue was the sun, and she the moon, and so she glowed. Only for him.

"Pardon me," Tiziano said to his acquaintances, excusing himself from his group and coming to meet her.

And she was sure that had they been alone, he would have caught her up and set that sensual mouth of his on hers, for a start. She could sense the savagery in him, barely contained, and what was the maddest of all was that she could feel it in her, too.

She felt like a mess. Like everything she had always prided herself on had no meaning, here between them.

And yet stranger still was the way everything in her thrilled to that.

As if this was the true perfection. The way all the longing turned into heat, and held them both close. If they were alone…

But they were not.

So Tiziano did not fall upon her and Annie did not fling herself into his arms, heedless of their surroundings.

Instead, he reached out and took her hand. Then he led her out to the dance floor.

And she had things to say, but none of them found their way to her lips.

There was only this, the dancing. The music, the dark room, the way he held her close, his eyes burning into hers.

It was only later, after the music stopped, that she remembered those women in the lounge. She saw them again in the crowd, with others just like them, all wearing those speculative, jealous expressions.

Because they all thought they knew exactly what she and Tiziano were leaving the hotel to do.

"People are staring at us," she told him as he helped her into her coat, lingering a little too long as he drew it closed and buttoned it up.

He smiled, though his eyes were dark.

"You're a beautiful woman," he said, almost offhandedly, though his gaze was tight and hungry on her. Then his smile widened. "And I am remarkably handsome. Ask anyone. Naturally people stare. What else can they do?"

"That's not why they're staring, Tiziano. They think they know what we're headed off to do now."

It seemed to take him much too long to step back. To shrug into his own coat, then loop his own scarf around his neck.

"Benissimo," he murmured. "That is what we want." He studied her face then, every touch of his gaze like a caress. One dark brow rose. "Is it not?"

Annie felt her lips part, but no words came forth. No sound. Something moved over Tiziano's face, some storm she dared not investigate too closely.

Because they had to run yet another gauntlet, walking with the rest of the guests of the gala as they all exited the venue. Then they were out in the London streets as fleets of gleaming cars lined up to whisk them off to their glamorous lives.

By the time she and Tiziano got into his car, it was a relief to escape all the scrutiny—so little of it friendly. His driver pulled out into traffic, so there was nothing to do but sit in the back, listening to each other breathe.

Except Annie's breath couldn't seem to settle into a reasonable rhythm.

"I assumed that parading about as your mistress would be unremarkable," she told him.

He shifted in the seat beside her. "I'm offended, *cara*. Nothing about me is *unremarkable*. I feel certain we have touched on this simple truth before."

She ignored that. "I thought I would simply be one in a crowd, able to fade into obscurity once this ended, and spend the rest of my life testing oils against acrylics with the odd watercolor period for fun. But I'm beginning to realize that there will be no obscurity. This is how people will know me, always and forever. As Tiziano Accardi's mistress that one holiday season."

Annie remembered telling him there needed to be

penalties if the rules between them were broken. It hadn't occurred to her that she would be the one to pay them.

"Some would consider this the role of a lifetime," Tiziano murmured in that way of his, sounding so deeply lazy that most might think him about to lapse off into sleep. When she could hear that dark, electric current beneath that told her he was wide awake.

"You knew this would happen," she said softly. "You like to appear to throw your money around, but the real reason you were happy to discharge all my debts and give me so much money up front is because you *knew*, didn't you? It's entirely possible that these weeks will haunt me for the rest of my life."

Tiziano's voice was dark. "I do not believe in ghosts."

She turned to him then. "I didn't understand. There's no possible way I could have understood. You knew that, too. That's why you picked me."

"Part of what makes this so believable is that you are not my usual fare." He looked at her, the lights from outside the car playing over his face and making him look like something more than just a man. She thought of that great big cat again. A jaguar prowling about the ballrooms of London, always hunting—even when he seemed to be at rest. Maybe especially then. "I told you that, though perhaps your attention was on other things at the time. Even so, it seemed the gentlemanly thing to make sure that if you wished, you could live off these weeks without ever having to worry about what became of your reputation."

Annie laughed at that, though it came out far scratchier than she intended. "And what reputation do you suppose I have? University dropout and failed secretary?

Oh, yes. I imagine there will be quite a scandal to worry about there." She laughed again but he only looked quizzical. "I think you're misunderstanding me. I'm not complaining. I didn't understand the whole of it, but now I do."

"Brava," he murmured then, and it was not the first time he'd reverted to Italian when he was feeling especially sarcastic.

Annie liked that she knew that about him. Just like all the other things she knew about him. She was tempted to believe that of all the women he might have had along the way, she was the only one who knew such things about him. Because she was the only woman alive, except possibly the mother he talked about so seldom, who had ever spent this much time in his presence without taking part in what was widely held to be his favorite pastime.

What she didn't like was the fact that even random women in a loo knew parts of him that she didn't. Not that she was jealous of them. Not in the least.

But it seemed deeply unfair that she should have all of the work and all of the notoriety ever after...yet without ever tasting the sweetness that drew all these women to him in the first place.

Yes, she told herself stoutly, *what I am concerned about here is* fairness.

She turned to face him fully in the back of the car, leaning closer, because she wanted—needed—to look straight at him while she said this. While she broke the rules she'd made.

And became the woman the whole world already thought she was.

Tiziano Accardi's mistress. For real this time.

Because it was only *fair*.

"If I'm going to be whispered about like this for the rest of my life," she said quietly, watching his gaze sharpen, "then it doesn't really seem fair that I'm not getting the full package, does it?"

CHAPTER EIGHT

TIZIANO SAT THERE in stunned silence.

He searched her face, but he could see nothing there save that same steady gray gaze, fixed on his. And a certain patience, as if Annie was prepared to wait as long as it took for him to come to grips with what she'd said.

"The full package?" he managed to ask after a small eternity dragged by. "I'm afraid I do not take your meaning."

"I think you do," she replied. And he could see the laughter all over her face then, transforming her from simply a beautiful woman into Annie. His extraordinary Annie, who never seemed to lose herself in this glittering world he inhabited. When he knew full well how easy it was for that to happen. He'd watched it a thousand times. It didn't take much for wealth to alter people. But Annie's gaze was full of mischief, her face suffused with a kind of joy, and she was still entirely herself. "You might be above propositioning women for sex in stairwells, but it turns out I'm not above doing the same in the back seat of a car. I don't know what that makes me."

"Dangerous," Tiziano bit out as his heart punched

at him, a sledgehammer in his chest. "What it makes you is dangerous."

She was sitting in the seat next to him, but as she spoke she pulled her knees up, curling her legs beneath the billowing skirt of her gown like it was a throw blanket.

Tiziano had been propositioned too many times to count. In a thousand different ways, but all of those proposals had something in common. The women were usually sophisticated. In on every joke. If they came at him in a cheeky fashion, they were usually already naked.

And even though, while in Annie's presence, he found it difficult to recall the face of any other woman, he was certain he had never before had a woman sit with him like this. So artlessly, so easily.

As if what she was suggesting was not the very thing that he found himself lying awake at night imagining.

It was the intimacy of it, he thought as the car pulled off the road and into the lane that led to his Hampstead house. He had spent time with Annie. He'd made a study of her. He'd danced with her and defended her. He'd even told her things he told no one.

That had to be the reason this all sat on him differently tonight when normally, offers of sex were as notable to him as a handshake.

"Are you thinking of saying no?" she asked in disbelief when the silence between them dragged on. "You must be having a laugh, Tiziano. I would need a calculator to add up all the women I know that you've been with who were at tonight's gala alone. You're the least picky man alive. How much of a hardship could it really be—"

"Annie." His voice was far darker than he meant it to be, when inside he couldn't decide if he wished to laugh, or perhaps let out the sort of deeply male victory cry he knew was frowned upon in these enlightened times. "It is extremely indelicate to pester a man for sex. You must allow me to come to my own decision." She scowled at him and he really did laugh, then. "I have no intention of denying you anything."

She looked neither shamed nor set back. Not his Annie. If anything, her gray eyes sparkled, turning them into a shade of silver that made his chest feel tight.

"Are you secretly a romantic?" she asked, a kind of wonder in her voice. "Is that the real secret heart of Tiziano Accardi after all?"

His actual heart stopped for a moment. Then kicked back in, hard.

He had no intention of answering that.

The car drew up to the front of the house, and Tiziano had no idea what he intended to do with himself. With all this mad energy winding around and around inside him. He was very much afraid he might simply…explode.

But he knew several things at once.

This was not any old run-of-the-mill proposition. And while he was not the romantic she was accusing him of being just now—because he refused to be anything of the kind, it had been beaten out of him years ago—what he wanted from her wasn't as simple as sex, either.

A surprising position to take for a man who had long considered sex his art.

Still, the fact remained. Annie was not like his other women. For one thing, she was innocent. He was not allergic to innocence, like some. But he had also not encountered much of it in his time. Tonight he understood that it was a gift, and he intended to honor that gift as best he could.

But there was one other extremely important thing about Annie. The thing that made her different from all the others, and always would.

She was his.

Something inside him seemed to fall open, then. It was a rending, a tearing apart, but he didn't resent it. He didn't even fight it.

It was as if his life divided itself in two in that moment. There was before and there was after. Before the moment he understood what this woman was to him, and then after, when there was nothing to do but live with it.

He, who had never had the slightest intention of allowing anyone that close—

But she was looking at him, with eyes turned silver and an unmistakable invitation stamped all over her lovely face.

And much as he liked to tell anyone who listened that he was as close to a god as any they were ever likely to meet, the sad truth was that even he was no more than a man.

Just a man, in the end.

He could not have resisted this moment if he tried. And the real truth was, he had no intention of trying.

He drew Annie from the car and waved his driver off. And when she started for the stairs, he caught her by the hand and pulled her back to him.

She looked at him, her head tipped back. The cold

night was making her cheeks flush, but that wide smile made him feel as if he'd staggered home drunk.

But if he was drunk tonight, it had nothing to do with alcohol.

Tiziano swept her up into his arms, enjoying the way she gasped a little, then laughed, and did nothing to conceal either response from him.

And he could feel that kind of unselfconsciousness in his sex.

He carried her toward the stairs, then in through the great doors that the staff, ever watchful, opened before them.

Once inside, he carried this woman who'd been playing his mistress—and would, tonight, become his mistress in truth—toward the gleaming white stair that flirted with the glass windows as it rose before him.

And with every step he took, Tiziano relived every moment they had shared. Every look, every breath. Every touch, played perfectly in public.

Every kiss alone.

All leading here, as if this had been their destination all along.

He wondered.

The fact of the matter was, he'd seen a great many thongs in his time. Pink lace or otherwise.

But there was only one Annie.

It was possible he had always been helpless before her.

He made it to the top of the stairs, then headed for the guest suite that Catriona, in her usual efficiency, had made certain to tell him was the one they'd used for this project, as she called it.

And he might not have been in this house in a long

while, not since he'd hired a cutting-edge, of-the-mo-
ment decorator and had come to marvel at the bizarre
choices made in the name of fashion. But he still found
his way down the hall easily enough, and carried Annie
into the rooms that she'd lived in for weeks now. Long
enough that they smelled like her.

"What is that scent?" he demanded as he walked,
looking for her bedchamber. "Is it you?"

She looked almost dreamy as she gazed up at him,
one arm slung around his neck. "There are usually flowers in this room," she told him. "They reappear every
day, like magic, in full bloom even though it's nearly
Christmas."

"But there's a scent you wear, specifically." His voice
was gruff. But that scent was all over him, and here in
these rooms it bordered on unbearable. "And you wore
it before you came here."

She blinked, then her nose wrinkled in that way
that meant another laugh was on its way. Sure enough,
that infectious sound only she made followed a moment later.

"That's my soap," she told him, and now her eyes
were dancing. "It's the only one I use. You can't get it
in your fancy soap studios, or wherever it is the likes
of you get such things. For this soap, with a bit of lilac
scent to make a girl feel special, all you need to do is
nip down to the nearest Boots."

"Boots," he repeated blankly.

"The chemists. One on every corner. Bog standard,
I'm afraid." And she smiled, but her gaze was gray
again. "Just like me."

"Annie," he told her, and by this time he had mercifully located the bedroom. "You are a great many things, but not one of them is bog standard."

And then he set about showing her precisely what he meant.

Though as he set her down on her feet, there at the bed, he felt a wave of an unfamiliar sensation move through him.

It took him much too long to identify it.

Was he…anxious in some way? It hardly seemed credible. He prided himself not so much on his prowess, but on the simple delight he took in uncovering his lover's needs, then meeting them. Those she knew about and those she didn't.

But Annie was different. Everything about her was different.

It was possible that he was, for the first time in his life, worried about the outcome of this particular adventure. Not that he worried about his ability to perform. Instead, he found he was deeply concerned that she had the time of her life.

Always before, he understood then, he had simply assumed that anyone who was with him would, by definition, be having the time of her life.

And yet there was a comfort, he thought as he shrugged out of his coat and tossed it to the bench at the foot of the bed, in knowing that if this woman was unsatisfied, she would tell him so. Quite directly.

"Is something funny?" she asked, watching him closely.

"It is the package that you asked for," he told her. "I want to make certain you get exactly what it is you feel you are owed."

"That would be the full mistress experience, of

course," she said. She started unbuttoning her winter coat, but he moved to brush her hands away, so that he could take pleasure in unwrapping this finest gift before him. The better to enjoy it fully. "I'm sure you know what that entails."

"A man does not usually set out to seduce his own mistress," he told her.

And the way that she looked at him, her eyes more silver by the moment, made something deep within him shudder. "Maybe if men did, they would find the experience more joyful for everyone involved."

He smiled down at her as he slid the coat from her shoulders, then let it pool on the ground at their feet. "Let us find out."

And this time, when he took her mouth, it was a different kind of claiming. Because they were alone in this room. In this house. They stood within reach of a bed. No one was watching. They were not stood in the dark outside, spinning around in the aftermath of a complicated evening.

It was as if time ceased to exist. There was only them. There was only this.

The heat. The sweet, drugging heat, that spun around and around between them, the flames higher by the moment.

"It took a team to put me into this dress," she told him, smiling as she said it. "You will have to get me out of it."

"With pleasure," Tiziano said.

And that was what he did, moving behind her and indulging himself.

He laid kisses along the line of her neck, moving his way down toward her shoulder as his hands busied themselves with the fastening of the ball gown she wore, opening a space at the bodice so it could fall to her feet. When it did, he helped her step out of the circle it made.

Tiziano drew her to him, her back to his front, and once again tasted her shoulder, her neck. He moved his way up to the delicate place behind her ear, then turned her head so he could take her mouth, too.

He wasn't sure he was going to survive this.

What he was certain of was that he'd never in his life wanted anything as badly as he wanted Annie.

So he slowed down. And made himself wait.

Because it seemed to him now that he had already waited an eternity.

He spun her around again, and finally got his hands on her as he'd imagined over the course of these last weeks. He freed her breasts from the corset-like thing she'd worn tonight and tossed it aside. And then, a wicked dream come true, she stood before him wearing nothing but a scrap of lace.

Champagne colored this time, but he found he did not mind that it was not pink.

It was still all for him.

She was breathing fast, and he liked that.

"Do you have any idea how long I have wanted to taste you?" he asked. But it was a rhetorical question at best. "Ever since the moment you crawled at my feet, and I found myself measuring your hips in my mind. Just like this."

And he set his hands there, enjoying the flare of her hips. He slid them up to her narrow waist, then finally tested the weight of her round breasts in his palms.

"You are the perfect hourglass," he told her. "Across the ages, men have gone happily to war over figures like yours. And all this time I have sat idly by, pretending I hardly noticed."

For once, it seemed his Annie could find nothing to say. He started to take off his own clothes, dispensing with his jacket, tie—

But he was too impatient and she was nearly naked, so he went down on his knees before her. He gathered her to him, getting his mouth on her last. He tasted her breasts, her nipples. He teased them into tight little peaks, and then he found his way down to that breathtaking indentation at her waist before playing with her navel, as well.

And then, at last, he moved lower, and breathed in deep.

Not lilacs, or not only lilacs. There was the faint scent of the soap she liked, but far better, the sweeter scent that was all woman and only her.

Her arousal.

Tiziano shifted her so she could lean back on her mattress. Then he settled himself between her legs, using his shoulders to keep her thighs apart. He could have removed the little bit of lace she wore, but it had figured so hugely in his imaginings that he kept it there.

He looked up the length of her body, grinning when he found her staring down at him in a kind of dark wonder.

"Hold on, *dolcezza*," he murmured. Because he already knew she was sweet. His sweetness. "This might take a while."

And Tiziano leaned forward, taking the heat of her into his mouth. He sucked on her, through the lace she wore, and felt her jolt. Then she buckled all around him.

It was not nearly enough. He pulled back, just enough

so he could hook the lace to one side, and then he truly indulged himself. He licked his way into her, reveling in the scalding, sweet heat of her core, that told him she wanted him every bit as much as he wanted her.

He felt her hands move to his shoulders, then the sides of his face, before she settled on his hair. She gripped him in tight fists, and he exulted in the pull of it, the tiny hint of pain.

Then he licked his way into her, settling in to glut himself.

Fully.

As he set a rhythm, and a pace, she quivered all around him. And then slowly, as if her body was coming alive beneath his mouth, she began to lift her hips to meet each stroke.

He felt a kind of dark triumph roar through him, setting him alight.

Tiziano was so hard he ached, but the ache was part of the pleasure, so he took it all and gave it to her.

With every lick. With every scrape of his teeth against that proud center of hers. He took her up and up. He pushed her further and further. He kept going until she stiffened, tightening all around him, and then she fell apart on his tongue.

Still he kept on going, carrying her through one peak and then taking her higher. Then higher still.

And this time, when she fell apart around him, the sob she let out was his name.

Tiziano stood, gathering her up and placing her in the center the bed. She lay there, breathing heavily. Her eyelashes were a sooty sort of smudge against her cheeks, where he could see the freckles he'd ordered her attendants to never, ever cover.

Tonight he intended to taste every last one of them.

He made short work of the rest of his clothes and then, finally, he was naked, too. He crawled into bed with her, gathering her to him, and only then did he strip the lace from her body.

And instead of concerning him, the odd sort of eagerness he felt—to do this right, to make her happy—made him almost…joyful.

As if all of this was unknown.

As if they had made this up together, the two of them, and it was only and ever theirs.

As if they were sharing this new endeavor with each other.

Tiziano felt as if he was new.

He settled in beside her and found himself something like reverent, though it was layered in with all that fire that was Annie to him. His Annie. His sweetness.

And her fathomless eyes were wide, flooded with pleasure, and fixed to his.

"Are you ready, *mia dolcezza*?" he asked, his voice a rasp in the dark.

She didn't say a word. She lifted a hand, running it over his jaw to test the dark shadow of his beard there. She followed the line of one cheekbone, then the other. Only then did she trace the shape of his lips, smiling when he pulled her thumb between his teeth.

"Because none of this is necessary," he told her, suddenly desperate that they both want this, and in the same way. With this same wildfire passion. It seemed to him then that nothing had ever been more critical. "Our arrangement does not include this. We agreed."

He shifted, rolling her body even tighter into his.

And suddenly he could feel her all over him, shoulders to toes, with nothing between them.

It felt as if he was naked with a woman for the first time.

"What is this?" she asked, her eyes silver and her lips in soft curves. "Tiziano Accardi himself, worried that a woman might not want him?"

"I'm never worried about whether or not women want me," he told her, though he was a far cry from his usual charming self. He felt stripped raw. The taste of her was in his mouth, the scent of her in his nose, and he had the strangest sensation that he would not recover from this. Not in any way he would recognize. He flipped her over onto her back and stretched out above her, as if that might give him control. "But you are not *women*, Annie. You are mine. And I find it matters a great deal to me that you…"

He couldn't say it. Because the stakes were too high. When he had never thought that there were any stakes to bedroom play.

But then, this was Annie. And he was not playing.

Tonight she was his entirely, her red hair freed from its sophisticated chignon at last, here in the dark. She was open and inviting beneath him, his sex pressed just above the place he most wished to be, and she was already shifting against him, sighing a little, a rose-gold flush taking over her skin.

"Tiziano," she said, and her gray eyes were steady again. Her voice solemn. "Don't you know? I have never wanted anyone else."

With a low groan, he fused his mouth to hers. And then everything was a mad whirl as she surged up to meet his kiss and wrapped herself around him with a grace that made him think she had made for this. Made for *him*.

And then, at last, his lungs aching as if he'd run a whole marathon to reach this moment, Tiziano twisted his hips, drove inside, and claimed his Annie at last.

CHAPTER NINE

It was already too much, and then he was *inside* her. And *too much* suddenly became bigger, hotter, encroaching into everything.

Taking her over from the inside out.

For a moment Annie couldn't breathe. She felt as if she was being crowded out of her own skin, as if she'd *become* her own heartbeat, for it was so loud and so jarring in places she had never felt it before.

But she only realized that her eyes were screwed shut when she felt the touch of his lips to her temple, and his dark, raspy voice in her ear.

"Open your eyes, *dolcezza mia*," he murmured.

Annie felt as if every possible alarm inside her was going off simultaneously, each one louder than the last. She couldn't catch her breath. She couldn't *think*. And that heartbeat only got louder, wilder—

So she did the only thing she could do and opened her eyes.

Tiziano was braced above her, an expression she had never seen before on his darkly gorgeous face. He looked…more finely wrought, somehow. As if the glorious sculpting that had made him was tighter tonight. And his stormy eyes blazed a brighter blue.

Almost as if he was a different man, lodged deep inside her, than the one she'd known when they were two separate people. Two separate bodies.

Annie shuddered, and he shifted somehow, and then it was deeper, hotter… Or maybe it was that he moved and then that he kept moving. Just a little. Just enough to send sensation crashing through her, this way and then that.

Just a little. Just enough.

First it was all too much noise, and she felt battered by it, as if she was being tossed about between her overwhelming heartbeat and the intense physical sensations, the knowledge he was *inside her*, thrown one way and the next as if she might spin out into the ether without ever managing a full breath.

But slowly, surely, it changed.

She pulled in a breath, and suddenly she could pick out the different parts of all that sensation. The deep, thick, hard-steel length of him, so deep inside her. Moving slightly, causing ripples of heat and sensation as he went. A kind of ache inside her, but it wasn't pain. It started in the place they were joined, but then it radiated out from there, connecting to all the things she'd felt about him across all these weeks, as if it had all only been waiting for this to connect.

To glow.

"Are you hurt?" Tiziano asked quietly.

And she thought he sounded different—or maybe it was because she could hear his voice and feel it beneath her skin, the way she always did, but now he was part of her body as he spoke.

It was almost too much for her to bear.

"Am I meant to be hurt?" she asked, not sure if she

felt…cross. Or possibly like crying. Or as if she'd some-how become a kind of sob herself and she wasn't cer-tain if she was trapped somewhere or if she had already broken wide open.

Annie moved beneath him, restlessly, not sure if she wanted to move closer or farther away. But whatever she chose, the heat followed her.

Not only did it follow her, it grew more intense every time. So intense that part of her wanted to stop—

But not enough to actually stop.

"Haven't you heard the grim and gory tales of vir-ginities crudely taken?" Tiziano asked, sounding so deeply indolent that it was a wonder he could hold him-self above her the way he did. So epically languid that she wanted to dig her nails into his arms, that she hadn't realized she was gripping so hard. When she did, he smiled. "And depending on how medieval the story in question, bloody sheets waved before the cheering peasants and so on."

"Of course I've heard stories," she said, frowning up at him, even as her hips followed his movements. As if they knew things she didn't. "But I assumed it was because the poor women in those stories were in the hands of inexperienced lovers. Not…you."

Tiziano laughed, and Annie felt her chest seem to split wide open, because it was a real laugh. And while she'd heard it before, this was different. Because he was naked and inside her, and she knew, with a surge of some kind of wisdom she'd never touched before, that this was the real him. All Tiziano, no show.

Her heart kicked at her again, but this time in a kind of awe.

Because his eyes were always blue. But never quite like this.

Never so intense that she felt as if she was the same storm in him.

"I am delighted to live up to your expectations of me, *dolcezza*," he said then, and his voice was still so low. Still so raspy. And yet he sounded something like hushed, as if these were vows. As if this was a ceremony, here in the fire they'd built between them. "It will be an honor."

And then, as if he had all the time in the world, Tiziano bent down and began to press kisses to her face. All over her face, but never quite finding her lips.

When she made a sound of complaint, he only laughed again. And it was darker this time. He switched his attention to her neck, her collarbone, each kiss more maddeningly decorous than the last when he was still huge and hard within her.

Annie pushed at him, outraged, though she couldn't have said what she wanted. What she did feel certain of was that he knew. He *knew* and yet he was playing games with her. And she had never been more sure of anything in her whole life than the fact that this was no *game*. It was too important. It was life-altering and he was *languid*—

But Tiziano pulled her over with him then, so that she sprawled on top of him, and that was new. And when she moved, she felt him inside her in a variety of new and concerning and marvelous ways.

"Sit up," he told her.

He helped her rise, and then watched her through narrow, proud eyes as she tested the new fit. She liked it.

Annie pulled her lower lip between her teeth and then slowly, carefully, began rocking herself against him.

And maybe she got carried away that way. Maybe she lost herself a little. She rocked and she rocked, chasing the wonder of it. The slick fit. The crash of light and longing inside her every time she dragged herself against him.

At some point, his hands moved from her hips and started to do magical things to her breasts, her nipples. And then, when she thought it could not possibly get any better, Tiziano reached down to the place they were joined and pressed, hard.

And this time, when she spun apart, Annie heard his laughter all around her. And it helped her find her way home through all those spinning, dancing stars that swept her away for a while.

She was panting, she felt bright red everywhere, and she didn't know they'd moved. It was a surprise, then, to find that she was on her back again and he was between her legs, pulling her knees up and wide so he could settle comfortably between her thighs.

Impossibly, she felt all that fire inside her burn brighter. Hotter.

When she would have said it had clearly burned itself out.

He said something in Italian, a dark, lyrical thread that seemed to wrap itself around her, and yet she could feel the way he held himself back. She could sense it, somehow, in the way he looked at her.

And she didn't want that from him. Not here. Not now.

"There's only so much generosity a woman can take, Tiziano," she whispered, and she hardly recognized her own voice. But then, she hardly cared. "Please, I beg of you, be selfish."

"I live to serve," he said then, his eyes glittering and a certain kind of gravel in his voice.

And Annie thought that by now, she knew. She understood what was between them. All the many contours of this fire. Hadn't he thrown her into the heart of it tonight? Too many times to count?

But as Tiziano moved over her at last, sweeping her off into a dark glory she could not begin to comprehend or explain, she understood that while she'd understood he was holding back, she hadn't understood what that meant.

Because this was the storm.

This was him.

At last.

It was a wildfire run amok. It was wave after wave, a tsunami of sensation. It was thunder forever, endless flashes of lightning, and she lost track of how many times he threw her off into the electric glory of it, burning her alive.

Yet each time, he brought her back.

Because every time, there was more.

Until, at last, he found a fire so hot that even he burned up.

And finally, as Annie tipped off into ash once more, Tiziano came with her.

She thought maybe she'd died. She wasn't certain that she hadn't. She had no idea how long it was, there in the dark. The two of them together, half stars, half fire, and not quite themselves again.

He had moved his weight off her, but lay beside her, his heavy arm anchoring her to the bed. And there were too many new things to parse, so Annie didn't try. She concentrated on the weight of his arm, all that smooth muscle, holding her here. Reminding her she was still a part of the earth. She lost herself a while in the scent of his skin, something that reminded her of the seaside, a windswept salt. Or the faint near-abrasions she could feel on her skin that made her prickle all over in a dark delight, because she knew they came from the scrape of his beard.

It felt like an intimacy almost too much to bear.

Annie lay there in the dark, slowly learning how to breathe again, and she didn't know if Tiziano was asleep or awake. But it hardly mattered. There was light outside the great glass windows and she turned her head toward it, pleased to feel the moon all over her tonight, like a kind of holiday blessing.

And after all these parties, balls and gowns and gatherings of every type, this was the first time she found that she felt the slightest bit of Christmas spirit at all.

A little bit of moonlight, and her very first lover, was all it took.

Her breath left her then, hard. And Annie had a sudden, stabbing moment of clarity so intense that she thought it might have knocked her off the bed if she hadn't been lying down. If his arm wasn't holding her tight, keeping her near.

Tiziano was her first lover, yes. But she would not take another. Despite the fact that she had made herself notorious in some circles as this man's mistress, a role she now inhabited in full, this was not a lifestyle. Mistresses moved from one man to another, she knew. It was why the men at these parties looked at her the way they did, as if inspecting merchandise.

But she would be a mistress to one man only.

If anyone other than Tiziano had come up those stairs that day, she would have been unmoved. She would have gathered up her documents and gone about her day. Even now she would be lying in her bedsit, glaring stonily at her ceiling. Concentrating not on the moonlight, but on the sounds of her busy neighborhood outside and the debt she couldn't pay.

Tiziano was the only man alive who could have tempted her away from her life. Not because she'd liked her life so much, but because only this man could have convinced her to agree to behave in a way that was fully alien to all she'd ever thought she was before.

More than that, she liked it.

Oh, my God, she thought to herself, lying naked beside him. *I'm in love with him.*

He murmured something in Italian beside her, and pressed his mouth to her shoulder. She shivered, just a little, the flames licking at her once more. But when he did not move again, Annie released the breath she'd been holding and turned back to the moonlight.

But she didn't feel like Christmas this time.

Instead, she felt a surge of grief. Not because she was in love with him, but because she wished—with an intensity that she would have said she'd healed from long ago—that her mother was still alive. That her grandmother was still here. That her aunt had been a warmer guardian. That her sister was less…herself.

Because she would have given anything to have someone to talk to, just now.

She would have given everything she had to have someone to tell that she felt these things. To be able to say it out loud. To sit with someone who already loved her and try to imagine that she would survive this. Him.

Of all of them, it was her wise, warm grandmother she would have killed to see just now. She wished she could sneak from this bed and go find her nan in her sweet little cottage in the Cotswolds. She had always been delighted to hear from her girls. She had never been impatient, or disinterested, or anything but engaged when they'd told her stories about their lives.

The cure for broken heart, she had always said, *isn't wallowing, though of course you must wallow first. With cake, in my opinion. But the true cure is time. And the best way to honor the passing of that time is to grow things.*

She would take Annie out into the garden, in those years when Roxy refused to visit. And that thickly overgrown garden was the only place she'd ever felt safe enough to express how low she felt. How much she'd missed her parents and how little she felt she could show that in Aunt Sharon's house. Because she knew that she and Roxy were her aunt's act of charity. Not love.

Her nan never told her she was wrong for feeling as she did. Together, they would get their hands in the dirt. They would talk about seeds and water, rain and sun. When Annie would come next, seeds she'd planted would be in bloom. And later in the summers, there was fresh veg to eat.

And her grandmother was right, always. There was no cure for grief. But the tomatoes were plump and juicy. The flowers were bright and happy. The roses smelled sweet and the wisteria could never be contained to its trellis. And somehow, the water and the sun, the earth between her fingers and the wind in her face, helped her heal.

Beside her, Tiziano stirred.

Annie thought of seeds in the earth. Grief and love, mirror images of each other. She turned toward him, smiling even though she felt that huge sob inside her again. Because this time it felt far more unwieldy.

His eyes were closed and so, for a moment, there was nothing to do but behold the singular beauty he wore too easily. Those dark lashes that were entirely too long for a man. His sculpted face in repose, nearly angelic, when he was anything but.

Then his eyes opened, for once not the least bit sleepy, and he pinned her with all of that impossible blue.

"You've never had a mistress before, have you?" Annie asked.

She had no earthly idea why she'd led with that. She hadn't even known the words were on her tongue. She blinked, not sure she if was appalled with herself or was secretly pleased.

And in any case, Tiziano only laughed.

"There are established responses in moments like these, *cara mia*," he said, as if he was chiding her, but she could hear the laughter laced in his voice. "I will compliment you, you will compliment me, and we will both note—perhaps at the same time, how clever—that we are yet naked. So many possibilities might present themselves. I might carry you into the bath, where even greater pleasures await. I might make better use of this bed." He shook his head, his gaze warm and blue, all over her like the moon. "But no. Not my Annie. It must always be an interrogation."

She wanted to apologize, but settled for a smile instead. "No one's around to watch us here," she said, reasonably enough. "It seemed as good an opportunity as any to ask you the real questions."

"The real questions that most wish to ask me involve my bank account." Tiziano's eyes lit with that dark amusement she found she craved. "The content of my wallet. The art on my walls and whether it has been recently appraised. The exact number of sports cars I have at my disposal. Whether or not my brother seeks a woman to provide him with the Accardi heirs everyone knows must someday appear. Normal questions." He moved to prop himself up on one elbow, letting his other hand move where it would over her body. He seemed to find the curve of her hip most entrancing. "Are you certain you wish to know the history of my mistresses at such time? I feel that can only lead to tears and dismay."

"I think you've been putting on a show," Annie said quietly. And since he was moving his hands where she liked, she did the same—finally indulging herself. There were those pectoral muscles of his that were so fascinating, and even more so because, when not hidden away beneath his shirt, they were dusted with dark hair. Something she would have said, in the abstract, she didn't find attractive. And yet when she touched him it made her shake, deep inside. And it made that ache between her legs intensify. "And you don't like anyone backstage. So no mistresses. Not like me. I reckon I'm the only one."

His gaze was still a gleaming thing, but it was no longer amusement she saw there. There was something much darker. Still, his voice remained light. "The first and the last," he agreed, but not in his usual careless tone. She clung to that. "Does this please you?"

"Well, yes." And Annie smiled at him, not caring the way she should that he might see things in her yes, all over her face, that were better hidden. "I was worried there was a standard I needed to live up to. But I am the standard."

That wariness in his gaze eased. "Indeed you are."

Annie followed the urge inside her and pressed her mouth to that hollow between his pectorals, then followed the spear of dark hair down over his ridged abdomen, tasting him, inhaling him, imprinting on him.

And when she reached those fine V-shaped furrows that seemed to guide her directly where she wanted to go, she paused and looked up at him. He was on his back now, one arm behind his head looking down at her with an indulgent sort of heat that made everything inside her seem to catch on fire.

"Just wait," she told him quietly. "Now that I have all the tools at my disposal, I'm going to be the best mistress that ever was."

"Is it a competition?" he asked.

As if he felt it, too, this impossible need. This same longing she felt inside.

But she knew him well enough to know that he would never admit these things. Maybe he couldn't.

"It could never be a real competition," she said, striving for a lightness she did not feel. "We are set to end this the moment your potential arranged marriage is taken off the table."

And it was only once the words were out, hanging there between them, that she admitted to herself that what she wanted was for him to argue the point. To tell her he needed more. That he needed *her*.

That this night had changed everything for him, too.

His eyes seemed a particularly dark shade of blue as he gazed at her, though his mouth did not curve. "What cannot last is all the sweeter for the swiftness of its passing, I think. *È così.*"

She didn't believe he truly felt that way. But she also didn't want to argue the point. Not now. Not when she was so raw, and this was so new, and everything was different whether he wanted to admit it or not.

And so Annie did not speak to him of love. Or grief. Or the state of her heart. She did not tell him what she had to lose here, or share with him her deep certainty that for every bit of pleasure he brought her—and she had never known such pleasure existed—he would be sure to bring her pain, too.

She planted all of those things inside her, deep, and knew that they would grow. In their own time. In their own way.

Annie held Tiziano's gaze, and she angled herself over the hardest part of him, already bold and ready for her again. Long and thick and so inviting it made her mouth water.

"You tell me if this is a competition," she suggested. "You are the one with experience."

There was that hard glittering thing in his gaze, then. She felt it echo deep within her own body. "It can be whatever you wish it to be, *dolcezza mia.*"

Annie moved lower, because all the ways that he was male where she was female fascinated her. And what a strange sort of fascination this was, that it wasn't something to think about. She didn't want to analyze this. She wanted nothing more than to explore him.

Preferably with her mouth.

"Let's see how it goes," she told him. "Because between you and me, I think I'm going to win."

"I have no doubt," he said, his voice little more than a growl.

And when she felt his hands in her hair, she bent down and set about exploring him. Learning him.

Inch by glorious inch.

CHAPTER TEN

CHRISTMAS EVE CAME too soon, Annie thought.

She stood in the ballroom of one of London's most exclusive hotels surrounded on all sides by a variety of decked halls, brightly decorated Christmas trees, and the usual crème de la crème of British society, dressed in sumptuous jewel tones and happy metallics. She didn't know which charity ball this was. They all ran together. Annie only knew that she was looking forward to Christmas. She needed the quiet. She needed a bit of the expected peace on earth, so she could see if there was any peace to be found inside her.

Because she was ready for a little break from being Tiziano Accardi's mistress. Even if thinking such a thing made her whole body ache, as if she'd already lost him. Not that she *wanted* to lose him, but this much intensity, day and night, when she already knew how it would end…

It was a lot, that was all. Annie needed to regroup.

And besides, tonight was supposed to be the night Tiziano's engagement to Victoria Cameron was announced. Despite his very public affair with Annie that the tabloids had talked about exhaustively for the past six weeks, the engagement plans had not been called off.

The last she'd heard, his brother was still determined that the match should take place.

Tiziano had informed her almost offhandedly the other day that if the announcement was made, nothing would change. They would carry on as they had all along, though it was a certainty that the tenor of their tabloid coverage would change.

But you were so sure this would work, she had said, not sure if she was upset for him that it hadn't—or pleased that she was getting more time with him than the original two weeks he'd promised. *It must be upsetting that this is not going according to plan.*

It is fine, he had said, though he neither looked nor sounded like it was fine. *The tabloids will focus on my wickedness, not yours. That might be the push Everard Cameron needs to do what he should have done weeks ago.*

But as he said it, he toyed with her fingers in his, and the look on his face was not the one he'd worn in that long-ago stairwell. It was too...intense.

Annie tried to tell herself that made it all better when the truth was, she loved him too much, too hard. And there was no possibility that she would not feel what was done to him even more keenly than anything that might be said or done to her.

That he didn't understand that, or feel the same, was its own ache.

The past couple of weeks had been a kind of waking dream. On the one hand, nothing had changed. Outwardly. Annie lived the life of a kept woman because that was what she was—in every respect, now. She swam her laps, she let her attendants turn her into a nightly swan, the same as ever. And then she and Tiziano would go out to yet another function to convince even more people that theirs was a scorching love affair with no equal.

But the difference was, when they left their engagements at the end of the night, he didn't drop her home with a few growled words and the odd kiss.

Sometimes he couldn't bear to wait out the drive and so he took her there in the back seat of the car, surging into her as London rolled by outside the windows while she muffled her sobs of joy in the crook of his neck. Sometimes when she was dropped off at his flat before an event, he threw her over his shoulder, and carried her to his bed there, a pageant in itself, where he would undo all the hard work her attendants had done and laugh while he did it.

Sometimes everything was too intense, too wild. It felt as if they'd opened a kind of Pandora's box of need and hunger, and Annie was very much afraid that there would never be any return to something like normal. That she would never, ever be herself again.

Other times, she didn't care if she was normal again, whatever that was. At night, they would sleep tangled up together in some bed or another, in these places he owned but did not truly inhabit, and she would try to caution herself. Every spring turned into fall, she knew that. And there was no escaping the winter that would follow.

She told herself these things again and again.

But it was hard to remember what she knew when Tiziano smiled at her. When he called her all manner of florid Italian endearments in public, for show, but only ever called her *dolcezza* in private.

Dolcezza mia. My sweetness.

Annie had never felt particularly sweet. But for him, she was. For him, she felt like a confection. A dessert of a woman instead of the meat and two veg, stolid and unflashy sort she'd been before she'd met him.

If she was sweet, he made her that way.

After that first night they'd finally come together, she'd stopped looking for other people's reactions. Maybe she didn't want to know if they could see how things had changed, stamped all over her face. Annie felt too raw. More, she was afraid she was a kind of walking billboard of love and sex and a heart already half-broken, because this was never meant to last.

But as the days passed, that eased.

Because it was impossible to love Tiziano without surrendering entirely to the moment, each moment, she had with him.

Annie stopped trying.

I don't want to get ahead of myself, Roxy had said in one of her calls. She'd started ringing almost daily now, though neither one of them commented on it. *But you do seem to have...lightened up a bit lately.*

I'm a very famous mistress now, Annie had told her grandly, because she knew her sister was perhaps the only one who would laugh at that—in the spirit intended, that was. *And do you know what mistresses do all day?*

Everyone knows what mistresses do all day, Roxy had replied dryly. *Much as all the riches and jewels and fancy parties seem appealing, the sex on tap does sound a bit like work, to be honest.*

Annie had been going to talk about all her spa visits and general loafing about, but had sighed instead. *Some people are allergic to work, I know.*

But her sister was unrepentant, as ever. *I think I'm more interested in being a bit of a spoiled wife*, she'd said, as if she could choose such a thing from a menu. *All the fun and games of the mistress life, but you're allowed to have a headache. And all you have to do is pop out a kid, and there you go. Lifestyle assured forever.*

Merry Christmas, Roxy, Annie had said, and she'd even laughed. When she knew that if her sister was in Britain, she would have felt honor bound to go and wring her neck. Something about the distance made it all right to talk like this, as silly as if they were still young. Or it made it better, anyway.

And how could she complain, really, when Roxy's betrayal had led straight to Tiziano?

Because even though Annie knew that she was on a speeding, out-of-control train that had no possible chance of doing anything at all but crashing, she couldn't regret him.

Not one moment of him.

One of these summers I'll have to come back, Roxy had said yesterday. *We can go to Whitby the way we did with Mum and Dad. Eat wretched, soggy sandwiches by the sea and complain about the cold.* She'd seemed to remember herself then. *If you're not, you know, traipsing in and out of various castles or whatever it is rich people do.*

There were so many things Annie could have said to that. She could have demanded a kind of reckoning. She could have reminded her sister that they still needed to have a frank word about debts and responsibilities and all the rest.

But she found herself thinking instead of swimming by the sea. Of dancing around and around in a caravan, with all that helpless, reckless laughter, because they'd no idea what was to come.

Because no one ever knew what was to come.

If they'd known, if they'd had the slightest idea, they would never have done those things in the first place. They would have wrapped themselves up in cotton wool and locked themselves away.

I'd like that, she said softly. *But I'll be hiding my wallet.*

That's fair enough, Roxy had replied. *As long as your flash bloke doesn't, it'll be all right.*

Annie would have said that her relationship with her sister could never be repaired. But each time she put down the phone these days, she felt better. Lighter.

As if she'd gone ahead and forgiven Roxy when she hadn't been paying attention.

Maybe it made sense, she thought now, as Christmas was nearly upon her and this was the season for that sort of thing, wasn't it?

Meanwhile, she and Tiziano were still playing their same game. Because his brother showed no signs of backing down. And even though Tiziano had been certain that the father of his supposed intended would sort this out long since, the man hadn't yet done it.

Remember when you thought this would take a week, maybe two? she'd asked in the car over tonight.

Tiziano's hand had been on her leg, his thumb moving in that restless manner that let her know that he was not satisfied by the way they'd made each other groan at the house before they'd left for the Christmas Eve ball. *I'm devastated that you no longer enjoy my company,* dolcezza.

He looked more handsome tonight than he ever had,

but then, that was true every night. The more time Annie spent with him, the deeper into that she got, the more beautiful he became.

It was unfair. But then, it all felt unfair these days.

I don't want this to carry on past your engagement announcement, she'd said. Though every word felt like a knife between her ribs. *That's to be tonight, isn't it?*

There will be no announcement, he'd growled at her.

Because it's all fun and games to play at being a mistress, she'd continued softly. *But not if there's an actual wife waiting in the wings.*

She'd come to that decision in the pool. And she'd contained the sobs that had surged up in her to beneath the smooth surface of the water. And until she'd said it out loud, she hadn't been sure she would say it at all.

There will be no announcement, Annie, Tiziano had said again, darker still.

And then he'd spent the rest of their ride to the grand hotel giving her a great many other things to think about.

It was one of his talents.

Now Annie stood in a fairy tale, just like a princess, but she wasn't one. The mistress didn't get to swan off into the sunset with Prince Charming. Everyone knew that.

While Tiziano was off having his usual tense word with his brother, Annie did what she always did at these functions. She kept to herself, smiling mysteriously, and doing her best to look as if she was perfectly at her ease. The usual people were busy whispering the usual things all around, but now that she really was the woman they'd imagined her to be all this time, Annie found she was far less interested in the things they might have to say about her.

Because it didn't matter what happened. They didn't know him.

Annie was the only one who did.

Though she sometimes wished she didn't, because one of the things she knew about Tiziano was that he would always be more committed to the show than to her. Than anything else at all. Because he thought the show was all he had.

And she knew better than to try to convince another person that she could make up for the things they lacked. Look at her sister. She'd imagined she could take the place of their parents for her sister—but she hadn't. Roxy had mourned them all the same, and turned that mourning into all kinds of bad decisions. Annie's credit rating being only one of them.

She finished off the last of the one glass of wine she allowed herself—because it was best to keep her wits about her, here in this lion's den—then turned to place it on the nearest table. And when she straightened, she found another woman standing before her.

But not just any other woman.

It was Victoria Cameron. The saintly woman that Tiziano's brother had every intention of announcing as Tiziano's fiancée by the end of the night.

For a moment they gazed at each other, and Annie braced herself. Even as she told herself that there was no need, surely. Tiziano had the right to be with anyone he wished.

But she was still ready for a slap.

Instead, Victoria smiled. "I thought we should meet."

"Whatever for?" Annie found herself asking, idly

enough that she could almost have been doing a Tiziano impression. "Surely it gives everyone far more to gossip about if we stand on different sides of the ballroom, glaring daggers at each other."

Victoria was a willowy, effortless blonde, a monument to poise and good breeding in a golden dress. Everything Annie was not—and yet somehow, Annie didn't feel diminished standing next to her. Maybe it was because Victoria's smile looked real. And she didn't seem aloof and snobbish like so many of the others Annie had encountered in ballrooms just like this one.

Not to mention the bathrooms.

"They'll do that anyway," Victoria said with a shrug. "Whether they have ammunition or not. Between you and me, I think that's all they know how to do."

"I wouldn't know." Annie took a chance and grinned. "Haven't you heard? I'm common as muck."

Victoria laughed. And then, to Annie's great surprise, leaned in and linked her arm with Annie's.

"My father is the one who wants me to marry Tiziano," she confided. "And I've been all for it, because the only thing I want in this life is to escape my father. It sounded like fun, to be honest. He's famously unserious and so I thought everything would be fizzy and funny, and then he'd go off somewhere and leave me on my own. Bliss in an arranged package, to my mind."

Annie felt as if her chest was in a tight fist. It was hard to get a breath.

"He's not unserious at all, actually," she managed to get out.

It seemed such a foolish thing to say. Especially when Victoria looked at her with a wealth of compassion in her gaze and she understood that somehow, she'd given herself away to *this woman*, of all people.

"I've seen the way he looks at you," Victoria said softly. "I would have said he didn't have it in him. I don't like that he does, because what I want is something shallow. Easy. A business arrangement, nothing more."

Annie felt a sudden, strange responsibility for this woman, which didn't make any sense. She was a stranger. A stranger who might marry the man she loved, no less.

"You should marry because you love someone," she said, frowning at the Cameron heiress, who could not possibly have known a moment's struggle. "And for no other reason."

Victoria smiled at her then, but there was something sad in her gaze. "I'll leave the love to you, I think. I'm afraid that for some of us, that will never be in the cards. Don't worry," she continued when Annie started to argue that. "I'll tell Ago Accardi myself. He and my father like to make decisions between themselves, but the good news is, Ago is the gentleman my father is not. *He* won't force me to marry his brother if I don't want to. And I don't. That's what I wanted you to know."

Annie wanted to tell her it wasn't necessary. That she might as well go ahead and marry Tiziano, because the kind of surface-only relationship Victoria was talking about was exactly what he wanted. It was the only thing he knew. It was the kind of show he liked best. This deeper, soul-shifting nonsense couldn't last, no matter how sweet he thought it was for now.

And she doubted very much he would allow it to happen with anyone else.

Besides, she needed to get some space from all of

this. The character she was supposed to be, according to the tabloids. The mistress, the jumped-up secretary. Tiziano himself. She needed to catch her breath, at the very least. An engagement announcement would be the perfect opportunity to bow out of this whole mad circus.

Annie opened her mouth to tell Victoria all of this, but instead, all that came out was a soft "Thank you."

And then she stood there, trying to reconcile that response with the swirling ache inside her, as Victoria nodded, squeezed her arm once more as if they were friends, and then walked away.

She was still standing there, unsettled, when Tiziano came to find her.

"Dance with me," he commanded her, his mouth at her ear. She had to fight to keep her eyes from falling shut. She had to fight to keep from leaning into him. "It's nearly midnight and there's still no announcement. Ago blustered about, as he does, but I think we might well be in the clear."

Annie could have told him there would be no announcement. She didn't know why she didn't. Instead, she let him draw her out onto the dance floor. And then she let herself ache as they swayed together, as he gazed down into her eyes. Then, eventually, she had to close her eyes and rest her cheek against his shoulder, because she did not wish him to see the way that ache grew and grew inside her.

Because Tiziano loved nothing more than his show.

And later, even as he moved inside her with that fierce, possessive look on his face, pinning her to the bed with his masterful strokes, she knew that no matter what he felt, he never would.

Tomorrow, or soon after, his brother would tell him that he'd received the reprieve he wanted.

Tiziano would tell her that his plan had worked.

And soon enough, this arrangement would end.

Maybe not immediately. But what good would it do to draw it out?

Sooner or later, Tiziano would remember that sharing himself led nowhere he wished to go.

Sooner or later, he would end it.

There was no avoiding her broken heart. Even the woman who wanted to marry Tiziano could see how in love Annie was. She probably also saw how doomed that love was, though she had been too polite to mention it.

The only thing Annie could do was choose the *when* of it.

And so, much later that night, when it was already turned Christmas, she crept out of that sprawling house in Hampstead. She took only a few of the things she'd brought with her, and a very few of the things that had been provided for her. She wrapped herself up against the cold and then headed for the village, though it was a long way to walk at that hour and the night smelled like snow. She found a cab discharging merrymakers and offered the driver an astonishing amount of money to drive her out of London.

Because the seeds she'd planted inside her had started to bloom into despair, and there was only one place in the world she could think of to go and nurse them.

Just until they could be flowers again. And she would be close enough to whole by then, she hoped, so she could appreciate them for what they were. Just what they were.

What they had always been despite her foolish heart. Just what they were, and nothing more.

CHAPTER ELEVEN

WHEN TIZIANO WOKE to find the bed empty, he didn't like it, but he didn't think much of it. He stretched in the early morning light, congratulating himself on having worked things out so well.

For Christmas Eve had come and gone, and Ago had made no announcements. Everard Cameron had made no claims. Despite all the pressure of these past weeks, Tiziano's engagement had not been announced—whether he liked it or not—to all of those people crowded into the ballroom last night.

He'd won.

His brother might not have admitted it yet, but Tiziano knew the truth. He had won the battle. This engagement was not going to happen.

More importantly, Ago had made a threat and been unable to carry through with it.

This meant two things. One, that his brother was going to think twice before he tried to come for Tiziano again.

And two, that Tiziano was perfectly free to indulge himself completely without having to worry about rumors, tabloid coverage, or the grind of so many formal events.

He prowled into the expansive bathroom suite, expecting to find Annie curled up in the tub. Or perhaps in the adjoining room, tending to her reflection in a way he'd never seen her do, but assumed all women must. Or perhaps selecting items from her wardrobe.

But she was nowhere to be found. Not in the guest suite that had been allocated to her. And not, he ascertained after an irritated tour through this absurd mausoleum of a house, anywhere else.

It was only then that he inquired about her whereabouts, only to discover from his staff that she'd left sometime before dawn.

He was on the phone to Catriona within seconds, because he had to do something. Because Annie couldn't leave him. How could she have *left* him?

The way that his heart thumped at him might have knocked him over if he hadn't taken some kind of action.

"Give me her London address," he barked down the line.

"There's no need," Catriona replied smoothly. "We broke her lease when she moved into your Hampstead property. The assumption being that once the project is at an end, she would have the means to ensure that wherever she lived next, it need not be a bedsit of such questionable quality."

"Where would she go?" Tiziano gritted out. He could remember every last thing Annie had said to him, and tried to go through it all, looking for clues. "She was raised by an aunt, was she not?"

"She was," came the crisp reply, and so quickly that Tiziano knew Catriona was not consulting any notes. She'd committed all of this to memory, because she was a gem without price. "But I believe her aunt's Christmas traditions center upon Spanish beaches. Even if Miss Meeks did intend to meet up with her, it's unlikely she could manage to get on a commercial flight this early on Christmas morning."

That was when Tiziano realized that it was, in fact, Christmas morning.

He'd known that, clearly. Because he'd known last night was Christmas Eve. But somehow, that hadn't given him so much as a moment's pause when he'd pulled out his mobile to phone Catriona.

Something he knew wouldn't have occurred to him at all if he hadn't spent these last weeks in the company of a secretary. Who had always been quite vocal about his privileged behavior when it came to his staff.

"I apologize," he said now, though the words felt strange in his mouth. And if he wasn't mistaken, shocked Catriona as much as they did him. "I'm not myself. You should not have to field unhinged calls for me on Christmas morning."

There was a short pause. And then, his unflappable assistant coughed, as if she was as uncharacteristically taken aback by this moment as he was. "It's no bother," she said after a moment. "The grandchildren aren't due for another hour."

Tiziano then had the distinct impression that they both stood there, in their respective homes, contemplating the fact that while Catriona knew every single detail of Tiziano's life, this was the first he had ever heard of any grandchildren. And, by extrapolation, that she was a mother. Possibly a wife in possession of a partner. And presumably had an entire rich life of her own.

Perhaps it is not so surprising that Annie left you, he told himself acidly.

"And speaking of grandchildren," Catriona said, in a tone that made it clear she did not intend to speak about her own, possibly ever again, "Miss Meeks and her sister were the only beneficiaries of their grandmother's will." She cleared her throat, which was as good as another woman's entire emotional breakdown, and then it was done. "If I had to wager, I would guess that if she went anywhere it would be to her grandmother's cottage in the Cotswolds. I will text you the address at once."

"Thank you, Catriona," Tiziano said, with excessive formality. He paused. "And I hope you have a very happy Christmas."

Catriona made a strangled sort of noise, then rang off.

Tiziano stayed where he was, in the oppressively over-white foyer of this house. He was concerned about the state of his heart. Because the house around him felt like a hospital already, and because his heart was making all kinds of noise. Every beat of it seemed to hurt, as if something was terribly wrong with him. As if he was cracking apart—

But there was no time to worry about such things, he told himself darkly. He had to find Annie.

In short order, Tiziano threw on some clothes and drove out of North London grateful that not all of his cars were fanciful, low-slung, sporty affairs. Because as he headed into Gloucestershire, the weather got worse, matching his mood by the mile, and he was grateful that he was in a Range Rover instead of an Aston Martin.

By the time he reached the village he was after, according to his navigation software, the world had become a proper Christmas card.

He drove down winding lanes piled high with snow. There were thatched roofs piled with snow and curls of smoke in the wintry air. There were candles in windows, twinkling lights on trees, and Tiziano was so agitated by the Christmas of it all that he felt like some kind of ravaging beast by the time he found the place he was looking for. A tiny little thatched cottage at the very end of an untouched lane.

It looked cozy and inviting, with hints of lights in the windows, and he resented it. Deeply.

At least she was warm. Even if she would have been far warmer if she'd stayed where she belonged, right next to him in bed.

Tiziano's temper was black and darkening by the moment as he threw himself out the Range Rover and stomped through the snow toward the front door, such as it was. It had clearly been fashioned for people a tenth of his size. He felt as if he was in some kind of fairy tale—and had been cast in the role of the hulking villain, a seething black roar across all of this pristine whiteness.

A feeling that only intensified when the door opened a crack. Then wider, to reveal Annie standing there.

Frowning up at him as if he was a stranger.

"What are you doing here?" she asked, as if that was not obvious.

"At the moment, *dolcezza mia*, I am freezing to death," he growled at her.

But she didn't move. She only peered up at him, looking about as happy to see him as he had been to find her gone. It did nothing to soothe his frayed temper.

Just as it made something in him turn over to find her looking so effortlessly lovely, here in this lonely cottage so far away from the world. So far away from *him*.

He did not often see her this way. Unstyled and wholly natural. Tiziano had woken up with her these many mornings, it was true, but there were always more pressing things to do with her. Then there were calls to take and engagements to avoid, and by the time he saw her again in the evenings, her attendants had always had their way with her. And they had proved remarkably talented at creating the vision he'd had of her from the start.

But it was this Annie who made his chest hurt.

Her red-gold hair was piled on the top of her head, but not in some elegant chignon. It was a mess of curls, pinned haphazardly to sit slightly off-center at the top of her head. Her eyes were big and gray, and rimmed with red. And all he could really focus on was that spray of freckles like stardust over her nose and the way she pulled her lower lip between her teeth that would now and forever remind him of the night she'd given him her innocence.

And she had *taken* all of this from him.

"Annie," he said, and there was an urgency in his own voice he barely understood. "Let me in."

For a moment that stretched on far too long, she appeared to consider it.

And for the very first time, possibly ever, Tiziano Accardi had to confront the possibility that a woman might, in fact, slam a door in his face.

More, she might mean it.

But instead, Annie blew out a breath. Then she

stepped back and waved a hand, as if she was *surrendering* to his presence.

Tiziano wanted nothing so much as to stalk inside in a manner clearly showing his displeasure, but the house was tiny and ridiculous. More suitable for a mouse than a man. He was forced to stoop down, then pretzel himself inside, following her down a haphazard hallway to what passed for a sitting room.

He could see in an instant that this was likely the only room that Annie had ventured into since her arrival, which could only have been a few hours ago. Some of the furniture was still covered. There were Christmas carols playing on an ancient wireless. She'd made a kind of nest for herself on a faded-looking sofa, piled high with quilts. And there was a fire in the grate, crackling merrily away and throwing about the only light.

She went and sat on that couch, looking prim and proper, but she was dressed in clothes he didn't recognize. Because he hadn't seen her in anything but gowns or workwear. Ever. And it was astonishing to him that the simple sight of a woman in an offhandedly elegant cashmere sweater thrown so carelessly over an old pair of jeans should make his heart flip around in his chest. Quite like it was trying to escape.

"Tell me, Annie," he said, hearing too much darkness in his voice but doing nothing to stop it. "Why is it you have come to this abandoned house in the middle of nowhere, to sit by a lonely fire, without bothering to leave so much as a note?"

She studied him. And he, who normally adored being stared at, found that today, it made him… Not uncomfortable. Not exactly.

But it was harder to remain still than it should have been. "It's Christmas," she said.

"I'm well aware." Though he could not say that without a pang of guilt, thinking of Catriona and her family. Not to mention the staff in Hampstead, who he had gruffly ordered to take the rest of the year off.

"It's Christmas, Tiziano, and I spoke with Victoria Cameron myself last night." Annie's gray gaze was solemn, but this time, he found it far less steadying. "She has no intention of marrying you. So you see, our arrangement is already at its end. I saw no need to draw it out."

He stared at her. "You saw…?" He shook his head, as if that could keep him from feeling as if his ribs were tearing him open from the inside out. *"You saw no need?"*

And though she was dressed more like the secretary he'd met in that stairwell than the pampered lover he'd made her since, the way she folded her hands in her lap and smiled at him was 100 percent the fantasy mistress he'd created for his own purposes these last weeks. Her expression was serene. Her smile bordered on lazy.

There was even a hint of something like pity in her gaze.

Meaning, none of it was Annie.

But she was speaking. "I fulfilled all my contractual obligations to you. You're welcome to check."

"I do not make it a habit of wandering about with contracts in my back pocket. Odd, I know."

Annie only looked calmer. "This was always to be our end date. I think you know that. Just as I think your objection has nothing to do with me personally. Or anything that passed between us. It's simply that you're used to being in control of these kinds of things." She inclined her head. "And I apologize. I should have given you the option to end this yourself this morning, as we both know you would have."

Tiziano knew no such thing. It hadn't even crossed his mind to end things with her today.

And the ramifications of that hit him, then.

Hard enough that if he hadn't already been standing near a wall, he might've stumbled back to find one, the better to prop himself up while a different sort of storm swept him away.

And all the while, Annie was watching him closely. Looking something like vindicated, as if she'd expected precisely this response.

But she couldn't possibly have done. Because he hadn't been planning to end things with her this morning.

He hadn't been planning to end things with her at all.

Last night, when they'd left the Christmas Eve ball with no hint of the threatened engagement, the Tiziano he'd been when this had all started would have ended things in the car. He would have dropped her at the hotel of her choice and would have had Catriona pop by in the next day or two to help sort out where she intended to go next. He would have washed his hands of her and forgotten her by morning, when he would have jetted off somewhere warm to reacquaint himself with his love of the bikini.

Because the game had been successful. The show had done what it was meant to do. And Tiziano had always known exactly when to draw the curtain.

Instead, he'd taken Annie home. Because that crypt of a house was as much a home as anywhere else. He had taken her to her bedroom, to be more precise, because he would have gone anywhere she was.

It hadn't even crossed his mind to finish with her.

And it still hadn't.

Clearly.

For here he was. Standing in a house he barely fit into. It was as if he'd crawled into one of those gingerbread houses that had never featured much in his Italian childhood. He might as well have inserted himself among the gumdrops, and why?

Because she was here.

Against his will and despite his best intentions, Annie Meeks had not simply threatened his languid unconcern—the hallmark of his identity, he would have said.

She'd upended everything.

And Tiziano had been so busy telling himself that he was playing a part that he'd completely missed the fact that he'd stopped *playing* a long time ago.

He hadn't been *pretending* to fall in love. He hadn't been *acting* as if he'd lost the plot completely over an inappropriate secretary who his brother would consider excluded from consideration by virtue of the simple fact she'd agreed to this game in the first place. Not even getting into her social status or the fact she'd been a secretary in their company.

Tiziano hadn't been *putting on an act* at all. He hadn't been faking a thing.

He'd shown Annie more of himself than he'd ever shown anyone, save his own mirror.

And she'd left him anyway.

Something rolled through him, a dark kind of anguish, but he told himself it was outrage.

"It turned out we were both a bit better at this than we expected," Annie was saying, still watching him in that way he didn't like. But then, he didn't like any of this. "But it's time we retreat to our separate corners and finish the way we always planned. To be honest, I'm ready for it to be over." She lifted her chin, possibly in response to whatever expression was on his face. For once, Tiziano had no idea. "The holiday season is all but over. This level of intensity won't be necessary going forward, even if the threat of engagement was still hanging over you. It's better this way."

He let out a laugh then and it must have sounded as unbalanced as he felt, because her eyes went wide.

"But I do not agree," he said, his voice low. That current of anguish wrapping tight around him, until it became him. "Perhaps you have forgotten, Annie, that I have had a great many lovers in my time. You have had only the one."

And he could admit it was a pleasure to see an emotion he hadn't seen a hint of so far move over her face then. Her cheeks lit up, red with temper, and he liked it.

He reveled in it, in fact.

"I don't need a reminder of your favorite pastime, Tiziano." Her eyes shot fire at him. "I can't wait to live it with you through the pages of all your favorite tabloids as you take it up again."

Once upon a time, some six weeks ago, Tiziano would have told anyone within earshot that jealousy was the province of the childish, the unfashionably *intense*.

Now he felt it was, truly, the very least of the things she should feel at the prospect of him with other women.

Given that the notion of her with any other man,

ever, made him feel as close to murderous as he had ever been.

Still, he was not so far gone that he did not recall that the woman he'd met in that stairwell—the woman who had been completely unimpressed with him in every respect—would not have cared in the least what he did or who he did it with.

That blaze of red on her cheeks wasn't only temper.

To him, it was hope.

"I think you are in love with me, Annie." His voice was quiet, but he aimed every word with deadly accuracy. "I think that you raced away in the night, on Christmas morning, no less, because you know you've broken the rules."

He watched her pull in a breath, as if to steady herself. He watched a kind of misery move through her eyes, and he hated it.

But the hands in her lap curled into fists. "You bought my performance, Tiziano." Her voice was cold. "And my performance is what you got. You have no right to my feelings, and thank goodness. Because you're wrong."

He might have accepted that, or tried, but he heard that little hitch in her voice.

"I don't believe you, *dolcezza*," he murmured.

And as he watched, as he *hoped*, something rolled through Annie. He could see her go pale, then flush bright again—before she dissolved into tears.

She pushed to her feet, so that they were now facing off in this tiny little room, surrounded on all sides by the ghosts of a long life, shrouded in old sheets and surrounded by dusty pictures.

It felt entirely too much like his childhood for his liking.

But even as he thought that, he knew that everything had changed. It wasn't only that he was older. Hopefully wiser, if only by default. But that he recognized himself now, the way he never had before.

And Tiziano had no intention of being a dusty portrait on this wall or any other one.

"You got everything you wanted," Annie threw at him, her voice thick and those tears wetting her cheeks. "And it's all been a rousing success. I haven't broken any rules. No one works on Christmas anyway. Even if we have to make another appearance, it won't be today. There is no reason at all for you to be here."

It was as if he'd never seen her before. Because he'd been so busy pretending, hadn't he, that he didn't see what was so plainly in front of him now.

But now he did. It seemed to him, suddenly, that he always had.

"Try again," he suggested.

She vibrated a little, there where she stood with her cute little feet in thick, patterned socks. That glorious scowl of hers taking over her face. As if, he thought then—understanding dawning—as if she was fighting the urge to cry.

"Tiziano," she said, and her voice was different now. Lower. Rougher. "I know who you are. And I know what you want. I've watched you all these weeks, in your element. You like a show." Her voice cracked on that, and so his heart did, too. "There's nothing wrong with that. But the show can only go on for so long. Sooner or later, reality reasserts itself."

He started to say something, but Annie shook her

head, looking even fiercer. "Not for you. I understand that. But for *me*. And I..." The breath she sucked in sounded ragged. "I can't go on pretending to be madly in love with you every night. I can't carry on acting the part of your besotted mistress. I can't do it."

"Because it isn't true?" he asked, with a kind of soft menace. "Or because it is?"

And he thought she would throw something at him. Call out another storm, put her temper to work. But instead, she seemed to deflate before him, and he liked that far less.

She hugged herself, but this was Annie, so she kept that steady gray gaze on him all the while.

"You're right," she said, as if it cost her dearly to say it out loud. "I love you."

Something in him roared, deep and long.

Yet she wasn't finished. "But I love *you*, Tiziano. And I know who you are. Please do me the favor of recognizing who I am, too. You told me it would be two weeks. It's been six. I can't do it anymore. I'm not cut out for acting. I can't pretend."

"No, *dolcezza mia*," he agreed. "You're a terrible actor." He laughed a little when she scowled at him again. "But don't you see? When it comes to boring parties where someone is called upon to be entertaining, I have never encountered a spotlight I could not hog. When it comes to tedious dinner parties where there must always be a clown, who better to assume that role than one such as I, who has never taken himself seriously? But when it comes to love, *amore mio*, I have never managed to convince anyone that I've even heard of such a thing."

She shook her head at that as if she didn't understand

him. "Then we're in agreement. It's over. No more performances. No more pretending. No more—"

"Annie, *dolcezza mia, amore mio*, I have been acting all my life," he said, cutting her off. "The bad influence, the disappointment—I played down to the lowest expectations of me wherever I went. When I was sent away to school, I was the Italian clown, because it was easier to make them laugh than sit in my own loneliness." He had never said that out loud before, but this was Annie. He could tell her anything. "I have never met a moment I couldn't make a stage, and there has never been a bit of scenery available that I couldn't chew. Because the best way to disappear in plain sight is to make the whole world think that you're nothing but a shallow puddle."

"That is not who you are," she threw at him, fiercely.

"No," he agreed, his gaze intent on hers. "But you are the only one who took one look at this disguise that has fooled countless people in all walks of life and saw straight through to the real me. The only one. Ever."

"Tiziano…" she whispered.

"This has never been acting," he told her, from that place where his chest hurt the most. "I think I loved you from the first moment I saw you, laid low before me, yet uncowed. Undiminished. Completely yourself from the very first. It was impossible to be near you and not wish to do the same. To be completely me, however I could."

Her eyes were too bright. "You don't mean that."

"I have never meant anything more."

He moved to her then, because he could no longer keep himself away. Then he took her in his arms, knowing in the moment her hands came to rest on his chest that he could breathe again.

For the first time since he'd woken up to find her gone, he could breathe.

"I don't want a mistress, Annie," he told her, as if the words came from him of their own accord. Called out from the deepest part of him, all for her. "I want *you*. I want every part of you. I don't want to hide any longer. I don't want all of these parties and all of these pointless people, not when I have you. Because everyone looks at me, Annie. I imagine they always will. But you alone see me."

"Since the very first moment," she whispered, her fingers gripping him as if she needed to hold on as hard as he did. "It's as if I've never truly seen anything else."

"You must decide if you are ready for this," he warned her. "Because I intend to be demanding." And he shook his head at the expression on her face then. "Not only in bed. I want every part of you. I want to marry you and grow old with you. All of these things that never made sense to me before, I want to build with you. I want babies who we can raise, you and I, to be more than heirs and spares, shunted off into roles we pick for them before their births. I want them to be so loved, so adored, that it would never occur to them to spend a lifetime pretending to be things they are not."

"Oh, Tiziano," she breathed, and the tears flowed openly down her cheeks now. "I think I must be dreaming."

His heart was beating hard again. This time, he liked it. "Then I'm dreaming with you."

"I love you," she told him, tipping her head back so he could see that she meant it, all over her lovely face. It blazed there in her gray eyes, as sure as steel. "And I thought that loving you meant leaving you, because I don't want you to feel badly that you can't give me the things I want from you when you don't even know what they are. Because how could you know? But then, everyone I love has died, or betrayed me, so it's not as if I'm any expert, am I?"

"I will never betray you," he promised her, and something lit up within him when he said it. As if he had branded himself with that vow, deep inside. "Everything I know of love, I have learned from you, Annie. I promise you, no matter what happens, that love will come first. We will make it so."

"I don't think life works like that," she whispered, though her eyes were gleaming.

And he smiled then, running his thumbs over her cheeks to capture the excess moisture there, and wiping it away.

"I am Tiziano Accardi," he told her. "Life works precisely as I wish it to work." He waited for her to smile, and then he bent his head to hers. "Come, *dolcezza mia*. Let me show you."

And he did.

CHAPTER TWELVE

THE SNOW KEPT COMING, but Annie didn't care. Because inside her grandmother's spellbound little cottage, she had a fire. Better still, she had her love.

It was, by far, the most magical Christmas ever.

When the weather cleared on Boxing Day, they ventured out, but only to gather enough supplies at the small local market that they could come back and hunker down some more.

But Tiziano was Tiziano, after all, so by the time they returned there was a Christmas tree, decorated with all the trimmings, standing near the fireplace as if it had always been there.

Annie thought that her nan would have been pleased.

Then she and the billionaire who had made her his mistress sat on the floor near the fire and ate beans on toast, which Tiziano found vile no matter how many times Annie assured him it was a true British delicacy.

And as the years rolled by, they regarded that funny little Christmas as their true wedding and the two weeks they spent in her grandmother's cottage their real honeymoon.

They had a proper wedding two years later.

Tiziano insisted that it be a proper paparazzi-friendly

affair, complete with a church ceremony and a star-studded reception, because the most notorious mistress of the modern era deserved her happy ending.

Printed in all the same papers that had spent so much time speculating about her.

"No one cares about the fact I was your mistress," she told him the night before the ceremony. Tiziano flatly refused to spend the night, or any night, apart— no matter how traditional it was meant to be. "No one cares about us, either. The only time they ever will again will be when we break up."

He pulled her to him, there in the bright and cheerful kitchen of the only property they lived in these days. It was a property they had found and moved into together. Then made a home together. Unlike his other London properties, now rented out, this one was filled with warmth. Light. *Them.* Annie had made the attic her studio and had found her way back to painting—after finishing her degree course at Goldsmith's.

She had even dared to have her first show, which the papers had all begrudgingly admitted was not bad. For a novice.

Tiziano, in the meantime, had stopped pretending he didn't know how to get to Accardi Industries headquarters.

Together, they had figured out not only how to love each other, but how to follow their dreams. No hiding required.

Here in his arms in the home they'd made, Annie smiled up at this man, the love of her life. She could have told him that they would begin raising their family here sooner than planned, but she didn't. Because she wanted to enjoy his reaction without having to worry about entertaining half of Europe the next day, as it was certain to be epic.

"It is a shame, then," Tiziano said, smiling down at her, his blue eyes warm and bright and hers. All hers. "We must resign ourselves to the obscurity you once longed for, *dolcezza*. For we will never break up. Not as long as we both live."

And to the great disappointment of the phalanxes of women who remained hopeful they might yet get the chance with him, they never did.

Though there were a lot of tears at the wedding, all the same.

Roxy, back from Australia and charmed, despite herself, by her sister's solid relationship, walked her down the aisle.

"I should steal your credit card more often," she said as they made their way toward the altar, where Tiziano stood like a dream come true, dressed entirely in hand-crafted Italian glory and Annie's favorite smile. The one that was all for her.

Annie slid a look at her sister. "Don't push your luck."

But they were both laughing. And later that year, they went, just the two of them, to the holiday park they'd visited as kids. They sat by the sea on typically frigid British summer days. They danced to old songs on the radio, and burnt their sausages in the pan. And then, afterward, went and got their feet in the dirt in Nan's garden.

After the ceremony was done and Tiziano kissed her far longer than necessary in the church, Annie danced with his best man. And despite the occasion, Ago was no less stern than she remembered him from long ago.

"You once told me that your brother's duty would never be me," she reminded him.

But Ago had been changed by these years, too, and he laughed. "Never," he agreed. "Thank goodness." His stern gaze found hers, and lightened. "It appears what you are instead is his heart, and I think he'd be the first to agree that he's a better man for it."

Annie's smile trembled a little on her mouth, then. "I hope so."

And as the years passed, there were hardships. There were tears. There was no one season to life. For all the flowers that spring brought to bloom, there was always the coming fall.

But what she remembered most were the summers. The endless sunshine and the sweetest, softest days.

So bright they seemed to make the harder, colder seasons fade away.

And a few times a year, she and Tiziano stole away from their lives, and their gray-eyed, dangerously charming children. They holed up together in that little cottage in the Cotswolds. If it was winter, they sat by the fire and told each other stories of their brighter days—some already past and some yet ahead. In the spring, they wandered the garden, where Annie taught her aristocratic husband to plant seeds. How to put his hands in the earth. How to plant hope into dirt and wait for the rain to make it into flowers.

In the summer they would dance beneath the stars, the garden dizzy with flowers and vines. And in the fall, they would walk hand in hand in the cool mornings, the nostalgia all around them like mist. Yet laced straight through with joy.

And then, without fail, they would steal away to their

favorite bed beneath the eaves and learn each other all over again.

Again and again, as if they were new.

* * * * *